ONE
THAT
GOT
AWAY

A NOVEL

LEIGH HIMES

hachette
BOOKS

NEW YORK   BOSTON

Hachette Books
Hachette Book Group
1290 Avenue of the Americas, New York, NY 10104
hachettebooks.com
twitter.com/hachettebooks

Originally published in hardcover and ebook by Hachette Books in May 2016
First Trade Paperback Edition: June 2017

Hachette Books is a division of Hachette Book Group, Inc.
The Hachette Books name and logo are trademarks of Hachette Book Group, Inc.

The publisher is not responsible for websites (or their content) that are not owned by the publisher.

Library of Congress Cataloging-in-Publication Data

Names: Himes, Leigh, author.
Title: The one that got away : a novel / Leigh Himes.
Description: First edition. | New York : Hachette Books, 2016.
Identifiers: LCCN 2015050560 | ISBN 9780316305730 (hardback) | ISBN 9781478909491 (audio download) | ISBN 9780316305723 (ebook)
Subjects: LCSH: Working mothers—Fiction. | Women blue collar workers—Fiction. | Wealth—Fiction. | Reality—Fiction. | Self-realization—Fiction. | Philadelphia (Pa.)—Fiction. | Psychological fiction. | BISAC: FICTION / Contemporary Women. | FICTION / General. | GSAFD: Fantasy fiction.
Classification: LCC PS3608.I485 O54 2016 | DDC 813/.6—dc23 LC record available at http://lccn.loc.gov/2015050560

ISBNs: 978-0-316-30570-9 (paperback), 978-0-316-30572-3 (ebook)

Printed in the United States of America

LSC-C

10 9 8 7 6 5 4 3 2 1

For Shelby

PROLOGUE

Fuck you, Marc Jacobs. Those were the words running through my mind right before I fell backward and flipped over the side of the Nordstrom escalator.

It was ten o'clock on a Saturday morning. The store was already filled with shoppers succumbing to the addictive, wallet-emptying lure of new leather and hundred-dollar face cream. I should know; I had fallen for this store's siren song too, and was paying the price. Before I fell, I was gliding up the escalator, cursing and mad, bracing myself to go head-to-head with customer service.

My plan was simple—to beg. They just *had* to take back the glossy red leather purse, even though I had carried it for a few days, and even though my five-year-old daughter had recently decorated one side with a deep scratch, an accidental maiming from a chopstick turned light saber. My hope was that whoever was manning customer service today had terrible eyesight or a forgiving heart, or both. As I made my way up the escalator, I balanced the glossy silver box up and away from my rain-spattered coat and dripping umbrella, careful not to inflict any more damage. In my other hand I held a coffee.

Its steaming liquid sloshed onto my fingers, my sleeve, and the slow-moving metal below my feet.

I was steaming inside too, having just run into two "friends" from high school, their not-so-thinly veiled insults embarrassing me more than the current state of my hair.

"Don't you look so cozy?" cooed one as they took in my outfit, then exchanged glances under perfectly blown-out bangs. "I wish I could wear something like that, but I have to be careful in case I run into one of Bill's clients," said Betsy, looking crisp and confident in her Main Line mom uniform: designer jeans, fur-lined boots, and puffer coat.

"I guess not all of us can be 'sweatpant moms,'" sniped Ellen as she brushed an invisible piece of fuzz off her Pilates-toned stomach. I was so caught off guard, I just stood there, wishing I could sink into the gleaming marble floor. I couldn't even think up a lie and found myself admitting to returning a purse that was too expensive. They smiled their close-lipped smiles of pity before rushing off to the shoe department.

Betsy Claiborne was the daughter of a single mom just like me and she never even finished college and now she acts like she's Jackie Kennedy. And Ellen Hadley gave out hand jobs like Tic Tacs before she lost forty pounds and married the heir to a dry-cleaning fortune. Now they spend their days driving around in Range Rovers, taking their kids to "the club," and ambushing sleep- and gym-deprived moms at department stores. I was so furious, I stomped up the escalator trembling in fury, cursing them, my bank account, my husband, and even Marc Jacobs himself, whose $598 bucket bag would be returned in favor of running water and pediatrician co-pays.

I loved that bag, and I got to carry it for only two weeks—to work, Rite Aid, Grange Hill Elementary, the Springfield School of

Irish Dance, Rite Aid again, and Mario's Bake-at-Home Pizza. Not to a trendy restaurant, not to a boutique, not even to the posh Bryn Mawr library the little guy and I crashed for its better Thomas the Train set and less disgusting rug. That bag was like a tree falling in the forest. If no bitchy Main Line moms saw it, did it even exist?

To be fair, it meant more to me than just making people jealous. That bag was a quilted red leather anchor, tethering me by its thin gold chain to a former life. Its links were links to the *real me*, the one who was cool and fun and spontaneous; who wore hip, clean clothes and ate dinner later than five thirty p.m.; who watched foreign films and read the latest novels; and who still recognized her face in the mirror. That bag meant I was still "Abbey," not Mommy or Mrs. Lahey. And it could have kept my former self alive and afloat for a little while longer, before the chain, so taut under the pressure, snapped for good, setting me forever adrift in the suburban-mom abyss.

But given the way everything was going lately, maybe it was a good thing I knocked myself out on the cold marble Nordstrom floor.

After all, I really needed a break.

CHAPTER ONE

The day before my accident started like every other morning of my life: pure chaos. The dog was barking, the baby was screaming, my daughter had wet the bed again, and my husband, Jimmy, was long gone to one of his landscaping jobs. Jimmy usually left around five in the morning, silently finding his clothes, lunch, and work boots before slipping out the back door like a cat burglar.

He was always so careful not to wake us, moving as quietly as his burly physique and heavy gait could manage. But early rising must be hereditary, because no matter how stealthily he left the house, one of his small children would feel the change in the parental atmosphere and wake the moment his truck left the driveway. Today, it was both of them.

So at just twenty minutes past five in the morning, right when Channing Tatum was about to hand me the keys to the HGTV dream house, I found myself jarred awake. And just two minutes after that, I was wrestling thirty-two-pound Sam from his crib-in-the-closet and heaving him down the hallway to the sound of muffled whimpers. I saw the telltale yellow stain and the tangled bedclothes before I found a little-girl-shaped lump in a white plastic laundry basket.

"You hate me; I know you do," said the dirty-clothes-covered heap.

"It's way too early for psychological warfare, Glo," I told her. "It's just a little pee, no big deal."

"It is a big deal!" screamed the basket. "No one else in kindergarten wets the bed!"

"I think there are a lot of kids who wet the bed," I said. "Look at Sam. He's covered in pee twenty-four hours a day."

"But he's a baby; he doesn't count," she argued. "I'm never going to kindergarten ever, ever, ever again!"

Think fast, Mommy, I said to myself, shaking off the early morning fog. We were four minutes into the day, and already one of us was making threats of monumental proportion.

I slid the baby down my legs, letting him toddle off toward some contraband, and crouched down beside the lump of laundry. I dug my daughter out of the underpants and sweatshirts and leggings and pulled her close, feeling her familiar warm breath, the messy brown curls, the scratchy pajamas.

"I'll tell you a secret," I whispered. "You know who used to wet the bed until he was ten years old?"

"Who?"

"Daddy."

"Our Daddy?"

"Yes, our Daddy," I white-lied. "He did it all the time."

She quieted, so I kept going, embellishing the lie with extra drama. "And because he slept on the top bunk, it would drip down on Uncle Pat too."

Her eyes widened. Her mouth opened.

"But one day his bladder became big and strong enough to get through the whole night and he never did it again. And that's what will happen to you. You just have to keep growing, and eventually your bladder will catch up, just like Daddy's did."

"Really?"

"Absolutely," I said, hugging her tiny body close. She felt so light in my arms, three and a half years older than her brother but only a few pounds heavier.

She must have bought the Daddy story because she looked up at me with those big brown eyes, and for a moment, it looked like I was going to get one of those gorgeous Gloria grins. But before I knew it, her little-brother sonar caught Sam as he chewed aimlessly on Celebrity Chef Barbie's pink plastic whisk. She jumped up, knocking me back hard against the bookcase. An epic tug-of-war ensued, one that was sure to test the very limits of Mattel engineering, leaving me just enough time to run downstairs and start the coffeemaker.

Today would require extra caffeine. Possibly even an intravenous drip.

After the three-hour morning madness, everyone was buckled in the car with their various backpacks, folders, lunches, snacks, sippy cups, nap mats, animal-shaped umbrellas, and, just in case, extra underpants. I had my various necessities too: laptop, week-at-a-glance calendar, refillable water bottle, travel toothbrush, and next to me on the passenger seat—perched scarlet-faced with embarrassment at its shabby surroundings—my new purse.

I had wanted to do the bag proud with a hipper-than-usual outfit, but comfort beat out style once again. For a moment, I stared at my best work outfit, a fitted black J.Crew pantsuit, and imagined the TV version of myself clipping down the sidewalk and being brilliant in the boardroom. But then I pushed the image out of my mind, already too tired to deal with the high heels it required, not to mention the added dry-cleaning expense. Instead, I went with my usual weekday uniform: skirt, cardigan, and flats.

Today's version was a machine-washable charcoal gray pencil skirt, a long-sleeve white T-shirt, and a nine-year-old lavender cashmere cardigan, its "pearl" buttons chipped to reveal the burnished silver underneath. Though technically I would be classified by most as "skinny," at least when seen fully clothed, I still needed a pair of super-control-top tights to corral and conceal the flabby postpartum flesh that stubbornly clung to my middle. One of these days I would deal with those extra ten pounds, perhaps take up spinning or yoga or some such thing, but for now, spandex was my strategy. It worked well enough; the zipper on my skirt went up with a few quick tugs. I finished up with some black mascara over my blue-gray eyes but skipped the under-eye concealer and blush. No one important ever came into the office, anyway.

My hair was another story. Once my pride and joy and the subject of much research and development, it currently featured an inch of brown roots on top and an inch of split ends on the bottom, and its highlights had long ago turned brassy. Today, as on most days, there was no time for styling, just a quick look in the rearview mirror as I pulled my hair into a messy bun. Also in the rearview was Gloria, glowering at Sam, still miffed about the morning's fight. She was no doubt plotting revenge, even as Sam cheerfully tried to woo her with a bungled version of "Itsy Bitsy Spider."

"Shut up!" cried Gloria. "That is not even the right words!"

"First of all, don't say 'shut up.' Second, it's 'those aren't the right words,'" I corrected with my most confident Mom voice. "And please don't scream at your brother."

"But he's soooo annoying," she cried, her tiny hands clenched in frustration.

"Well, that may be true," I told her. "But you better be careful; he'll soon outweigh you."

I realized too late what I had said, and I cursed Wisecracking

Mommy under my breath. Mentioning Gloria's size was never a good idea, but especially not on the way to school, where she was painfully aware of being the smallest in her class.

But she surprised me with a question, not tears: "Why am I so small, Mommy?" she asked, the question I'd learned to dread.

"You're not small," I lied.

"Yes. I. Am. Mommy," she said, her clipped tone giving me a sneak preview of teenage Gloria. "Why?"

"Well, people come in all shapes and sizes, and you just happen to be petite," I explained. "You'll grow. Just be patient."

But I knew that wasn't true. Gloria was tiny and she probably always would be. According to the many specialists we'd visited before and immediately after Gloria was born, she'd suffered from intrauterine growth restriction due to a problem with my placenta. In what should have been an all-you-can-eat buffet, Gloria's in utero experience was more like nine months at Canyon Ranch. She didn't have any cognitive problems, but she was tiny, didn't eat much, and never made it above single digits on our doctor's height/weight chart. Not fair for a kid whose parents were above average height and whose brother was breaking all-time pudge records. Luckily we hit the school parking lot before she could think of any more questions.

Grange Hill Elementary looked cute from a distance, with a cherry tree–lined drive, wide lawn, and brick- and flower-ringed flagpole. But up close, it was proletarian Russia: all rough cinder-block walls, flimsy wooden doors, and a few bricked-in windows. It hadn't been renovated, or even thoroughly cleaned, in decades. The classrooms were overcrowded, security was nonexistent, and in winter its boilers ran so hot, the students sweated through their T-shirts. No one seemed to notice or complain, all of us public school veterans.

I unbuckled and unloaded, caught Sam before he toddled into traffic, and then steered both little bodies toward the school door.

Smiling and nodding, but moving fast, I maneuvered past the conga line of silver minivans, the stay-at-home moms desperate for conversation, and a confused grandfather holding a dripping lunch box. He was probably hoping someone might take pity on him and stop to help, but today it wouldn't be me. I knew I had exactly twenty-eight minutes to get Gloria inside, drop off Sam, and get to my office, ten miles up the Blue Route in Conshohocken. I pretended not to notice the lunchroom coordinator motioning to me but managed to wave to my heavily pregnant neighbor Mary Anne as she waddled past with her three boys. I'd catch up with her over the fence this weekend. Or in fifteen years.

Inside, a quick kiss and Gloria was on her way, a bobbing fuzzy hat, giant backpack, and boots disappearing down the hall. Both Sam and I paused to watch her go. She looked so confident and capable, the morning's incident forgotten in the shrill of the morning bell.

"Sissie bye-bye," babbled Sam, jolting me back to the task at hand.

"C'mon, little guy, let's get you to Grandpa's," I responded.

If Gloria's school was Communist Russia, then Sam's day was a visit to Middle Earth. Jimmy's dad, Miles, a gentle but absent-minded Irishman, took care of Sam while I put in face time at the office. Over the years, Miles had owned a variety of companies: carpentry, house painting, auto repair, even a short-lived stint as an Irish DJ (surprisingly popular in our town). His house was a little boy's paradise, full of tool belts, handmade wooden toys, rusty fishing poles, sixties-style turntables, and old car parts. Sam probably wasn't getting much circle time at Grandpa's, but at this rate, he'd be able to fix our car's transmission or reroof the house by age six.

Miles's house hadn't always been such a man cave. When Jimmy's mother was alive, the two-story brick row home had been bright and orderly, even with four boys at home. But since she'd died five years ago, there was barely a trace of her—except for one room. It was the front parlor, and even Sam wasn't allowed to trespass. Miles kept it just as his beloved Jane had left it. As if she'd walk in at any moment and ask who moved her figurines and why the shades were still drawn.

Pulling up to the curb filled me with the usual dose of stomach-tightening Mommy guilt but, in my case, not just for my son, but for my father-in-law as well. How did this happen that a seventy-nine-year-old retired housepainter, himself someone who could use a little looking after, was taking care of our rambunctious toddler? Sam should be in day care or nursery school, gluing together Popsicle sticks and singing "Wheels on the Bus," not watching *The Price Is Right* and going on Powerball runs. And Miles should be reading the paper and napping under an afghan, not struggling with tiny snaps and butt paste and temper tantrums. But since the recession had hit the lawn care business with a wallop, Jimmy and I didn't have the money for day care, or even a regular babysitter. I knew Miles adored Sam, and Sam adored Miles, but still I worried. The old man was becoming more and more forgetful, and he moved much slower than he used to.

"It's only temporary, it's only temporary, it's only temporary," I repeated to myself as I lifted Sam out of his milk-stained car seat and onto the tiny patch of grass. I grabbed his bag and beloved stuffed giraffe and walked behind him as he toddled up the front walk.

The door opened and out stepped Miles, looking like an artist's rendering of a grandfather in his wool cap, chunky cream sweater, and carved wooden cane.

"Good morning, little laddie!" he shouted as he shuffled to meet Sam, his gnarled, work-weathered hand gently taking Sam's baby one.

"Hi, Pop," I said, reaching out and handing him Sam's daily supplies. I kneeled to give Sam's head a kiss, then ran back to the car, calling out last-minute instructions over my shoulder: "Make sure he naps today. There's diaper cream in the bag. And no more bean dip!"

As I cranked the ignition, I watched Miles help Sam navigate the front steps. I should have been comforted by their easy camaraderie, but as I backed out of the driveway, thinking of the next eight hours away from him—and all the babbles and giggles and little tumbles I'd miss—I bit my lip to hold back tears.

I arrived at Elkins Public Relations mere seconds before my boss, threw my new bag under the flimsy gray cubicle, took the lid off my coffee, and stared intently at my computer as if I'd been reading e-mails for hours.

"Hiiiii, Abbey," purred Charlotte, my former underling turned boss with the perfect bob, perfect blouse, perfect butt.

"Good morning," I said, eyes not moving from my screen. "See you in a few minutes."

"Actually, I really need to talk to you before the meeting," she insisted, not even turning her head as she glided toward her corner office.

Of course you do, I thought. *You want me to bring you up to speed on the account, since you're always too busy schmoozing to actually do any work.* I sighed to myself as I kicked off the purse straps still tangled around my feet and grabbed my notebook. As I walked by, I made a face at my best friend, Jules, also pretending to work but really stalking the new FedEx guy's Instagram.

Seconds later, standing in Charlotte's light- and leather-filled office, I told myself *not* to give up any info, and *not* to fill the silence with my usual blabber. After arranging herself neatly in her chair but not offering me one, Buns of Steel began her usual inquiry:

"Sooooo, what's new with our friends at Maxim Pest?"

I took a breath.

"Jules and I have the fall e-blast all set for today, just waiting on one last photo from the client," I told her, pretending not to notice as her eyes slid from my faded sweater to my scuffed ballet flats. "And I've been working really hard to get the word out about the new stink-bug promotion. I've got some interest from reporters, but nothing definite yet."

Actually, I did have a really good lead. For weeks, I'd been doing some schmoozing of my own, and I was very close to getting a reporter at the *New York Times* to interview our client Max DiSabatino regarding a top secret bedbug product he was developing. Max was the founder and owner of Maxim Pest, the biggest pest-control franchise in the Philadelphia area and a man so intimidating and irascible that he kept me up more nights than my teething toddler. His company's communications strategy was my main responsibility at the firm.

Before I got on the mommy track, I had represented some of the agency's best and most creatively challenging accounts: Web developers, restaurants, architecture firms, and the Fine Arts League. But now that I wasn't as available for travel or late-night drinks with clients—and since Charlotte was promoted to vice president of public relations—I was assigned all the clients nobody wanted: exterminators, chemical manufacturers, mushroom farms. If an account involved something that people tried to *avoid* thinking about, it was mine. And if it was something that I *wanted* to work on—something with museums or artists or medicine—Charlotte always either snatched it for herself or gave it to one of the straight-out-of-central-casting clones she had recently hired.

Still, stories by the *New York Times* didn't come along all that often, and if I could pull this off, I could ride this placement for a few months without the client or Charlotte asking me, "What's next?" And with holiday bonus checks coming out in November, the timing couldn't have been more perfect. But I also knew I couldn't say anything about it just yet. If I told her, she'd announce it at the staff meeting as if it were her idea and then hound me about it from then on. And if the story didn't happen, then I'd look like I'd failed at something that had always been a long shot to begin with. *Don't say anything,* I told myself as I tried to slowly back out of her office.

But she wasn't letting me go so easily. "Abigail. Surely you have something you're working on," she asked, nose wrinkling in disbelief. "You know how important this account is to the firm. To Richard."

"I promise, I'm working on it," I replied, my voice growing terser at the mention of Richard Elkins, our firm's owner. "But it's not exactly the most exciting account. There's been another mass shooting and it's an election year. No one cares about bugs."

"It's our job to make them care," she said sharply. Then she leaned closer, her expression disbelieving. "You've been running this account for a while now. Don't you have *any* leads?"

She was questioning my abilities. And it made me roar inside. *Despite my disheveled appearance, I am very good at my job,* I wanted to scream. *Of course I have leads. I get more story leads in a week then you've gotten your entire career.* But I stayed silent, staring at the little crystal clock on her desk.

A moment passed and I heard her sigh. "If the account's too tough, we should consider getting you help with it. Perhaps Britney. She's got some new ideas."

My head snapped up to see her expression. She was serious. If I didn't give her something, she would stick me with some pretty young thing, maybe even demote me. *Nicely played, Charlotte.*

"Well, there is one reporter who seems interested…"

Her eyes narrowed and she leaned back in her chair, victorious. "Well?"

"I had a brief conversation with Marty Alyward at the *New York*

Times. Turns out he's working on a story about new technology in pest control and he wants to talk with Max next week."

"Fabulous," she said, picking up her silver pen and beginning to scribble.

"Well, it's still not definite, so let's not get too excited," I told her. "Seriously, it's just a 'maybe.' I really don't want Richard to know; he'll think it's a done deal. So please don't say anything—"

"Of course not. I totally understand." She nodded, all wide eyes and false concern. "My lips are sealed."

"And, well, I had to offer him the exclusive," I said, almost under my breath. "I hope that's okay."

She stared at me, considering. Then she sighed and said, "An exclusive? Without asking me first? Well, I hope you at least put a clock on him."

"A clock? It's the *New York Times*, Charlotte," I told her, incredulous. No one makes demands on the Gray Lady. You wait for them. As long as it takes.

"Put a clock on him," she repeated, "or pull the offer."

I opened my mouth to protest but then stopped. She looked down at her iPhone and starting responding to a text, and I swear I noticed a smile curving on her lips. She was probably already texting our boss to tell him that *she* had a lead on the *New York Times*.

I waited for her to finish and cursed my big mouth. Despite her threats, I should have kept my mouth shut. But once again, I'd given in.

"One more thing," added Charlotte, with fake nonchalance. "I need all the current Quaker Chemical clips analyzed, including impressions and ad equivalencies, by Monday morning."

I should have refused, told her it would have to wait until next week, but I was tired, and I figured it was just easier to acquiesce. "Okay," I said. "No problem."

She smiled, then turned her perfectly painted crimson lips and professionally blown-out hair toward her computer screen, showing me her Pilates-toned back. I was used to it and I knew what it meant.

The stained sweater, scuffed shoes, and I were dismissed.

Three hours later, I was seated in a booth in the only lunch spot within walking distance of my office, a little café promising Conshohocken's biggest bagels (my happy place). As my sesame-and-light-garlic-cream-cheese monstrosity cooled, I checked my e-mail, praying for word back from the *New York Times*. I debated internally whether to contact the reporter again and composed several versions of a "just following up" e-mail before deleting them all in frustration. I then proofread a press release and cringed, dreading the thought of spending all afternoon pushing "Maxim Pest's Five Tips for 'Sinking' Stink Bugs in French Drains" on innocent reporters. I sighed and closed my laptop.

Looking out the window at the pretty, quiet streets of Conshohocken, a nineteenth-century factory town trying to reinvent itself as a small business enclave, I sighed. Sure, it offered views of the Schuylkill River, no city wage tax, and old brick warehouses turned into open-concept office space, but I missed working in the city, where the hustle and bustle made even stink bugs seem important. I took a bite of my bagel when a text appeared from Jules. She was going to "need a few more minutes," which could mean anywhere from three to thirty-three.

Jules, my best friend since college, was chronically late. She'd grown up the last of six kids born within ten years to hippie parents, so things like schedules, rules, and deadlines were only words, and time was arbitrary, not finite. At times her lateness brought tragic consequences—failed classes, big arguments, missed flights—but she never changed, or thought to buy a watch. And when she became a graphic designer, and a darn good one, she had no incentive to change, her constant tardiness discounted by her bosses as "artistic idiosyncrasies." Usually it annoyed me, especially when it ate into my comically tight daily schedule, but after today's long morning, I needed a moment to collect myself. I took another bite, then a breath, and repeated the sequence until I was halfway through the enormous bagel. When I washed it all down with a sip of coffee I was in a better place, my mood buoyed by the carbohydrates, not to mention the luxury of five minutes spent without anyone asking me for anything.

I lugged my heavy workbag up onto the table, setting salt and pepper shakers dancing. I should have started with the latest *Pest Control Technician* and *Bugs Today*, but I bargained that I deserved a few minutes to peruse the latest feel-bad-about-your-skin/thighs/ life fashion monthlies instead. That was one of the few good things about working in PR—free magazines.

I pulled out my nine-hundred-page September *Vogue*, now a month old. I flipped through the blur of colorful stilettos, long limbs, and glossy lips before digging into an article about a young mother in irresponsibly high heels and a red taffeta ball gown. Her two toddlers roamed between cypress trees and sculpture in gauzy white dresses, oblivious to the world beyond. The idyllic scene seemed galaxies away from the sizzles and clanks and beeps of Bagel Towne.

Finishing *Vogue*—and still no sign of Jules—I moved on to my other guilty pleasure, *Town & Country*. The pages revealed a world so decadent and beautiful, it was like peeking at life on another planet, a place where roses never wilted and every house fronted a sapphire-blue sea.

I was only a few pages in, somewhere between the fancy rugs and the fancier watches, when I saw it. Or rather, him.

There on the party page, looking slightly uncomfortable at having his photo taken, but very comfortable in his perfectly tailored tuxedo, was Alexander Collier van Holt. His smile was straight and wide, his hair thick and dark, his eyes as blue as I remembered. Pulled apart, each feature was impressive, but together they created an image so rare among the scruffy, bearded looks of today—the traditionally handsome man. The kind you might see advertising cologne or watches, not sneakers. Beside him were two women in plain gowns, one older, one younger, but each with hair and eyes the same color as his. Their hands placed protectively on his arms told me they recognized his uniqueness too.

I leaned in and peered at his face, then let my thoughts escape out loud: "Oh my God," I said to anyone listening.

This man, who I knew simply as Alex, had worked in the same building as I when I was a year out of college. He had been interning at Philadelphia First, a big foundation that gave away tons of money to the arts, schools, and health care. My employers at the time, a small PR firm run by two ex–*Philadelphia Inquirer* reporters, shared a floor with the foundation, and we often benefited from the proximity. Many of our firm's clients were recipients of Philadelphia First grants, eager to give us at least part of their new capital in exchange for some media recognition.

It had mostly been grunt work, but I loved Sharon and Barbara, my smart and sarcastic bosses. I had learned more on my first day with them than in a whole semester's worth of Image versus Morality: Best Practices in Media Relations, even if I was just typing up media lists, faxing press releases, and pasting newspaper clips in spiral-bound books. I also loved the building, a former nineteenth-century department store once known for its elaborate window displays. Walking through the lobby each morning, I hunted for the peeling gold cherubs who peeked down from the ornately carved ceiling. At one time they presided over shoppers buying bowler hats and rose-water perfume, but that summer they watched, chortling, as a young blonde in an Ann Taylor suit and Payless heels shuffled by each day.

It was on a warm day in late April, while waiting in the line at the lobby coffee cart, that I first saw Alex. The morning sun threw curved patches of yellow across the lobby, lighting up women's stockings and men's briefcases as they crossed. He stood behind the crowd, at the farthest elevator, hitting the up button over and over and looking around for help.

He was tall and angular and boyish, his looks still a rough draft of the masterpiece they would become. His cheeks and nose were tanned, as if he had just stepped off the slopes, and his thick dark hair had loosened from the grip of its pomade, falling into his startlingly blue eyes. He wore a classic navy blazer, crisp white shirt, and tan pants, all expensive looking and well tailored, but with contrasting muddy boat shoes and a fraying red-and-black REI backpack. The overall look was one of Outward Bound counselor turned management trainee, the kind of young man who made both mothers and daughters swoon.

Still befuddled by the elevators, he looked up with anxious eyes as I walked up, attempting to be cool and nonchalant. "Need some help?"

"Thanks," he said, smiling with relief. "It's my first day today, and I can't figure out how to make this thing open."

"You need a key card," I told him. "They're locked."

Juggling my coffee and my bag, I tried to slap my electronic card against the keypad nonchalantly, but it slipped from my grip and went flying. I watched as it hit him squarely in the groin and then dropped to the ground with a clatter.

He cringed for a second and then bent to retrieve it. Too mortified to speak, I stepped into the elevator, hoping the dim lights would shroud my face, now red and blotchy with embarrassment. He hopped in after me, apparently not seriously hurt.

"What floor?" I whispered, finger hovering above the numbers.

"Six," he said as the door slid shut.

"Oh, same as me."

"Philadelphia First?"

"No. I work at Salmon and Sisley Communications."

As the elevator ascended, I kept my gaze on the blinking buttons inching closer to floor six, still too mortified to make eye contact. It was not every day that I found myself alone with a man like him. Most of the guys I met smelled like cheesesteaks and cheap shampoo; this guy smelled like Christmas morning.

"I'm starting at Philadelphia First. An internship in their public policy department. I'm Alex." His voice, deep but warm, filled the elevator.

"I'm Abbey. Nice to meet you."

"Nice to meet you too," he said, extending one hand while keeping the other one protectively over his groin. I looked at him, horrified, then realized he was joking. I shook his hand and we both laughed.

The door slipped open and he motioned me out first. I turned and walked slowly toward my office, wishing I could have prolonged the conversation. Then I heard his voice—"Abbey, wait, I think this is yours."

I turned around and saw his arm extended again, this time with my elevator key card. As I walked back toward him, our eyes locked. Silently and slowly, I took the card from his hand, our fingertips touching. It was a moment that felt dangerously intimate for an office hallway. And sure enough, another elevator opened, adding others— nameless, faceless strangers—to our private moment. Alex smiled, then turned toward the walnut-and-glass doors of Philadelphia First.

I stood and stared, watching him walk out of my life.

Or so I had thought.

Two days later, while I was busy faxing press releases, a call caught me off guard. I had almost missed it, its ring barely audible over the screeching fax machine.

"Hi, Abbey," said a male voice, a bit timid. "This is Alex. We met the other day?"

"Hi! How are you?" I swiveled in my chair and leaned down, a finger over my other ear. This was important.

"They let me come back, so I guess I'm doing okay. And you?"

"Fine, thanks." My voice was higher than I wished. I cleared my throat. He did the same but didn't say anything else. The uncomfortable seconds ticked on. Finally, I broke the silence with a question: "Um, do you need some PR or something?"

"No," he said with a nervous laugh. "I'm not calling for that, though I'm sure you would do a fantastic job. I...I was calling to see if you wanted to go out with me sometime. Maybe Friday night? My friend's band is playing...and there's this new Thai place nearby and..."

His voice began to fade in and out as I struggled with what to say. Even though every bone in my body yearned to say yes, even though I was twenty-three years old with every reason to play the field, and even thought this guy seemed nice, sweet, and more than a little sexy, I did what any good, rule-following girl would do. Told the truth.

"I'm really flattered," I said, my heart thumping in protest, even my internal organs disbelieving what I was about to say. "But I have a boyfriend."

"God, I'm so sorry I'm late," said Jules. "But Charlotte made me change a layout even though the client already approved it."

She slammed her giant key ring on the table and then slid herself, her giant woven purse, and her brown-bagged lunch into the seat across from me. "So now I'm totally caught between the client and her and I really don't know what to do. I think I'll just send the file as is and tell her the client was not happy. Or maybe I'll change it and let her take the…take the…why aren't you listening to me? What's wrong? Please don't tell me it's the termite mailer."

"No, the mailer's fine. It's termite-tastic. Really."

"Well, what, then? You look like you saw a ghost."

"Well, I kind of did."

"What? Who?" she said, first sinking back with relief, then sitting back up and waving her hands. "Wait! Don't tell me until I get everything out."

She threw her cell phone and keys into her bag, unstuck her long reddish hair from her striped sweater coat, and pulled out three plastic containers of food. I peeked over the table, anxious to see what bizarre, low-calorie cuisine she would be dining on today.

To a (mostly) skinny, flat-chested gal like me, Jules was curvy and voluptuous and lovely. But to the rest of the world—and in her own mind—she was about twenty-five pounds overweight. Every few months she would try the latest fad diet, cooking up a week's worth of recipes in her tiny studio apartment kitchen, but usually giving up by day three. I'd seen her try the no-carbohydrate diet, the caveman diet, the blood type diet, and even eat only red and yellow foods. I didn't dare tell her what I really wanted to: that none of these "guaranteed" diets would ever work and to me, she was perfect and beautiful just the way she was. Whenever I made any comment about her looks, she always glared at me and said the same thing: "Easy for you to say. You have a husband and kids. My time is running out." To which I would always respond, "Nonsense. You have plenty of time."

Though because she was just shy of her thirty-sixth birthday, we both knew Jules was probably more right than I. Time was a cruel and discriminating bitch, and she preferred to leave slightly pudgy, often wifty, dog-loving hippie chicks behind. No matter how sweet, beautiful, and talented their best friends thought they were.

So as she pulled out her current surefire weight-loss solution, I didn't say anything, just watched her open small plastic containers and pour all the items onto a paper plate snatched from Bagel Towne's counter. At least this week's choice—the Pacific Rim diet, which promised that if you ate with chopsticks you would eat slower and feel full faster—had lasted all the way until Friday. I acted like eating homemade pad thai with chopsticks at a bagel place was perfectly normal and continued with my news.

"Do you remember when I worked at that little agency after college, and I met that guy in the elevator? The one doing the internship?"

"Not really. Why?"

"Come on. You remember. The really cute one? The one I almost castrated with my key card?"

"That sounds familiar. Didn't he ask you out or something?"

"*Yes!* And like a dope, I said no," I said, then turned the magazine toward her and stabbed his face for emphasis. "Well, there he is."

"Wow, he sure knows how to wear a tux," she said as she pulled the magazine closer.

"Well, he should. He's a van Holt."

"And apparently an ardent supporter of botanical gardens," she said, reading the caption. "How admirable." She rolled her eyes as she handed it back to me.

"I never even gave him a chance," I said, my voice serious and quiet. "My bosses were horrified—they couldn't believe I turned down a van Holt. Or understand why someone who was twenty-three wouldn't say yes, boyfriend or not."

"Oh, well," said Jules. "He's probably a weirdo anyway. A coke-head or serial killer or something."

"No, he seemed sweet. Not like a rich jerk or anything. Not that I knew who he was then."

I pulled the magazine and stared even closer, then looked up. "Why was I so stupid?" I continued. "The boyfriend I had at the time—the one I was so devoted to—broke up with me, like, three minutes later. Couldn't he have realized he didn't want to be tied down, like, *before* Alexander van Holt asked me out?" I felt my heart drop, as if that phone call was just yesterday, not years ago.

"Stop," said Jules. "Why are you getting so upset? It doesn't matter."

"I know it's silly, but I can't help but think about what my life would have been like if I had just said *yes*," I said.

"Oh my God, Bee," said Jules, using my college nickname and a softer tone. "It wasn't a mistake. You have a great life."

"I know, I know. I love my kids. They are more than wonderful," I replied as tears welled. "But life's just so much harder than I thought it would be. There's no money and no prospect of money, and Jimmy's gone all the time, and the kids are always fighting and work is overwhelming and I'm just so tired. So, so tired."

Inexplicably, I began to cry, tears dripping down my face and splashing onto the orange Formica tabletop. I pushed over the bagel and magazines and laid my forehead down among the sesame seeds. I started sobbing uncontrollably, right in the middle of Bagel Towne's lunch rush. Jules, always the supportive friend and never one to be embarrassed, reached out and stroked my hair, shushing me quietly while using her other hand to stab my bagel with her chopstick. After a few minutes, I began to calm down, letting the cool of the plastic tabletop and the hum of the restaurant lull me to silence.

When I had quieted down, Jules spoke. "Well, Abigail Owen Lahey, I, for one, am glad you never went out with that rich guy. I can't imagine you all Botoxed and blown out and lunching with the ladies."

"Me neither," I said, head still resting on the table. "But I bet Mrs. Alexander Collier van Holt never has to worry about the mortgage. And by the way, don't think I can't hear you eating my bagel."

"Shut up, you dirty whore," she deadpanned.

Leave it to Jules to make me laugh through tears.

Jimmy was picking up Sam on his way home from work, and Gloria's carpool didn't drop her off until later, so I knew I had a few minutes to change into sweats and slippers, start dinner, and maybe even use the bathroom without an audience. I was able to sneak out of work a half hour early, thanks to Charlotte needing a polish change before tonight's Young Friends meet-and-greet at the Rodin Museum. As soon as she was safely out the door, computers were powered down and bags packed so fast you'd have thought there was a bomb threat.

I turned up our street of seventies-era brick boxes and stone bungalows and arrived at the Lahey residence. It was typical of the area, its front door facing the neighbors' in the Pennsylvania Dutch style, its white wood siding accented by a blue-gray stone chimney. Nothing spectacular, but solid and well built. It was one of the few houses on our street without an ugly addition tacked to its rear. In other neighborhoods, our family of four was average; in Catholic Grange Hill, we were just getting started.

Ours was a commuter town, a lower-middle-class Bermuda Triangle wedged between West Philadelphia, the prestigious Main Line, and the rolling horse farms of Chester County. It was the kind of place where parents still yelled at their kids in public; lawn ornaments and birdbaths were considered chic without any sense of irony; and stores were named after what they sold: Fruits & Veggies, Beer/Soda, and Lamps! (the exclamation point the Grange Hill version of branding). The town seemed to suffer from decades of both overuse and neglect, the entire zip code in need of a good power washing.

Turning into the driveway on autopilot, I slammed on my brakes, narrowly avoiding the side of a shiny red sports car parked sloppily across the asphalt. Its vanity license plate—"GRRRR"—did nothing to help identify the owner.

"Who the hell...?" I said, shutting off the ignition and grabbing my stuff. Running up the back porch steps, I noticed every light in the house was on and the door was not only unlocked but slightly ajar, swinging inward easily as I rushed inside. I also noticed that the dog, usually pawing at the door, was already out in the yard.

Panicking, I threw my bags down on the kitchen table and ran from room to room, though not sure what I was looking for. Thieves? Meth-heads on the hunt for drugs? A neighbor, already drunk from happy hour, mistaking our house for his and passing out on our couch? (That had actually happened once before; we gave him a cup of coffee and drove him home.)

And then upstairs I heard voices and the sound of water running.

"Jimmy?" I whispered as I crept up the steps, feet moving quietly on the worn runner.

And then another sound, a high-pitched giggle. But this I recognized.

As I opened the bathroom door, steam flowed out, revealing my daughter, Gloria, sitting on the toilet with a white towel wrapped tightly on her tiny frame and a second towel wrapped atop her head, framing her rosy-pink face. And standing just in front of her, someone even more sinister than a burglar, a desperate addict, or a drunken neighbor—my mother.

Roberta Eleanor Owen DiSiano was not your typical grandmother, or your typical mother. Hell, she wasn't your typical woman.

At sixty-two years old, she had short, fluffy blond hair, layers of makeup, and long, dangly earrings that touched her shoulders. In the summer, she lived in tennis skirts and halter dresses, but on a cool fall day like today, she sported tight jeans, a fuzzy sweater, fur-trimmed boots, and plenty of turquoise and silver jewelry. She looked like she should be bartending at a Reno nightclub, not grand-mothering in Grange Hill.

I had to admit Roberta looked good for her age—fit and firm and painted and plucked—but for decades now she had embarrassed me with her choice of attire. Day or night, her clothes were always a little too tight, a little too short. She said she dressed to match her "tiger spirit," but I had no idea what that meant and wasn't about to ask. All I knew was that she was desperate for attention: from men, from women, from bank tellers, from bartenders, from Gloria, from me, from anyone with a pulse.

"What are you doing here?" I asked, catching my breath. "And what is Gloria doing with you?"

"Relax, Abigail," she said, her eyes not straying from the nail polish, the exact flame-red shade as her lips, she was carefully applying to my five-year-old's toes. "I got off work early, so I thought I'd pick up Gloria from school and show her my new car."

"Mom, you can't do that. They have rules," I said, exasperated. "I have to let them know in advance if we change the pickup person."

"It's just elementary school; it's not the Pentagon."

Gloria chimed in, emboldened by her new nails and an hour spent with the tiger spirit—"Yeah, Mom, it's not the Pentagong."

I closed my eyes and took a breath, trying to remain calm. "I really don't want Gloria wearing nail polish, and you know this. She knows this. Mom, I wish you would respect—"

"Well, us girls just have to look great on a Friday night, don't we?"

she asked, steamrolling over me, then turning back to her grand-daughter. "And when we're done we can go downstairs and eat ice cream and talk about boys!"

"Eeeewwww," shrieked Gloria, jumping off the toilet and racing out before I could say no to the ice cream, the nails, the fun.

I reached in and turned off the shower, then started picking up Gloria's discarded clothes.

"Mom, how many times do I have to tell you? My life is *not* an episode of *Sex and the City*, and my five-year-old daughter is *not* one of your girlfriends," I said. "I am not Miranda, Gloria is not Charlotte, even if *you* are Samantha."

"Of course not, Abigail," she replied, her eyes locking with mine for the first time since I entered the room. "Even Miranda wouldn't be caught dead in that outfit."

After the kids were asleep, the dishes washed, and the laundry folded, I carried a cup of herbal tea up to bed. I padded carefully into the room, trying not to wake Sam, sleeping profoundly, as only a toddler could, just a few feet away. We kept his crib in our closet since the nursery radiator stubbornly refused to get hot. (When we had first bought the house, our plan was to renovate the back bedroom and add a bathroom, but with money being tight, what should have been a blue-and-brown monkey-themed nursery was now just a catchall for out-of-season clothes, old speakers, hockey sticks, and tax files.)

I climbed into bed, holding my steaming cup carefully as I sank back into my stack of pillows. I had just cracked the Edith Wharton novel I was reading—only a few pages from the end—when Jimmy appeared carrying a white envelope.

"What's up?" I whispered.

"Can you tell me what is a 'bucket bag' and why the hell is it five hundred and ninety-eight dollars?" he asked, half-laughing, half-serious. "I'm really hoping it's some sort of marketing stunt that you'll be reimbursed for."

"First of all, I'm in PR, not marketing, and second of all, it's none of your concern," I said, attempting to grab the envelope.

He held it out of reach, knowing I was trapped by hot tea on a lumpy bed. He stared at me until I confessed.

"It's a purse, okay? I bought it a couple weeks ago."

"Why?"

"I don't know. I was having a bad day. And I guess it caught me in a weak moment."

"So you spent six hundred dollars on a purse? That's crazy."

"No, it's not. Lots of women I know carry purses *way* more expensive." *And those women don't work half as hard as me*, I wanted to add but didn't. We glared at each other.

"Abbey, you know we can't afford it." He sighed and looked away. "God, why do you always do this?"

"Do what?"

"Make me the bad guy."

"You're not the bad guy; obviously I am for wanting to spend *my* money on something for me."

"*Your* money?" he whisper-shouted. "How come when you make money, it's yours, but when I make it, it's ours? That's not fair."

What's not fair is that you're not making any money at all, I wanted to scream back. *You sit in your office just waiting for the phone to ring or drinking at your brother's bar, while I run myself ragged with work, the kids, the house, and the four thousand other responsibilities that somehow got dumped on me when I married you.*

But instead, too tired to fight any longer, I told him, "I'll take it back."

"Tomorrow." He threw the envelope down in front of me, his

brown eyes almost black with anger, and walked out, the creaking floorboards underscoring his rage.

I picked up the bill and attempted to toss it back at him, but its pages separated and fluttered back down into my lap, mocking me. I shoved them onto the floor, set aside my mug, then flopped back onto my pillows.

I should have gotten up and brushed my teeth and wiped the mascara off my eyes. But I didn't care. I turned off the light and curled up under the bedspread, the bitter taste of tea still on my lips.

The next morning I made Jimmy watch the kids while I headed straight for Nordstrom. I was dreading it, knowing the saleslady would take one look at my fake Uggs and even faker diamond studs and give me that "we both know you shouldn't even be in here" look. As I turned onto Route 1 toward the City Line Mall, I found myself thinking of that photo of Alex van Holt in *Town & Country*. What was his Saturday morning like? Was he married? Did he have kids? Had he ever thought about me again after that day?

At a stoplight, I pulled up behind a smooth navy BMW, its glossy windows hiding the glossy family inside, and wondered why the choices you make when you are young don't ever seem to matter until you're too old to go back and fix them. Or too tired to even try. I was a thirty-seven-year-old woman who had worked full-time her entire adult life, yet I belonged wholly to other people—my kids, my husband, my boss, my clients, even my mother. My daybook was filled with grocery lists, half-written press releases, dry-cleaning receipts, appointment reminders, overdue cable bills, and a prescription for something my vet swore would heal those spots on the dog's back.

And I wasn't even allowed a designer bag to carry it all in.

So it was with a mix of irritation, anger, and self-pity that I walked into the busy first floor of Nordstrom and onto the escalator, feeling exposed and vulnerable, not just from the Betsy/Ellen run-in, but from the department store's overly bright lights. Clomping up the moving steps and muttering to myself, my hands occupied with an umbrella and coffee and bags and boxes, my heart beat fast and my body felt strangely unsteady. As the first-floor accessories receded, I lost my footing—and my balance.

What happened next was so fast, there was no time for me to be truly terrified, and I must have looked to others as if I was performing some strangely choreographed high dive. I swooned backward, my hands windmilling, as coffee flew upward in a thick arc. I tried to connect to the railing but overcompensated, so when I turned toward it, I hit it like a gymnast on the uneven bars, flipping over easily. Together with the umbrella, my old purse, and the silver box, my body twisted downward.

A second later, my head hit the Nordstrom piano bench and then smacked the floor, a one-two punch of the most unforgiving wood and marble. I saw the red purse free itself from its box, then skid away on its little gold feet.

And then I smelled roses and heard a few bars of a classical tune, the overly sweet scent and dramatic music making the whole incident seem all the more ridiculous.

CHAPTER TWO

I woke to the soft, repetitive drip of an IV machine in an otherwise still and silent room. As my eyes opened and began to focus, I saw spotless cream paint on smooth walls, the warm glow of a crystal lamp on a walnut dresser, and a small silver frame with "No Smoking" stenciled in calligraphy. Also on the dresser—and strangely out of place in this perfectly curated room: a blue plastic pitcher of water and some gauze.

I lifted my head, then shut my eyes and grimaced. It felt like someone had hit me with a hammer, leaving a pulsing ache above my right ear. I reached up and gently touched the spot, expecting to find matted blood and a gaping wound, but felt only smooth hair over a slight lump.

I took a few deep breaths, and when the pain subsided, or I adjusted to it, I took another look around. And better understood. I was lying in a bed, in a hospital. But not one of the shared and shabby rooms in Delaware County Memorial, where I had given birth to my children. Here, there were tasteful watercolors on the walls; a flat-screen TV; a private, en suite bath; and beside me on another pretty mahogany table, an obscenely large bouquet of peonies. Eyeing the explosion of pink petals, I became scared. Just how long had I been here? And how badly was I hurt? The only way Jimmy would spend more than $12.99 on flowers was if something was *really* wrong.

Oh my God, I'm paralyzed. I'm permanently disfigured. Or worse, I'm bleeding internally and have only days to live. I'll be the first person in history to die from shopping…how humiliating.

But then, before my racing heart could accelerate into a full-blown panic attack, in walked the most gorgeous doctor I'd ever seen, all straight teeth and bright eyes and strong shoulders, smiling at me like I was Marilyn Monroe back from the dead. He wore a beautiful suit, not scrubs, so I wondered if his shift was ending and he was heading out for a meeting or for dinner. If it was a date, she was one lucky lady.

"You're awake!" he said as he moved alongside my bed, grabbing my hand. "Sorry, I wanted to be here when you opened your eyes."

Wow, this hospital keeps getting better and better, I thought, staring up at the man. Then, slowly, as if he were a blurry photo coming into focus, I recognized the hair, the jaw, and the face from the magazine. His eyes, then dulled by the limitations of print, were sparkling and intense in reality. What a weird coincidence after all these years. I had no idea that Alex van Holt had planned to go to medical school.

"What happened to me, Doctor?" I asked, hoping he didn't recognize me.

"Doctor?" He smiled adorably. "That's a new one." He laughed for a moment but then turned serious as he registered I wasn't joking.

"It's me, doll," he said quietly. "Alex."

"Yes, I know," I said, attempting to smile. "Small world, huh?"

His concern only intensified as I babbled, "Why am I here? What happened? And where is my husband? Did anyone call Jimmy?"

His eyes got wider, and he squeezed my hand. "What do you mean? *I'm* your husband."

I blinked at him, confused.

"Don't you recognize me?" he continued. "We've only been married for ten years."

I moved my eyes up and down, taking in his anxious expression, his warm hands, his thick silver Rolex, his thin gold wedding band. I figured I must have been dreaming, so I closed my eyes and took a few deep breaths, expecting to open them and see Jimmy's tattered baseball cap and five-o'clock shadow.

"You're in the hospital. You had a fall while you were shopping. The doctors say you are going to be just fine. No permanent damage. Nothing but superficial bruises, really."

I opened my eyes again. He was still there. I snatched my hand from his and pulled down the sheets, looking for the nurse's call button. I started to get out of bed, but with the sudden movement came a rush to my head that sent me reeling back toward the pillows.

The handsome nutjob claiming to be my husband started shouting to the nurse's station, and in rushed two women clad in scrubs the same tasteful color as the walls, urging me to be still. "Mrs. van Holt, please lie back!" Their warm hands gently but insistently held me down.

The older nurse began to speak loudly and slowly: "Mrs. van Holt, Abigail, you've been in an accident. You're going to be fine but you must calm down. You've suffered a head injury and we want you to be still..."

I kept thrashing, trying to get up, looking around wildly for my family. And then I felt a prick in my arm, warmth rush over my body, and a heaviness in my head.

As I drifted away from them, I heard the words "my wife" and "Mrs. van Holt" several more times.

"But, I'm not...," I said, fighting to hold on to consciousness. "I'm not..."

And then I was sinking into a pharmaceutically induced sleep the same deep blue as the eyes of the man beside me.

When I woke again it was dusk, the setting sun turning the walls orangey pink. No one else was in the hospital room, so I had a chance to take it all in and—and think.

What the hell was going on? If this was a dream, when would I wake up? I eased myself up on my elbows by degrees, waiting for the pain to subside, until I was sitting up. I kicked off the thick sheets and swung my legs around until they hung off the bed like overcooked spaghetti. The top of one knee had an angry black-and-purple bruise, fortunately more ugly than painful.

I heard a male voice in the hall, and I strained to hear—

"The doctor says it is not unusual for someone with head trauma to experience confusion...We're canceling St. Joe's and KYW; let's see what happens tomorrow...Well, yes, Mother, I am concerned about the press...kids okay?...No. Yes. Okay. Ciao."

Was he talking about me? My kids? *Our* kids? And why was he concerned about the press? And what kind of a man calls his mom "Mother"? Or says "ciao"?

I was still pondering, my brow quizzical, when he appeared in the doorway. Even more handsome than when I'd last seen him, if that was even possible.

"You're up. Are you feeling better?"

"Uh-huh."

"Does your head hurt?"

"Not as much."

"Do you recognize me?"

"Yes. You're Alexander van Holt. We met years ago," I told him. Then I smiled and asked, "Did Jules put you up to this? How did she find you?"

This time when his blue eyes looked into mine, I saw tears.

That night, thanks to another shot from a nurse, I slept deeply and dreamlessly from nine at night until eight the next morning. When I woke, I was still confused and anxious, but the throbbing in my head had quieted. In fact, I felt better and more rested than I had in months, miraculously caught up on five years of lost sleep.

With no one in the room and no sound from the hallway, I decided to have a look around. Clad in fuzzy hospital socks and wheeling my IV pole around with me like a dance partner, I tiptoed around the room. I read the cards on the flowers and balloons, all addressed to "Abbey van Holt." I looked at the clipboard hanging from the foot of the bed and learned I had been admitted on Saturday, the twenty-fifth of October, at ten thirty-five in the morning.

I found some clothes in the closet that definitely didn't belong to me: Rag & Bone boots, Current/Elliot skinny jeans, a J.Crew T-shirt, and a yummy cream sweater from Theory. In the pocket of the jeans was some cash and an appointment card for a facial at Bellevue Salon & Spa. The appointment was for Saturday at two o'clock. Guess I missed that one.

On the back of a chair near the door hung a man's size forty-two long black cashmere sports coat, presumably Alex's. I patted down the pockets and found an iPhone. I slid it on, but it was locked. I slipped it back into the breast pocket, jiggling the fabric. I heard something clang the metal arm of the chair. I reached into the lower inside pocket and found a BlackBerry. Unlocked.

DATE: *October 26, 2014*
TO: *Alex <avanholt@vanholtforcongress.org>*
FROM: *Larry Liebman <lliebman@philadelphiainquirer.com*

Van Holt—
  The city desk got wind of Abbey's accident. If you can give me something on your wife's condition, it would hold them off at least a day or so. Otherwise, who knows what they'll write. The election is nine days away.
  Larry

DATE: *October 26, 2014*
TO: *<lliebman@philadelphiainquirer.com*
FROM: *<avanholt@vanholtforcongress.org>*

She's going to be fine. She slipped and fell on an escalator. Doctors kept her here last night only for observation. Canceling all campaign events until tomorrow, though.
  AVH

DATE: *October 26, 2014*
TO: *mirabellevanholt@vanholtfoundation.com, aubynvanholt@vanholtfoundation.com*
FROM: *avanholt@vanholtforcongress.org*

All—
  Abbey is still confused. The doctors can't find any reason for it on the X-rays or CAT, and there's some talk of transfer to psych ward if she's not better. No mention of this to anyone—not even other family. Canceling all events today.
  More later,
  AVH

Van Holt for Congress? Election? Events? The man claiming to be my husband was also running for office. And apparently that made me, and my retail swan dive, front-page news. Before I could read further, I heard footsteps approaching.

I quickly shoved the BlackBerry back in its pocket and then dragged the IV pole back to the bed. I was just smoothing the sheets over my legs and catching my breath when two little children came running toward me in a blur of navy blue and white.

"Mommy," they cried as they flung themselves at the bed.

There they were—my children. Gloria's hair was a little darker, a little thicker, and her eyes were blue, not brown. Sam was just as cute and pudgy, but with a tiny cleft in his chin and close-cropped hair, not his usual dark blond ringlets. And yet, despite these differences, it was still them, all shiny cheeks, bright eyes, and unbridled enthusiasm. They stretched their tiny arms across the hospital bed, with Sam's little fingers just barely reaching my thighs. I pulled them both up on top of the bed and breathed them in.

"Whoa, whoa," said Alex from the doorway. "Let's not hurt Mommy."

"It's okay," I said. "I'm fine, really."

After hugs and kisses and giggles and testing out the nurse's call button forty times, they plopped back down with double slaps of leather-soled shoes, eager to inspect the room's bounty of balloons. Their clothes were neat, their faces jelly-free, and their voices low. Even Sam's cowlick was behaving.

Alex looked relieved. "So you remember them?" he asked quietly. "How about me?"

I knew that I would never get out of here and find out what was really going on if I kept on about Jimmy. "Of course," I told him with a smile. "You're my husband, these are our kids, and I had some sort of an accident. But I feel fine now." I gave him a little jazz-hands maneuver for emphasis.

"Are you sure? Yesterday you insisted you were married to someone named Jimmy."

"I did? That's funny," I said, trying to act natural. Then I put my hand over my mouth as if to whisper and added, "They must have way overserved me." He didn't laugh, just continued to stare, so I told him again, "I promise you I feel fine." And I wasn't lying about this; I really did feel pretty good.

I looked up and around the room, then back at him. "Can we get out of here?"

Finally he smiled, and I couldn't help but smile back. I had no idea how this happened, or what was going on. But I also knew that I wasn't going to figure things out from the confines of this hospital room. Or on lockdown in a mental ward.

I needed to be there for my kids, who obviously had no problem with the new me or the new Daddy. I also figured that if this was a dream or an out-of-body experience or temporary insanity, I might as well enjoy it. And him.

Since I had no dizziness, nausea, or double vision, and since there was no swelling or bleeding detected by the CAT scan that Alex had insisted upon, the hospital had to let me go. I signed oceans of paperwork with a smile, promised to be more careful, and, following hospital protocol, even relented and used a wheelchair. After a ride across town in a huge black Suburban with tinted windows and a quick trip up a wood-paneled elevator, I found myself rolling along the top floor of an ornate mid-rise condo on Philadelphia's exclusive Rittenhouse Square. Because I was being pushed by a tall black man named Oscar, whose warm smile and joking attitude clashed with his secret service–style suit and sunglasses, and whom the kids knew well enough to call "Big O," no one could tell I didn't know which door was mine. But then again, on this entire floor, there were only two to choose from.

Alex let Gloria and her jumble of balloons walk ahead, while Sam rolled along with me, perched proudly on my lap. It seemed like an excruciatingly long roll, but eventually we made it to the door marked with a cursive "Twelve," which Alex pushed open without a key. On the other side was a living room the size of a Banana Republic.

Two lacquered consoles lined the short entryway that led to an open-plan living and dining area decorated in various shades of cream and white. In the center, wide beige velvet couches flanked a low glass-and-metal table perched on a soft white carpet. On one wall, a built-in bookshelf housed decorative bowls, gold Buddha heads, and oversized books, and to the right, a long polished-wood dining table gleamed under the largest drum shade I'd ever seen. The walls were filled with large canvases of modern paintings, some with just a few smears of color, some antique-looking mirrors, and, in the dining room, a massive black-and-white photograph of sheep. It was the kind of effortlessly elegant look that only the very rich could pull off.

I lifted Sam off my lap and stood shakily. I began to walk around the room as if in a trance. I ran my fingers down the glossy dining table and felt the soft cashmere throw on the sofa. I breathed in the faintly lemony smell of all-natural cleaner mixed with orchids in full bloom. Moving to the windows, I pushed aside the filmy sheer curtains and looked down at the tops of the trees, their leaves just beginning to turn yellow and red, that filled the square. Between the branches, I could make out the fountains, the strollers, the wrought-iron benches, and the large bronze statues. I could also see people moving around like windup dolls, walking straight, then turning, then disappearing from view. They moved in ordinary clothes toward ordinary jobs and ordinary houses, oblivious to the luxurious paradise that floated just twelve floors above.

I turned back to the living room and the people in it: Alex intently scrolling through messages on his phone; Oscar trying to maneuver the wheelchair back out the door; Gloria untangling her balloons.

Only Sam stood motionless, his big blue-gray eyes fixed on mine and his mouth slightly open. We stared at each other for a few seconds, our eyes locked and knowing. I shrugged and gave him a funny look. He grinned and giggled his baby giggle.

This will do just fine, he seemed to say.

It had been two days and two nights since I'd last showered, so that became the next order of business. Alex led the kids away, promising them cartoons. When I heard the click of the television and the shrill voice of Dora the Explorer, I walked toward the opposite hall in search of a master bedroom.

It was much like the living room, but in shades of white, gray, and a blue somewhere between slate and robin's egg. Anchoring the room was a king-sized bed with a smooth, spotless white duvet and four stiffly arranged pillows. The tables and dressers were equally clean and uncluttered—with no car keys or pennies, no dry-cleaning slips, no single socks or errant Lite-Brite pegs. Just wide expanses of polished wood with an occasional silver-framed photograph or ceramic elephant.

The bathroom continued the same white, gray, and blue color palette, but this time in marble. I saw a walk-in shower with a massive showerhead, a double vanity sink, and a huge rectangular soaking tub. Open shelving held stacks of white towels, plush circular rugs dotted the floor, and a separate room housed the toilet. It looked like a hotel bathroom, the maid having just left, except for a toy boat lying on its side beside the tub's drain.

Though I wasn't sure what I was looking for, I turned on every light and began opening the vanity drawers. Little boxes clacked into one another, all solid black or silver and emblazoned with simple monograms: "Chanel," "Bobbi Brown," "NARS." The second drawer held designer face creams and body lotions; the third was full of fancy perfumes and shampoo. I pulled out a pot of Crème de la Mer and touched a tiny bit on my face. It smelled as one would expect—like the sea.

Opposite the shower was a door that opened to a long room anchored by a marble-topped island. On each side hung clothes and coats interrupted every few feet by floor-to-ceiling shelves housing neatly folded clothes, as if for sale in a fancy boutique. At the back, two full-length mirrors faced each other, allowing whoever stepped before them an infinite look at both front and back.

Everything was organized by type and then color, the stacks of blouses, T-shirts, skirts, jeans, sweaters, and dresses creating fabric rainbows around the white room. One section of hanging clothes held an array of black satin, smoke gray velvet, and silver sequins, the most elegant collection of formal wear I'd ever seen in person. Tucked to one side were zippered garment bags, the fabrics underneath too vulnerable to be exposed. At home, there was only one garment awarded a home in plastic—my wedding gown.

But all that paled in comparison to what I saw when I looked up. Perched on a thick shelf that ran all the way around the top of the closet was a cavalcade of leather. Not just bags, but designer purses, all polished and poised for action, their gleaming leather and heavy gold chains begging to be touched.

I reached up and took them down one by one. There was a tasseled gray Balenciaga, a purple-and-black Stella McCartney, a large white YSL Muse, a straw-and-leather Michael Kors, a pebbled orange Prada, and twin quilted Chanels in cream and black. There was an Alexander Wang tote, a sparkling Anya Hindmarch clutch, a caramel Céline shopper, a boxy Botkier, and a spiked Valentino. It was the Twelve Wonders of the purse world.

I started to put them all back when a large orange box stowed away in a corner caught my eye. I pulled it down, put it on the marble counter, and opened the lid. Inside, underneath silky monogrammed tissue, was the mother of all designer purses, the it bag of it bags, one that outshone all the others like a movie star in a room of civilians.

A bright red Hermès Kelly bag. The leather was dulled with age (read vintage), but in exquisite condition, its handles still stiff and upright, its lock and key shiny and unscratched. It looked like it hadn't been touched in years.

Inside was some tissue paper and a card that read "Happy 30th Birthday." I quickly rewrapped it and put it back on the shelf, wondering what kind of person gets a Kelly bag for her birthday and then never uses it.

Standing before the wide mirror in the van Holt bathroom, I began to peel off my clothes. I slipped off my boots and then my jeans and was surprised to find a perfect pedicure. And my soles—usually so cracked and dry—were as smooth and unbroken as the marble they stood on.

Quickly, I pulled off the thick cream sweater I had thrown on during my hasty hospital exit and stood up straight, taking it all in. With a look of disbelief on my face, the same look I imagined one might have when looking at a new Lexus in their driveway on Christmas morning, I saw my body in the mirror. My stomach was flat and smooth, with no droopy skin or love handles, just taut, firm skin as if pulled across a drum. My legs were free from stretch marks and broken capillaries; instead they were long and lean, and still tan, as if I were just back from the islands.

And my breasts. There was something definitely different about my breasts.

I looked down at them sticking out of my chest, then again in the mirror. I tentatively touched one with the tip of my finger, the way you touch a cake to see if it's done. I cupped each in a hand, feeling their soft weight. Gorgeous, full, awesome...

And fake.

As boob jobs went, this was peerless work. These were the Cadillacs of implants: pliant, under the muscle, any incision scars artfully concealed.

I stood slack-jawed, wondering what had made Abbey van Holt decide to go under the plastic surgeon's knife. Especially since I had always claimed I never would. And secretly looked down on women, like my mother, who did. (Breast cancer survivors excepted.)

But, then again, maybe I was against plastic surgery because our financial situation meant I never really had the option. I stepped closer to examine my face and hair and see what other improvements, surgical or otherwise, might have been made.

Where were the two deep grooves in my forehead and the little lines around my eyes? The skin was smooth and poreless, as if someone had blurred it in Photoshop. My hair was shorter and blonder, with a razor-sharp edge that just barely grazed my shoulders. I smiled to reveal straight, alabaster teeth.

"Holy shit," I mouthed to myself in the mirror.

I was still naked and admiring myself when Alex walked in. I reached down for my towel and covered myself as best I could as he walked to the double sinks and dropped his heavy silver watch on a crystal tray.

"So, I guess we should figure out tonight," he said, removing his sports coat and unbuttoning his shirt.

"Okay?"

"I know it's a lot to ask, but if you are feeling up to it, it might be good for you to come. It'll stop all the rumors, the media barrage."

"Sure," I said, stealing glances at him in the mirror.

"But are you feeling well enough?"

"Surprisingly, yes. I feel fine. And you heard the doctors; they said I can go back to my normal life."

"I know, but still. Why don't you just stay for a few minutes, shake some hands, get your photo taken, and then Oscar can bring you back," he said. "If it runs late, I can always just sleep at the house. You know how long-winded the Presbyterian League can be."

"No kidding," I said, trying to keep up. "Those Presbyterians are so...so..." My voice trailed off as I watched him step out of his pants.

"Frank thinks that with their endorsement I can pick up more of Montgomery County, maybe some of Bryn Mawr," he continued. "Important votes."

I had completely tuned out what he was saying, too distracted by his reflection in the mirror. As he lifted his undershirt, he revealed the muscular arms, hairy chest, and six-pack abs of a *Men's Health* cover model. When he stepped out of his pale blue boxers and kicked them across the room toward a hamper, my mouth fell open. He walked over to me, his skin looking healthy and tan against the white walls. He wrapped his arms around me and kissed my forehead, not noticing my racing heart and frozen stance.

"I was worried about you," he said, whispering into my hair. "I'm so glad you're okay."

Except for Jimmy and Sam, I hadn't seen another naked male in twelve years, let alone had one pressed against me. It felt so strange, so ridiculous, but also exhilarating. I tried to regain some composure, but when I felt his naked cock pressing against my hip, my heart stopped—and I emitted a little involuntary gasp.

"What?" he said.

"Nothing," I said. "Just tickled."

He laughed, then disappeared into the shower.

Our chauffeur, Oscar, opened the door and held my hand as I stepped down from the big Suburban and landed with a crunch on a circular pebbled driveway. Alex followed behind, still talking on the phone. He was speaking to who I presumed was his campaign manager, and together they had dissected poll numbers and voter maps during the entire half-hour ride. I always hated it when Jimmy talked business in the car—hearing just half of a conversation is worse than hearing the whole—but on this ride, I had listened closely, trying to learn anything I could about this man, this life.

Outside, the early evening light was fading, which made the building before me more potent and magical, like a fairy-tale castle from one of Gloria's storybooks. It was a massive gray stone mansion, covered in ivy, with too many chimneys to count, a gray slate roof, and one rounded turret. The windows glowed golden, lit from within so brightly the interior seemed ablaze. This was Bloemveld, Alex's childhood home and the family estate for more than a century.

I would learn later that prior to this gray stone mansion there had been a smaller brick version, and before that, a log cabin. The land had been in the family since Alex's ancestor Alexandre van Hault purchased it from William Penn in the late 1600s. The first van Holt living on American soil had been a farmer and a tender of sheep, but his great-grandson found coal on the land, which led to investments in steel, which eventually led to real estate. The poor, illiterate Dutchman in the log cabin would never have believed that his descendants now owned a third of Philadelphia, half of the Main Line, and enough of Manhattan to be invited to the Central Park Conservancy gala and the Met Ball every year.

As I started for the front door, Alex caught me by the elbow. Holding the phone in his hand, he whispered, "What are you doing? You know Mother hates it when we use the front door."

"Right," I said, abruptly changing course and falling into step behind him. This would be the first of many pivots—both physical and conversational—I'd be making that evening.

It was a warm night for October, almost muggy. I had played it safe with a simple sleeveless black shift and plain gold jewelry. But I couldn't resist when it came to choosing shoes, picking a pair of crystal-covered Jimmy Choos. They sank past the pebbles into the dirt, but I didn't care. If these got ruined, there were plenty of other "cocktail" heels back in the apartment: a pair studded with gold, one with little mirrored shards, another topped with a black lace bow so stiff it felt like plastic.

As we crossed in front of tall windows with pencil-thin mullions, I peeked into each room, taking in the overstuffed upholstery, watered-silk wallpaper, and paintings of bright-eyed, pointy-eared stallions in gilded frames. Passing the dining room, I noticed an enormous crystal chandelier lit by candles, not bulbs. I wondered if wax would drip onto the massive table beneath it and whose job it was to snuff the flames each night.

At last, reaching the side of the house, we stepped onto a raised stone terrace covered by a taut green-and-white awning. Alex took my elbow and steered me indoors, into a room abuzz with clanking silverware, harried footsteps, and slamming oven doors.

Actually, it was a series of rooms culled together into one big kitchen, the needs of modern entertaining gobbling up old closets and butlers' pantries into a massive, noisy ode to all things culinary. A small army of cooks and maids and servers rushed to and fro, like commuters hurrying for their trains, their arms laden with trays and linens.

Amid the monochromatic tableaux—black-and-white uniforms, stainless steel appliances, and granite countertops—two women stood out like Jordan almonds: one in a pale blue wool suit, the other in a pink sweater set. The middle-aged woman, in blue, inspected a tray of champagne flutes while the younger one, in pink, flipped through a magazine, a bored expression on her face.

When we approached her, she looked up lazily from her magazine and spoke with obvious sarcasm: "Nice of you to join us."

"Oh, calm down. People aren't even here yet," Alex replied, sliding his phone off and slipping it into his chest pocket. "I had a radio interview that went long, and I'm not sure if you heard, but my wife was in the hospital."

Not knowing her name, I just stood there as she cut her eyes toward me for a moment, then returned to Alex. I thought I should say something, but the best I could come up with was a whispered "Yeah, I was in the hospital."

She turned back to me and glared. "Yes, *I know*, Abbey. You were in the hospital. We would have visited but Alley told us not to."

"That's not what I meant," I stuttered.

"Whatever. I really don't even know why I bothered to come to this," she said, turning back to Alex. "I'm telling you, Alley, this is the last night for me. The old bags better have their checkbooks with them this time."

"Hey, watch what you say," said Alex with a glance around the room. "Last thing I need is for that to end up on YouTube."

"Chiiiiildren," wailed the older woman in blue as she moved toward us. "Please stop bickering. Let's get through this as best we can. It's important for Alex, for all of us."

Then, turning to me and putting her manicured hand on my

shoulder, she looked at me with loving concern. "Abigail, we were so worried. Is there anything we can get you?"

I opened my mouth to respond, but the woman, who I guessed was "Mother," continued to speak, though her eyes were glued to a passing server's tray: "What an absolutely bizarre accident. You know, someone should really investigate those escalators. For someone as fit as Abigail to fall, there's a problem. But the most important thing, of course, is that she is fine." She turned back to me and smiled, and I smiled back.

Then she leaned in closer to me with a wink. "Though I have to say, we so enjoyed having the children here with us. You should have seen Van with Cook. What an appetite that little one has."

Van, I thought. *That's what they've been calling him. Oops.*

Then I saw her eyes flick over my dress and land on my sparkling heels.

"What wonderful shoes!" she exclaimed. She seemed delighted by them, but I couldn't help but feel slightly embarrassed.

"Thank you," I whispered shyly. "I thought so too."

But she didn't hear, instead focused on a half-filled ice bucket floating toward the swinging doors. She darted away, leaving tendrils of gardenia perfume in her wake.

"Mrs. van Holt?"

I heard someone talking behind me but ignored the sound as I took in the enormous wood-paneled room. Despite all the bodies flowing in, and the crackling fire in the stone fireplace, I was shivering in the cavernous space, realizing only now why everyone else wore thick tweeds, wools, and cashmere.

The voice behind, this time closer and louder, asked again, "Mrs. van Holt?" and I wished whoever she was addressing would just respond.

It wasn't until Alex whispered, "Abbey, answer her!" that I remembered. Mrs. van Holt was me.

I whirled around, and not realizing how close the server was, I upset the wide silver tray she was balancing so neatly in one hand. She and I watched in horror as the tray—filled with champagne flutes—flew up in the air, the glassware hitting the carpet without incident but the bubbly liquid flying farther, smacking a group of party guests as if they were sitting front row at SeaWorld.

And thus began my foray into Main Line society.

A woman who doesn't even know her own name. A woman red-faced and shaking with embarrassment and wondering what one can possibly say to a bunch of elderly Presbyterians one just baptized in booze.

"Jeez, Abbey," said Alex after the help swooped in to clean up and the room returned to its conversations. "If you weren't feeling like champagne tonight, you could have just said so."

I looked up at him in anguish, mortified, before I saw a smile curve on his lips. He was joking. I laughed in relief, then leaned toward him and whispered, "Oh my God."

"Seriously, what's with you? Are you sure you're okay?"

"I'm fine, really. Just...just nervous for you. The election and fund-raising and everything."

"Well, don't be. You know I've known these people forever."

He slid his arm around my back, guiding me protectively, and for a moment, the rest of the room disappeared. It came back into focus quickly, though, as a photographer hired for the event jumped in front and asked us for a few photos, and then, as the flash went off, couples from around the room noticed us. They looked over and moved toward us like a leather-heeled herd, all wanting to be the first to greet the guests of honor.

I clung to Alex's side, even standing a few steps back, like a small child hiding behind a parent. I quietly smiled and nodded, trying my best to go unnoticed. But almost every person who approached expected me to say *something*, if only small talk. After all, Alex was the reason for this party, and I was the reason's wife.

Even the simplest question was fraught with danger, and never in my life had I felt so uncomfortable in a social situation. My body language was as taut as a drum, my expression anxious, and when I spoke, my voice came out either too soft or too loud. It was as if I had been thrown onto a Broadway stage on opening night with no script.

And the audience? Not only strangers, but strangers from another land, talking about things and people and places I knew nothing about. And the *way* they spoke was problematic too. I had no idea that people—aside from the Thurston Howells on *Gilligan's Island*—actually spoke like this.

"Abigail, dear, are we mucking through?" asked a silver-haired matron with golf ball–sized pearls.

Mucking through what? This party? My recovery? Life in general?

I whispered a benign "yes" and she began to drone on about the demise of our country now that there was a "colored man" in the White House. Was I hearing her correctly? I hoped not.

After her, a silver-haired gent with an enormous overbite mumbled questions at us between bites of shrimp. Though I couldn't understand but every fifth word, Alex answered deftly and with ease—he being well-versed in this secret Wasp language—before he pitched the conversation to me.

"You'd have to ask my wife," he said as he put his hand on my shoulder. "That's her domain." *Oh no.*

I bought time by pretending I couldn't hear him. "Excuse me?"

The old man shuffled closer, his sour breath making my eyes sting. "I *mumble mumble* Alexander here *mumble mumble* the cottage. Is it coming along?"

A cottage? What cottage?

"Fine," I replied. "Just fine."

"*Mumble mumble.* So by New Year's?"

I wanted to tell him, *I have no* mumble *idea*—anything to get him and his halitosis away from us—but I took a stab at an answer: "Yes."

Alex started to laugh. "Are you kidding?"

I guessed again—"I mean maybe"—figuring that was safer. But at this, Alex turned and stared, eyebrows raised. Next, I went with the only remaining option: "No?"

Alex leaned over and yelled into the old man's ear: "George, with the way my wife fires architects, we'll be lucky to be in by *next* New Year's."

The two men laughed. I joined in a beat later while making a mental note: The van Holts were building a "cottage" so magnificent it required multiple architects and many years to build. Somewhere.

From another direction came a tall, steely-haired woman in a dark green plaid suit hanging like Spanish moss on her gaunt frame. Her skin was so pale and thin I could see the web of her veins, as if she'd just risen from the dead and rushed right over to Bloemveld. Her only adornment? A diamond salamander with sapphire eyes trying to escape over her bony shoulder.

"Abigail," she snapped, stepping in front of the mumbler. "There are too many people here. Why don't you van Holts pare down your lists?"

"Um, well…"

"And the crab is almost gone. Mirabelle should have used my man. He does a smacking good job."

I nodded, smiling, but that seemed to irritate her more. She stood straighter and spoke louder. "And you haven't responded to my note. We *will* be seeing you and the children at Jamaica Hill over the holidays, right?"

Jamaica Hill as in Jamaica? Count us in!, I wanted to say. But then I noticed Alex looking down at the floor. I took a stab at an answer.

"I'm sorry. But we don't have plans to travel this year."

Her black eyes flew open in surprise, then narrowed with irritation. She stomped away.

"Really, Abbey?" asked Alex, annoyed. "I don't think driving a mile down the road constitutes 'traveling.' Surely we can work her in."

"I'm sorry," I said, just then realizing that Jamaica Hill wasn't a resort in the Caribbean but the name of her estate. And it was close to Bloemveld, maybe even just next door. "I didn't mean to be rude."

"Yes, you did. You've always hated Aunt Tickle."

Aunt Tickle? Who would tickle her? Rich people and their stupid names and their stupidly named estates. Didn't they realize this was the twenty-first century?

"Should I go apologize?" I asked. But before Alex could respond, we were approached by yet another couple, these two looking like they'd just stepped off the Scottish moors, their tweed jackets, thick wool turtlenecks, and riding boots perfectly matched. Their most marked difference was their eyebrows: hers were drawn on messily while his stuck out like steel wool. I braced myself.

"Abigail, we're so sorry about your little fall," said the woman languidly. "I trust you're feeling better?"

Finally, someone had asked me about something that had happened in the last twenty-four hours. Something I could easily answer.

"I'm fine, thank you. Overnight in the hospital was just a precaution."

"But what happened?" she asked. "Did you slip on something?"

"I . . . I just lost my footing. Everyone's worst fear on an escalator, right?"

"I've warned her before about those high heels, but she won't listen to me," said Alex, shrugging.

"Wives these days never do," added the old man. Everyone laughed except me.

The conversation turned to the campaign and then life in general. I listened intently, trying to pick up any information that might help me. From what I could gather, this couple was Mr. and Mrs. Brindle of the now defunct Brindle Department Store chain. They lived nearby and were old friends of the van Holts; Alex was even their godson. And perhaps benefactors too: At one point, the old man pulled Alex aside and slipped him an envelope. Alex put it in his coat and stepped back to me, and we all stiffly shook hands good-bye (no one hugged here, not even godparents).

We were almost free of them when Mr. Brindle turned back, suddenly remembering something. "Oh, Abigail, I forgot to ask. How did you like the seats last Sunday? Helluva night, huh?"

Last Sunday? Last Sunday I had been home watching the Eagles get crushed by the Giants as Jimmy threw things at the TV. I guessed he meant the game?

"I know! What a disaster. Heads are definitely going to roll for that one."

The group turned silent; then Alex jumped in. "Oh, I don't know, doll. I know it's not the philharmonic, but I thought the new strings were terrific."

Huh? "Oh! You meant the symphony! Yes. Terrific."

Alex laughed. "What did you think we were talking about?"

"I thought you meant the Eagles."

A confused-looking Mrs. Brindle spoke next. "Who?"

"The Eagles. The Philadelphia Eagles."

The woman looked at her husband and then back at me. "Excuse me?"

"She means the professional sports team, Edith."

The old lady and I stared at each other without speaking, she still confused and me stunned. To not know Katy Perry or *Finding Nemo* or Blue Man Group, I understood. But to live in Philadelphia and not know the Eagles? Unbelievable.

The couple smiled and walked off, leaving me a few seconds to take in the room and everyone in it before the next conversation. These people were the last of the great robber barons and society matrons of the Main Line, a group of people so out of touch with reality, so protected in their own tweed- and mahogany-coated world, it was like they were their own species. Or a lost tribe— hidden not by jungle but by high stone walls and curling iron gates. And lots and lots of money.

And here was I—or some symphony-loving, cottage-designing, estate-visiting version of me—living among them.

Or "mucking through," that is.

After another twenty minutes of "fines," "greats," and "uh-huhs," plus a lot of napkin dropping, drink refreshing, and talking about the weather—so much so you'd have thought a fifty-five-degree day in late October was like a snowstorm in July—I realized I had better get away from Alex. Even though he was so polite it was hard to tell what he was thinking, I had made so many gaffes, he had to be suspicious. Or think I had suddenly turned into a moron. Thank God I could always fall back on my "head injury" if I needed to.

I excused myself and made my way slowly through the crowd, examining the world around me. There were so many people jammed into the large room—more than one hundred guests, all drinking heavily, barking orders at servers, and crowding around two bars (one raw, one wet)—that no one seemed to notice me.

Adding to the commotion were three loping Irish wolfhounds, which mingled along with everyone else, knocking into knees and begging for bits of Camembert when not lounging like furry maharajas on the flowered couches.

Across the room, I spied Alex's sister and mother, both at ease in their natural habitat. There was no sign of a father, and no one mentioned one, so I figured he must be dead or out of town. Not that I was one to question a broken home; I hadn't heard from my dad in more than twenty years.

I moved into a corner, eager to further examine my in-laws. Alex's sister was Aubyn, much younger and even more patrician looking than her brother. She was tall, ballerina thin, and very pretty, but her preppy pink sweater and plain black pants made her look matronly, dull. Her eyes were just as azure as my husband's, and her chestnut hair was thick and glossy, piled on her head like a Gibson Girl painting come to life. *She could use a pair of jeans, a T-shirt, and a hair out of place,* I thought as I took a seat beside her on a long leather bench. When she rose and walked off just seconds after I sat down, I began to understand our relationship. She hated me.

Alex's mother, Mirabelle, on the other hand, showed only sheer delight in all her guests, including me, treating each of us with warmth and rapt attention. She had dark hair like her children, but hers had touches of silver and was cut in a soft bob that curled up under her chin. Her skin was smooth and rosy, suggesting she wasn't above a good facial or two, but with enough laugh lines to indicate she viewed Botox as vulgar. An impeccably tailored suit accentuated her petite frame. Her shoes were stylish but not too high; her jewelry was expensive but tasteful; and her hair shone as if it had been brushed with a good fifty strokes.

I watched her move from group to group, making each person feel welcome with her direct gaze, easy smile, and quick wit, social skills no doubt honed with decades of practice. With no patriarch around, I deduced Mirabelle was used to being the sun around which this family orbited. I couldn't take my eyes off her. She was mesmerizing.

Not only that, but she was so different from my "other" mother-in-law. I couldn't help but think of tonight compared to the first night I met Jimmy's parents. That night there were certainly no staff, no suits, no shrimp tower.

It began with Jimmy driving me home after our first night together, which I would have liked to call a date but was really a one-night-into-the-next-day stand. I'd met Jimmy at his brother's bar in Bryn Mawr when Jules and I snuck out of a client event early and hightailed it across the street. Though this was certainly not a detail I was proud of or planned to tell our children, I had spent the entire night and the next morning and afternoon with Jimmy in his cluttered one-bedroom apartment above the health food store in Ardmore. I remember it smelled like patchouli and peppermint, the scents making our drunken sexcapade seem more exotic than it was.

That afternoon, my clothes slightly rumpled from twenty-four hours of wear, Jimmy had insisted on stopping by his parents' house to pick something up. They lived in Upper Darby, a working-class neighborhood below the Main Line that was on the way back to my apartment in the city. After being stuck behind a trolley for fifteen minutes, we turned onto a narrow street of tiny row homes, their identical brick facades interrupted only by alternating Flyers, Eagles, and Phillies flags.

"I'll wait in the car," I told him as we pulled up to a tidy house with a white metal fence and overflowing window boxes. A painted sign marked *"Fáilte"* hung instead of a wreath on the door. As Jimmy shoehorned his truck into a tiny spot effortlessly, then jumped out, I slumped in the seat so no one could see me. He went inside but then burst back outside a few moments later. Next thing I knew, he was opening my door and pulling me out.

"My mom saw you from the window and is insisting you stay for dinner," he said. Mortified, I yanked back my arm and scrunched down even further.

"Don't try to hide from her; she won't take no for an answer," he said, laughing. "She has a radar for any female within a hundred feet of our house."

I cringed and shook my head, wanting to disappear into the upholstery.

"Why don't you have mercy on a mom of four boys and come in?" Jimmy begged.

"Oh God, no!" I remained immobile, but my eyes made contact with his oak brown eyes, and I knew going into the house was inevitable, the same way I had known the night before, after just a few hours of talking, that I was going home with him.

"Tell her that we met at lunch today," I implored. "Don't you dare tell her I met you last night."

"Right, okay, I'll tell her I met you pounding shots at lunch," he joked. "That's definitely classier."

I laughed in spite of myself, then sighed. *I'll never see this guy again,* I reasoned, *so I might as well enjoy a free meal.* I tucked my wrinkled work blouse into my skirt and stepped out of the truck.

Four hours and four thousand calories later, I was enjoying myself as Jimmy's one younger and two older brothers regaled me with tales of their hockey triumphs, their Catholic school misadventures, and their hundreds of adolescent fights. Jimmy's adorable, auburn-haired mother, Jane, brought so many dishes out of her tiny kitchen, I wondered if more people were supposed to show up. There were enough clams, pasta, ham, green beans, potatoes, and rolls for the entire block.

I didn't say much, but I laughed the entire time: at Jimmy's imper-
sonation of their drunken uncle Seamus; at older brother Chris's
tales of selling telephone cable to mobsters in Atlantic City; and at
father Miles's Irish-brogued rendition of Nat King Cole's "Unfor-
gettable." For just an average Sunday night at six thirty, it was pretty
rollicking, and certainly different from the silent, heat-and-serve
meals my mother and I ate in front of *Entertainment Tonight.*

All of the Lahey brothers were handsome in their own way, but
Jimmy's younger brother, Patrick, was just plain hot. Where Jimmy
was more rounded out and soft-spoken—with thinning dark blond
hair, warm brown eyes, and broad shoulders perfect for leaning
on—Patrick was bad-boy handsome, with a wiry, muscular build,
thick black hair, and an icy green gaze that suggested he knew
exactly what was under your clothes. He also had several tattoos,
rode a motorcycle, and tended bar, hitting the twentysomething-
party-girl trifecta. To say he was good with the ladies was the under-
statement of the year, but to me, his brand of bad-boy sex appeal
was a little scary. I knew just where that would lead. Jimmy was
more comfortable, warmer, and, back then, really funny. Like that
favorite sweater you look forward to wearing every fall.

Luckily, Patrick never let on how drunk we were the night
before, or that when I stumbled out with his brother after last call
he was pretty sure what was going to happen. I guess it was a brothers' code, or perhaps a bartender's: never kick a gift one-night stand
in the mouth. And never deny your poor daughterless mother the
chance for female company, even if she might never see the young
lady in question again.

Not that Jimmy's mother ever acted as if I was anything less than
a formally invited guest. Despite having just met me a few hours
earlier, she laughed at all my jokes, asked me lots of questions about
work, and insisted I take the first piece of homemade key lime pie.

After several hours and an after-dinner Irish coffee, I realized I'd better get back home, and we said our good-byes. I don't know if it was the booze, the stories, the Nat King Cole, or the carbohydrates, but by the time we'd climbed back in the truck and started making out over old coffee cups and the parking brake, I knew I was in love.

When I heard my name this time—"Mrs. van Holt?"—I answered readily. It was yet another server, touching me on the arm and pointing to Alex, who was waving me over. He was standing beside a handsome young couple, one of the few here under forty, and perhaps friends of ours. I couldn't do it, though. If I made any more missteps, he would be suspicious, and I couldn't risk him getting worried and sending me back to the hospital. I held up my finger to indicate I needed a minute, then went in search of a bathroom.

The server directed me toward "the main hall," but the promised powder room proved elusive. I looked around and eventually made my way toward the back, where the light from the large chandelier didn't quite reach, making it hard to see. I tried a few doors, but each glass knob led to a closet, a long back porch, and an even darker stairway, respectively.

I spun around and tiptoed back to the front, confused. Maybe this wasn't the main hallway? Maybe there was an even bigger, grander hall somewhere else? One with more ancestral oil paintings, bigger black-and-white marble tiles, and an even taller wood-paneled staircase?

Suddenly, a portrait underneath the stairs swung toward me, the van Holt ancestor it depicted coming at me like a Scooby-Doo ghost. I gasped and stepped back, making room, then steadied myself. From behind the painting stepped a tiny white-haired clergyman in a dark suit and collar, his eyes bright and blue. Seeing me in the hall, he held open the door from which he had just emerged and gave a little courtly bow: "It's all yours, madam."

"Oh, *that's* the bathroom?" I asked. "I...I forgot where it was."

"These old houses are a lot like churches. Hidden doors. Secret hallways. Little Scots that jump out from under the stairs." He winked and gave me a mischievous grin.

"Well, thank you for the warning," I said, laughing. "Now, if you'll excuse me."

I snuck around him and into the hidden bathroom under the stairs, ducking my head to avoid the slanted ceiling. When I came back out, the man was still there, gazing up at a painting of a shepherd fighting off a snarling wolf.

He felt me walk up beside him, then held out his arm without turning toward me. "My mother told me a lady should never enter a room by herself," he said. "May I escort you?"

"Funny, my mother will *only* enter a room by herself," I replied, thinking how Roberta always preferred all eyes on her. "But yes, thank you." I put my hand on his arm and we rejoined the party, finding a quiet space near the window. He introduced himself: "I'm Father Ferguson. I was hoping to speak with your husband, but he's been occupied for the last hour. Though it's quite possible he's avoiding me."

"Oh? Why would he do that?" I asked, intrigued.

"He knows why."

"Well, why don't you fill me in?"

"Your husband promised to speak with his uncle in the state senate to see if we could help my little community center qualify for state funding," he explained. "But that was before he was running for Congress."

"Well, my husband's got a lot on his mind," I said, remarking how I'd just referred to Alex as "my husband" so easily. "Maybe he plans to help you after the election?"

"Maybe," he said. "But I'm running out of time. And money." He sighed, then sat down on the edge of a sofa and patted the space beside him. "Perhaps *you* would like to come to the center and see what we're all about?"

"I would love to, but we have campaign events scheduled every single second from now until next Tuesday," I told him in a tone that I hoped sounded as elegant as Mirabelle's. "I'm sure you understand." *Plus, I am not sure how much longer I'll be living in this dreamworld.*

"But we're only five minutes from Center City. It's the Holy Rosary Settlement House on Pine and Fifty-Eighth."

"Holy Rosary?" I asked. "You do know this is a *Presbyterian* event?"

"Well, we won't tell anyone, will we?" he said, holding his finger to his lips. "You'd be amazed the places this collar can take you." Then quieter, in a confiding tone: "Besides, I've never been afraid of the Calvinists. They've got it easy. It's suffering, not salvation, that toughens us. Right?"

"I wouldn't know."

"Oh, for some reason I thought you were Catholic."

"Why would you think that?"

"Just a feeling."

He was sort of right. Though I was raised without any formal religious training, Roberta being an agnostic, Jimmy was Catholic, making me one by marriage. I changed the subject, asking my new friend how he came to be a priest.

Father Ferguson, or "Fergie" as he insisted I call him, seemed less socially awkward and more worldly than the priests I knew in Grange Hill, so I wasn't surprised to learn he had come late to his ministry. In fact, he'd been married once—to his high school sweetheart, who he claimed was the great love of his life. They lived together "blissfully" until 1972, when she and their son, his only child, were killed by a drunk driver. He spent two years trying to drink himself to death, finally got sober, joined the priesthood, and made it his life's work to help poor children and their families, asking the church to place him in the most crime-ridden sections of southwest Philadelphia. It was a tough job, full of heartbreak, but he credited it with rescuing him from despondency and keeping him sober these past twenty-five years. In his words: "It brought me back to life."

He told me one story of a four-year-old boy who showed up on Holy Rosary's doorstep too weak to stand. Turned out the boy had scurvy from a diet of oatmeal, mac 'n' cheese, and soda, the only foods his parents could afford—or, frankly, find—in the "food desert" of far West Philadelphia. Today, the boy was strong and healthy, and now about to graduate with a degree in economics from La Salle University.

"Growing up in South Philadelphia, we never had much, but we *always* ate," he said. "I can't bear the thought of kids going hungry. Have you ever seen the look in a mother's eyes when she knows her little ones are starving but there is nothing she can do about it?"

I shook my head. Even in Grange Hill, where people lived paycheck to paycheck and the bank owned at least one house on every block, no one ever went hungry. I promised to visit Holy Rosary later that week and made a mental note to talk to Alex about his promise. From across the room, I could see my husband watching us, but he made no move to come over. I told Father Fergie I had to go.

He reached up and touched my face, turning it toward him to ensure my complete attention: "Abigail, I've appealed to every person in this town and they've all let me down. Now I'm putting all my hopes in your sweet face," he said.

"I'll try my best."

"That's all I ask." He smiled widely and clapped his hands together, as if his job was done. Then, more quietly, he added, "I'm just sorry we haven't met before."

"Well, we might have," I said quietly, not wanting to lie to a priest. "You see, I don't really know. In fact, I'm not really who you think I am."

He chuckled as if I'd made a joke, and leaned in close to whisper in my ear: "None of us are, dear."

He stood up, lifted my hand to kiss it, like a knight kissing a lady after a tournament, and then walked out the door.

Standing up, I noticed the crowd had thinned, but only slightly, with most people still drinking and laughing, some in heated discussions, saliva spraying as they spoke, while others lounged their bodies across couches, almost motionless, their bellies full of red wine and oysters. I noticed a few folks still clustered by the raw bar and my stomach growled, and I realized then just how long it had been since I had eaten. But when I reached them, I saw that the bar was picked clean, the mound of ice bare except for a few lemon wedges and some frozen dill fronds.

Not easily thwarted, I strolled around the room searching for some leftover crudités or for a server passing a tray. But all I could fine was a solitary silver dish of dry brown crackers on a sideboard in the corner. I shoved a few in my mouth, grateful for any sustenance. Then I looked for Alex, figuring it was time for me to go.

But all at once the three white-gray wolfhounds leapt off their respective couches and came running toward me on their long legs. They jumped up on me and barked, knocking me backward until I felt the heel of one of my beautiful shoes weaken and snap off.

The massive dogs barked and snarled as if I were an intruder, as if they knew I was an imposter, and I wondered if it was true about dogs: They could sense visitors from another world. As they continued their attack, I cowered and sank to the floor in fear.

Alex yelled—"John Henry! Malcolm! Rex!"—and rushed over, then pulled the dogs away with hard tugs at their collars. Then I was up and in his arms as he carried me and my broken shoe across the room like a bride. From over his shoulder, I saw everyone I'd just met gawking, their mouths open and motionless. Even Mirabelle stared, her mask of gentility replaced with one of confusion. And perhaps a flicker of irritation.

Only when we reached the front door did Alex stop, pausing to look into my eyes and ask if I was okay, his brow wrinkled in concern, then cursing Aubyn for not putting those "damn dogs of hers" outside. He looked so worried about me—and angry at her—that if I hadn't already been in his arms, I would have swooned.

It wasn't until after he'd helped me into the back of the Suburban, after he'd closed the door and rapped on the roof, signaling Oscar to go, and after we'd pulled out of the circular drive and onto the winding road that would lead us back to the expressway that it occurred to me why Aubyn's dogs had attacked me.

Those hadn't been stale crackers in that fancy silver dish. They were dog biscuits.

CHAPTER THREE

The next morning, I opened my eyes expecting to see my red-numbered alarm clock, a basket of unfolded laundry, and Jimmy's pajamas strewn across the floor but was met by the bright white order of the van Holt household. I sat up with a jolt.

Beside me were an empty pillow and rumpled bedsheets, Alex already up and on the campaign trail. I wasn't sorry to be alone, though, needing time to process another day in this strange world, this pretty fishbowl I couldn't swim out of. I took a few deep breaths in an attempt to calm the rising panic and the sudden desire to run out of the apartment screaming. My mother always told me there's a solution to every problem if you just looked hard enough. It was time for me to do some looking.

I got out of the bed and stretched, then froze as I heard a child's voice: *"Maman,"* it said. *"Van se lève."*

I spun around and saw Gloria, her curls dark against a light pink nightgown.

"What did you say?" I asked. My own silk nightgown swished around my shins as I walked toward her for my morning hug.

"Van se lève," she repeated. *"Allez le chercher."*

"You speak French!"

"*Mais oui, Maman.*"

"That's so cool. Unbelievable, actually."

"Does that mean you want me to speak English?"

"Sure."

"Good. 'Cause I want Froot Loops for breakfast and I don't know how to say that *en français.*"

I laughed, then pulled her close. Her hair didn't have the touches of auburn I remembered, and her upper lip was more smoothed out, not pointed like Jimmy's Cupid's bow. She smelled different, too, less syrupy and more astringent, like she had bathed in lemon water. But it was still Gloria. Funny, smart, passionate, sometimes pain-in-the-ass Gloria.

I stood up, looked around, and then asked her: "Where's your brother?"

"In his crib."

I checked the time—seven thirty—and thought it seemed late for my early bird Sam. Who knew how long he'd been up, his room so far from mine? I squatted and put my hands behind me for Gloria to jump on.

"C'mon," I said. "Don't you want a ride?"

"Huh?"

"Don't you want a piggyback ride?"

"A what?" she said, confused.

I reached back and pulled her tiny body toward me, then grabbed her hands and laid them over my shoulders. She timidly wrapped her legs around my waist, and up we went in a swoosh of nightgowns and little-girl laughter. Her body was as light as a bird's, like always. Apparently intrauterine growth restriction knew all zip codes, even the posh ones.

We traversed the apartment like two adventurers, searching for a lost toddler somewhere in this elegant jungle. We avoided the bright light streaming through the windows, the two of us happy to be alone, undiscovered, in the dark hallway. I loved feeling Gloria's warm breath on the nape of my neck and her lungs moving up and down against my back. As always, she made me feel more alive. While Sam tied me to the moment with his simple toddler needs, Gloria freed me, her energy electrifying.

Past the living room and down the long hallway, I heard Sam—I mean Van—making morning noises. We followed the sound of singsong babbles and finally found him pitching handmade velour animals out of a boxy white crib. The room was sizable, a definite upgrade from the windowless closet. It was painted light gray with matching striped curtains, and its decor was punctuated with pops of color: a modern orange rocker, a round green leather stool, and a rainbow of ceramic animals on arty steel shelves. Taking up one corner of the room was a large red-and-blue wooden sailboat with "SS *Alexander*" painted on the stern. And above his crib, echoing the colors of the room, were eight-inch letters spelling "AVH IV." I puzzled at them until I realized they weren't a code, but my son's initials. To the van Holts, Sam was more than a little boy; he was an heir.

I picked him up, kissed his big blond head, and spoke my usual greeting: "Good morning, Mr. Magoo."

"Who's Mr. Magoo?" asked Gloria as she climbed onto Sam's rocker.

"Daddy nicknamed him that 'cause it was *his* father's favorite cartoon…" I stopped myself mid-sentence, remembering I was talking about Jimmy's father, not Alex's.

"Grandpa Collie watches cartoons?" she asked incredulously.

"Well, not very often," I replied, trying to cover. I paused for a second, more curious than ever about Alex's father.

I lifted Sam out of his crib and laid him on the matching changing table, then started unsnapping. I diapered him quickly and plopped him down on the circular rug. He toddled over to his sister, now standing on the arms of the chair, balancing her small frame like a surfer. I watched her move back and forth with ease, and it suddenly struck me that her nightgown was dry.

"Glo, you're dry," I said, swooping her off the chair and kissing her. "Good job, sweetie!"

"Well, of course, Mommy. I have my diaper on," she said matter-of-factly.

I set her down on the rug and peeked under her nightgown. Sure enough, she was wearing a diaper, and it was soaked. *Who puts a diaper on an almost-six-year-old?* And not even a Pull-Up, but an actual diaper, and from the looks of it, maybe even one of Sam's! I let the nightgown drop and stood there dumbfounded. Then I realized that "someone" was me.

"Let's take that off and get some panties," I said, leading both kids by the hands.

We made our way out of the nursery and across the hall to Gloria's room, a little girl's paradise in pink. I was rooting around in the top drawer of a white dresser when a small Asian woman popped into view from behind the canopied bed.

"Good morning, Mrs. van Holt," she said flatly as she picked up a hamper that was almost as big as she was. "Just getting the laundry."

"Oh…okay…great," I said, catching my breath and trying to act nonchalant. "I'll just get the kids their breakfast, then."

"It's ready," she told me.

"Oh?"

"In the stove."

"Right."

"Feeling better, Mrs. van Holt?"

"Yes, much better, thanks."

"You going back to bed?"

"No." *Why would I go back to bed?* "I need to get the kids ready for school. It's late."

She raised an eyebrow: Clearly this was out of character. I gently dropped Sam to the ground, then held out a pair of panties to Gloria. I watched her pull up her nightgown, rip apart the taped sides of her diaper, let it hit the carpet with a thud, and walk away. Two seconds later, the little Asian woman swooped the diaper up and headed toward the door. "Thank you, Miss Gloria," she said. As I watched my daughter ignore her, my face flushed with shame.

"Breakfast, you two," I said sternly, then corralled them toward the door. I would talk to Gloria about her attitude later. But for now, I was anxious to get them busy with cereal so I could look for a computer or iPad or anything with an Internet connection. I wasn't sure if there would be any chat rooms for women who wake up married to men they met briefly fourteen years earlier, but it was worth a search.

In the bright kitchen a massive rectangular island gleamed, its marble face like a giant block of streaky blue cheese, marred only where the stainless steel sink had taken a bite. Against the far wall was an eight-burner Viking cooktop, a swath of white subway tile, a chrome pot filler, and four—*yes, four!*—built-in ovens. Elsewhere, the walls held floor-to-ceiling white cabinets that were almost indistinguishable from one another. Large streak-free windows flooded the room in light, so there was no need to flip on any switches. Which was good considering I couldn't find them, the walls offering nothing but immaculate white paint, so clean it looked like freshly poured milk.

As Gloria scaled a white-leather-and-chrome barstool, I plopped Sam into a pedestaled high chair and snapped him in. I turned to search for the promised breakfast, but even after strolling around the island a few times, I couldn't find anything. I would have missed the food entirely if I hadn't felt warmth coming from one of the ovens. Actually, not an oven, more like a drawer. I pulled it open to find two perfectly plated breakfasts, including scrambled eggs, oatmeal, both bacon and sausage, and sliced strawberry garnish. I took out the plates, warm but not hot, and set one in front of each child. I then picked up napkins, forks, and two sippy cups I found beside the sink and pushed them over. I tied a monogrammed bib around Sam's neck.

Now I just needed something for me. Perhaps just some juice. And coffee. Surely Abigail van Holt hadn't given up coffee along with all the junk food?

I turned back and looked for the fridge. Nothing. The other side? Nada. I peeked in a closet, but it housed only crackers, pineapples, fitness bars, and champagne. I tried to open one of the cabinets but couldn't find a handle. I ran my hands over the edges, looking for an opening. I used my foot underneath, looked on the wall for a button or switch. I even wrestled a fork into the seam, but the damn cabinets wouldn't budge. Sweat was starting to bead on my forehead when I heard Gloria plop down and pad over. She reached up and pressed her tiny fingers against a spot about two-thirds up on a cabinet door. It popped open with a soft *pffft*.

"I said I wanted Froot Loops," she said, rolling her eyes at me and reaching for the large red box.

Well, of course. Why should anyone be bothered with something as pedestrian as a handle? I quickly popped open the rest of the cabinets, locating a hidden fridge, a separate freezer, dishes, serving platters, stacks of linens, and shelves alternating with boxed, canned, and foil-packaged food. But still no coffeemaker.

I was still looking for it when I heard a quick buzzing noise, like an intercom. Sam and Gloria both looked to a panel on the wall, so my eyes followed theirs. I found a control panel, touched a button, and heard someone talking.

"Mrs. van Holt?"

"Yes?" My too-loud voice reverberated around the room.

"There is someone here for you. A Mr. Cowan-Smith from Nordstrom. Shall I send him up?"

Nordstrom? Perhaps this person might know something. "Yes! Absolutely! Send him up."

"Very good."

I looked back at the kids, then rushed toward the front door and flung it open. Eventually, I heard the elevator ding and watched as a nicely dressed middle-aged man holding some large shopping bags marched toward me.

"Mrs. van Holt?" he asked in a posh British accent. "I'm from Nordstrom. I'm here to return some items from when you, ahem, when you had the unfortunate accident."

"Hello!" I said, stepping back and letting him inside. He was the very definition of distinguished older gentleman, with silver hair, rimless glasses, and a brown glen plaid suit with folded navy pocket square.

I noticed he looked everywhere but at me and that he didn't put down the large silver bags until I motioned toward the hall table. As I moved my arm to point, I felt my heavy breasts jiggle under the thin fabric and realized why he averted his gaze. I crossed my arms over my chest, embarrassed.

"Madame, everyone at the company is very concerned," he began. "And I can assure you we are doing everything we can to investigate the incident. We take the safety of our guests very seriously."

"It wasn't your fault," I said. "I'm such a klutz. I just remember going up very fast, and feeling woozy, and the piano music…"

"But thankfully you seem to be no worse for wear," he said amiably. "It is good to see you up and about."

He pointed to the first bag, which held a large box, and then another filled with some smaller bags and clothes. "This is your alteration, and these are some of your things that didn't make it into the ambulance. We tried to get them to you at the hospital, but they told us you had been discharged."

"Thank you so much," I said, eager to find what clues the bags might hold. "I appreciate you hand delivering them. How thoughtful."

"It's the least we can do for *you*, Mrs. van Holt," he replied. "And please remember, if there is anything you need, please don't hesitate to call."

He bowed his head slightly and handed me a business card. I took it and quickly recrossed my arms. I was hoping he might stay and answer some questions, but when I looked up he was back out the door. I ran after him in my bare feet, my arms still clamped across my chest.

"Sir, can I ask you something?" I asked as he neared the elevator.

"Of course."

"Did you see me fall?"

"No. But I did view the security tape. Looks like you were just juggling some bags and coffee and...well...muttering to yourself. Then you lost your balance and fell."

"But did you notice anything else? Like a loud noise? Or a bright light?" I cringed at how ridiculous I sounded.

"No. Nothing like that," he said, confused. "The escalators were fully operational. They had just been inspected last week."

"Sure. Of course. But I don't mean anything weird with the escalators. I mean anything out of the ordinary?"

"No. It all seemed perfectly normal. Just you shopping. Like you do every week." Every week? No wonder my closet held Nordstrom's entire fall/winter collection.

He looked at me with a sympathetic smile and asked if I need anything else.

I shook my head, defeated. He stepped into the elevator and turned around, taking in my unbrushed hair and bare feet.

"Good luck to you, Mrs. van Holt," he added with a note of

fatherly concern. "We hope to see you back very soon. We so appreciate our special customers." The door slid closed and he was gone.

I looked down at the business card he had given me. Listed below the gold Nordstrom logo was his full name—Mr. Bingham R. Cowan-Smith—and his title: Executive Vice President of Nordstrom Mid-Atlantic.

Pretty special, indeed.

I watched as the little Asian lady, name still unknown, dressed Gloria in a maroon-and-khaki Saint Andrew's School uniform, then sent her and her plaid backpack off with Oscar. Next, she insisted on taking Sam for one of his two daily walks. I tried to figure out her name, but all I could tell about her was that she liked Drexel University basketball, the team's dragon mascot visible through her white housekeeper's uniform. I kept catching her looking at me suspiciously as I loitered around her and the kids. She made me feel like a nuisance, as if she was the mother and I was a visiting in-law trying to help but really just getting in the way.

The minute she and Sam strolled out the door, I ran back to my closet, slipped on a pair of size 27 waist (!) jeans and a sweater, and headed straight for the Nordstrom bags. I carried them into the kitchen and dropped them on the floor near the island. Out of the bigger bag, I pulled out a large white box big enough to hold a bedspread. I placed it on the counter and took off the lid. Swaddled in layers of white tissue were seemingly endless folds of thick, heavy satin. I tried to lift it out, but the fabric kept coming. Eventually, I had to stand up and take a step back before it escaped the confines of the box and unfurled.

It was an evening dress—no, an actual ball gown—with pretty cap sleeves, a deep rounded neckline, and a long flowing skirt, of a color somewhere between black and navy, like a winter evening. It was lighter than it looked, and as I held it up, it sang a swishing song. The sleeves and neck were lined with more tissue, which I had to remove to see the tag. Embroidered in gold were four little words: "Oscar de la Renta."

I carefully draped the dress over one of the kitchen stools and opened the second bag, which held even more tissue, a folded khaki raincoat, and two small boxes containing the shrapnel of my fall: cracked sunglasses, a dented golden bangle, an umbrella, and a wallet holding a license and a black American Express card. The other box held an iPhone, scratched but still holding a charge. Bingo.

After pushing it on, I saw a wallpaper photo of Gloria holding baby Sam, but that's as far as I could go. It was locked. I tried my usual four digits, but they didn't work. Nor did my birth date or the last four digits of my cell number. Then I centered my finger on the round button at the bottom of the phone and pushed hard. I held my breath as it thought for a moment, then blinked open. Abbey van Holt might have different hair, a better wardrobe, and perfect tits, but there was one thing she was stuck with—my fingerprint.

I immediately began scanning e-mail, staring eagerly as it downloaded 170 messages. I read through them carefully, hungry for details of how Abbey van Holt spent her days. Mostly it was spam from shops and online retailers, but there were some appointment reminders, event invites, and missives from Gloria's school that helped fill in some blanks. The only e-mails that looked important (mostly because the subject line said just that) were from Alex's campaign manager, a man named Frank Klein, who, despite being someone who refused to use punctuation, was at least very verbose and detail oriented (thank God!). He e-mailed a daily schedule of campaign events, complete with type of event, address, time, and who was to attend. I noticed only a few were marked "abbey optional."

I closed the e-mail app and, on impulse, called my home number in Grange Hill. After fourteen rings, I admitted defeat and hung up. Then I tried Jimmy's cell phone. It rang twice, but instead of the usual "Lahey Landscape" greeting, I heard a man's gruff "Hello."

"Jimmy?" I whispered.

"Who is this?" said the voice. My throat went dry.

"Is this Jimmy Lahey's phone?" I asked.

"No, you've got the wrong number." *Click.*

Then I tried the only other number I knew by heart—Mom. I dialed and waited. After four rings, I heard her voice and was flooded with relief. "Mom, it's Abbey," I started to say, before realizing it was her voice-mail greeting: "Roberta here. I may be ignoring you, but I have good reason. I'm cruising the Mediterranean until November fourteenth. Leave a message and I'll get back to you when I return. *If I return, that is.*"

Shit, I thought, gone until the fourteenth. That was more than two weeks away. What in the world was she doing on a cruise? She hated cruises, called them "floating Ruby Tuesdays." I left a message asking her to call me as soon as she could. I also sent her an e-mail with a simple subject line: "Call me."

I opened up the phone's browser and began to type but found it maddeningly slow. I stood up and began searching for a computer or an iPad, looking in all the cabinets again, the kitchen's one wide drawer, and even the pantry. Finding nothing, I moved into the family room.

It was cozier and more lived in than the rest of the apartment, with a thick red-and-blue Oriental rug, floor-to-ceiling cherry shelves, a big leather sectional, and a huge flat-screen television. A few puzzles and children's books littered the floor, and stacks of decorating magazines were piled on the coffee table. In one end table were some remotes, tissues, and a hairbrush, while the other stored more magazines. I was about to give up when I noticed an inch of matte silver peeking out from beneath the coffee table. I pulled out an Apple laptop, opened the lid, and pressed it on.

It was time to find out what had had happened to me. "C'mon, Google, don't fail me now," I whispered aloud as I watched the screen load.

My first search term? "Head trauma." Google offered a vast list of causes, symptoms, and case histories, but way too many to examine. I narrowed the search by trying "head trauma and confusion." Again, Google produced pages and pages of Web links, but most pertained to memory loss, and I knew that wasn't my problem. If anything, I had too many memories, not too few.

More clicking revealed additional diagnoses. One doctor argued that head trauma coupled with psychological trauma could result in "delusional psychoses." But that didn't seem right either. Returning a Marc Jacobs bag was disappointing, sure, but certainly not traumatic enough to make someone crazy. I kept typing.

One promising explanation was called dissociative fugue, where an individual is confused or unaware of his or her identity and will travel "in psychological journeys away from known surroundings." But, again, that wasn't me. I knew exactly who I really was.

An hour and a half later, most of the Internet-proposed theories dismissed, I turned my attention to the scientific community, more specifically to physicists. A June 2013 issue of *Physics Today* described a young MIT professor's belief in the concept of a "multiverse." The prize-winning Japanese physicist presented a new theory of existence: Our world is just one bubble in a giant foam of bubbles, with universes separated from others only by thin, fragile membranes. I stared at his photo, his face smiling from a podium, while I tried to grasp his words. Had I gotten mixed up in someone else's bubble? Had my bubble burst? Or was this bubble running alongside my real one, with this Abbey and the real Abbey separated by just a thin, glistening wall? Perhaps she was still out there somewhere, begging Gloria to eat, brushing her teeth in the car, and downing Nutella by the jarful.

With trembling hands, I typed in my name, my fingers zipping on the familiar ten letters. I held my breath as I waited for the results. But the only matches were for a college kid in Texas and a school board superintendent in Boise. I tried it again, this time using "Abigail." But still, there was nothing relevant, nothing pertaining to me.

Next, I tried "Jimmy Lahey." It returned a million hits, but none of them referred to *my* Jimmy. I tried "James Lahey," but again the links led to other men with different jobs, different families, different faces. I paused and forced my mind to bring up Jimmy's face, but the image that appeared was one of the last ones I'd seen: his angry scowl from our fight over the purse. I shut the computer, leaned back, and closed my eyes.

When I opened them again, my gaze landed on the shelves across from me. Mixed in with the books and burnished silver bowls were several silver-framed family snapshots. I looked closer and saw my own face staring back at me.

I walked over and examined them, one by one. Gloria covered in pink frosting on her first birthday. Aunt Aubyn on a horse. Me awkwardly holding Sam in a long, embroidered christening gown. Alex and me together in some tropical paradise, him shirtless and me with a flower behind my ear, both of us tanned and laughing. Alex on skis; Alex with his parents; Alex and me with Colin Powell at a charity function.

I looked at the few photos of me and saw my eyes, my smile, my slightly lazy left eye. I scrutinized my shoulders, my long arms, and, with toes sinking into soft sand, my size-nine-and-a-half feet. I was there at these parties, on these trips, a part of this picture-perfect family. But these were cherished memories I had no memory of.

They belonged to another Abbey, whose younger self had made a different choice and now lived in a very different world. One small word—*yes*, not *no*—had very big consequences.

Curiosity gnawed at me. Who was this woman?

I started pulling open drawers and cabinets. I found the usual evidence of family life—board books, diapers, Vaseline, markers, and Barbie limbs—along with some receipts, DVDs, instruction manuals, power cords, and some marked-up blueprints for a house with several balconies. The cottage, perhaps?

From the back of one cabinet, I pulled out some dusty yearbooks from Mercersburg Academy, which I took to be Alex's prep school. I flipped through to find his teenage face grinning out from a variety of group photos—glee, debate, lacrosse. I put them back and kept searching.

In the last cabinet, I found an enormous black leather box embossed with a date: "June 19, 2004." Inside was a silver-tipped album so heavy I needed two hands to lift it out. As I opened the heavy cover and gazed at the first photo, I swallowed hard. It was twenty-seven-year-old me. On the day I became Mrs. van Holt.

I stood in a long, lacy veil and 1930s-style white gown, its train artfully pooling around my feet and spilling onto the lawn at Bloemveld. My dress was elegant and demure, and I looked pretty and poised, if perhaps a bit too thin, the diamond bracelets slipping down from my wrists to circle my palms. My cheeks flushed gently pink and my hair shone in its tight, flaxen chignon. I held a bouquet of white tulips, their stems encased by a tight white ribbon. With Alex beside me in his black morning coat and striped tie, both of us leaning languidly against the side of an antique car, we looked like a duke and duchess from another era, only with better teeth.

Each page of the album was more achingly beautiful than the next: Alex and me next to a rose-and-ivy-covered pillar; flower girls (eight in all) in their cream-on-cream silk; me with Jules, her auburn hair so pretty against her sage green bridesmaid dress; and then the entire well-heeled wedding party, all walking toward the camera on a lawn so thick it looked like a rug. One photo showed Alex and me with our mothers, and I couldn't help but cringe at how different the two women looked, one in an oyster-colored skirt suit and the other in low-cut electric blue satin with matching shoes. What had Mirabelle thought of Roberta? And what had she thought about me, for that matter? Surely she would have preferred a daughter-in-law with a more patrician lineage. But if she had, she certainly didn't show it. Of all of us, her smile was the widest.

I flipped back to the first photo, the official wedding portrait. I stared at the bland white flowers again, so different from the mixed bouquet I'd held on my wedding day to Jimmy. And at my hair, which was so sleek and tidy compared to the wisps that blew around my face as I said my vows to Jimmy in the warm September sand of Rehoboth Beach. I understood how different choices lead you down different paths, and how on those different paths you find even more choices.

But still I was baffled. I'd always hated tulips.

I was still sitting on the floor of the family room when the petite nanny returned with Sam. I had been so deep in thought, she startled me, and I returned the album to its shelf and hurried to the kitchen. The baby greeted me with rosy cheeks still flushed from the autumn cold.

"Do you want a snack, *nuu jaa*?" the nanny asked him.

I started toward the refrigerator to get it for him, then realized she was already on it. I watched her pick him up, wash his hands, and plop him in his high chair. I walked over and tickled his belly. He squealed and blew saliva bubbles.

She gave him some blueberries and sliced mango and instructed him to say "thank you."

"Tank yoo," he answered cheerfully, then dug his tiny hands into the bowl. I watched in disbelief as my carb-addicted son scarfed down the colorful fruit. And I mean real fruit, not the kind squeezed from pouches or molded into the shapes of Disney characters.

"No gym today?" It took me a minute to realize she was talking to me.

I shook my head. "Moving a bit slow today."

"Mr. van Holt will be here soon," she said, eyeing my jeans and unbrushed hair. "Saw his car pulling in."

"Oh." I smoothed my hair, and wished desperately that I'd brushed my teeth, when in walked Alex, looking like the movie version of an airline pilot in a navy suit and white shirt that set off his blue eyes and dark hair handsomely. Following him were two other men: a balding, bearded guy in a worn sports coat and olive corduroys and a young African American man in pressed jeans and a techy zip-up sweatshirt. All three were intently engaged in their phones; then, as if on cue, they thumbed them off, slipped them into their pockets, looked up, and smiled.

At the sight of his father, Sam started hopping in his chair, gurgling with glee. I understood how he felt, the room suddenly brighter and the air more electrified as Alex entered. My eyes couldn't help but follow him, and I felt a little tingle of excitement down deep. I recognized the feeling, one I hadn't felt in years—the giddy exhilaration of a new relationship. My cheeks reddened and my stomach fluttered.

I looked down, trying to hide it, knowing Abbey van Holt would have reacted more indifferently. Ten years of marriage would have muted the thrill, even with a ball and chain as gorgeous as Alex.

The older man, whom I took to be punctuation-challenged Frank Klein, turned my attention by shouting my name: "Abigail!" He walked over and grabbed my hand, then kissed it with mock chivalry. "Thanks to your little spill, our poll numbers are up for the first time in weeks. I know it wasn't fun, but your accident has captured the media's attention. And the public's sympathy."

"Glad I could help," I said, laughing. "I guess being a natural-born klutz finally came in handy."

"You're not a klutz," said Alex as he stared into the fridge. "You just never were any good on moving objects. Remember that elephant in Sri Lanka?"

"Of course," I bluffed. "That elephant."

"It's specifically with women over forty," interrupted the young black man. "Four points. I think it was leaving in the middle of that speech for the hospital. The clip is all over the news. Classy move, van Holt."

"Well, I guess my natural chivalrousness finally came in handy," he said, giving me a wink. I looked down and blushed.

Alex walked over and lifted Sam out of his seat, tossed him up in the air, and tickled him until he shrieked, then handed him to me.

"I have lunch at the police station on Spruce, and then I have that rescheduled KYW interview," he told me. "I figured you could use another afternoon to recover, so we didn't book anything for you today."

I looked at him, forcing another expression besides my usual "deer in headlights," and he added with an eye roll: "Except for tonight, *of course*. I know nothing will keep you from tonight."

Not knowing what to say, I just smiled and gave him the thumbs-up sign.

"You all right?" he asked, laughing. "Need some more coffee or something?"

But before I could answer, he turned and looked at the nanny. "Actually, I could use some too. May?"

May! And better yet, coffee! My eyes widened, eager to solve the mystery of the invisible coffeemaker.

May put down the sippy cup she was rinsing, smiled sweetly at Alex, and walked toward the back wall, pausing in front of a rectangle of black glass above a perforated steel box. She tapped the glass and it came alive with a row of glowing buttons. She hit a few and, thirty seconds later, handed him a steaming latte.

Alex took two quick sips and put it down. He moved toward the door, following the other men. He paused at the kitchen doorway, then looked back.

He stared at me like he was looking for words, and I found my body frozen under his gaze, eager for whatever charming remark he might leave me with.

"Oh, and, Abbey?"

"Yes?"

"Don't forget to pick up my tux."

With my oversized Gucci sunglasses and black cashmere wrap, I looked like every other woman on Walnut Street, but as they paused before window displays and opened heavy salon doors, I kept walking, my eyes dead ahead. I had only an hour or so before Sam woke from his nap and Gloria got home from school, so I moved briskly, weaving around anyone in my way and noting each cross street I passed: Eighteenth, Seventeenth, Sixteenth, Fifteenth, and, finally, Broad Street. I paused for the light and to recheck the map on my phone. I was almost there.

When the light turned green, I moved with the crowd and crossed over the wide avenue. But halfway down the next block I had to stop again, derailed by a truck pushing a Dumpster toward a storefront under renovation.

I stepped back from the cloud of dust and waited. Looking up, I watched construction workers chipping away at an old wooden sign. I tilted my head to read it: "Ochs & Ochs."

This, or what was left of it, was the old Ochs luggage store, one of Philly's last independent retailers, a holdover from the days when luggage cost more than a box of diapers. I covered my eyes from the sun and peered inside, remembering old Mr. Ochs and his brother, always in three-piece suits, always yelling at kids not to touch anything. Now the shop floor played host to a row of white mannequins, indifferent to their nakedness and the workers who moved around them.

A construction worker strolled outside for a cigarette and I asked him what store was moving in.

"Beats me," he said, lighting up. "I just do what they tell me." After exhaling his first drag, he examined me further, letting his eyes linger on my ample chest. *That's a first,* I thought. I decided to cross the street after all.

Finally arriving at Thirteenth Street, I entered a boxy concrete office building through revolving doors that spun me into an empty, dimly lit foyer. I scanned the directory of doctors' offices and law firms until my eyes found the name I was looking for: Agency X, Suite 1105. I stepped inside the elevator, hit the button, and waited for movement. Eventually, it jumped awake and heaved itself upward, each floor announced with a dull clink.

The eleventh floor was bright and open, with long white corridors punctuated with an occasional poster or plant. I breathed in Chinese food from one door and paint smells from another, and heard rap music from farther down. *This must be where they put all the creatives,* I thought, and I was right. The suites I passed were occupied by interior designers, Web developers, architects, advertising agencies... and a lone psychiatrist. How convenient for them.

I turned a corner and peered down another long hall. The last door at the end was bright white like the others, except for a large hot pink "X" painted stylishly and off-center across it. I smiled; this was definitely the place.

Hot pink had always been Jules's favorite color. Maybe because it looked so good with her green eyes or maybe it was the one girlie indulgence she allowed herself, but as long as I had known her, she'd insisted on pops of pink in her decor, in her artwork, or in her wardrobe. In college it had been hot pink pillows; in our early twenties, it was pink streaks in her hair; and, later, when life demanded a more "mature" palette, she downsized to a single pair of pink leather flats. Luckily, she had a partner in crime in Gloria. They would sit for hours coloring hot pink butterflies and hearts and flowers, bonding over the shade like two old ladies discovering their mutual love for Judi Dench.

Heart racing and anxious, I entered the office suite. At the stark white reception desk, a bored young girl with a nose ring looked up to see what I wanted. Yes, I was here to see Miss Xavier. No, I didn't have an appointment. Yes, she would know who I was. And no, thank you, I didn't need a kale-and-pineapple smoothie.

I sat on the edge of the first chair I found and waited. And waited.

For almost half an hour I sat there, twisting my heavy wedding rings and observing the daily grind of a small communications firm. I had toiled in agencies my entire adult life, so some of the sounds were familiar to me—phones ringing, fingers tapping, young staffers hurling insults at one another—while others were less familiar—the *beep-beep* of a far-off video game, the gurgle of a fish tank, the soft whir of a fancy blender.

I smiled as a Jack Russell terrier scampered up to investigate my shiny Rachel Zoe boots. I leaned down and scratched him between his ears and wondered what his name was. I certainly knew whom he belonged to.

If there was one thing Jules loved more than pink, it was dogs. While she was growing up, her family already overwhelmed with six kids, a ninety-six-year-old grandmother, and a decaying Victorian, they added to the fun with at least four dogs at any given time, most of them rescues. Ever since, Jules had a weakness for strays, letting them move too quickly into her heart and bed. Later, she would replace the dogs with men, and I knew exactly which species left Jules with more of a mess to clean up.

When we'd first met in college, Jules had been a sensitive, curly-haired art student with a fondness for bong hits and Billie Joe Armstrong. The first time I saw her—on freshman move-in day—she was sitting on her bed in our shared dorm room, tears streaming down her pale, freckly cheeks.

"Hi," I said. "I'm Abbey."

"Hi." She sniffed, wiping away the tears and looking up. "I'm Juliana. But everyone calls me Jules."

"Is everything okay?"

"I know it's only been a few hours, but I miss my dog."

"Oh my gosh. I'm so sorry," I replied, dropping comforters and books on a plastic-covered mattress. "They aren't allowed in the dorms?"

"No, not even to visit," she said.

"Maybe you can go see him on the weekends?"

"Her. And yes, but it's not the same. She's slept on my bed since she was a puppy. I'm worried she's going to think I deserted her."

I sat down on the bed opposite and tried to think of something comforting to say. She stopped sniffling, took a deep breath, and looked down at her shoes. We were sitting there quietly, both contemplating the psychological state of the abandoned puppy, when in walked my mother, interrupting the silence with a canary yellow tennis dress and matching visor. She dropped the floor lamp she was carrying with a clank and began fanning herself with overly tanned hands.

"No air-conditioning?" she asked. "Jesus, I'm paying twenty-four thousand dollars a year so you can sweat your ass off all day and night?"

I looked at Jules, cringing inside and wondering what this sweet-faced dog lover would think of Roberta DiSiano.

She looked at me with wonderment, then turned to my mother. "I hear you, lady. Let's burn the fucking place down."

I knew right then we were going to be best friends.

The bobbleheads on the receptionist's desk had long ago stopped wiggling and the dog was well into a running dream on his bone-shaped bed before the receptionist finally spoke.

"You can go back now," she said without raising her eyes from her computer.

I walked down a short hallway lined with posters from Philadel-phia events, all in the colorful-yet-clean style that had won Jules so many Ad Club awards. Stepping into a small office lit by one big window, I took in the white laminate desk, Lucite chairs, and a rug of converging pink and orange circles.

Behind the desk was Jules, glancing up when I entered. Her long reddish brown hair was blown out straight, and her green eyes shone under long black lashes. Her wine-colored blazer looked pol-ished and cool, its sleeves rolled up to reveal a contrasting striped lining and thick onyx and gold bangles. She said nothing, her eyes on some layouts, as I sat across from her.

"I am *sooooo* glad to see you," I said. "You are not going to believe what's happening. I can't even explain, but I'll try. Oh my God, how do I start—"

It took me a few seconds to realize she had barely moved, only her left eyebrow arching upward. I stopped talking and leaned forward, trying to make eye contact.

"Jules?" I said softly. "What's wrong?"

"What can I help you with, Abbey?" she asked, finally looking me in the eye. "I told you before I can't do any more free charity logos for you. I'm running a business here."

"No," I said, frustrated. "I don't want any work, I just wanted to talk to you."

"About?" Still with that chilly tone.

"This is going to sound totally crazy, but I think I am—we are—living in some kind of alternate universe," I said. Saying it aloud made me wince, but I pressed on. "And I think that maybe you had something to do with it."

"Me? What would I have to do with anything? I haven't seen you in years."

I sat back in my chair, confused. I turned to the side and saw two photos on a file cabinet: one of the dog I had just met, and one of Jules, her arms encircling a man with choppy black hair and Buddy Holly glasses.

"No. Listen. We just saw each other Friday at work," I explained. "That's what I'm trying to tell you. This isn't real; something really bizarre is happening."

"Saw each other at work? We haven't worked together in six years, remember? We started this agency together and you ditched me at year two. Too busy redecorating or something."

I ignored her and began to talk louder and slower. "I know it sounds batshit crazy, but this is not real. This is all a dream or a delusion or some kind of black hole," I said, desperate for her to believe me. "You and I are best friends and we work at Elkins PR in Conshy. We hate it, but we do."

She stared at me for a few seconds, then looked away. "I'm sorry, but I'm really busy," she said, returning her gaze to her paper-strewn desk. "I've got a ton of work to do. Lots of calls to return."

"Jules, it's me, Abbey. Bee. We've known each other for almost twenty years. You're my best friend." I reached out to grab her hand, but she yanked it back as if I was a monster.

"Look. I don't know what you're on or how much expensive chardonnay you've mixed it with, but I'm not your therapist. Or your friend, really. Now, if you'll excuse me…"

She stood up and I gasped. Not only was she perfectly put together and stylishly dressed—not to mention successful enough to rent this hipster office and then fill it with equally hip employees—she was thin. Model thin.

My eyes grew wide and a smile broke across my face.

"Jules," I whispered. "You're gorgeous."

But the look she returned was not only not appreciative but venomous, her lips pale and grim. She picked up the phone and punched some numbers, ignoring me. I stared, unable to move, unable to accept that my best friend could be so cold, so distant.

"Jules," I muttered again as my eyes filled with tears. "I don't understand. What's happened?"

But her green eyes refused to meet mine. Instead, she spun around in her chair and began to speak to someone about a press check. I sat for a few more moments but then felt myself starting to cry. I grabbed my purse and hurried out, scurrying past Little Miss Nose Ring like a scolded child.

"Don't let the dog out," I heard Jules yell as I let myself out. Then, more quietly, she added, "Bitch."

CHAPTER FOUR

When I arrived back in the apartment building, my red-rimmed eyes hidden by sunglasses, I was drained. Not only was the encounter with Jules terribly upsetting, but I had to visit five different Center City dry cleaners before finding a size forty-two long tuxedo for "A. van Holt."

Could what Jules said be true? That we hadn't hung out in years? That we only ever spoke when I needed a free logo? Even though we both looked so different, and lived different lives, it didn't seem plausible. In what universe wouldn't we be friends?

She said we had started a business together—an actual communications firm with real clients and a real copier—just like we always said we should but never did. We started it together, we worked together for two years, but then I "ditched" her? I would *never* have left softhearted Jules to fend for herself in the kill-or-be-killed world of public relations and strategic communications. But then again, she seemed to be surviving quite well.

Inside the elevator I hit the twelfth-floor button impatiently, eager to get upstairs to the apartment and the refuge of its clean, quiet space. Eager for a few moments alone, to try to figure out the more puzzling parts of Abbey van Holt's life.

But greeting me on the other side of the door were two strangers with identical faces and identical pained expressions, toting matching wheeled silver suitcases.

"Finally!" they said in unison, each throwing up his hands and widening his eyes, their exasperation announced in stereo.

"Where have you been?" asked the one holding a giant coffee. "We've been waiting almost half an hour. And you know my brother hates to wait."

"I *do* hate to wait," said the other man, moving closer to me. "Especially on such a big night." He pinched my chin with his fingers, tilting my puffy, mascara-smeared face toward the light.

He scowled at his brother, then at me, and let out a long sigh.

"Let's get going," he said. "We have a lot of work to do. *Serious, serious work.*"

They wheeled their shiny suitcases toward my bedroom, gesturing impatiently for me to follow.

Thus did I meet the Bacco Brothers, Abbey van Holt's longtime stylists. They were there to help me get ready for tonight's high-society fund-raiser at the Union League, the event that Alex had mentioned, the one I refused to miss. Despite their matching faces and physiques, Bobby was bossy and loud while Francis was soft-spoken and gentle. Bobby mostly did hair, while Francis concentrated on my makeup and nails. They both consulted on wardrobe. As I watched them flit around my bathroom, I smiled to myself. Only Abbey van Holt would have not just one gorgeous gay boyfriend, but two.

I stood between them shyly, watching them unpack. I was made to shower and instructed to shave everything. Despite having just met these men only three minutes ago, I did.

Once I was out—dripping yet clean—they seated me on my tufted stool and got to work, speaking to each other in a strange beauty shorthand. One dipped my hands in bowls of pink liquid, while the other massaged something slimy into my hair. They worked quickly and deliberately, as if I were a patient just wheeled into the OR with cardiac arrest. It might have been my bathroom, but once they started fluffing and plucking, brushing and painting, I realized I was completely in their care. Best to sit down, shut up, and let the trauma surgeons operate.

"These roots are crazy bad," said Bobby as he combed and separated a few wet strands. "I knew we should have come last week." Crazy bad? They looked perfectly acceptable to me. He paused and looked over at his brother. "Remember when we first met her? How her hair was?"

"Dreadful," said Francis. "So bleached it was almost green."

"But you were so cute." Bobby smirked. "So determined to try to be *you*." My ears pricked up at this.

"Mirabelle was just confounded," chimed in Francis. They both laughed.

I lifted my head at the mention of my mother-in-law, but Bobby gently pushed my head back down.

"Those days were fun, though," he reminisced. "Everything so new. You were one of our first clients. And now we do *everyone* in this town."

He looked down and saw me trying to understand, to catch up, and mistook it for annoyance. "But of course you're our *favorite*."

"Of course," I said with a smile.

"Oh my God, do you remember that dress?" blurted Francis, looking up from the footbath he was filling on the floor. "The one you wore the night of the engagement party? It was some god-awful flowered thing from Ann Taylor or somewhere."

"Hideous," added Bobby, shuddering for added emphasis. "And I believe, if memory serves, one hundred percent polyester." Their matching high-pitched laughter lifted and faded in harmony.

"It wasn't polyester," I said indignantly, but knowing exactly which one they were talking about. (I had bought it with my first paycheck and still wore it; in another universe it was waiting, along with a size 4T child's skating dress, to be picked up at Top of the Hill Cleaners.) I slapped Bobby's hand away and continued: "And a lot of working women shop at Ann Taylor. Their clothes are really good quality, especially when you're on a budget."

"Budget?" said Bobby with a horrified expression and comb frozen in midair. "Promise you'll never say that horrible word again."

This time when they began to cackle, I covered my ears and shook my head in irritation. But I also couldn't help but crack a smile.

For the next hour and a half, I was exfoliated, massaged, clipped, creamed, painted, and perfumed, until I finally emerged—transformed. I watched in the mirror as my new overcaffeinated, overenthusiastic courtiers turned a normal-looking mom into an aristocrat, one who was not only pretty but perfectly on trend. The dress—fetched from the kitchen and held by both brothers with reverence—slid perfectly over my board-certified size-six body.

Once the hair and makeup and nails were complete, Francis pulled out his iPhone and a small plastic speaker and the atmosphere turned into a party. As a group, we moved into the closet, opening velvet-lined trays and lacquer boxes as we searched for the perfect accessories. No detail was considered too inconsequential, and every decision—bracelet clasps, heel height, even color of just-in-case tissues—was open for debate. It was the most fun I'd had in ages, feeling so deliciously feminine and luxurious, and as the closet got messier and messier, I got more excited about the night ahead.

Having returned from an after-school playdate, Gloria and Sam joined us too, crawling between the Bacco Brothers' shiny track pants and trying on discards from the pile of rejected accessories. Eventually, with just a few minutes to spare before I was due to meet Alex, I was complete. My bag was boxy and beaded, my earrings long and sparkly, my stilettos boldly strappy.

And for the first time today, my happiness genuine. When the two men took a photo of the finished product—yelling "Smile like you mean it!" before they snapped—I couldn't help but do just that.

Underneath, though, I was nervous, anticipating my time with Alex. Would I be dressed right? Would I say the wrong things? Would he suspect I was an imposter? Would he like me? I realized I was feeling first-date jitters because technically it was one. At least for me, anyway.

Glancing at Alex's tux hanging on the back of the door, my mind slipped to Jimmy. God, how he hated dressing up; I only ever saw him in a suit at our wedding and his mother's funeral. He preferred khaki pants, work boots, and T-shirts, and if he felt the need to be more professional, a golf shirt.

On our first official date, Jimmy arrived at my doorway in a heavy army green parka and jeans, with something hanging over his shoulder.

"How do you feel about ice?" he asked.

"I feel cold. Why?"

"Because I'm taking you skating. So you better change out of that skirt and into something that can take a fall."

I laughed, then realized he wasn't kidding as he unveiled a pair of well-worn black-and-white hockey skates with gleaming, freshly sharpened blades. He walked into the apartment and suddenly the space felt even smaller.

I had been ready for hours and had painstakingly picked out this outfit to accentuate the positive: a tight pencil skirt to show off my pert rear and a shirred V-neck shirt to disguise my flat chest. At least he got to see me in it before I went to extricate my favorite jeans from the hamper. Though he had seen every inch of my body the weekend before, I hid in the bathroom to change, chatting with him through the white wooden door.

We drove out to Grange Hill and parked at a large seventies-style brick monolith called the Skatium. The imposing building looked like a windowless fortress, but teenagers, old folks, and families moved toward the doors happily, anxious to leave school and work and the bladeless world behind, if only for an hour or two.

"Don't worry that you're a first-timer," said Jimmy, helping me out of the green truck and pointing to a family up ahead. "See, there's a two-year-old."

"That's not making me feel any better," I said. "That little guy is going to fall."

"I have a feeling that the only thing that will be falling tonight is you," he replied, helping me across the snowy parking lot.

"Oh, you're on, big guy," I said, jogging past him and up to the door.

But Jimmy was right: I was terrible. On the ice, in my brown rental skates, my long arms and legs seemed to get even longer, while my weak ankles wobbled from side to side. I clung to the side of the rink in fear as the good citizens of Upper Darby breezed by in waves of Old Navy fleece. Even Jimmy, whose broad shoulders and heavy build made him slightly top-heavy, glided in and around the other skaters elegantly.

Two watery beers later, I was relaxed enough to make it around the rink without Jimmy's guiding hand on my back. Emboldened by the alcohol, I attempted to go faster, trying to mimic the easy glide of the skaters around me. Then a teenage kid in a T-shirt and hockey mask cut me off and I lost my balance, my hands windmilling around before I landed hard on my butt.

"Are you okay?" Jimmy asked, after shouting at the teenager to slow down.

I attempted to stand but kept slipping back down. "Ow, ow, ow."

He bent down and lifted me to my feet, then guided me safely to the wall, out of the fray.

"So sorry," he whispered, his eyes full of concern. "I was just joking before. I really didn't want you to get hurt, I swear."

"I'm fine. I'm having fun. Really."

"I know it's probably not the kind of dates you're used to," he said as he looked out onto the rink, now even more rowdy and crowded. "You're probably used to fancy dinners. With guys who wear ties. And went to college."

I appreciated that he thought I was such a sophisticated lady. And so in demand. But I also knew it was my time to be honest.

"This is the first date I've been on in a year. And I'm so glad you called. I didn't think you would, especially after that, uh, crazy night," I said quietly. "And I know you probably won't believe me, but I have *never* done that before. Go home with a guy I just met, I mean."

He didn't say anything; his only response was to pick up my hand and pull me back onto the ice, a smile crossing his lips.

"I feel honored," he said. "And certainly have no complaints. In fact, I hope you'll come out this way more often."

"I think I just might have a reason to," I said, feeling confident enough to release my fingernails from his arm. "But only if my butt heals. I have a feeling I'm gonna have a bad bruise."

"I'll take a look at it later," he said, putting his arm around me as we slid around a curve in unison.

I flushed with embarrassment. But not so much that I spent the night alone. I invited him back to my place that time.

The Union League was housed in an oversized mansion set back about ten feet from the rest of the buildings on Broad Street, their plain gray facades providing the perfect counterfoil to its rosy redbrick facade. I had been there once before with my mom, years ago, so its curving double staircase and age-blackened statues were familiar, though no less daunting. Roberta had dragged me to a Princeton University admissions seminar she had read about in the paper. I didn't want to go, and knew we would never be able to afford Ivy League tuition anyway. I suspected she just wanted to meet divorcés, preferably those who were old, rich, and susceptible to her kind of in-your-face femininity.

Tonight, the grande dame of a building was abuzz with people, noise, lights, and a long line of limos stretching all the way to city hall.

"Do you want me to circle and get closer?" asked Oscar from the front seat of the Suburban.

"No, thanks," I told him. "I'll just get out here and cross over."

Alex was MIA due to a late interview, so I would have to brave the elaborate steps, TV cameras, and hordes of high society alone. It was not what I was hoping—I was nervous enough—but I guess it couldn't be helped. I walked carefully across the street in my delicate heels, avoiding puddles and taxi exhaust before falling in line with the other ball-goers. Gowns and tuxedos lined the steps ahead of me like a scene from a Disney movie; some of the older women even wore long white gloves and tiaras.

Once inside the crowded main entrance hall, its wide expanse filled with people, busts of soldiers, and an inordinate number of grandfather clocks, I kept a low profile by studying the program. The event was a fund-raiser for the Ballantine School, a West Philadelphia private school for lower-income kids, and as I learned from the program booklet, the social event of the season. The more than eight hundred guests were a mix of Philadelphia's wealthiest, be they scions of business, politics, high society, or, like us, all three. I was reading the names of donors—which included Alexander and Abigail van Holt at the "Platinum" level—when I felt someone come up beside me smelling of expensive perfume and, very faintly underneath, of hay.

I turned and found myself face-to-face with my sister-in-law, Aubyn. She looked plainly elegant in a black velvet dress and pearls. Beside her, a twentysomething man with slicked-down, flame-red hair stared blankly at me, then looked down.

"Where's Alley?" she said with eyes only half open. "I thought he was coming."

"He'll be here," I said brightly, smiling at her and her young man. "He's just running late."

"Oh."

"You look lovely, by the way."

She ignored my compliment, then flicked her gloved hand toward her escort, looked up at the ceiling in boredom, and gave a perfunctory "You remember Kipper?"

"Sure," I lied, shaking his hand. "Nice to see you again."

"Likewise," he said, a weak smile on his lips.

As we exchanged hellos, I felt her critical gaze fall on my dress, my hair, and my shoes, and suddenly I felt self-conscious, silly. But I decided not to let her intimidate me. I forced myself to stand up straighter and imitated her tilting chin, her bored expression.

Her eyes narrowed and her voice lowered as she looked at my ears. "If my grandmother saw you in those earrings, she would roll over in her grave. Our people never wear diamonds before eight o'clock."

"Oh," I said, my hands moving to the dangling diamonds in fright. "I didn't know...I mean, I just thought they were pretty." The Baccos had plucked them out of a worn velvet case, declaring them "dazzling." I'd had no idea they were real.

"Just be careful," she added. "They've been in my family forever." Then she turned to Kipper, who was busy staring into his bourbon, and pulled him away by the sleeve.

"C'mon," she said. "I see the Cresheims. They must have just gotten back from Longport." She walked off without saying good-bye.

What the hell was her problem? Why did I always seem to say the wrong thing? And why did I suddenly feel like Meg in *Little Women*, looking pretty and polished but not fooling anyone?

I needed a drink. I followed the crowds toward the main reception room and stood in line at the bar. I took a few deep breaths, hoping my blotchy neck—the aftermath of my run-in with Aubyn—would return to a normal shade. I ordered champagne and took a sip. Touched and smoothed my hair. Counted the portraits on the walls. Checked my phone again. Watched silver-haired society matrons and their portly, red-faced escorts mill around. Admired the few mavericks who wore red or yellow or silver in the sea of dark gowns.

A young couple approached and asked me about "the club." I talked about how terrible I was at putting before realizing they meant the Racquet Club. I stuck out my hand and introduced myself to a stately older gentleman, only to find out he knew me *very* well, having delivered both my children ("exceptionally quick both times—and no epidural!"). And I agreed to a Saturday playdate for Gloria, even though I had no idea who the tall blonde proposing it was, where she lived, or if Gloria even liked her kid.

I had been at this ball for a mere twenty minutes, and already I was mentally drained. Who knew that simple conversations, and being able to respond quickly and with confidence to a question, would be such an elusive treat? Would life as Mrs. van Holt ever get any easier?

Sighing, I placed my half-drunk glass of champagne on a passing tray and maneuvered through the crowd back to the hallway. I looked around for the restroom and found it without too much trouble. Unlike the hidden one at Bloemveld, this door was marked with a thick brass plaque and a cursive "Ladies."

After an epic battle of woman–versus–ball gown in the bathroom stall, I washed my hands and checked my voice mail. Still nothing from Alex. I leaned against the tiled wall, letting the cool quiet of the room still my nerves. Finally, after some small talk with the ancient bathroom attendant, and glancing at my reflection one last time, I worked up the courage to exit.

In burst two beautiful yet brittle-looking women, cackling as they rushed toward the mirror. I saw them before they saw me: Betsy Claiborne wearing a creamy silk confection that set off her black bob, and Ellen Hadley, in emerald green satin that matched the emerald ring blazing on her right hand. I felt the same rush of dread and humiliation that I'd felt when I—er, Abbey Lahey—spotted them Saturday in Nordstrom. I froze, praying they wouldn't notice me.

But they did, spying me in the mirror, then snapping around like velociraptors scenting prey. I braced for impact—and insults. But instead, I was hit with a mix of smiles and awe, followed by a lot of giddy hopping and finger clapping.

"Abbey!" exclaimed Betsy. "We've been looking for you everywhere!"

"You look *stunning*," said Ellen, emphasizing the last word with closed eyes. "I just knew you were going to wear navy. You look so good in blue. Doesn't she, Bets?"

"Beyond. You're just beyond," replied Betsy. "But then you always look *parfait*."

Ha! I thought, how times had changed.

Before I could respond, or return a compliment, Betsy leaned closer and whispered, "Nobody good is here yet, just the mayor and his cronies."

"Yeah, and your sister-in-law and her boring horsey set," added Ellen. "She leads that poor boy Kipper around like a Shetland pony."

"I know," I said. "What's his story?"

"Who cares? I'd rather talk about that gorgeous husband of

yours," said Betsy, her voice dropping to a feline growl. "Please tell me he's coming. And please tell me he's planning on coming to our little fund-raiser next week. It would be so nice to have a *congressman* there."

"He's not a congressman yet," I snapped. "But don't worry. He'll be there. Here, I mean."

"At least he has a good excuse for being late," added Ellen. "We had to drag Bill and Robbie here kicking and screaming. The only reason they agreed to come is because of the auction. Y'know, any chance to gamble."

They used the rest of the primp session to dissect the outfits, rumored affairs, and recent plastic surgery of the other ball-goers, and to reapply lipstick and smooth hair that didn't need it. As they headed for the door, they turned back to me in unison.

"Aren't you coming, Ab?" said Betsy. "We're going to miss the intro!"

I realized that they expected me to come with them, and, more shockingly, that they considered me a friend. A good friend. It felt so odd and unnatural, and I wanted to ignore them altogether in payback for a thousand previous slights. But right now they were among the few people in the building I could positively identify, so I followed them.

"Can you introduce me to Kelley Radomile?" whispered Betsy as we made our way down the hall back to the reception area. "You know I would just love to have a Radomile on the benefit committee next year."

"Uh, sure," I said. "Just point her out when you see her."

"Oh, Abbey, you're so wicked," said Betsy, putting a hand to her mouth and snickering. "All that stuff about him being a cross-dresser is just a rumor."

Their cackles ricocheted off the marble walls like gunfire.

*   *   *

We separated to our assigned tables but promised to meet up after the dinner, and I was glad to be rid of my fair-weather friends. I found my table up front near the emcee and auction tables and sat down with a sigh. I looked around for Alex, hoping he'd get here soon. I checked my phone one more time and then silenced the ringer in irritation. I scanned the crowd taking their seats and noticed the Phillies' most recent star pitcher, one of our high-profile restaurateurs (and newly crowned Iron Chef), and a billionaire real estate developer and his much younger girlfriend of the month, among the rest of the doctors, lawyers, and CEOs. To my relief, Aubyn and Kipper, followed by a few other matriarchs and titans in training, headed toward a table in the back. I was just pulling apart a roll when a flurry of activity surrounded my table.

Across from me, taking their seats, were a handsome older couple and a mountainous black man who didn't make eye contact and inadvertently revealed a badge and gun holster as he unbuttoned his jacket and sat down. Then, to my left, first pulling out the chair for his wife, and then settling down with a sigh, was the mayor.

The mayor of Philadelphia. The fifth-largest city in the United States. Inches from me. Once again, my neck turned blotchy and hot with nerves.

"Good evening, everyone," he said, nodding all around.

"Good evening," I whispered back in disbelief.

"Nice to see you, Mrs. van Holt," he said as he turned to me. "Your husband running late?"

"Yeah," I stammered. "You know Alex…"

"Well, he'll fit in really well in Congress," he said with a guffaw.

The lights flickered, then dimmed, and a spotlight illuminated the podium. The crowd hushed as the evening's emcee, a veteran local TV anchor named Wally McNamara, took the stage. He opened with some jokes about the Eagles' running game and my heart returned to its normal speed. With all these surprises taxing my little ticker, I was going to need a doctor by dessert. But looking around at the well-dressed crowd, I figured that wouldn't be a problem. There must be a cardiologist or two in this group.

I perused the program, flipping absentmindedly through the Flyers tickets, Tiffany bracelets, and Kimmel Center seats before finding one item that held my interest. It was a vintage Cartier tank watch that once belonged to Sarah Lippincott Biddle, a Philadelphia name so old and esteemed it made even the van Holts sound like white trash. Made in 1917, the watch was one of the first of this style, said to reflect Louis Cartier's fascination with World War I tanks. I had always loved them, ever since I saw a photo of Princess Diana wearing one. I wished I could have bid on it.

Then I realized I could. The van Holts certainly had the money, and we were there to support this cause. In fact, we were probably *expected* to bid on something. I waited in anticipation for Wally to get to Lot 22.

When he did, indicating a minimum bid of five hundred dollars, I raised my paddle timidly. Someone else raised theirs. Eight hundred dollars. I raised mine again. One thousand. We continued to do paddle battle, the price increasing faster and faster, until it was my move again at six thousand dollars. Wally and the entire crowd looked at me with anticipation, but I couldn't do it. Outside these doors, in the real world, six thousand dollars was a lot of money. Three mortgage payments. Almost a year of groceries. A new roof. I shook my head and dropped my hand, and the bidding continued without me. A couple near the back finally won it for twelve thousand.

I sighed and picked at my salad, deflated. And not because I'd lost the watch. Because here I was at an honest-to-goodness ball, and I wasn't having much fun. But then a waiter touched my shoulder and handed me a note. I unfolded a white-and-gold Union League napkin. Scrawled in blue ink was a message:

Meet me in the lobby? AVH

Alex! He was finally here.

As a cheer went up for a ten-thousand-dollar bid on a date with the Fox traffic girl, I quietly grabbed my purse and excused myself. A few people waved at me as I tiptoed among the tables, but I ignored them, my eyes searching for the nearest door.

Out in the hall, my high-heeled sandals clicked on the checkerboard marble floor as I hurried toward the lobby area and looked around—but it was empty. I poked my head into the library but found only a couple of hedge-funders puffing on cigars. Then I heard a long, low whistle and someone clearing his throat.

He was waiting at the other end of the hallway, leaning against a fluted column casually, with his hands in his pockets, but with a serious gaze fixed on me. Not checking e-mails, not talking with voters, not surrounded by his entourage, just him in a perfectly tailored tuxedo with French cuffs exposing a glint of golden cuff links. His hair smooth and almost black with pomade, making his eyes the bluest blue, even from far away. So handsome, like a Tanqueray ad come to life.

I was overjoyed to see him. Other than Sam, and occasionally Gloria, he was the only person in this new world who seemed to genuinely like me. As I moved down the hall, I couldn't help breaking into a run. When I got close enough, I threw myself into his arms. He laughed, surprised at my enthusiasm, then lowered me to the ground.

"Hey, gorgeous," he whispered into my hair, his strong arms circling me. "Where have you been all my life?"

If you only knew, I wanted to tell him. But I stayed silent, looking away, embarrassed that I'd almost tackled him into a potted plant. He tilted my face up to his, then leaned in for a kiss.

His lips on mine felt strange, and my first instinct was to stop him, not only because it felt unnatural to kiss someone other than Jimmy but because someone might see me. But then I remembered that in this world, this man *was* my husband, and it would be much more alarming to be seen kissing a landscaper from Grange Hill. Still, out of guilt or shyness or nervousness, I didn't respond, my lips impassive and my torso leaning slightly away from his.

Then his hand moved around my waist and his lips moved down my neck, sending a tingle from my throat down to someplace lower. Thoughts of Jimmy—of anyone else—floated away. When his lips moved back to mine, I kissed him back. Hard.

"Brought out the big guns, huh?" he said, breaking away and noticing my earrings.

"Yeah, why not?" I replied.

"Yeah, why not, why not," he repeated softly, back to kissing me. When a woman passed, he stopped, then moved us back farther into the shadows and took both my hands in his.

"Don't be mad…" He looked at me, sheepish, and I understood now the reason for all the sweetness, the kissing. He was buttering me up.

"But I'm not staying," he continued. "I'm tired, and frankly, I know these people are going to vote for me. Maybe the *only* votes I can count on right now. But I don't want to ruin your night. Go have fun." He looked down, as if bracing for my response.

"If you're going, I'm going too." I smiled, happy to have the chance to get away from here. Happy to save myself from hundreds more epic conversation fails.

His head snapped up. "Really? Are you sure? This is your big night."

"It's not as fun as I thought it would be. Honestly, I'd rather be with you."

He looked at me in surprise, then grinned. "Oscar's waiting outside."

Beside each other on red leather stools, the only patrons at a small Greek-owned diner, my gown puffing up and falling down around me like a botched soufflé, and Alex's tuxedo deep black in the harsh lights, we looked like a couple from another era. The small side street was quiet, but the few passersby couldn't help but stop and stare. They giggled as they peeked in at the crazy couple eating today's special in diamonds and superfine wool.

We sat for a good ten minutes before the waitress finally sauntered over and took our order. "This place is great," said Alex without irony. "I love being ignored."

He was not very talkative at first, probably tired, but brightened after a few bites of his homemade souvlaki. He talked about the campaign, the city's crime and tax rates, and the million-and-one strategy "huddle-ups" Frank insisted on each day. His imitation of Frank was so spot on, complete with Yiddish profanity and wild hand gestures, that I laughed out loud. It also was clear he had a brotherly affection for Calvin, his communications wunderkind, who was helping Alex reach younger voters through YouTube, Instagram, and Tumblr, and who often met Alex for early morning runs along the Schuylkill River.

Alex vented about how hard it was, talking to representatives from the teachers' union, Rittenhouse Small Business Association, trash collectors, and meter maids. How much their expectations weighed on him.

"Guys like them work their asses off," he said, nodding toward two patrol cops near the register. "They deserve pay raises, better pensions, more days off, everything. But let's face it, no matter what I do or say, it's just not going to happen.

"It's so different from the DA's office," he continued, shaking his head. "As fucked-up as the court system is, every once in a while you put a bad guy away for good. I felt like I was making a difference, doing what I said I was going to do. But politics just seems like a lot of smoke and mirrors. I never thought it would be this frustrating."

Suddenly, I heard myself telling him what Jimmy always said when I was frazzled: "I know it seems overwhelming right this second. But you don't have to solve every problem right now. Just try to move the ball down the field a little bit every day. Eventually, you'll get to the end zone."

He looked up at me with a funny expression. "Thanks, Coach." Then he smiled and conceded, "You're right, though. Not everything has to get done today. And who knows? Maybe we will be able to deliver on some promises."

I couldn't help but smile back. Handsome and hardworking? A great kisser and compassionate? I was wrong when I told Jules that I thought Alexander van Holt seemed like a nice guy. He wasn't just nice; he was *amazing*.

Spinning toward me, he changed the subject. "Tell me about your day...how were the kids?"

"Great," I said. "School, naps, toys, fights. Typical little-person stuff."

"Did the Baccos come? You guys have fun?" he asked, loosening his bow tie and stretching his neck from side to side.

"They were there when I got home from—" I stopped myself. I longed to tell him about my run-in with Jules, but I wasn't sure how to explain it to myself, let alone another person. "Yep, we had fun."

"Good." He pulled out a buzzing BlackBerry and began to text.

I used the break to finish my gyro, careful not to drip tzatziki down the front of my gown.

"It looks like tomorrow's thing is moved to nine, so you better be ready by eight," he told me.

"Yep," I replied, clueless. "I'll be dolled up and ready, bright and early."

He raised an eyebrow. "Dolled up? For a bunch of union guys?" he asked. "Please don't overdo it. You're supposed to be the home-town girl, right?"

"Right," I said, nodding. "I was just kidding." But he barely heard me, his eyes darkening as he read another e-mail. "Shit."

"What's wrong?"

"Looks like my father is coming back for election night," he said, putting down his phone and looking up at the grubby cork ceiling. "Fuck. I wish we could have shipped him, not Roberta, off on that cruise."

"*We* sent Mom on that cruise?" I asked, forgetting myself.

He looked up. "It was your idea, not mine."

"Yeah, I meant—"

Alex interrupted: "All I can say is he better behave himself." He pushed his plate away, his meal only half-eaten.

I wanted to ask more, to find out about this mysterious—and apparently unwelcome—father. But a decade of marriage had taught me when to leave it alone. Instead, I put my finger under his chin and turned his face toward me.

"Guess what?" I said, a silly expression on my face.

"What?"

"Do you want to know all the interesting things I learned tonight?"

"I'm not sure. Do I?"

"Oh, yes, you do. For starters, Kelley Radomile is a cross-dresser.

And Dr. Farley is giving free Botox to any lady who lets him see her tits. And Jennifer Delacourt is not only screwing her psychiatrist, but also the maître d' at the club. The Racquet Club, that is."

"Wow, you're up-to-date on all the sordid misdeeds of the Philadelphia elite," he said, the glint returning to his eyes. "Speaking of sordid misdeeds, let's get out of here."

We rode home in the back of the Suburban in silence, the space between us electric. Outside, rain began to fall, smearing the city lights, and inside, with Alex's hand on my thigh, my thoughts felt just as blurry. When the car stopped in front of our building, we said good night to Oscar, then ran toward the front doors, water staining the edges of my satin shoes. The doorman was gone for the night, leaving Alex to fumble with the key card, just like when we met all those years ago. As I waited, my mind swam with the nearness of him, with the events of the evening, with what might come next.

Inside, the elevator doors opened and we stepped in, our hair and shoulders moist from the rain. The door slid shut and we were alone.

He stepped over to me and took my face in his hands, kissing me on the mouth while maneuvering me gently to the back of the elevator. His hands moved down my neck and up under my breasts, with all the sureness and haste of a husband. When his hands started to move lower, I pushed him away, thinking of a different marriage, a different man.

The elevator paused at our floor, then slid open. I stepped out and walked as fast as I could in the masses of fabric. His footsteps followed behind me, but slowly, and I beat him to the door.

"Oh, that's how we're going to play it," he said in a funny/sexy voice, teasing me as if I were playing some lover's game of hard to get.

I opened the apartment door and slipped inside, then moved quickly through the wide rooms until I found myself back in my closet, where the night had begun. I stood in the dark catching my breath, knowing I should feign a headache but also knowing I wouldn't. Couldn't. The crystal chandelier snapped on and I felt his arms around my waist.

"You're not getting away this time," he whispered, his voice lower and more urgent.

He spun me around to face him, then moved me back against one of the long mirrors, its smooth glass cold on my bare back. He kissed my face and neck, while his hands made their way up under my dress, finding my black lace thong and pulling it down. As his fingers moved up inside me, I stopped thinking of anything but how it felt, how he looked. I stopped resisting, started matching his intensity with my own.

I pulled off his tie and ran my hands up his chest, loosening his shirt out of his pants. His eyes locked on mine, he stepped back, shrugged off his jacket, and unbuckled his belt and pants. He stepped back to me and fumbled for my zipper, but finding only silk-encased buttons, ripped apart the top few and yanked down the dress. I stood there panting in my black lace bra and heels. He lifted me up and held me against the mirror, then entered me.

The motions felt familiar but also dangerously different. This was not the typical weeknight lovemaking or the fastest way to an orgasm or even silly, dirty fun. This was uncompromising desire having its way—the kind that makes even reasonable women turn Lifetime movie crazy. I let myself enjoy every thrust, every part of my body on fire for this man, every motion tipping me further and further toward the inevitable, first for me, then him.

Afterward, we clung together for a few moments, our breath slowing, the sweat on his brow leaving dampness on my forehead.

He separated himself from me and lowered me gently onto the carpet. But my legs were jelly, and we both laughed as I slid down the mirror with a squeak.

He bent down to touch my cheek, then stood up and buckled his pants. I watched as he turned and stepped over me, leaving me a jumble of limbs on a cloud of navy silk. I sat there a moment after he'd left, then stood up and kicked the dress under the hanging clothes and searched for some pajamas.

It was only as I was brushing my teeth that I noticed one of my earrings was gone.

Who cares? I thought. For the first time in a long time, I felt invincible.

CHAPTER FIVE

The cloudy glass-and-chrome light fixtures hanging in the Lansdowne Lions Club looked like they hadn't been cleaned in decades, and only about one in four bulbs was working. Tiny pools of light shone down on the crowd, illuminating people as they darted here and there for coffee and doughnuts, and creating a pretty undersea effect, despite the dreadful metal chairs and faux-wood paneling.

The scene felt very familiar to me. The noisy chatter was the same as before a PTA meeting, and the low wooden stage looked like it was set up for one of Gloria's dance recitals. Plus, Jimmy's older brother was a Lions Club member, and his six children, my nieces and nephews by marriage, had had their christening and first holy communion parties in rooms as ambiance challenged as this one.

Alex was at the front, chatting with a man in jeans and an untucked golf shirt. In a few minutes, he would be addressing the club members as well as, and more important, about ten percent of the seven-hundred-strong International Brotherhood of Electrical Workers, Local 654. He was standing behind a scratched wooden podium on the stage, in front of a wall covered with plaques listing veterans from four wars and flyers selling everything from guitars to snowplows. Behind him, in a corner, was an American flag that once hung over Saigon. Front and center, though, looking conspicuously dust-free and bright, was a large blue-and-white campaign sign: "Van Holt for Congress."

We had made the half-hour drive in Frank's beat-up Camry because he was afraid a chauffeured Suburban or Alex's Porsche would have sent the wrong message. And yet, despite Frank's careful consideration, no one noticed us as we pulled up, and we had to ingratiate ourselves into a crowd of smokers in order to start schmoozing. No one seemed particularly friendly, except for the elderly veterans and their wives, with their soft, papery handshakes and twinkling eyes. One old lady held me in a hug the entire time I spoke with her.

Now I sat in the second row sipping coffee from a paper cup and waiting for the speech to start. After adjusting and readjusting myself in the hard metal folding chair, I forced myself to sit still with my legs crossed at the ankles, hands in my lap, and an "Isn't this wonderful?" expression on my face. The devoted candidate's wife.

Beside me on the aisle sat Calvin, preparing to video the event on an iPad, while on the other side sat two Van Holt for Congress staffers: a pretty Indian intern named Sunita in a Bryn Mawr College sweatshirt and Carol, a professorial-looking volunteer in red glasses, a tweedy pantsuit, and an "Equality Now" pin.

At the end of the row sat a large bearded man, his too-small argyle sweater and khaki pants straining from his girth, his purple socks begging for attention. Sunita leaned over and whispered, "Hi, Gerald," then rolled her eyes at me. I would learn later that Gerald was one of Alex's groupies.

If elected, Alex would be one of eighteen congressmen from Pennsylvania, and, at thirty-eight, the youngest. His district, the second, encompassed a swath of Center City, University City, and West Philadelphia as well as part of two suburban counties. To win, he would have to appeal to a wide variety of voters, including suburban blue-collar families; Center City hipsters, socialites, and professionals; the ultraliberal University of Pennsylvania and the middle-class African American neighborhoods that surrounded it; as well as the poorer, high-crime areas of far West Philadelphia where Father Fergie worked. It was a district that almost always went to an ex-union guy or former city commissioner, but since the 2012 redistricting, which added the affluent Main Line to the mix, it was a whole new ball game. If anyone could get the district to vote for a young newcomer, and one with a lineage that included two state senators and a governor, it was Alex. His commercial on You-Tube already had more than a million views.

But, still, Frank was nervous. The latest polls had Alex well behind his opponent, a cool-headed ex-judge from Center City named Amanda Bullock. She was smart and tough and she knew how to work the media to her advantage. Just that morning, the *Daily News* quoted her saying Washington didn't need another "limousine liberal," especially one who had never struggled to feed his family or pay his bills. It was a tired sound bite, and a little beneath Judge Bullock, but it would resonate, especially here in working-class Upper Darby. Alex had better be prepared.

This morning's event, a blue-collar double dip of Lions Club members and union representatives, was designed to counter Alex's image of a bored rich guy with nothing better to do. And if you wanted something done in Philadelphia, unions were a good place to start. I looked forward to hearing what Alex would say; I was pretty sure the only time a van Holt entertained this many union members was when Bloemveld needed a new roof.

It proved to be a tougher room than even Frank expected. Really tough. When Alex began to speak, there was no head nodding or clapping, just poker faces, audible sighs, and chatter. As he segued into the state of the economy and "making sure we have a strong middle class," someone actually guffawed.

Alex looked down at his notes. The crowd was getting to him. He began to speak again, but with even less authority. His voice cracked. I thought of all my years of public relations and willed him to keep going, just finish the speech. If he gave up and walked out now, he'd look foolish. Or worse, like a quitter. And here in the front row, ready to document it all—the press.

"Come on," someone said, irritated. Uncomfortable laughter ensued, and people began to whisper and chat. One man got up and left—signaling to everyone present that Alex wasn't worth their time, much less their vote. Then someone in the back of the room articulated what many might have been thinking: "Goddamn rich kid."

My head whipped around to find the wise guy, an overmuscled, unshaven man in a paint-spattered T-shirt, baggy canvas overalls, and an Eagles ski cap, smirking proudly. I knew this type of guy—the kind who spoke too loud at movie theaters and refused to curb his dog—and wished I could walk over and slap him. I fought the urge, turning back to Alex. I realized then that I felt protective of this man on the stage. Like a wife.

I stared at him until I caught his eye, then mouthed three words: "Fuck that guy." In an instant, his expression changed from fear to amusement. He slipped off his jacket, rolled up his sleeves à la Bobby Kennedy, and began to speak, this time off the cuff and with confidence: "You're right; it's true. I *am* a rich guy. And I don't *have* to work. If I wanted to, I could spend my days going to the club and buying expensive cars. But I don't. I never have."

The room quieted; bodies stopped twitching.

"I've *always* worked. Every day. Since I was sixteen. First as a volunteer at my local Boys and Girls Club, then with the Peace Corps, and later as an assistant district attorney with the special victims unit. Because, to quote JFK, 'Of those to whom much is given, much is required.'"

With the mention of our thirty-fifth president, an Irishman and a veteran, the room silenced, the only sound the quiet hum of the ice maker.

"But mostly I worked, well, because..."

He paused, put his hand over the microphone, then looked back at the crowd with a grin. "Because I fucking hate to golf."

People laughed and nodded; there was a smattering of applause. Alex had won them over, the mood in the room shifting from uncomfortable to amiable.

I clapped too, my eyes locked on Alex's sexily sheepish smile. I flashed back to his naked back and sweat-soaked brow, not realizing everyone else had stopped clapping. A while ago.

"Thanks, doll, but you're the one vote in here I can definitely count on," he said to me. "At least I think so."

My cheeks burned and I thrust my hands in my lap. People seemed to like it, though. They laughed and wolf whistled.

After shaking hands outside a day care, then a quick tour of the new dementia unit at a retirement community, Frank informed us that our next appointment—a lunchtime meet-and-greet at a community center—had been canceled due to low interest. We were all sitting in Frank's car again, Alex and I in the backseat, the passenger seat filled with a laptop, brochures, maps, and a box of breath mints.

"Well, kids, we've got an hour to kill, so I guess we should find a place for lunch," Frank announced, looking back at us. "Preferably a place with voters in our target demographic."

"And what is that, again?" I asked, trying to sound nonchalant.

"Same as it's been all year, Abigail. Men aged twenty-five to forty-five." He laughed and added, "We're doing well with women and old people. But the men around here—"

"They hate me," interjected Alex.

"No, they don't," said Frank, rolling his eyes at Alex. "Look at this morning. You won them over. We just have a long way to go."

"Maybe you need more press. Something big and splashy," I suggested.

Frank seemed to be mulling it over, but Alex said, "No! Slow and steady wins the race. And besides, Philly press can smell a stunt from a mile away."

Well, not a well-executed stunt, I wanted to say, but stayed quiet.

"If memory serves, there's a diner around here," said Frank as he put the car in gear. "It's noon, so it should be packed. Let's go check it out." He hit the gas harder than he intended, sending Alex and me backward with a jolt. We laughed and held on.

But Frank's idea of a "blue-collar" haven, a sixty-year-old diner with torn leather seats, a sloping floor, and a TV tuned to *The Price Is Right,* was almost empty. Only four booths were occupied. Those folks, plus the two waitresses and one host/manager, meant twelve potential votes. Alex would not catch up to Amanda with twelve votes; he needed more like twelve thousand. Alex introduced himself anyway; then we huddled together by the rotating pie case, deciding what to do.

"I don't get it," said Frank. "Don't guys who work blue-collar jobs love diners?"

"Not today," said Alex with a shrug. "Maybe tomorrow?" The two men looked at each other in commiseration.

"Not tomorrow either," I offered timidly. "No one I know has time to sit down at a diner in the middle of the week. And certainly not one as slow as this one." I motioned to the man in the second booth, anxiously drumming his fingers on the table as the waitress ignored him.

Both men turned and looked at me.

"And it's not just that," I continued. "Most 'blue-collar' guys, as you call them, eat lunch at, like, eleven o'clock, because they've probably been up since five. And a lot of them eat in their trucks." I thought of Jimmy and the red Playmate cooler he filled every night before work: a sandwich, apples, chips, plus at least a liter of unsweetened iced tea he steeped himself.

"Really?" asked Frank, disbelieving. "How did you become such an expert on the daily rituals of the Delaware County working class?"

I smarted at his tone, but Alex stepped up to my defense. "Don't forget that Abbey grew up around here." He turned to me. "Where do *you* think we should go?"

I gave it some thought. It was Tuesday at half past twelve. Libraries would be somewhat empty, as would grocery stores. A dead time at the YMCA, except for a handful of Silver Sneakers. The mall at midday? A ghost town.

There was only one place I could think of that always had a line...and a rather long one, at that. In fact, last time I was there, I almost gave up.

"Chipotle."

"Where?" Alex looked confused.

"Chipotle. You know. The Mexican place. The guy was on *Oprah*." He looked at Frank, who immediately whipped out his phone.

"Sustainable...organic beans...recycled napkins...blah, blah, blah," the older man mumbled as he clicked. "All good messages, so okay." He shrugged at Alex, then pulled out his keys and held the door.

"After you, Mrs. van Holt," he said with a hint of sarcasm.

When we arrived at the Chipotle on Sproul Road, close to where I used to drop off Gloria for 4-H camp, the line ran out the door, just like I had promised. Frank excused himself and darted off to the adjacent supermarket to find something kosher, leaving my husband and me alone for the first time that day.

Watching Alex at a fast-food restaurant, I began to suspect this was the first time in a long time that he had been inside such an establishment—the kind of place where menus hung above your head, not handed to you in a leather folio, and where everyone carried their own tray. But after the Bloemveld cocktail party and the Ballantine Ball, it was nice to share a meal with Alex in a place foreign to *him* but not to me. Funny to watch him struggle a bit, even if it was just figuring out the difference between carnitas and barbacoa.

Alex seemed delighted by the array before him, choosing almost all of the fixings and taking forever to get through the line. When the lady at the register asked if we wanted "chips and guac" too, he looked at me to translate. When I told her "of course," he seemed thrilled.

And a bit surprised. As we filled our drinks, I reminded myself that Abbey van Holt didn't get a body like this by eating burritos. I would try my best to eat just half. But after the long morning, and two days of barely any food, it smelled wonderful.

We found the last two available seats at a group table next to two thirtysomething guys in Adam Mechanical shirts. I nodded my head in their direction and mouthed, "Told ya so."

Alex nodded back, then began to unwrap his burrito.

"Wow, this thing is giant," he said as he pulled back silver foil and surveyed the tortilla, wondering where to bite first. "And it was only eight bucks!"

"I know. Sam loves it."

"Who?"

Shit, I slipped up. *Note to self: Never get too comfortable.*

"A friend of mine. Nobody." I laughed and swatted the air like it wasn't important.

He took a bite, rolled his eyes in ecstasy, then leaned over and whispered: "Tell me, Mrs. van Holt: Are you cheating on me with a man named Sam? At Chipotle?"

"Yes. Yes, I am."

"Well, I don't blame you. This place is awesome."

He took another bite, sending rice and salsa down his shirt, across his paper-lined basket, and dangerously close to the large, burly man beside him.

Alex wiped up the drippings and told him, "Don't mind me. I just got out of prison." The guy laughed and I could see that it pleased him.

God, he's cute, I thought. Even while perched on a round metal stool, sipping diet lemonade out of a paper cup and making an absolute mess of himself. If voters knew this Alex—this funny, self-deprecating burrito lover—they couldn't help but like him and accept him as one of their own. So what if he sometimes used words like "brilliant" and "vexing"? And that he dressed like Matt Lauer twenty-four hours a day?

He was more than that. Much more.

Even Frank had to agree that the Chipotle whistle-stop was a shrewd move. Alex had been relaxed and made some real connections, like his bearded tablemate, who, after discovering their mutual hatred of green peppers, had shaken his hand and told him, "Good luck, bro." On the car ride to the next event, I made sure to let Frank know how many hands Alex had shaken—more than two hundred!—and how cool it had been when the manager let him come behind the counter to try his hand at burrito folding.

But Frank acted dismissive, droning on about how much more

work we had to do. I was beginning to understand that Frank was a bit of a taskmaster, while Alex could be more loose. Which was probably what made them such a good team.

The next event had Alex serving as moderator for a mock debate about gun control at South Westbrook High School. After that, he would stay and speak to members of the PTA at their afternoon meeting. It was a good idea: South Westbrook was an enormous 1950s-era brick public high school, with a student body of twenty-five hundred from the surrounding middle-class neighborhoods. Its sprawling campus felt more like a small college, with a gym, classroom buildings, and a huge new theater.

Here, Alex didn't seem nervous at all; he came alive interacting with the students, listening intently as they awkwardly debated Second Amendment rights versus the threat of gun violence in a free society. When one girl froze, he walked up and whispered a joke. She laughed and was able to continue.

He was giving the debaters some tips when a long buzz sounded, and in an instant, the students were packed up and pushing for the door, then schlepping off toward buses, ten-speeds, and beat-up sedans. When they'd gone, I helped Frank and Calvin arrange chairs in a circle on the stage for the PTA, while Alex talked to a potential donor on the phone. Twenty or so women wandered in, and with their tied-back hair, exasperated expressions, and Big Gulps, I felt at home.

Strangely, though, not one woman spoke to me. And when I did catch someone's eye or attempted to introduce myself, I received only a quick, grim smile. In my tight-fitting Calvin Klein wool suit and high-heel Altuzarra booties, I was out of the club.

Eventually, they settled into metal chairs, like an Arthurian council in mom jeans. Alex opened with a five-minute overview of his platform, then took questions. Hands shot up all around and several women started talking at once, so he pointed at a middle-aged brunette to begin. I thought she would ask about schools or health care, but she asked about Pakistani militants.

Another mother asked about his stance on the two-week waiting period to own guns. Another peppered Alex about tort reform. And yet another asked what Alex could do to protect her husband's solar-powered factory job now that the governor had repealed the three percent "Wind, Solar, and Geothermal" incentive.

Wow. These women were hard-core. I was ashamed to admit it, but I thought they would ask about "women's issues" like education and health care. But they knew everything about everything, even the most confusing amendments and the most obscure foreign policies. I made a mental note to start reading the paper more.

In return, Alex gave them specifics, discussing policy, legislation, and his beliefs in detail. As he paced back and forth, he cited statistics and personal stories and even conceded when one woman's argument topped his own. When he spoke about crime, a subject he knew well, he sat down and told an anecdote about why he became a district attorney. A childhood friend of his had lost his only brother in a botched convenience store robbery, and the day after the funeral Alex changed his major from business to prelaw. If the moms weren't on the Alex train before, they were on board now.

I left them there—discussing alternative energy sources—and slipped out to check on the kids. Outside, the crisp fall air felt good after a day spent indoors.

May picked up the house line after six rings.

"Hi, May, just checking in," I said.

"Huh?"

"It's Mrs. van Holt. Just checking on the kids."

"Oh."

"Did Sam—excuse me—Van have a good morning?"

"Yes."

"Did he eat a good breakfast?"

"Yes."

"Did he have any outdoor time?"

"Yes."

Will you please stop yessing me to death and tell me something specific about my son's day? I wanted to scream at her. May never seemed to volunteer any more info than the bare minimum, in the fewest possible syllables. I knew it wasn't a language barrier; her English was really good. This morning, she'd read Gloria a page of Rainbow Loom instructions without hesitation and in the woven tote bag she brought each day I glimpsed a thick textbook on applied calculus and a copy of the latest *Atlantic Monthly*. I also heard her tell Alex a dirty joke at breakfast. Perhaps she only became an introvert around Mrs. van Holt.

"Well, kiss him for me when he wakes up, and we'll see everyone when we get home. Probably five thirty or six. Seven at the latest."

"Yes."

I took my time going back into the auditorium, wanting a few moments away from policy talk. I pulled my jacket tighter and strolled along the covered walkways, painted with various iterations of Buster the bulldog, the school's mascot. I knew Buster well: my high school tennis team got crushed by the Lady Bulldogs every year.

I found a courtyard filled with picnic tables and trash cans full of the remnants of today's lunch. Dropping down to a bench, I parked my leather tote beside me and kicked off my booties. I tucked my sore feet up under me and took a deep breath.

A young girl walked by, her head down and shoulders hunched under the weight of her overstuffed backpack. She wore too-short, too-blue jeans and a dowdy, plain sweatshirt, her face hidden by glasses and long, stringy hair. Her lone attempt at style—red-and-green bowling shoes—backfired horribly, making her look even younger and gawkier, instead of the subversive coolness I knew she was after. With her eyes downcast, I could tell she was trying to be as inconspicuous as possible, even here, with only a stranger watching.

I thought of myself at that age and remembered my own teen-age self-consciousness and my constant slouch to hide my height. I thought of my mother too, who would chide me for not standing up straight and, even worse, for my wanting to be like everyone else. Roberta was a woman who lived to stand out, to be noticed.

But she also liked that I was smart and never encouraged me to abandon my studies to be cool or popular. She admired people who knew Latin and calculus and read something other than celebrity biographies and horoscopes. She liked that I always had my nose in a book, even at the expense of a prom date. And in fact, that's why we lived in Tallymore. It may have been a sad little low-rent village tucked between fancier neighborhoods, but it fell squarely in the Lower Merion School District, one of the best in the country.

Life with Roberta was a constant battle. She embarrassed me with her tight outfits, her loud jokes, and her complete lack of subtlety. I avoided mentioning or including her as much as possible, trying hard to hide the fact that I didn't have a father and that we lived in an apartment. I wanted to fit in with the popular girls, the pretty, bubbly ones who lived in old stone colonials, played field hockey, and rode horses, and whose dads left each day in suits, hot coffee steaming from law firm–logoed mugs.

Despite Roberta's urging, I never invited girls back to our place for sleepovers. I discouraged my mother from attending tennis matches and cello recitals, even stooping so low as to giving her the wrong times. And when Joshua Freeman was making fun of the lady in the grocery cart ads wearing a short, tight tennis dress and proclaiming herself as the "Main Line's Real Estate Ace," I laughed along with the crowd, too ashamed to admit that not only did I know her; I was her only child.

As a mother myself now, I wasn't proud of the way I had acted, but I understood: To a gawky, smart kid with borderline social skills, a suspect wardrobe, and a 34A bra size, having a mom like Roberta was one liability too many. There were only so many aberrations the popular kids could ignore.

So it was with sheer terror that I found out days before the senior trip that Roberta had signed up to be a chaperone.

"You hate flying, you hate humidity, and you hate mosquitoes," I screamed at her one afternoon in our apartment's galley kitchen, not caring if the tenants who lived below us could hear. "Why are you doing this?"

"Principal Myrtle asked for chaperones," she replied calmly, pouring herself some iced tea, then taking a sip. "And since I've never done much for your school, I figured my number was up."

"Well, call him back and tell him you can't," I pleaded, following her into the living room, with its white wicker couch and conch-shell-strewn coffee table. "Besides, I really don't think they'll need you. I heard they have enough chaperones."

But she wasn't buying it, waving me away with her hand and plopping onto the couch. I switched tactics, this time going with the brutal truth.

I sat down beside her, my hands in my lap. "Mom, I really don't want you to go."

"I can see that, Abigail," she said, setting down her tea and grabbing the *TV Guide*. "But I already committed. So deal with it."

This prompted a week-long sulk, until one night after a conversation-free dinner, she asked, "What's the big deal, baby? It will be fun. I *promise* I won't embarrass you."

"Yeah, right," I said, then stormed out of the room.

Scheduled for fall break of my senior year, the trip was a seven-day "working vacation" to Costa Rica to help build a one-room schoolhouse in a small village near Puerto Limón. I had worked the entire summer at our local grocery store in order to afford the $450 fee and was looking forward to my first time out of the country. The farthest away from home I had ever been was to visit Grandma Gloria in Virginia Beach, and that was only for a long weekend, my mom and her mom in agreement that four days together was plenty of intergenerational bonding.

And now Roberta was going to ruin my trip by chaperoning. I continued doing everything I could to dissuade her—the silent treatment, tears, bribery—but she had made up her mind. She was going.

So we went. And for the first six days, the trip turned out to be pretty uneventful. Roberta kept her promise, sticking mostly to the other chaperones, biting her tongue, and pretending to not mind what the humidity was doing to her hair. Her outfits were as demure as the heat would allow; it was the first time I'd ever seen her wear a one-piece swimsuit. She also didn't try to hang out with us or pretend she was a teenager, like some of the other parents with their bad jokes and dated references. She played the part of den mother and grown-up convincingly—keeping a watchful eye on us, but a healthy distance too.

Despite the differences in social status of the students—soccer players, theater geeks, cheerleaders, art-school wannabes, and cliqueless kids like me—everyone seemed to be getting along. Maybe it was living among the Costa Rican villagers, who lived so simply, or the incredibly hard work, or simply being two thousand miles from school, but the artificial walls that normally kept us confined came crumbling down, leaving room for real friendships to bloom. And my mother, not usually one for physical labor, seemed to be enjoying herself too, hammering roofing nails by day and leading lantern-lit games of charades at night. I didn't dare tell her, but I was almost happy she was there.

And then, on the last night—disaster.

A group of adult chaperones decided to celebrate having survived the week without losing any kids to snakebites or human trafficking. They planned a night out at one of the local cantinas, leaving us with Principal Myrtle and his wife. They thought they made plans stealthily, but one of my classmates, felled by an attack of Montezuma's revenge and camping out in the latrine, overheard their plans, then generously relayed them. It was the perfect time for an illicit outing.

A few ringleaders spread the word and collected money for a couple of fifths of *guaro*, the sweet Costa Rican moonshine we saw advertised everywhere. Feeling emboldened by the new friendships and wanting to impress, I agreed to go too.

We waited until ten thirty, after Principal Myrtle completed his final cabin check, then slipped out of the concrete windows like teenage commandoes. There were just seven of us: five boys and only two girls, me and head cheerleader Melanie McCarthy. We tiptoed quietly behind the cabins and down the jungle-lined path to the village, our footsteps muffled by a chorus of insects.

In the small "downtown," a few locals were out enjoying their Friday night, strolling along wide dirt streets, chattering with neighbors. Occasionally, a motorbike or doorless minivan would bounce by, leaving a flutter of angry chickens in its wake. My friends and I found an abandoned stone courtyard that overlooked the water, sat down, and took turns passing the bottle. A cute soccer player sat next to me, eventually putting his arm around my waist. A welcome breeze blew in from the Caribbean Sea, making the humidity bearable and chasing away the bugs.

The time ticked by lazily as we laughed and talked and teased one another, our voices getting louder as the alcohol dimmed our senses. When the two bottles began to get low, and not one of us as drunk as we'd hoped, we headed toward the main part of town, searching for a shop still open.

Knowing our chaperones were somewhere nearby, possibly seated outside, we stayed away from the center "street" and stuck to a small path that ran behind a row of stores and restaurants. Melanie and I giggled as the boys chased us, our bodies moving fast despite the dark. Coming almost to the end of the village, we'd turned down a small alley that would take us toward a bodega, when we saw her. Or, I should say, *them*.

Roberta was leaning against a wall, her blond hair and white cotton dress bright in the tropical moonlight. Pressed against her was Mr. Johnson, our high school guidance counselor, the only other single chaperone, and the only black person on the trip, who was kissing her neck, his long legs wide so their faces would meet. They were so engrossed they didn't notice the sound of fourteen flip-flops approaching and then stopping, or the little cloud of dust lifting and wafting over.

"Mom!"

They looked over, their mouths in surprised O shapes.

"Abigail?"

Mr. Johnson quickly took a step back and smoothed his shirt. Someone behind me dropped a bottle; it fell with a thud.

Mom and I stood there staring at each other, our minds in a race to recover from the shock and move to a more actionable emotion— anger. I got there first.

"What the fuck?" I said to her. I couldn't believe it. Here it was, just hours from when we would leave for the airport, and she couldn't stop herself from yet another attempt at seduction, this time aiming her charms at sweet widowed Mr. Johnson, a man who lost his wife just last year.

She ignored my word choice and addressed the entire group. "What are you kids doing out here?" she asked loudly, using her chaperone voice.

"Way to go, Mr. J," a boy behind me called. A couple of others laughed.

"You kids are not supposed to leave the camp," he responded sharply, stepping toward us but tripping on a half-exposed root and stumbling. As he righted his lanky frame, the kids turned and ran, leaving me alone with the two adults.

"You promised," I whispered, then turned and ran.

"Abigail, wait," I heard her say, but I didn't stop.

I kept running until I was back at my cabin, panting hard. I hauled myself up through the window, scraping my shins, then threw myself on my metal cot. I didn't bother to change my sweat-drenched clothes or even to take off my shoes, just curled up on my cot and prayed for sleep.

But it did not come. I knew the story was already spreading across the camp like wildfire, whispered from cot to cot, embellished at each retelling. I knew how quickly this story would make the rounds through school on Monday. And I knew that, thanks to one minute in one night thousands of miles from Tallymore, my senior year would go from what should have been one of the best years of a girl's life to one of giggles and teasing, my social status downgraded from unspecified to outcast.

And all because of Roberta. I couldn't wait to go to college and be rid of her.

It was past eight o'clock before Frank pulled the car off the Vine Expressway and through the dark, tree-lined streets that would lead us back to Rittenhouse Square.

"Abbey, I have to admit, you were great today," Frank said, over his shoulder. "It's the first time I've ever seen you so comfortable with voters. Keep it up, kiddo. For at least another week."

"What happened to you?" Alex teased. "I thought you have a no-hugging rule."

"I do?"

He laughed again, then turned back to his phone, leaving me to wonder about the other Mrs. van Holt. I guess life on the campaign trial had led me to become a real germophobe. Or a cold fish.

Still, I was happy to hear the approval from Frank. All day, I tried to be the best Mrs. van Holt I could be, greeting everyone with a big smile and a handshake, listening to my husband speak with a demure and devoted look, and admiring as many babies and dogs and knee replacements as possible. But it wasn't easy being "on" all day, especially while remembering to keep Abbey Lahey "off."

It also wasn't easy listening to Alex's "bootstraps" version of me. I heard him tell one father that he understood the difficulties of paying for college because his wife had had to rely on scholarships. That wasn't true; the only scholarship I ever received was five hundred dollars for winning the *Tallymore Local* "Young Voices" essay contest. (I wrote about how dangerous our town's bike lanes had become, and I suspected I was the only entrant.) Then at the PTA meeting, he told one woman he understood the special struggles of the single parent all too well. "My mother-in-law—also a single mom—told me there were nights when she had to choose between paying the power bill or putting food on the table," he told the crowd, shaking his head at the thought. I shook my head too, before realizing he meant me.

Roberta was much too proud and organized to pay a bill late. The only time we had ever lost electricity was when a drunk driver ran into our street's transformer, knocking out lines for a three-block radius. It actually was Roberta who saved the day, Erin Brockovich–ing the power company with her cleavage and not-so-idle threats.

I had spent the ride debating whether to say anything to Alex about his exaggerations, but now, as Frank doubled-parked in front of our building and Alex ran around to open my door, I wondered if it was such a big deal. With my hand in his hand as we walked to the door, I decided to forget about it.

Inside the apartment, Alex changed for an evening run while I washed off my makeup. I moved into the closet to take off my clothes and jewelry but stopped as I slid out the worn velvet jewelry case. In the center, alone, sat one diamond chandelier earring.

Feeling guilty, I spent the next twenty minutes on my hands and knees in the closet, the bathroom, and the bedroom. I then retraced my steps from the night before, walking slowly down the hall and into the elevator. Down in the lobby, I scanned the floors, peeked into corners, and rifled through two silver trash cans. I left a note on the day manager's desk, asking him to call me as soon as possible. Then, remembering the diner, I found it on Google Maps and called. They remembered us, but no, there was no earring. I asked them to check again and waited, but eventually I had to just leave my name and the promise of an exorbitant reward.

Though futile, my last chance was outside, so I searched around the front door and the large concrete planters. I was holding my phone's light over a large abaca plant, digging through the dirt and hoping for a miracle, when my phone rang.

"Mrs. van Holt?" said a voice that was vaguely familiar.

"Yes?"

"You promised to call me."

"Oh! Father Fergie! How are you?" Hearing his voice, gravelly with age, reminded me of my father-in-law, Miles. I swallowed hard.

"Is something the matter?" he asked. "Should I try you again later?"

"No, it's just, I lost something important."

"Oh, dear. Perhaps it will turn up," he said. "Things always do."

"Yes, but it's not the kind of thing someone is likely to return. And it doesn't belong to me."

"Well, I promise to say a novena to Saint Anthony. He rarely lets me down. Now, when am I going to see your sweet face over here at Holy Rosary? Perhaps tomorrow?"

"I don't know. I mean, I'll have to check with Alex."

"Why don't you leave Alex out of it? I'm sure he won't mind sparing you for a few minutes. Come after lunch. We're at three twenty-two South Fifty-Eighth Street, a brick building with a sign out front. Just ask for me when you get here."

The tone of his voice was so calming, so soothing, that I found myself agreeing.

"And, Abigail?"

"Yes?"

"I really do hope you find what you're looking for."

Back upstairs in the apartment, admitting defeat, I went to check on the kids. I stared at each of them for a full five minutes, listening to the peaceful rhythm of their breathing. I tucked Sam's pink foot back under his blanket and, in Gloria's room, pushed her sweaty curls away from her brow, her face so serious in a little-kid dream. I felt a pang of guilt for not being home to put them to bed, for missing the thousand and one moments that make up a day spent with small children.

Exhausted, I moved back to my closet and looked for something comfortable to wear to bed. In the back of a drawer, I found something I recognized: a faded, wash-softened Villanova T-shirt. I put it on and then pushed aside the satin thongs and sheer bikinis to grab the biggest panties and the tallest socks I could find. I tied my hair in a sloppy knot. Cinderella was dead tired. Cinderella wanted some fuzzy slippers, a cup of herbal tea, and an *Us Weekly*.

Alex was still not back, so I padded into the kitchen, starving.

I grabbed a glass from a cabinet, then opened the fridge. There was no leftover mac 'n' cheese, no peanut butter, no cheese sticks, not even a baby yogurt. Just some uncooked steaks, salad greens, grapes, and rows of organic juices: kale, carrot, and beet. I moved to the cabinets but was equally disappointed. Finally, I scored a box of organic dark chocolate truffles from the walk-in pantry. I bargained that just a few bites wouldn't ruin my new figure, especially since I had barely eaten since Chipotle.

But the one half turned into three more halves, then four complete truffles, so that by the time Alex returned from his run, I had eaten the whole box.

"Wow," he said, eyeing my T-shirt and topknotted hair. "I thought our kids actually had to play soccer to be married to a soccer mom."

"Ha-ha," I replied, though I'm not sure he meant it as a joke. I pulled my hair out of its messy knot and sank lower on the barstool.

He grabbed a bottled water, twisted the top, and paused, watching me as I licked chocolate off my thumb.

"Are you okay?" he asked.

"Sure. Why?"

"You never eat after eight. And never chocolate."

"Oh," I said, pushing the empty truffle box away, embarrassed. "I was just hungry. And tired."

"Just tired? Because you've been acting a little strange. Is it your head? Maybe you should make an appointment with Dr. Cohen."

"I'm fine. Really."

"You sure? Because at times you seemed like you had no idea what was going on. Like this was all new to you."

Shit. It showed. I bit my lip and looked around.

He raised his eyebrows at me, expecting a response. When I remained silent, he sighed and continued. "I don't think you have any idea how hard this is, how many people are counting on me right now."

Was he kidding? Like I wasn't with him on forty-seven stops today, playing the dutiful Mrs. van Holt all day long. I wasn't even supposed to be here. I was *supposed* be in Grange Hill, folding laundry and packing lunches. Now I was getting angry.

"I *know* how important this is," I said, matching his ire with my own. "And I am *trying* my best. Trying so hard to be the person you want me to be!"

"The person *I* want you to be?" he said sarcastically. "Please."

He slammed his bottle into the trash and walked out, leaving me shaking and confused. All this because of a T-shirt and granny panties?

After a few minutes sitting in the blindingly bright kitchen wondering what had just happened, I stood up and followed him. I heard the shower running, so I slipped into bed with my iPhone. I checked e-mail, hoping there might be a ship-to-shore response from my mother. But there was nothing but a bunch of "urgent" messages from Betsy about a charity fashion show next week. Another fund-raiser? It was a wonder the van Holts had any money left, they were so busy giving it away.

I waited for Alex, but the shower just ran and ran. I pulled the heavy white duvet up to my chest. I rubbed my tired eyes. I chewed my lip, then my nails. Finally, I looked around for something to read.

The sleek, modern bedside table offered nothing but a lamp and a crystal alarm clock, and the long dresser by the window was equally bare. I was about to give up when I noticed a small brass lever, like a windup knob on a snow globe, at the back of the bedside table. I turned it slightly and the back opened toward the wall, revealing two interior shelves.

Inside were tissues, face cream, hand cream, foot cream, a relaxation candle, and a few books and magazines. I pulled out two catalogues (DwellStudio and Neiman Marcus), a copy of *Born to Run*, and a book about art collecting. I dropped them beside me and dug farther back in the table. From deep inside, I found a copy of *The Custom of the Country* by Edith Wharton. Go figure! It was the same book I was reading at home. Only Abbey van Holt was just a few pages in. She had yet to find out that Undine Spragg marries Ralph Marvell, and the French count, and finally good old Elmer Moffatt, but still isn't satisfied. That like in most Wharton novels, there would be no happy ending.

I started to page through to the end when a little voice from the other side of the bed called my name. It was Alex's bedside table, beckoning me to find out what was inside. I leaned over and very quietly clicked open his table's latch. Inside was an iPod and earphones; also a box of Benadryl, loose change, nail clippers, and two biographies: John Adams and Jay Z. I opened the Jay Z biography, curious to see if Alex was actually reading it, and a bookmark fluttered out: a photo of me holding Sam. How sweet.

The shower stopped. A door popped open and shut. Footsteps. I scrambled to return everything inside the two tables, just barely making it. I was panting and flushed and feigning interest in my nails when Alex padded in wearing thin-striped pajama bottoms. I watched him walk over to his side of the bed and sit down, ignoring me. His smooth, muscular back was still damp from the shower.

I waited for him to speak, to continue our conversation. But instead of saying anything, he turned to me, winked, then laid back in bed. He then picked up a remote and hit a button, and the room went dark.

That was it? A wink? Surely he would say something else. Surely we would talk this out.

But after a few minutes of silence, his breathing slowed. He was about to fall asleep.

"Alex?"

"Yeah?"

"I'm sorry." I wasn't really sure what I was apologizing for, but I figured it was a good place to start.

"Forget it."

I waited for more, but nothing. I sat up and turned on the lamp beside my bed.

"I know you're stressed, and I know it must be tough, but—"

"I said 'forget it.' "

"Can't we talk about it?"

"There's nothing to talk about."

"But you seem so upset. Was it something I did?"

"No. It's fine." He clicked the light back off.

But I knew he wasn't okay. He had picked the fight for a reason.

After a few moments of silence, I reached out and rubbed his arm to let him know that if he wanted to talk, I would listen. But he must have misconstrued my meaning, because he rolled over and started nuzzling my neck and put his hand on my left boob.

It was startling, this change in demeanor, and I wasn't ready to kiss and make up. And yet as the scent of him hovered around me, and I felt the weight of his chest and hips against mine, I found myself struggling to stay focused on our "fight," struggling to keep my thoughts G-rated.

Maybe Alex was right. Just forget it. I started kissing him back.

But, still, when he started to pull up my T-shirt, I swatted away his hand playfully.

"Can you handle it?" I asked. "We soccer moms can be pretty hot."

"I can handle it," he said.

And that he did.

CHAPTER SIX

It was a room I didn't expect I would ever find Mirabelle van Holt in. Or myself, for that matter.

I felt like I was on the set of a mafia movie—standing under a single bulb, surrounded by goods in boxes and stacked on shelves, examining contraband. The "really good stuff...*imported.*"

But this fabric shop behind a shop on South Street was where Mirabelle wanted to come, so this was where we were. Assisting us was a small man in an impeccable navy suit that remained surprisingly clean in the messy shop. He owned the shop but he moved like a worker bee, unfolding bolts, unpacking boxes, and laying out sample after sample, some of them so old, a wave of dust and acrid air floated up as they were unfurled.

I watched Mirabelle's eyes cut to one fabric, then another. Occasionally, she shook her head or flicked her wrist, spelling doom for whatever piece lay before her. The little man, his balding head shiny with sweat, would then snatch the offending sample away as if it were an unthinkable insult. I imagined each rejected selvage would be destroyed, execution-style, its guts ripped apart in punishment for a too-thin pinstripe or a ghastly polka dot, then left for dead in the Dumpster out back. Right beside a rotting polyester blend.

"I just can't decide, dear. What do you think?" Mirabelle sighed and turned to me. "Abigail?"

"Sorry," I replied. "I don't know. They all look nice to me."

"But this one's too cadet. And this one is too . . . royal."

"They're not the same?"

Mirabelle frowned and the shopkeeper threw up his hands. "No! Not the same. Very different!" His wild gesticulations roiled another cloud of dust and fibers. I sneezed and he offered me a linen handkerchief.

"Oh, right. I see the difference now," I lied as I leaned in for a closer examination. If only Jules were here, I thought. At home, she picked our paint colors, rugs, and throw pillows, and I always loved them.

Mirabelle instructed the shopkeeper to bring a bolt of brocade over to the one small window, preferring to examine it in "natural light." I sighed and bit my lip in boredom. And frustration. When she'd showed up unannounced at the apartment this morning and insisted I accompany her on a "little expedition," I didn't think it would take so long. And I thought we might talk about something other than pima cotton versus blends, the benefits of blind stitching, and why certain Armenian importers—not this one—were crooks. I wanted to talk about Alex. If anyone could illuminate me on life as a Mrs. van Holt, it was one who had been doing it for forty years.

"I just can't decide." Mirabelle sighed and thrust the final two contenders under my nose. "You pick."

I studied them again and pointed to a pale blue silk embroidered with darker thread in the shape of chrysanthemums.

"Wonderful. That's the one I preferred too," she said. "I'm so glad we have the same taste. When you and Alex are to have Bloemveld, I don't want you sleeping every night in a room with drapes you *despise*."

It took me a minute to understand that she meant after she was gone and we inherited the place—a thought that gave me pause on multiple levels. Not only did it mean my children and I would live in a mansion where the gatehouse was bigger than the apartment I grew up in, but it assumed a future for me in this world decades down the road, something I hadn't yet considered. Every morning I woke half expecting to be back in Grange Hill, with Jimmy. But as days turned into weeks, and the weeks into years, would that always be the case? Or would that life fade and become hazy—like a half-remembered dream?

"Dear?" Mirabelle waved a hand in front of my face. "You left us for a moment."

"Sorry."

"We were thinking about this one," she reminded me, pointing to the blue silk. "For the master bedroom."

"It's perfect," I reassured her.

She smiled and turned back to the shopkeeper, who was holding an enormous pair of gleaming scissors, hoping to cut before either of us changed our minds.

Mirabelle turned to me with a question. "Help me with the math?"

"Three yards? Five?"

"Total, dear, not per window." She seemed annoyed, pulling out a piece of paper from her purse and jotting down some numbers.

How many windows could there be in her bedroom? And how wide and tall was one window? And what about seams and a hem? I felt like she expected me to know this, as if calculating drapery yardage was included in some van Holt instruction manual I received on my wedding day. Little did she know I had never purchased decorator fabric in my life and couldn't tell you how many inches were in a yard if my life depended on it.

I deflected her question with a question: "Maybe you should ask your interior designer?"

"Interior designer? Heavens no. I never use them," she said, wrinkling her nose. "I thought you knew that."

I started to reply, but she looked away, almost wistful. "Besides, I rather like sewing, always have. Did you know before I married Collier, I had two years at Moore College of Art studying fashion design. I was going to be the next Edith Head! But then I had Alex and, well..." Both her voice and her smile faded.

I wanted to tell her I understood. Things change; life sometimes has other plans. Instead, I leaned over and helped her finish the math. We came up with seventy-seven yards total, plus another five "just in case." The shopkeeper turned bright red with excitement.

Out on the sidewalk, the noontime sun blindingly bright after the dark room, Mirabelle paused to put on oversized seventies-style tortoiseshell sunglasses while I slipped on my gold Ray-Bans. Then she began to stroll south toward Queen Village, her medallioned flats silent on the grimy sidewalk. I thought she was looking for her driver, but she pulled me close and linked her arm with mine. We fell into step together.

She was remarkable, my mother-in-law. In my entire life, I'd never met anyone more effortlessly refined, with a personal style that was so timeless yet approachable. It was as if Queen Victoria, Grace Kelly, and Michelle Obama had been blended together and then poured into a crisp blue shirtdress and Valentino flats.

"Now. Abigail. Are you all right?" she asked, her brow knit with matronly concern. "Let me know if you need to sit down or take a break."

"I'm fine. Why?"

"Alex tells me ever since the accident you've been..." She paused, searching for the right word. "Different. Not yourself."

I tensed, suddenly nervous. Did Alex suspect I was an imposter? Did she? I tried to relax, imitating her careful tone: "I can assure you, Mother, I'm perfectly fine."

"Well, if you say so. But the Brindles thought you seemed out of it on Sunday. And Aunt Tickle said you insulted her."

"She did? Oh, my apologies. I was just having a bad night. I was exhausted."

"Of course," she said, with a wave of her hand. "Just promise me you'll be careful. I think we both know we can't have any more distractions. Alex is far enough behind as it is."

We turned right, onto a narrow street blanketed with yellow leaves. I started to speak but she pretended not to hear, continuing, "And I'm concerned about Alex. I was with him all day on Monday and he seemed so tired. Probably just concerned about you, my dear, but still…"

Funny, Alex hadn't mentioned he'd seen her. If she wasn't so gracious, and if her arm wasn't wrapped lovingly around my waist, I would think she was making a point of letting me know that she had been with him, not me.

"No, he's okay," I replied, noting that he certainly hadn't seemed tired last night. Or the night before. "But honestly, I don't know how he does it. It's so much pressure."

"Well, you know Alex. Such a hard worker. And such a good boy. He always does what he's told."

I couldn't tell if she meant that as a compliment or a failing. Either way, I felt a chill run up my spine.

She continued. "Still, Abigail, too much is riding on these next few days." She stopped, turned to me, and peered over the tops of her sunglasses. "I need to know we're still on the same page."

"Of course," I replied, though I had no idea what page, or even what book, she was referring to. But since she seemed so worried about the election, I attempted some reassurance: "Don't worry. Frank told me this morning Alex was up another point since Sunday. He's been calling it the 'Abbey's bump bump.'" I pointed to the side of my head where I'd hit the piano bench for emphasis.

"Oh? How wonderful," she said, dropping her arm from around my waist. "I guess I should thank you again for making time today, then. Now that you're so valuable to the campaign." I detected an undercurrent of hardness in her silky-smooth voice.

She paused, and I looked up to see the fabric store from which we'd emerged a few minutes ago. We had circled the block without my realizing it.

And to my left? Her car and driver pulling up, as if she had willed them to do so.

I walked home, hoping some fresh air would clear my head. I strolled by pizza places, cheap jewelry stores, and a crowded Whole Foods, and into the boutique-filled "gayborhood." With May watching Sam, and Gloria at school, there was no rush—or any reason—to get home.

I popped in to a baby boutique and bought Sam three complete outfits without once checking the price. Then, at an art supply store, I picked up some colored pencils, a few jars of glitter, and a Halloween I Spy book that I knew Gloria would love. And in yet another shop, I bought her a hot pink cashmere cardigan I had seen in the window.

Back home at the apartment, I asked the doorman for the time. One o'clock—Sam would be napping. I gave the man my packages, then hailed a cab.

As the taxi made its way from Rittenhouse Square and across the Schuylkill River to University City, I leaned back to enjoy the midday sun. We passed college dorms, fast-food restaurants, a new IMAX movie theater, and colonial homes turned frat houses, their large Greek letters marring their lovely facades. Then, as we moved farther away from the university, each block had less brick, iron-work, and grass and more chain-link fences, vinyl siding, and barred windows. We turned south off Walnut Street onto Fifty-Eighth, and the street scene became quieter, even the people sitting on stoops and porches appearing motionless.

The cabbie pulled up to the address I'd given him, a low brick building that must have been a mid-century expansion of the now derelict stone church beside it. I swiped my credit card, punched in a tip, and then got out, stepping over broken bottles and sidewalk cracks as I moved toward the facade. The windows were wide but covered with iron bars. The red brick was dulled by pollution and bus exhaust, except for one cleaner, darker swatch in the shape of a cross, the emblem either stolen or removed in recent years. Now, a hand-painted sign stuck in the small patch of grass announced the "Holy Rosary Settlement House, established 1977," the year I was born.

I knocked a few times with my knuckles at first, then louder with the palm of my hand. I peered through the door's mesh window and called "Hello?" but still no one came. A few minutes later, I saw a small plastic buzzer and pushed it hard. I was about to give up when a small black woman in a nun's wimple walked by. I rapped on the door to get her attention and she almost jumped out of her bright green Crocs.

"Heavens, you startled me," she said as she pushed open the door and let me in.

"I'm sorry," I said. "I tried the buzzer, but no one came."

"That old thing hasn't worked in years," she said, smiling.

"Well, that explains it."

"How can I help you? You don't look like you are here for lunch."

"Well, no. I'm here to see Father Fergie. I'm Abbey van Holt."

"Follow me, child."

We walked down a hall lit by humming fluorescents and smelling of dust, bleach, and instant mashed potatoes. My heels clicked loudly while the nun moved silently. I tried to walk more softly.

At the end of the hall, we turned into a cafeteria-like room where twenty or so people from the community were seated at long tables, some still finishing their lunches, others reading the paper, some just staring out the windows. At one table, two young mothers were chatting as their toddlers played with Legos, while at another, three elderly men sipped coffee from mismatched mugs. By the windows, a baby in a wash-faded sleeper rolled an empty water bottle back and forth while her mother talked on her phone. A grinning boy slightly younger than Gloria, eyes bright and mischievous, scooted from table to table playing a solitary game of hide-and-seek.

"Stop that!" yelled a woman I took to be his grandmother, who was busy feeding a teenage girl in a motorized wheelchair.

The nun placed a coffeepot on the table in front of the men, then turned to me. "Wait here," she said.

I smiled at the baby and took a seat at an empty table. Not knowing what to do, I pulled out my phone and pretended to be engrossed in an e-mail. I felt all eyes on me for a few seconds, but by the time I looked up, conversations and playing had resumed.

"Mrs. van Holt! You came!"

I stood up as Father Fergie came toward me with outstretched arms.

"You seem surprised," I said as I extended my hand.

He ignored it and went in for a bear hug. "I *am* surprised," he said, embracing me a little too long. "Cocktail party promises are usually broken."

"Well, here I am."

"Yes, you are," he said, one arm still around my waist. "Welcome to my little piece of heaven."

He waved his hand proudly at the room as if he was introducing a play. Our tour was to begin, and off we went.

The building consisted of the cafeteria/fellowship hall, an office, a smaller room with couches and TVs, and a supply room stacked with boxes of paper towels, off-brand diapers, and canned tomatoes. In the modest kitchen, two rusty ovens competed for space with a dented refrigerator, a six-burner stove, and a restaurant-sized dishwasher. The little nun was there, wiping down the biggest, blackest pot I'd ever seen.

"How many meals do you cook in here?" I asked Fergie.

"Three a day, except Mondays. Only one oven works, but we manage. But that's why I need your help. If we could get Alex to help push our reclassification through, we could start getting HHS funding. Maybe even some grant money."

"And if he can't?"

"We'll have to close down by December. If not sooner."

"But where will all these people—these children—eat?"

He sank back on his heels, tilted his head to the ceiling, and quoted scripture: "Count it all joy when you meet trials, for you know that the testing of faith produces steadfastness. Let steadfastness have its full effect, that you may be perfect and complete, lacking in nothing."

He opened his eyes, watery and pale blue, and whispered, "The Good Lord won't let us down. And hopefully, neither will your husband."

As he walked me out, I thought of the money I had spent that morning on the kids' clothes and felt sick. We passed the room where the little baby played with her crinkly water bottle, and I thought of Sam and his wooden boat, his shelves of handmade BPA-free toys. And I couldn't help but think of Jimmy, who insisted we give two hundred dollars to the Salvation Army every Christmas, even when we were broke, and even though he knew it would start an argument between us. Fergie's words "lacking in nothing" were not meant to be ironic; he truly believed that through faith, Holy Rosary would persevere.

At the door, Fergie paused to greet a homeless man he hadn't seen in months. As he assured him there was still some lunch left, then sent him on his way, I opened my quilted Chanel purse, rifled around for my Tiffany pen, and grabbed my Tory Burch pink leather checkbook case.

"Let's give faith a little help, shall we?" I asked, scribbling.

Then I pressed a ten-thousand-dollar check into his hand.

That night as Sam and Gloria and I ate dinner at the kitchen island, Alex out campaigning again, I couldn't help looking at my children and feeling lucky. Sam looked like an ad for baby cereal with his glossy pink cheeks and pudgy knees. And even though Gloria was tiny and completely indifferent to any food except high-fructose corn syrup and red dye number 4, she was strong and smart and hardly ever sick. After what I'd seen today, I knew I was lucky, and not just because I was living in a four-thousand-square-foot apartment that had been featured in the September 2010 issue of *Architectural Digest*.

Gloria caught me looking at her and smiled. "Hi, Mommy," she said.

"Hi. Did you have a good day?"

"Yep."

"Did you learn anything good?"

"No."

"Do anything fun?"

"No."

"Nothing happened at all?

"Well, Blake Randleman threw up all over his shoes."

I wrinkled my nose, sorry I asked. "That must have been pretty gross."

"Gos," mimicked Sam.

All of a sudden, I felt an overwhelming sadness. Jimmy and Gloria liked to count all the words Sam could say: "Mama," "Dada," "sissy," "baba" (for bottle), "bye-bye," "ball," "car," "Pop" (for Miles), "toot," "night-night," and now "gross." Sam had just said another word—his eleventh—and Jimmy wasn't here to hear it.

I was still thinking about Jimmy two hours later. The kids were in bed and I was on the long couch in the family room, alone, flipping through channels and sipping a glass of red wine. I wished I had someone to talk to, someone to tell about my visit to Holy Rosary.

Before we had kids, Jimmy and I often met on our front porch to catch up after eight or ten hours apart. The summer we had moved into our new house, we had no outdoor furniture yet, so we sat on beach chairs and rested our feet on wooden crates Jimmy stole from work. We would watch the sun sink low, turning trees and houses and steeples into black cutouts.

One night, when I was four months pregnant with Gloria, we were out later than usual, enjoying a cool breeze that kept the mosquitoes at bay. I had already finished the takeout dinner from our favorite Thai place, but, my pregnancy cravings not yet sated, I had moved on to a jar of salsa, using a tortilla chip as a spoon. I couldn't get enough tomatoes that summer, eventually replacing salsa and red sauce with the real thing, sprinkling raw beefsteaks with salt and pepper and eating them like apples. Jimmy sipped on a beer while listening to me ramble on about baby names I liked.

Out of the blue, off subject, and in his usual nonchalant way, he said something that would change our lives forever.

"I think I want to start my own business."

His words seemed to hang in the air. I stopped chewing. "Really? What kind?"

"Cupcakes," he deadpanned. "What do you think? Lawn care, maintenance, installation. But more than that. I want to design too. Using native plants and succulents and natural drainage systems. Maybe even tree care."

He paused and looked at me shyly. "Do you think that's stupid?"

I was stunned. Jimmy had never seemed the creative type. But come to think of it, he was always sketching ideas for neighbors, always offering his boss suggestions for a better plant, a prettier tree line. And though we'd lived in this house for only six weeks, our yard was already beginning to look like Longwood Gardens.

"I don't think it's stupid," I said. "I think it's a *great* idea. But do you need a degree? Or at least a certificate or something?"

"Well, yes and no. I've been in the business for ten years. I've probably installed a thousand new lawns. But I would need to finish college and maybe get a master's."

"You could do that. They have night programs."

"Yeah, but it's a big time commitment. And money. And you were hoping to cut back to part-time with the baby coming and all…"

I attempted to wipe the sprinkling of chips off my stomach and sat up straighter.

"You're right," I said sarcastically. "Wife and kids ruin everything. The bastards."

I expected a funny remark back, but Jimmy said nothing. He took off his cap, wiped his brow, and put it back on. He then reached over, took the jar from me, and put it on the ground. He pulled me up to standing and lifted my face to his. Our bellies touched.

"That's just the thing, Ab," he said, his eyes shining in the porch light. "I'm going to have a kid. Can you believe it? Me, a dad. And I have you. Right now, I feel like I could do anything. Make it a real success. Even if I have to pull every weed from here to Pittsburgh."

It was the longest speech he had ever said to me, longer even than when he proposed. I hugged him and snuggled into his shoulder, feeling that all was right with the world, in the way that only pregnant women really understand.

CHAPTER SEVEN

I was flying, all the shops and people and cars a blur as I breezed by them. For the first time in my life, I was jogging—no, *running*—and I was really hauling ass. With the light morning traffic, I had made it all the way across the city to Front Street in twenty-five minutes. Sweat soaked my Lululemon sports bra and mesh-trimmed shirt, but I was barely winded, my ponytail bouncing back and forth, up and down.

In Grange Hill, I had tried many times to become a runner, not for the cardiovascular benefits or stress relief but to melt the muffin top that clung stubbornly to my waist. But my attempts usually ended with me giving up less than a quarter mile from home or bailing minutes into a charity 5K. I told Jimmy I just didn't have the talent or the lung capacity, but inside I knew the real problem was dedication. And motivation. Why should I work out when Jimmy never did?

But today, after waking early and wandering around the apartment aimless and anxious, and feeling guilty about secretly finishing off Gloria's box of Froot Loops last night, I'd decided to give it another try. I also figured from the sheer volume of running shoes in the closet, this body could handle it. Time to take it out for a test drive.

As I ran with ease, I wondered where Abbey van Holt found her inspiration. It had to be more than just a desire to stay model thin. Perhaps she had learned to love it from Alex, so committed to his late-night runs? Or maybe she was a member of an elite city-moms running club, the kind that tracked mileage on special watches and posted their Broad Street Run finishes on Facebook, shaming the rest of us for our slovenly ways? Whatever the case, I added "discipline" to the long list of traits Abbey van Holt possessed that I did not.

I slowed to a walk, paused to check my pulse (a mere 142 beats per minute), then descended a small flight of stone steps toward the Delaware River. I paused to watch the cargo ships gently slipping by and saw the cars rolling over the Betsy Ross Bridge. The city was waking up, ready for another long day.

It was Thursday, October 30—almost a week now in this new life. Already it was feeling familiar, and more routine, less like a fabulous vacation. And already my old life felt muted, like a seventies photograph. The faces were still familiar, but the edges less sharp, the colors fading.

It made me feel scared, as if I was having one of those dreams where I lost Gloria at school, me running the long, bright hallways of Grange Hill Elementary in terror, searching for her pink backpack, her tiny flowered sneakers. Had she gone home with a friend? Did Jimmy have her? Was she waiting for me somewhere else? Panic rose, and I started to run again, turning back toward Center City.

With commuters now rising from subway stations and cars at every intersection, I found myself having to slow. I tried to weave around them but gave up by Eleventh Street. I looked up and realized I was near the building where Jules worked. I began to circle her block.

On the third lap, I noticed a coffee shop across from the entrance to her building and went inside. A young woman with short black hair and a knit fisherman's cap was filling metal baskets of gluten-free bagels, muffins, and scones. A large chalkboard announced prices and I winced. Even their specials were double what the same pastry would cost in Grange Hill, just six miles away. I pulled out a credit card from the tiny zippered pocket on my thigh and bought some scones, a bagel, two organic fig bars, and a coffee and then settled onto a stool by the window to wait. Like a cop on a stakeout.

A little after eight o'clock, I saw her. She was wearing dark gray skinny jeans, a silky aqua T-shirt, and a black leather blazer. Loops of thick silver chain hung low to her waist while knee-high black boots reached up toward them from the concrete. White plastic headphone strings emerged from her jacket and up into her long auburn hair, still her best feature, even when stick straight.

She was moving briskly, one arm on a black workbag, another holding a silver water bottle. I put down my coffee, grabbed the bag of baked goods, and sprinted across the street, catching her on the arm before she reached the revolving door.

"Aaaaahhh! What are you doing?" she cried in alarm, yanking back her arm and then removing her earbuds. "Trying to give me a heart attack?"

"I didn't mean to scare you," I said. "I just wanted to talk. Got a minute?"

"I've got to get to work."

"Please, Jules," I said. "I really need to talk to you." And then, holding up the bag, I added, "And I have snacks."

She eyed the bag and took in my sweaty clothes, messy hair, and eager expression. Then she glanced at her watch and sighed. "Five minutes."

We crossed over to the coffee shop and plopped into opposite sides of a booth. I laid the pastries I had just bought on the crinkly brown bag, a little buffet of breakfast delights I hoped would sweeten her expression. But she didn't touch them, just watched as I took a large bite of a cinnamon scone, raining crumbs on the table.

"Mon't mu mant mum?" I asked, the scone turning to cement in my mouth. For a moment, I thought I saw a glint of craving in her eye, but she turned away.

"I don't eat that stuff anymore," she said flatly.

I cleared my throat, steeling myself for what I'd come here to say.

"Jules, I know that somehow I screwed things up. But I want to make things right between us. Please tell me what I can do so we can be friends again."

She sighed and looked away, a bored look on her face. But I could tell she was listening. I could also tell she was not having it.

"I promise you I'm not this so-called socialite you think I am. I'm the same Abbey you met in college. I swear."

Still nothing, but at least now she was making eye contact.

"Look. I appreciate the apology. But I'm not sure there's a place for me in your life or for you in mine. You're busy. I'm busy. I've got Lucas. My business. It may not seem very glamorous to you, but I'm happy. Happier than I've ever been."

"I can tell," I said, beaming at her. "And I'm so happy for you. But I could really use a friend. Alex is stressed out and—"

"That's just it, Abbey. It's always about what *you* need and what *you* want," she said. "Or what Alex needs, what Alex wants."

"What?"

"Oh, come on. You know what I mean."

No, I don't, I wanted to tell her. *Please, Jules, please explain it to me. It is beyond comprehension that I don't see fourteen texts from you every day, that you haven't updated me on every calorie you've consumed in the past forty-eight hours, that we let another himbo get chucked off* The Bachelorette *without a word exchanged between us.*

Was I really the self-centered socialite she thought I was? And even worse, was I all about Alex van Holt, all the time?

"Don't you like Alex?" I asked.

"I like Alex just fine. It's *you* I have a problem with."

I reeled back as if she had slapped me. Then she seemed to regret being so harsh, her expression returning to the gentle Jules I knew. Her voice fell to a whisper. "Bee, you were always the independent one. The one who knew what she wanted and went after it. It was me who was always morphing for the guy of the moment. Their music. Their food. Their side of the bed. Oh God, I even took line-dancing lessons for that guy from Lancaster. What was his name? Patrick?"

"Peter," I told her.

"Yeah, Peter." As she sat cringing at the desperation of a much younger self, I sat frozen, anxious—and scared—to hear more.

But it came. "But then, after Gloria, you started to change."

"Kids do that to you. It just happens." Jules just didn't understand the grind of being a working mother. If she did, she'd understand why I quit working. I knew plenty of mothers—rich *and* poor— who quit their jobs after childbirth. I felt defensive, wondering when she'd become so judgmental.

She lifted her hands in a gesture of self-defense. "I know, I know, how could I get the mom thing? But you and I both know it was more than that. You stopped calling so much. Stopped doing all the stuff you liked to do. Started going to fancy fund-raisers and hiring decorators and doing *cleanses*. It was like the Abbey I knew disappeared. Or got swallowed up."

"That can't be true," I said, speaking to us both.

She looked at my fancy running gear and beige-blond highlights. She eyed my fake breasts and perfectly painted nails. "Really? Have you looked in the mirror lately?"

I started to refute her, getting angry. The demise of our friendship couldn't be all my fault. But then again, it wasn't like Jules to exaggerate. She always gave it to me straight; it was one of the things I valued most about our friendship.

She sighed and stood up, then grabbed her bag. "I have to go."

I watched her move to the door and felt so helpless. But I also knew that nearly twenty years of friendship couldn't end like this. I wasn't about to give up.

"Jules, wait," I said, jumping up to catch her before she reached the door. "Is there *any* way we can start again? Maybe just have lunch sometime. Or coffee. I could bring the kids."

She paused, thinking it over.

"Maybe," she said. "I'd really like to meet Van."

Then she was gone, leaving me covered in crumbs and self-loathing. The situation was even worse than I'd thought; it was utterly unimaginable. Was I so wrapped up in myself and my husband and my new life that my dearest friend, the maid of honor at my wedding, the person who felt more like family to me than my own family, had never even *met* my son?

I gathered the half-eaten goodies and the coffee and stuffed them into the trash. I hurried outside and began to run again, wanting very badly to be home. And not at the apartment, but at the Grange Hill house, with its drafty windows and sloping porch. I ran and ran and ran, trying to ignore the cramp in my stomach and the even more painful thought in my mind: *I may never see home again.*

As I stepped off the elevator, I saw May coming out of the apartment door with Gloria and Sam. I hid on one side of the hallway, listening to her sing a funny song to them, one they knew well.

"Ladybug, ladybug, what do you say?" she sang.

And the kids sang back: "Ladybug, ladybug, have a good day!"

"Ladybug, ladybug, what do you hear—" She stopped, both the smile and the song, when she saw me.

"Oscar is taking Mr. Alex, so we are walking to school," she said, all business. I was relieved that Alex was already gone, not here to see me looking so sweaty and gross, but also sad. I could use a quick hit of his smile right now.

"I'll take her," I told May.

She looked surprised—and suspicious.

"But you never...," she said, her eyes opening in horror as I held out my hand for Gloria's backpack.

I took it and then grabbed Gloria's hand. But except for her arm, which hung between us like a clothesline, the little girl didn't move.

"Gloria," I said. "Let's go." I gave her my patented "Don't test me" look.

"Let me take her," offered May, pulling Gloria's other arm up and out. "I'm sure you have things to do."

"No. I don't. I'll take her." By now I was getting angry, and so when I pulled Gloria again, it was with a little too much force. She smacked into me and yelped. May was aghast.

But she let Gloria go and instead reached down to pick up Sam. She wasn't giving *him* up so easily.

"I'll take the little guy too," I insisted, curling my hand in a "give it here" motion as if he was a piece of a contraband I'd just seen May hide behind her back. She took two hesitant steps and gave him to me, but not before wiping the drool off his mouth and smoothing down his hair.

As we walked down the hall toward the elevator, both children looked back at May with longing. It filled me with curiosity. Was Abbey van Holt too busy and important to take her own kids to school? Did they prefer May to her? I tried not to target my frustration at them, but I couldn't help it. It hurt and, at the same time, felt ridiculous. Two women fighting over who gets to take a little girl to school. In Grange Hill, it was the opposite: Jimmy and I always argued over who would be forced to take them, neither of us able to spare the twenty minutes it took to maneuver the kiss-and-go line.

"Go relax, May," I said. "I can handle the kids. I *am* their mother."

But then halfway down the hall, I had to yell back: "The stroller?"

"I called down for it," she said, still not moving, watching.

"Right," I said, herding the kids into the elevator.

Waiting for us downstairs in the lobby was a fancy chrome-and-red-canvas stroller with oversized all-terrain wheels. I lifted Sam and turned him around a few times before I figured out which direction he should face. There were no straps; the hammock-like seat used his own body weight, of which there was plenty, to secure him. Gloria was already to the front doors, so I gave the stroller a push. It shot forward like a hockey puck on ice, the motion lifting Sam's soft blond hairs up like a halo.

We cruised along Walnut Street toward the intersection, Gloria skipping five feet ahead. My suburban parental instincts told me to grab Gloria's hand, but since I had no idea where we were headed, I had no choice but to let her lead the way. After a few blocks I realized I need not have worried; she charged through the busy city streets with the focused gaze and pumping arms of a mall walker. Pedestrians moved out of her way; one couple even dropped hands and separated to let her pass. *Watch out for this one,* I thought, *she's got the eye of the tiger. Just like her grandmother.*

We dodged people and dogs, and the occasional delivery cart, until the commercial buildings gave way to residences, and the sidewalks turned from smooth and concrete to bumpy and bricked. Stately old town houses loomed over foot-softened marble steps, and carriage houses, long ago emptied of horses and coachmen, beckoned young professionals with their wide-planked doors and clay roofs.

I admired the curving iron handrails, the professionally decorated flower boxes, and the mullioned windows as Sam and I bounced along behind Gloria. I saw some equally confounding strollers heading in the same direction and figured we were close.

Gloria led the way to a pretty yellow church with a modern stone-and-glass addition. An etched gold sign announced the place: "St. Andrew's School for Children, Established 1886." A wrought-iron fence enclosed a slate courtyard and a mulched playground, while two rows of teachers, all looking like Jennifer Garner on her errand days, were clapping and singing a "good morning" song.

On the sidewalk, our trio waited in line, competing with kids jumping out of Land Rovers and nannies pushing double strollers. Gloria gave me a quick kiss good-bye and then ran through the gauntlet of teachers, while Sam looked around with glee. For a school built in the center of one of the nation's grittiest cities, it felt more like a day with the von Trapps, but I guess this was the kind of educational environment that five-figure tuition buys you.

A few other mothers mouthed hellos under the din, but none stopped to chat. Most of them looked just like me in their expensive exercise tights and bright sneakers, their morning runs either complete or imminent. I saw one mother in a gray pinstriped suit kiss a little boy and then rush off down the sidewalk, thumb-typing on her iPhone. She was no doubt sending a clever but apologetic text to her boss, explaining why she was late for work—again.

The crowd thinned and the singing died down, so Sam and I made our escape. We were just turning out of the gate when a monstrous white Mercedes SUV ran up onto the sidewalk, dangerously close to the entrance. Twin boys burst out of the backseat door and raced inside, not bothering to say good-bye to their exasperated mother stepping out from the driver's side. Against the white car, her hair gleamed black, while her overly bronzed skin skewed orange.

Apparently she knew me, because the moment Sam and I passed by, she screeched, *"Aaaaaaabbey,"* and ran over to us. I stopped strolling and braced for impact as she came toward us at top speed, her giant breasts heaving.

"I'm so glad I saw you," she said as she caught her breath and then extracted some long black hairs from her lip gloss. "Did May quit too?"

"What do you mean?" I asked, noticing her overly penciled eyebrows and platform heels.

"My nanny quit last week. Missed her boyfriend, so she moved back to Sweden. Didn't even give notice," she said as she leaned over and gave me a quick hug and a *mmmm-ah!* kiss. "I figured the same happened to you!"

"No, just decided to bring the kids myself." Why was this so shocking to everyone?

"I've been e-mailing Betsy, but she never responds," she continued. "Where the hell is the next benefit committee lunch? I've got updates on the caterer."

"Um, I don't know," I said. "Is that today?"

She gave me a look: *Duh.* "Yes, it's today, silly. We always meet on Thursdays."

This woman had a little too much of everything—jewelry, teeth, cleavage—but I liked her smile and her blatant disregard for school policies: a sign directly above her car said "Absolutely No Parking."

"Oh, right. Today is Thursday," I said slowly, awkwardly. "And Thursday is when we meet. For the benefit...committee...lunch." I was beginning to get used to sounding like a total moron.

I watched her face drop and realized she didn't think I was stupid; she thought I was being coy, trying to evade the question. Luckily, an idea surfaced.

"Let me check my phone!" I whipped it out and held it up as if it was the first phone ever invented. I scrolled through messages while she cooed over Sam, and eventually I found one from Betsy marked "Today."

"Looks like it's at twelve thirty at a place called Le Jardin on Broad Street," I told her.

"Never heard of it—but I'm sure I can find it," she said, happy again. She bent down and touched Sam's cheek, then attempted to get her bracelets away from his grasp. This time she tickled him hard and he let go, gurgling with delight.

"You're such a little roly-poly cannoli," she said as she kissed his head. "God, I just love them at this age. Once they start talking, the bullshit begins." I laughed out loud, and as I heard my own voice, I realized it was the first time I'd done so since Saturday. It felt good.

A long honk from a blocked taxi sent her scurrying back to her car, her big boobs and hair bouncing in sync. She flipped off the driver, told him to fuck himself, and then sped off in her oversized Mercedes. The few remaining mothers looked aghast but then quickly moved on, shaking their heads.

"Well, my little cannoli," I said to Sam, mimicking my new friend's South Philly accent. "I guess Mommy's going out to lunch today."

At noon, dressed and ready for lunch, I was relieved to hear my phone buzz. I ran to my purse and picked it up. It was Alex.

"Hey, doll, just wanted to let you know that Dr. Cohen can see you this afternoon."

"Okay. But I didn't know I had an appointment today." I had scoured my e-mails earlier, eager to find out how Abbey van Holt occupied her day, but found nothing.

He ignored me, continuing: "It's at two. No, three. Wait, let me double-check." I stood with my phone to my ear until he got back on the line. "Mother says get there around three and he can work you in. But don't be late because he's playing squash at four."

"Got it," I said, looking around for a piece of paper and a pen.

"And don't forget I have that dinner thing tonight and then tomorrow I'm gone all day for debate prep."

"Got it; doctor, dinner, debate prep."

"Bye, doll. Gotta jump."

I started to ask about Dr. Cohen, but the line went dead. I stared at the phone for a moment, then slid it off. Mirabelle made the appointment? I almost laughed out loud. Jimmy's mother, Jane, wouldn't even buy me a plant without checking with me first.

I sighed, then caught a glimpse of myself in the wide gilded mirror that ran the length of our foyer. I couldn't help but punch out my hip and pose like a Heidi Klum selfie.

In my leather-trimmed leggings, white silk tank, and cream cashmere cardigan cinched with silver buckles, it dawned on me that I looked like one of those magazine women I'd always longed to be. *Excuse me,* I said to myself with a sly smile and some eyelash batting, *I'm just dashing out for a quick lunch to hatch a plan to save the world, before picking up my incredibly well-schooled and adorable children, then rushing off to meet my male model turned congressional candidate husband for a night of dancing and champagne.*

In the mirror, I was the Abbey I always knew I could be.

Le Jardin was one of those restaurants that was billed as a café but was actually more like a ballroom at Buckingham Palace. The main dining room was octagonal, with mirrors on all sides that reflected its incredible views of both rivers. The soft, plush, Louis XIV–style chairs beckoned, as did the smell of fresh roses at every table. There was no entrée under twenty-two dollars, including the cheeseburger.

Not that it mattered—I was the only one at the table who ordered more than a side salad or cup of soup.

Betsy stared at me as I asked the waiter for an iced tea with no lemon.

"I hope you're joking," she said as she flicked out her folded napkin. "The waiter is bringing us that fumé blanc you like. I already ordered it."

"Super!" I said, playing along. "Just needed a quick hit of caffeine first. Barely slept last night."

"Stop it with your fabulous sex life," she said in mock exasperation. "It's too depressing."

"Sorry?"

"I can't take any more stories about you guys," she said with a laugh. "Bill and I can barely manage once a month. And even that's a chore."

I cringed to think Abbey van Holt bragged about her sex life to these women. Wasn't she envied enough?

"About time," Betsy chided the waiter as he set up a silver bucket beside us. "I really need a drink. This morning, the builder told me I can't have the pool tiles I wanted because they take eight weeks to make. In Italy. And the chandelier I picked for the library is too heavy for the custom plasterwork. I know he just doesn't want to do it. He lies to my face."

"You poor thing," said Ellen, staring hungrily at the bread basket. "Contractors are just the worst, aren't they?"

"The absolute worst..." Betsy's voice trailed off as she saw someone enter the restaurant. Her hand hit the table and the ice in our water glasses tinkled in protest.

"Who told *her* where we were meeting?" she seethed. I turned around and saw my foul-mouthed friend from this morning checking a black patent trench coat. She waved and smiled and gave us the "one-minute" sign.

"Oh, I did," I said, turning back. "Sorry, I didn't know it was a secret."

"What? I thought that was the whole point of a new restaurant," said Ellen, chiming in. "It's embarrassing enough to have her on the committee, but now she's going to ruin our lunch with her constant chatter. And all her tacky ideas."

"But she said she has info on the caterer," I added, trying to be helpful.

"Well, thank God for that," quipped Betsy. "That's the only thing these South Philly girls are good for—food. That and recommending a good plastic surgeon."

Apparently Betsy had forgotten that my maiden name was DiSiano and that my dad was born and raised on Two Street. I hadn't had any contact with him in decades, but I was still offended.

"Does it really matter?" I snapped at her. "It's just lunch."

She started to say something back, and then, amazingly, she shut up and greeted our friend sweetly.

"Mindy, don't you look adorable," Betsy cooed.

Mindy! I practiced a mnemonic device so I'd remember: Mindy drives a Mercedes and wears minis.

"What?" said Mindy, plopping down beside me in a satin blouse and short stretchy skirt, her best guess at a ladies-who-lunch outfit. "You have to be kidding. I just threw this on." But I knew better; she'd probably agonized over it. I smiled and winked at her, and I saw her shoulders relax.

We spent the next half hour gossiping about another absent committee member's upcoming anniversary party, why bangs were always a bad idea, and at what age a child was old enough for a WaveRunner. I listened for a while, but then started looking around, losing interest.

Finally, Ellen placed a folder marked "Benefit" on the table, and I snapped back into focus. I took out a pen and a note pad and wrote "To Do" across the top. Time to get to work.

The Philadelphia Animal Rescue Center Gala was to be held in the art museum's foyer on Thursday, November 6, just two days after the election. All of Philadelphia was invited, and we expected it to sell out, despite charging five hundred dollars for a two-hour event that didn't even include a sit-down dinner. When I heard the theme—a fall fashion show featuring local celebrities' pets, all wearing miniature couture outfits, including jewelry—it was all I could do to keep from choking on my crab cakes. Even after ten years in public relations, it was one of the more absurd, and out-of-touch, ideas I'd ever heard of. I cringed when I found out the genius idea was Abbey van Holt's.

I sighed and took a sip of wine. At the very least, I should help it to be a success. I began to ask questions in rapid fire: "How many more tickets need to be sold? How much do you think we'll raise? What media is confirmed? Who have we yet to reach out to?"

No one responded.

I turned to Mindy. "And the caterer. Is he locked in?"

She just looked at me and shrugged. I looked at Betsy and Ellen. But only blank stares from them, too.

Had we already been over this last week?

"Sorry, guys, it's been a long week," I said. "Just thought we could recap what's been done, what's yet to do."

"But, Abbey," said Ellen incredulously. "We don't need to worry about any of *that*! The museum handles it. As long as we got our RSVPs to Alistair, we're fine."

"Oh. Right," I said. "I forgot."

Betsy hit me with a strange look, Ellen giggled, and Mindy swallowed the bite she had been working on for twenty minutes. But then Betsy took over the conversation again, and I realized what was going on. This wasn't a planning lunch; this was just a lunch.

And we weren't going to roll up our silken sleeves and help Philly's unwanted dogs and cats; we were here simply to donate money, put our names on the invitation, and make important decisions like whether to serve French or Italian wine, whom to blackball from the event, and whether "festive cocktail" meant Ellen could wear a strapless dress. Not knowing the answer to any of these questions—or, frankly, giving a shit—I quietly sipped my wine.

Back in my old life, whenever a deadline was pushed or a client quit the firm, I was secretly giddy. Nothing thrilled me more than found time or scratching an item off my list. But now, as I put away my notebook—the blank page practically neon white without my slanted handwriting—I felt untethered.

It wasn't just that I had no to dos. It was that the ones I did have didn't really matter. At least, not to me.

Two hours later, the food everyone pretended to eat long ago taken away, the conversation turned back to houses. Everyone at the table was in the midst of a major renovation. I tried to contribute as best I could but was pretty sure they weren't talking about installing new garbage disposals or tearing out old quarter round. We also talked vacations, a hot topic given the looming fall break.

"Oh, I meant to ask you," said Ellen nonchalantly. "What is that little hotel you recommended in New Orleans?"

"Excuse me?"

"The one near where you and Alex lived? The one with the great coffee or something?"

"Uh, I can't remember. Can I text it to you later?"

New Orleans? Alex and I had lived in Louisiana? When? For how long? I put down my wineglass and sat up straighter. But just as it was about to get interesting, everyone started checking their phones and lifting their heavy quilted purses onto their toned shoulders.

Ellen motioned for the check as Betsy took a call. As I waited, I tried to ignore her conversation, but her voice was loud, fueled by white wine.

"I am sorry, Principal Murray, but there is no way my son did this. No. Possible. Way." A hush fell over the table. We were all listening now.

"I am not coming over there for this," she continued. "Especially because I know it simply did not happen. My son would never say *those* words to a teacher. He simply wouldn't. Now, if you'll excuse me."

She tapped the call off and slammed down the phone, then slammed back the rest of her drink. Then she checked her watch, smoothed her hair, and looked around for the waiter as if nothing had happened.

"Was that the school? Do you have to go pick up your son?" I asked. It seemed a natural enough question after what we just witnessed.

"No. I'm not going. They are always making up lies about Cranford. He would never insult a teacher. They just have it out for him. *You* know how they are there."

She didn't wait for me to answer. "And besides. I know Cranford would never disrespect an authority figure."

"Doesn't take after his mom, huh?" I chuckled but then stopped.

Betsy stood motionless, glaring at me. Ellen looked up at the ceiling, pretending not to hear. Only Mindy moved, turning and smiling at me and then Betsy in anticipation, unaware that in high school, the year we hosted the all-county basketball play-offs, Betsy Claiborne streaked naked across the gym floor, weaving around players, referees, and an angry rent-a-cop while her long black hair and the smell of really good weed trailed behind her.

"What did you say?" asked Betsy.

"Nothing. Just, well, you remember."

She flicked her eyes to Mindy, who was slack-jawed with anticipation, and then back to me. "No. I. Don't."

"Oh, c'mon, Betsy. In high school. Streaking across the gym. You used to wear your arrest as a badge of honor!"

"Abbey, I don't know why you are making stuff up, but I really don't appreciate it. I think that accident has you all mixed up. You better go back to the doctor." She looked at me with total seriousness, as if I *was* making this up. As if I hadn't been there to witness it myself. As if it hadn't made the local paper.

I watched her snap her purse closed and stand up with a jolt, and realized that it was okay to laugh about it back then, but not now. The reckless and carefree Betsy I knew in high school no longer existed. That person had been replaced with what stood before me: an elegant, sophisticated swan.

"Betsy, wait..." I stood up and tried to grab her arm, hoping we could all just laugh it off. Or change the subject. But she was so livid she wouldn't even look at me or say good-bye. She hoisted her purse on her shoulder, motioned for a blank-faced Ellen to join her, then weaved around tables to the exit, her black hair and lipstick-pink jacket reflected in mirrors and glassware as she moved.

Once they were gone, Mindy and I settled the bill in silence. I tried to concentrate on the credit card slip and spelling my new name correctly, but my hands were shaking so much, it turned out illegible anyway. I was scared, the altercation with Betsy giving me an uneasy sense of foreboding. She and Ellen might have been insufferable, but they were Abbey van Holt's good friends. Possibly the only two she had. And right now, I needed as many as I could get.

Alone, just the two of us in the small elevator, Mindy finally spoke. "I'm sorry, but I have to know. Did she really streak across the gym naked?"

"I plead the Fifth," I told her, holding up my hand as if in court. "Apparently, anything that happened before 2002 is not approved lunch conversation."

"Well, she should just own up to it. It actually makes me like her better."

"I know," I replied with a sad smile. "But, honestly, I'm not sure being liked is her primary objective these days. I think she'd rather be admired."

"Is there a difference?"

"Absolutely."

My tone was serious, but Mindy howled with laughter anyway.

After the epic lunch, I had fifteen minutes to figure out which of the seven Dr. Cohens in the Philly metro area was the one Mirabelle had gotten to squeeze me in. As I flagged down a taxi, I checked the list Siri had found, eliminating Dr. Gerry Cohen, who specialized in holistic healing; Dr. Emily Cohen, age twenty-eight; and J. J. Cohen, who, though a general practitioner, operated out of Fishtown. It was unlikely the van Holts would travel above Spring Garden Street, and even more unlikely for them to go to a doctor named "J. J." So William R. Cohen, an internist at Pennsylvania Hospital, just *had* to be the guy.

As I looked at his photo on the practice's Web page, I hoped he was kind and patient and maybe a little unorthodox. And a lover of movies—particularly *Freaky Friday*.

His office was on the third floor of an old brownstone on Washington Square. The waiting room was empty, quiet, and genteel chic, with a worn Oriental rug and mahogany furniture, a world away from the crowded, noisy, urgent care centers we used in Grange Hill. A nurse, one of the few I'd ever seen who still wore a white skirt and blouse, led me back to the examination room, which was more modern, except for two high-backed upholstered chairs beside a bay window.

Dr. Cohen was a soft-spoken man in his sixties, with a trim gray beard and sparkling blue eyes shining through his rimless glasses. He was shorter than me and slight, wearing a conservative yellow bow tie and maroon sweater vest that may have been purchased in the boys' department. But despite his miniature stature, he was handsome and confident, and I noticed he wasn't wearing a wedding ring. He was exactly the type of guy I wished Roberta would fall for, but her halfhearted attempts at dating men her own age always ended badly. Ditto for her attempts at dating short guys.

"Abigail, my dear," he said as he hugged me hello. "You gave us all quite a scare last weekend. How are you feeling?" He stepped back and looked me in the eye, with genuine concern.

I smiled and let my shoulders drop. Something about doctors, especially older ones, always made me relax. Like they could fix anything, from broken bones to broken hearts.

"I feel fine, really, just thought it wouldn't hurt to check in," I said. "It was such a bizarre thing that happened."

"I'll admit, I was baffled," he said. "You were unconscious for hours."

"You saw me? At the hospital?"

"Oh yes, I came right over when I heard," he said. "I got called away before you woke up. But I spoke with Dr. Aaronson and went over the scans. They were perfectly normal, like nothing had happened."

But something did happen, I wanted to tell him. *Something huge.*

"Let's take a look, shall we?" he said. He asked the nurse to come in, and while she checked my blood pressure, he asked some routine questions. He had me stand and perform various balance tests that felt more like a field sobriety check than a neurological work-up. Then he peered into my eyes and ears and at the area above my right ear, where my head had slammed into the piano. His hands were cold on my neck; I shivered in my flimsy paper gown.

"Tell me, Dr. Cohen," I said, trying to be nonchalant. "Do head injuries ever cause delusions?"

"Delusions?"

"You know. Like some sort of reverse amnesia or memory loss or something like that?"

"I'm not sure I follow. There is no such thing as 'reverse amnesia.' And clinical amnesia is extremely rare. And usually only temporary. And from what we could tell, your injury was superficial, with no effect on the intracranial areas."

"What about some sort of psychiatric episode? Like, alternate reality–type stuff?"

"That's just in the movies," he said with a laugh. "Pyschoses or psychotic episodes are from a chemical imbalance, not blunt trauma. Or from taking drugs—like PCP."

He put down his penlight and looked at me: "Why, Abbey, are you having some sort of problem? Strange thoughts? Anxiety?"

"No, nothing like that," I said, trying to be nonchalant. "Just curious."

"You sure?" he said, touching my arm in concern.

"I'm sure. It's nothing. Though sometimes I do feel like I'm living someone else's life." I laughed at my own joke, but he didn't. Instead, he picked up my hand and took my pulse, then peered into my eyes once again.

As he began to examine my bruised knee, I couldn't resist more questions. "But let's say I did have some sort of chemical imbalance. What would you do for me? Pills? Electroshock?"

"Psychiatry isn't really my specialty," he said, grave faced. "If you feel like you need to talk to someone, why don't I write you a referral? I have a colleague who would be a great fit for you. She's very good with housewives."

I smarted at the term "housewives" but nodded assent.

"It's not a bad idea," he continued. "Mirabelle tells me you are under tremendous stress with the campaign—and the new beach house. And of course your charity work."

He walked over to a drawer, took out a prescription pad, and scribbled down a name and number. Then he slid the pad back into a drawer, locked it, and turned back to me as I sat motionless, wondering why Mirabelle was discussing my health with Dr. Cohen. I guess she felt the same way about doctor/patient confidentiality as she did about calling before stopping by someone's apartment. Those silly rules didn't apply to *her*.

"I almost forgot!" said Dr. Cohen, spinning around again. "I have that referral for Gloria. Dr. Ramsey. He's at Cypress Street Psychiatry, so not too far from you. He said he could see her right away."

I stared at him.

"To help with her enuresis," he continued.

"Enuresis?"

"Bed-wetting."

I stopped mid-buckle and stood up straight.

"You want to send a five-year-old to a psychiatrist for bed-wetting? It's a perfectly natural thing. Especially for someone whose bladder is as tiny as Gloria's." I had done enough online reading to know that the worst thing a parent could do was make a big deal out of it, to turn what is a mechanical issue into a psychological one. Nine times out of ten, children grow out of it by second grade.

"Of course, I didn't mean to say she was abnormal," he said. "But, well, her grandmother thinks this would be a really good thing for her."

I don't give a flying fuck what Mirabelle or anyone else thinks would be good for my little girl, I wanted to shout at him. Jimmy and I had decided long ago, after a series of tests that made everyone miserable, most of all Gloria, we would not make her size, or any medical ramifications of her size, an issue. I was not about to start now.

"Gloria is already aware of the problem," I said. "And unless this Dr. Ramsey has some magical way of making her bladder grow bigger and stronger, I really don't think—"

"Abigail, I realize this is upsetting," interrupted Dr. Cohen, misreading my outrage as distress. "I urge you to give it a try. For everyone's sake."

For everyone's sake? Isn't the only "sake" of importance Gloria's? I was dumbfounded. Were Mirabelle and the van Holts embarrassed by this? And, God forbid, not just of the bedwetting, but of how tiny Gloria was? And had Abbey van Holt condoned this? Was this yet another aspect of parenting she had subcontracted? I was stunned. And furious.

I felt a sudden urge to hightail it to Gloria's school, yank her out of class, and run far, far away.

But I couldn't. This was my world now and I had to make it work.

"All right. I'll consider it," I said, taking the note and slipping it into my purse. He smiled and excused himself.

Later, walking across Washington Square, its dry concrete fountain full of toddlers writing their names in chalk and throwing tennis balls, I became angry again.

I knew what was best for Gloria; I had since the beginning. I tore the referral card in half and shoved the pieces into a trash can.

"Just a minute," said the ultrasound technician, a forced smile on her lips. "I'll be right back."

Not the words you want to hear in the middle of your thirty-week ultrasound, your protruding belly exposed and vulnerable, your husband nervously tapping his foot.

"Jimmy," I said, my head twisted toward him, my body heavy on the padded exam table. "Did you catch that? Did she seem worried?"

"No," he said, but he wouldn't look me in the eye. "I didn't notice anything. I think she's just going to get the doctor. She always goes to get the doctor."

I wasn't convinced, and I knew he wasn't either. I stared at the ultrasound, trying to decipher what could be amiss in the blur of black and white. Waiting for the door to swing back open was torture. Jimmy tried to distract me by asking me what I wanted for lunch.

"Mr. and Mrs. Lahey," said Dr. Zardari, a tall, thin Pakistani man who had a funny habit of ending every sentence with "okay?" like a Valley Girl. Everyone in Grange Hill knew him; he was the only ultrasound doctor at Delco Memorial and he had pretty much scanned every kid in town. More than once I heard a pregnant friend joke, "Don't tell Dr. Z!" before stealing a sip of wine or taking a drag off a friend's cigarette.

"Let's see how we are doing, okay?" he said as he squirted more cold gel on my tummy. He scanned the baby's head, limbs, and torso once, then twice, scribbling notes on my chart. He motioned to the technician and they spent a few minutes quietly conferring, ignoring Jimmy and me.

My heart was beating fast, my throat was dry, and Jimmy had stopped rubbing my arm as he focused on the doctor's face. Dr. Z sat down beside us and, in his lilting tone, told us words no expectant parents would ever want to hear.

"I've found something concerning."

Time stopped.

"It could be nothing, but it could be something," he continued. "We just don't know, okay?"

"Something like what?" Jimmy managed to say.

"The fetus is small. For thirty weeks, we would expect it to weigh at least two more pounds, possibly three. Are you certain you are thirty weeks along? Did you mistake when you had your last period?"

"No," I told him. "I know it was June eleventh, because that's my husband's birthday." He listened, scribbled more notes in the chart, and then looked up at me.

"We have to get you in for some more tests," he said. "The good news is that the baby seems to be functioning adequately, and the head size is disproportionally large compared to the body. That means the brain is getting most of the nutrients, which is what we want to happen. The body can catch up later, okay?"

"So what do we do?" asked Jimmy.

"We'll continue to monitor the fetus via ultrasound for the next few weeks and hope for some progress. But if we don't see any, we'll get the baby out early—thirty-four or thirty-five weeks—and put him or her on a feeding tube. We see good results with this in cases of IGR."

"IGR?" said Jimmy.

"Sorry. Intrauterine growth restriction. A condition where the fetus isn't getting proper nutrition—and no, Mom, it has nothing to do with what you are eating or not eating. It could be a problem with the umbilical cord, could be a placenta issue. Sometimes we never find out why. So again, we'll monitor it closely and schedule a C-section if we have to, okay?"

"But thirty-four weeks is so early. Too early," I pleaded.

"Having the baby early isn't the risk. We deal with preemies all the time. What we can't ascertain at this point is if the nutrient deficiency has affected development, in particular the baby's cognitive function."

This time he didn't finish his sentence by asking us if we were "okay?" We weren't.

Jimmy continued to ask a stream of questions, but I stopped

listening, overwhelmed. Had I not been eating right? Or enough? The panic I felt was physical, my skin tingling, my stomach churning, and my lungs working double time. It didn't help that the room was small and dark; now it felt like it was filling with water.

Jimmy looked over at me, saw my face, and began overcompensating as a way to distract me. He spoke louder and louder and became weirdly cheerful. It was like we had switched personalities: me now silent and stoic, Jimmy talkative and awkward.

In the waiting area, me trying not to look at the other women with their perfectly normal pregnancies, the receptionist patiently helped us book five appointments and fill out some forms. She tried to calm us with smiles and two plastic cups of water, but to this day, whenever I use a pen attached by a silver chain to a clipboard, I feel sick.

Back home in our house in Grange Hill, I lost it. Jimmy held me as I cried and rambled, stopping me only when I started blaming myself. Together, we analyzed every word the doctor had said; the words "functioning adequately," "nutritional deficiency," and "cognitive function" repeating like the CNN scroll across our kitchen walls. That night, when I couldn't sleep, Jimmy came downstairs with me to watch *Project Runway* reruns. He held me in his arms on the couch, both our hands on my belly, both of us secretly willing the baby to grow.

The next five weeks were terrifying. I spent all day Googling "intrauterine growth restriction" until Jimmy finally had to confiscate the computer and hide it in the basement. I told total strangers at the grocery store about my baby's condition but kept it from my closest friends, too afraid of their looks of concern and pity, too afraid of making this nightmare an irreversible reality. I sleep-walked through work, my mind busy bargaining with fate for just a few more ounces, a few more centimeters. And I ate and ate and ate, gorging on avocadoes and mashed potatoes and Greek yogurt, hoping that the more I consumed, the better chance the baby would have to be normal.

If anyone asked me today what we did that winter, whom we saw, or what we gave each other for Christmas, I'd still have no idea. The only memories I have are of the five ultrasound appointments, two of which showed progress; three did not. My weight ballooned while the baby's stayed frustratingly the same. At the final appointment, at thirty-four and a half weeks, our anxiety having grown to near hysteria, Dr. Z asked us, "Time for the baby to come out, okay?"

"Okay," we replied in unison.

And then the strangest thing happened.

The next morning—up early and getting dressed, ready to leave for our scheduled C-section—I went into labor. It started as soon as I woke, an unmistakable twinge that progressed steadily. By the time I got out of the shower, I was into full-blown contractions. I waddled to the stairwell and called down to Jimmy that we'd better leave earlier than expected. Gloria, already smarter than both of us, knew it was time to come out.

And boy was she in a rush. By the time we made it to the hospital at a quarter past seven, I was eight centimeters dilated, too late for the operation or even an epidural. After half an hour of me clawing at air and screaming until I had no voice, she slid into the doctor's arms with barely a whimper.

Holding her birdlike body, barely heavier than a Diet Coke, was infinitely frightening. She was trussed up in a heating pad and foam neck support, her little blue-tinged face the only part of her visible. But looking into her wide eyes, and feeling her little fingers wrapped around my thumb, I felt her strength and her determination. Something inside told me she would be fine.

Gloria's first two weeks of life were spent in the crowded, noisy NICU at Delco Memorial, where we watched her suck milk from a syringe and cast irritated glances at her noisy roommates. When we were finally discharged, she slept the whole way home but then woke with a start as we stepped into the house. She looked around the kitchen, stacked with dishes and mail from weeks of neglect, then at each of us, haggard and unshowered, then at the large black Labrador who would be her childhood pet. Her expression was one of resignation and exasperation, as if she couldn't believe what she'd gotten herself into. But I couldn't have been happier ... after months of agonizing worry, our journey was over. And we had a small, but healthy, daughter.

In the days that followed, it was Jimmy's turn to lose it. He had held his own emotions back—in order to be what Dr. Z called "positive and supportive for the mother"—and now they burst forth like a violent summer storm.

"Why is she crying?" "Is she hungry?" "Is she still breathing?" "Is that a rash?" "What's that thing on her belly button?" "Why does she need *another* shot?" he asked, his questions peppering me wherever we went: the hospital, the pediatrician's, on a walk, in the middle of the night. I allowed the overprotective new father bit to continue as long as he needed, knowing it was my turn to be the strong one.

Only after she began putting on weight—slowly, but surely, half ounce by precious half ounce—did we allow ourselves to relax a bit. Jimmy turned his attention back to Lahey Landscape, which he hoped to launch by Labor Day, meeting with potential clients and researching zero-turn mowers. I was back at work too; my home life of sleeplessness, diapers, and onesie snaps interspersed with days in the now irrelevant and irresponsible world of public relations. And though it wasn't the perfect life portrayed in diaper commercials, it was still wonderful, each day electric with the heightened emotions and countless surprises that first babies bring.

And then later that summer, our relief about Gloria was overshadowed by another catastrophic event. But this time, we would wait for death, not life.

On a hot August Sunday, just weeks before Jimmy officially launched Lahey Landscape & Design LLC, his mother, Jane, announced that she had just months to live. After the lasagna, while dishing out slices of her famous key lime pie, she told us that the stage three breast cancer she had successfully fought four years before had returned with a vengeance. It had metastasized from her breast to her lymph nodes and finally found its way to its ultimate goal, her liver. She dutifully got her two scans per year, but this cancer had hidden from the technician, silently moving from organ to organ in the most devious and elusive way. The odds of beating it, she said, were slim.

As she broke the news, Miles kept his eyes on her face and held her hand. I was nursing Gloria under a baby afghan, unable to move. Jimmy and his brothers listened with their heads down, as if they were being punished.

After a few seconds of heartsick silence, Jane spoke again. "Now, boys. It's going to be all right. Really it is."

No one responded, so I ventured, "There are some amazing experimental therapies out there. I just read about this Temple doctor who invented this thing that helps target tumors. And there's holistic healing and herbs and—"

"Abbey," said Miles, but I kept talking. He said my name again, still gently but much louder, and I shut my mouth.

My father-in-law looked around the table, all of us crammed into the small daisy-papered dining room where the Laheys had eaten thousands of family meals. He took a deep breath. "We've been through this before. We know how hard it is even when you have a good prognosis. And we had a second opinion, a third, even a fourth. They all say the same thing. Surgery won't help, and if we did chemo again, well, at this point, that in itself might kill her."

The words "kill her" rang out. Patrick frowned, angry. "What? That's ridiculous. Of course you're going to fight this."

"I know it's quite a shock, my darling," said Miles, addressing his youngest son as if he were still a baby. "But try to understand. This is cancer, and try as we might to fight it, it fights harder. And dirtier."

Now Jane spoke. "I want my last days to be spent in peace with the ones I love, not on some fool's errand."

"How long have you known?" asked Jimmy, with hurt in his voice. "Why didn't you tell us before now?"

"You had enough to deal with, with Abbey and the baby, and the new business," Jane explained. "And there is nothing—absolutely nothing—any of you could have done. Now, someone please hand me my granddaughter." End of discussion. She was a sweet woman, but stubborn, and her boys knew when it was pointless to argue.

I passed her Gloria and she held the tiny pink face to her own. She breathed deep, taking in the smell of talcum powder and regurgitated breast milk. The smell of new life. Gloria let out a little gurgle and Jane laughed and looked around to see who else had heard the delightful sound.

She died five months later, four days before her granddaughter's first birthday. It was the same day we found out Gloria had actually made it to one percent on the doctor's height/weight chart, as if Jane had sent her that extra ounce as a parting gift.

Again, I found myself nursing my husband's heart back to health, but this time instead of questions, I got silence. He spent more and more time at work, leaving before sunrise and poring over paperwork late into the night. He was a new business owner with a lot to prove, toiling over lawns and shrubs and mulch, coming home grubby and exhausted and distant. I helped as much as I could. But I was a working parent myself, and time was a luxury that was becoming harder and harder to share.

Jimmy and I were still in love, and we were as happy as the next couple, but the sadness and stress of the past year filled our house with shadows. And the invisible chalkboard in the sky—the one that keeps track of who got up with the baby last, who unloaded the dishwasher, who folded the laundry—began to get marked more often, wiped clean less. We no longer watched the sunset from the front porch; instead, we texted updates on car repairs and day care schedules from different floors in the same house.

It was sometime during that year, with a one-year-old, two client-focused careers, and an eighty-year-old house in constant need of attention, that life started to get away from us.

Like millions of other families across the country, we went from living for today to simply getting through it.

Now, six years later, walking down the thickly carpeted hallway to this apartment in the sky, the pain of that pregnancy and Jane's death felt so far away, as distant and muted as the traffic outside. How different life was here with the van Holts. Instead of clogged drains and recycling schedules and late fees, and multitasking and running late and barely making ends meet, I didn't have to take care of anything; it was all done for me. My only responsibilities were to attend a few events, manage the help, decorate, and occasionally see the kids. And I had a handsome, charming husband who not only appreciated the few tasks I did manage to accomplish each day but rewarded me with anything I could possibly desire.

What a civilized way to live, I thought.

CHAPTER EIGHT

O*wwwwww!!!*" screamed Gloria as I accidentally jabbed her with a bobby pin. After twenty minutes of trying, I still couldn't get the red yarn Raggedy Ann wig to stay on right.

"Sorry, Glo," I told her. "This thing just won't lay right."

"It's stupid, anyway," she said, tugging her white pinafore down over the blue printed dress. "Why can't I be a vampire? I really want to be a vampire, Mommy."

"These are the costumes we were told you should wear," I said, eyeing Sam in his blue overalls, oversized buttons, and sailor cap. "I'm not going to argue about it anymore. Now, stand still."

Gloria might have felt miserable, but she looked adorable. And the pair of them, with her brother in a matching Raggedy Andy costume, were off the cute chart: two tiny dolls with red circles of rouge on their cheeks, shiny buttons, striped knee socks, and black patent shoes. These costumes might not have been what the kids wanted, but they were one hundred percent cotton and campaign approved.

Frank didn't believe in leaving anything to chance. Monsters were "too violent," witches "sexist," movie characters "too liberal

Hollywood elite," and ninjas or toy soldiers would highlight the fact that Alex had not served in the armed forces. That left us with animals, fairies, or dolls. Personally, I thought Depression-era Raggedy Ann and Andy were ridiculous for a wealthy family like ours, but Frank liked that they were red, white, and blue. May's sister had made them by hand, and Oscar had picked them up late last night.

The plan was for us to join Alex at a political rally after Gloria's school Halloween party, then have dinner and go trick-or-treating together as a family. May usually worked Fridays, but since we had the debate tomorrow, her day off had been switched. I was glad she wasn't with us. I was looking forward to spending time, just the four of us. After today, there were only three days left until the election, and we probably wouldn't see much of Alex again until it was all over. I made sure I looked good: a gray Lanvin suit with a dotted, white-on-white silk blouse, diamond studs, black leather boots, and bright red lips. The rally was outside, so I twisted my hair into a chignon and sprayed it until it shone.

With minutes to spare, I grabbed the kids' candy bags, my giant white YSL purse, and a pink cardboard box containing four dozen dark chocolate and buttercream cupcakes, each topped with a marshmallow ghost dipped in edible white glitter, with two minichips as eyes. Thank God for city bakeries; they'd honor any lastminute request if you didn't mind the rush charge. We didn't.

Downstairs in the lobby, the kids' patent leather shoes squeaked on the glossy black floor. When they spied Oscar waiting outside in a Darth Vader mask, they squealed with delight and ran faster, the doorman barely getting the door open in time.

I caught up and Darth wedged the giant cupcake boxes into the trunk while we waited on the sidewalk. Passersby oohed and aahed at the old-fashioned costumes, but Gloria ignored them, still fuming about the vampire costume veto. At least Sam seemed pleased, touching his head and repeating "hat" over and over. *Word number twelve,* I silently whispered to Jimmy.

He had always loved Halloween, as all landscapers do. It's the holiday that marks the end of their busiest season and kicks off the short lull before they start plowing snow and hanging holiday lights. He celebrated each year by going all out: decorating the yard with bales of hay, potted mums, and black bats hung from invisible wire. He also always insisted on full-size candy bars for the kids and a keg of pumpkin ale for the parents. Friends from high school or work would stop by with their kids, and the party would stretch well into the night, neighbors putting their sugar-crashed kids to bed and slinking back for one last beer.

Halloween in the city was sure to be different. The van Holts didn't even have a pumpkin.

In the car on our way, my phone rang. It was Alex.

"Please tell me you didn't write a check to Ronald Ferguson for ten thousand dollars," Alex said, clearly annoyed.

"Yeah, I did. Why?" My heart moved up into my throat.

"Are you kidding? Abbey, we've talked about this."

"We did?" Uh-oh.

"Didn't we have a whole conversation about him a few weeks ago?"

"I guess we did."

"You guess we did? Well, then, why the hell did you write him a check? I thought I made myself clear. If I can help Holy Rosary, I will do it *after* the election."

"Right. Sorry."

I heard voices in the background and Alex telling someone he needed a minute. "I swear, Abbey, I don't know why you do this. Are you trying to sabotage the campaign? I thought this is what *you* wanted."

"It's just a donation. To help them with food and electricity and stuff. How can it hurt the campaign?"

"Oh, I don't know. Maybe because your friend Father Ferguson has been doling out birth control to teenagers and Rome has him on some sort of watch list. Or maybe because he's rumored to have a girlfriend up in Kensington. And here I am—*right now!*—on my way to meet with the Catholic Coalition to ask for their support."

I felt sick to my stomach. "Don't worry; I'll call him and tell him not to cash it until after the election."

"He's already posted it. How do you think I found out? I know ten grand is just another day at Neiman's to you, but for most people, it's noticeable. Thankfully Randall at the bank is going to stop payment."

"Stop payment? Alex, please don't. Let it go through. I swear no one saw me. No one will know."

"I'm running for Congress, Abbey," he snapped. "*Everyone knows everything.*"

Five minutes later, as we pulled up to the children's school, picture-perfect with its trees of orange, gold, and maroon against gray stone, I was still shaking. And trying not to cry. I forced a smile, though, and thanked Oscar, then ushered the children through the gate while carefully balancing the cupcake boxes. Inside, as we walked through the noisy, bright hallway, the familiar smells and sounds of an elementary school calmed me. I began to feel a little better.

Gloria, Sam, and I dodged glitter wings and plastic swords to find her classroom and unload the treats. Gloria ran off to join her friends while Sam and I found seats in the child-sized chairs in the back of the room where we could wait. Sam wanted to run to his sister, but I distracted him with a lollipop I grabbed off the treat table. He sucked happily as I looked around, admiring the colorful rugs and decorations, as well as the wide windows that overlooked a lovely stone courtyard, a vegetable garden, and, if I wasn't mistaken, an Alexander Calder sculpture.

After a few minutes, a teacher just seconds out of college approached, so naturally pretty that even her Harry Potter wig, glasses, and painted-on scar didn't diminish her perfect features.

"Good morning, Mrs. van Holt," she said with a wide smile. "Gloria looks so cute."

"Thank you, Miss Regan," I said, proud of myself for learning her name before we came. "I'm sorry we have to leave early, but Gloria's dad has a campaign event and really wants her there."

"Of course," she said, pushing her costume glasses up her nose. "I understand." She stood smiling expectantly, as if waiting for something. After a few more seconds, she asked, "So is your driver bringing the pumpkins?"

"Pumpkins?"

"For the pies."

"I thought I just had to bring the cupcakes." I felt that same anxious feeling I'd had last week when I realized too late it was "pajama day" at Gloria's school.

"The cupcakes are for *this* class," she explained. "I believe you also signed up to bring pumpkins for the 'alt trackers.'"

"What?"

"The twelve pumpkins for her alternate track. For the 'snow leopards.'"

"But I thought Gloria was a 'manatee,'" I said, exasperated. Last night, I had painstakingly reviewed all of Abbey van Holt's e-mails yet again and had figured out that Gloria's classmates were nick-named the manatees, that her teacher's name was Miss Regan, and that for Halloween, I was assigned "ghost-, ghoul-, or witch-themed cupcakes" for the party. What was this "alt track" business?

Miss Regan continued: "On Fridays she has her other track, too. And for their party, they are going to make pumpkin pies. Bryant's mother already brought the gluten-free flour for the crust. And Kennedy's mother brought the organic butter from Shepperton Farms."

I would have been annoyed at all the dietetic pretense if she didn't look like she was about to cry. I had no choice: I had to find some pumpkins. And fast.

"Don't worry. I'll just run out and get some. I'll be right back," I told her in an overconfident tone. Then I grabbed Sam's hand and rushed out the door. So I needed twelve locally grown organic pumpkins. How hard could it be? It was Halloween after all.

But outside, I paused, not knowing which way to turn. If this had been Grange Hill, there would be pumpkins at every grocery store and corner market, but here in the city, I hadn't seen any stores, let alone pumpkins. I pulled out my phone to check for a Trader Joe's or any other grocery store, but the nearest one was north of Market Street, a mile away. I searched for a bodega or produce shop, but the only one I found and called didn't have any pumpkins. I even looked up and down the street, for a moment thinking of "borrowing" some from the steps of the nearby brownstones. But there was only one, and it was already carved. I stamped my foot in frustration.

A little Ninja Turtle—Donatello, I think—passed by, escorted by two fathers. I asked them if they knew of a place to buy pumpkins and they directed me to a farmers' market in Fitler Square, just a few blocks away.

"You're in luck," said the older man, his arms full of candy apple–making supplies. "This is the last weekend before they close for winter."

I thanked them profusely, swung the baby up onto my hip, and trotted off in the direction they had indicated. In my high heels, I limped a little as I jogged, like a sulky on its last lap.

My luck continued at the farmers' market, which was in full swing when I arrived. Moms with strollers vied with aging hippies for five varieties of kale, home-brewed kombucha, vegan soups, and apples ranging from light pink to deep red to lime green. One table held pyramids of handmade soap, another displayed hemp onesies, while another offered pamphlets for a Green Party candidate running against Alex. I picked it up and shoved it in my purse even though I knew the guy didn't have a chance; I'd never heard Alex or Frank even mention him. Finally, in the back corner near the bear statue, I found a young man selling beautiful green and orange "heirloom" pumpkins.

"I'll take *all* of them," I told him. "Provided they are organic. And that you deliver." He looked up from his guitar and smiled, his teeth bright against his long black beard and red-and-black-checked shirt.

"Yes to both, milady," he said, jumping up. "As long as it's not far. I only have an oxcart." He pointed to a rickety wooden contraption in the corner. It would work.

"It's just three blocks away," I assured him, then opened my purse. "How much?"

He did the math in his head and, with all seriousness, told me, "Two ninety-five." I almost fainted. But then again, thinking of Miss Regan's worried face, and given my new circumstances, I would have paid double that.

I set Sam down among the gourds, stretched my back, and pulled out my wallet. I had nine dollars. That wouldn't even get me one pumpkin, let alone twelve.

"Do you take credit cards?" I asked sweetly.

"Nope."

"Personal checks?"

"Sorry."

"Do you think you could just take a check just this once? I

promise I'm good for it...I'm married to Alex van Holt, the guy running for Congress." I was not above playing the husband card if it meant fulfilling my parent-teacher duties, especially now that I had no full-time job and no excuse for flaking out.

"I'm sorry," he said with a big smile. "I'm sure you're good for it. But I don't have a bank account."

I stared at him. He continued: "I'm cash only. Or barter."

Cash only? Barter? Was he serious? Did he not understand that there were twelve little alt trackers waiting eagerly to clean, cut, scoop, pulverize, mix, and bake these pumpkins into low-sugar, gluten-free organic pies they would take one bite of and then reject? Looking at his expression, blissful and somewhat vacant under his Fidel Castro–style hat, I realized he didn't. Nor did he care. Unless he was willing to exchange these pumpkins for a cute toddler with a really wet diaper, I would need to find some cash.

"Fine. I'll go to the ATM. But *please* don't sell these pumpkins. I'll be back in five minutes." I swung Sam back up onto my hip and shuffled off again.

I found a money machine outside a bar on the next block. I slipped in what looked like a debit card and entered my pin number, but it was rejected. I looked at the screen in confusion, then remembered. Of course. My anniversary date was different in this world. I remembered the date engraved on that heavy wedding album— June 19, was it?—and entered 0619 next. But no luck. I then tried my two kids' birth dates, also a favorite pin, but the machine spit my card back out. And worse—a message told me I had to wait twenty-four hours before I could try again.

I'd have to find where the van Holts did their banking and make a withdrawal from the teller. Surely "Randall at the bank" wouldn't have a problem with me buying my daughter some pumpkins on Halloween. I pulled out my checkbook to find the institution's name, only to have Google tell me the nearest location was ten blocks away, on the fourteenth floor of building across from city hall.

I was so tense, I didn't realize that I was holding Sam's hand in a death grip. He looked up at me with a pouty lip, whimpering.

"Oh, Mr. Magoo, I'm sorry," I said, picking him up and hugging him close. "This is ridiculous. The snow leopards are just going to have to get over it."

And they did. Except for one. Mine.

Finding Gloria and her classmates in the school's kitchen, each with a ball of dough at the ready, Sam and I attempted to slip in and nonchalantly explain to Miss Regan that we had an epic pumpkin fail but were able to find nine cans of Libby's easy pumpkin pie mix at the local bodega (which, thankfully, was happy to take a credit card). Miss Regan actually took the news better than I expected, but Gloria was furious. She stomped over to me with balled fists and narrowed eyes.

"Where are the pumpkins?" she said, glaring. "You were supposed to get pumpkins!"

"Gloria, calm down. You'll just use the canned stuff. It's fine."

"What? The Native Americans didn't have cans!"

Well, they probably didn't make pies either, I wanted to say. But I bit my tongue. Never in my life had I seen her so irate. Not the time I accidentally threw out her prized shell collection. Or when I told her she couldn't go with Roberta to the dog track. Not even the time Sam threw up on her beloved Lambie.

This was white-knuckled, teeth-baring, five-year-old fury.

I knelt down and tried to pull her close, whispering, "It's okay, GloWorm. It will be just as fun. And honestly, a whole lot easier." But she pulled away from me, her face growing redder, her little arms and legs taut with frustration. By now the class was silent, watching. Even the local pastry chef they had brought in to help was staring, his floured rolling pin poised in midair.

Gloria sucked in a deep breath and shouted "No!" so loud it reverberated around the room. Then she raised her hand and slapped me. *Slapped* me. So hard it took my breath away. And by the sound of gasps around the room, everyone else's, too. I think even Sam understood, his mouth opening in a silent "WTF."

It was one of those moments, like in the seconds just after a car crash, where the world stops turning. Where you are floating, and have time to notice things you wouldn't normally notice. Like a row of cherry-red mixers on the counter. The expensive bamboo flooring beneath your feet. How long and black your daughter's lashes are.

It's where the most painful reality—usually tucked away with old photographs and graduate school catalogues—finally escapes from its hiding place and confronts you head-on. Where you can see your child for what she is: spoiled, uncontrollable, and spiteful. But also a victim. A victim of indulgence, overscheduling, and a terrific case of "everything she wants but nothing she needs."

And where you recognize yourself, as the mother, as the main perpetrator of that crime.

With that clarity comes a strange exchange of emotion. You do not feel mad, as you would have thought. You do not even feel embarrassed. You feel sadness, to the point of heartbreak. So much so that you no longer feel the soreness in your feet and arms, or the stinging of your cheek.

It's the thinking about your daughter as Gloria van Holt—and the five and a half years of her life that have passed without you— that really hurts.

CHAPTER NINE

Inside the bathroom of a West Philadelphia electronics store, I could hear the noise of the crowd gathering for the rally. It got louder by the second, much like Sam's whining as he tried to wrestle himself out of my arms. I wouldn't let him down, though, the place dirty and cluttered, and his costume overalls suit so pristine and white. I looked for a changing table or any kind of shelf but found only a tall radiator too thin and rickety to hold Sam. I gauged the width of the plastic toilet seat and the back of the toilet but ruled them out as well. I cringed, knowing I had no other choice. The rally was about to start.

I tugged a cream cashmere wrap out of my purse and spread it out on the dirty tile floor, then laid Sam on top of it. Six minutes and forty wipes later—me sweating through my blouse, pieces of my hair freeing themselves from the tight chignon—I looked around for a trash can. There was none. Knowing Alex was waiting for us, probably growing desperate, I did what I had to do: bundled the dirty diaper in the cashmere wrap and shoved it deep into my purse. "Sorry, Yves," I whispered.

Half an hour earlier, when we'd met up with Alex under a tent near the rally, he'd acted like the phone call about Father Fergie had never happened, greeting us with hugs and kisses and telling me I looked "hot." I wanted to apologize, but we were surrounded by Frank and Calvin and a bunch of supporters, so I took Alex's lead and pretended everything was fine. I tried to read his eyes, to see if he was still mad and just playing nice for the cameras, but I couldn't tell. Either I didn't know him well enough or he was a really good actor. Or worse, he didn't care.

Or maybe he was just distracted. This event was huge. The main spectator area was the parking lot of a now derelict hospital, already so full that people spilled over into the surrounding lots, even onto the street. Television trucks pushed up satellite feeds on one side of the road while newspaper reporters paced and chatted on cell phones by the raised metal stage. Police rerouted angry commuters around the block.

A few people were there to hear Alex, but most were waiting for incumbent senator Doug Blandon, Philadelphia's hometown hero. Blandon was known as a salt-of-the-earth type, with a résumé that read like a political consultant's dream: Gulf War veteran, son of a waitress, college football star, and father to six—four natural and two adopted. He was a personal hero of Alex's, and I knew my husband was honored to be Blandon's opening act. But as the proud wife, and given the headway Alex was making lately, I couldn't help but think Blandon should have been honored too.

When Sam and I returned from our bathroom misadventures, we found Alex posing for photos with groupies, and this time not the creepy Gerald type, but the young, female, and "ready to do anything for their country" variety. I walked over and handed Sam to his father, hoping a messy, fussy toddler might scatter them like Kryptonite. But my plan backfired: seeing the handsome possible congressman cuddling a pudgy toddler in overalls made them practically ovulate in unison. Alex pretended to be oblivious, but I caught him stealing a few looks. Luckily, Blandon's aide pulled us away toward the stage, and the girls dispersed back into the crowd.

Ten minutes into the speech, sitting on the stage in a folding chair between Mrs. Blandon and a still pouting Gloria, Sam heavy and sweaty in my lap, I started to tune out what Alex was saying, listening only for certain words and phrases. I knew Alex's speeches so well by this point, I could clap on cue, nod at big moments, smile shyly and wave when he mentioned me, and feign indignation at the state of the nation's economy, unemployment rate, or educational malaise. I knew it was almost over when Alex took off his jacket—he always did this for dramatic pause before the big crescendo—so I prepared myself to stand. I placed my heels squarely beneath me on the metal stage and rearranged Sam, using my arm to hide the stain on his tummy.

Sure enough, the jacket came off, the sleeves went up, and ten seconds later we were standing and basking in the adoration of the crowd. Alex stepped over to us and picked up Raggedy Ann and then leaned over to kiss Raggedy Andy on his head. When he leaned over and kissed not-so-Raggedy me full on the mouth, the applause got even louder. Only Sam was unimpressed. Somewhere between "let's give our children the future they deserve" and "the American dream is still alive and well in Philadelphia," he had fallen asleep in my arms.

It was an overwhelming moment, one I wasn't likely to forget. The entire crowd was on its feet, and the chants of "van Holt" drowned out the sounds of the city. I could feel Alex beside me fill with pride and excitement and relief; it was becoming apparent he had a shot at winning this. I felt my own relief, too, that my screw-up with the check seemed to be completely forgiven and forgotten.

I looked out and smiled at the crowd as they began to sing along to the music spun by a local DJ. I read the signs and waved to kids on their parents' shoulders and let myself enjoy the warm October sun. Eventually we all sat down again for the senator's speech. Alex had been introduced by the local party chair; the senator was introduced by the Eagles' current cornerback.

Sam snored peacefully on my chest and my thoughts began to drift, when about two-thirds back into the crowd, I saw a face I recognized. I could just make out his head above the others, but I would know those eyes, that cap, and that white beard anywhere.

It was Miles.

I sucked in air in surprise and fought the urge to stand up and start waving. Instead, I simply stared, my eyes locked on his face, urging him to step closer.

Dear, sweet Miles. He was looking right at me. But what did he see? His daughter-in-law or Mrs. Alexander van Holt? Did he wonder why his grandchildren were up onstage? Was he confused that his beloved Sam was introduced as "Van"? Did he miss me as much as I missed him?

Then his eyes moved past us and back to the podium, and my heart sank. He didn't recognize us. His expression seemed to read like everyone else's—"When is this guy going to wrap it up?"

I leaned down to whisper in Sam's ear. "I just saw your Pop."

Alex looked over at me and put a hand on my thigh. He smiled a tight-lipped smile, but his eyes gave him away. *Shush,* they seemed to say.

As soon as the speeches ended and we filed off the stage and down the creaky metal steps, I shoved Gloria's little hand into Alex's big one. With Sam bouncing on my hip, I plunged into the crowd, heading in the direction of where I'd seen Miles. Alex called my name, confused, but I ignored him, losing myself in the human tide.

As we weaved through the crowd clumsily, I scanned faces, desperate for a glimpse of a wool cap, a limping walk. I squeezed around backpacks, stepped over strollers. Luckily, a few people recognized me and paused to let us pass.

I saw a black hat and rushed toward it, but the face that turned belonged to a much younger man. I ran after a fluff of white hair, but it, too, belonged to a stranger. I paused, and with my free hand, I shielded my eyes from the late afternoon sun, scanning the rivers of people as they moved across the concrete lot and onto the sidewalk. I was about to give up when I noticed a crowd of people funneling into the trolley station—and realized that Miles would likely be among them, taking the Route 100 line home. Slinging Sam onto my opposite hip, I started to run toward it.

Inside, the trolley platforms were shoulder to shoulder with people, all trying to force themselves inside two small silver cars. Sam and I pushed toward the doors of the one marked "Delaware County." As I got closer, my head straining over the sea of people, I saw Miles through the window. He was reading the paper, clueless.

"Miles," I shouted at the trolley. "Miles Lahey, please wait. Miles!"

Sensing my desperation, people parted to let me pass. But just as I reached the trolley, the doors slid shut and the conductor announced the first stop. I reached out, but my hand only grazed the cold, dirty metal.

He didn't hear me, didn't know that his precious grandson was just a few feet away. "Miles," I said again, but softer, as the trolley rolled away. I caught my breath, adjusted Sam, then turned and started back, fighting the current of bodies.

As we walked back to the lot, I laughed at myself. What would I have said to him? Miles was an old soul and a practicing Catholic with a healthy respect for fate and chance and the mysteries of life. But alternate universes? That would be hard, even for him.

By the time we made it back to the rally, only a handful of supporters lingered, and both Alex and Gloria were frantic.

"Where did you go?" they asked in stereo, Gloria desperate to start trick-or-treating and Alex worried.

"Sorry. I saw someone I used to know."

"Jesus, Abbey," Alex said. "You can't just run off like that. There could be nutjobs around. Seriously." I looked at my feet, contrite, and fell in step behind them as we made our way back to Oscar and the Suburban.

But we'd made it only a few yards when we were stopped again, this time by a pretty petite woman in a black shirtdress and giant witch's hat. Her skin was caramel colored and luminous, her hair long and dark, and her figure curvy in all the right places. But it was her smile that delighted above all: wide, warm, and genuine.

Which is why I was surprised when she spoke so bluntly.

"Van Holt! That was one bullshit speech," she barked at Alex, not caring who among the straggling supporters heard.

"Larry!" Alex's eyes flung open in surprise. "How are you?" He hugged her hard, almost lifting her off her feet, then stepped back. "Nice language in front of my kids, by the way."

She clapped her hands to her face in embarrassment and looked at me apologetically. Alex laughed, then introduced us.

"Abbey, this is Larry Liebman," he said. "Larry, this is my wife, Abigail."

"Actually, we met at your wedding," she explained. "But there were about a million people there, so I understand if you don't remember." For once, an easy out.

We exchanged pleasantries until I noticed the identification badge dangling from her neck. "Are you with the press?" I asked.

"I write for the *Inquirer*," she said. "City desk."

"You're that Larry Liebman!" I exclaimed. "I've seen your byline. I try to read your stories. But I always thought you were a man."

"Yep, everyone does. It's part of my cover," she said, pulling the brim of her hat down over one eye and winking at Gloria. "Only my mother still calls me Lawrencia."

"Are you covering this rally?"

"No. Since Alex and I went to school together, I recused myself. I just came by to enjoy a little sun. Certainly not those ridiculous speeches. Honestly, van Holt, you can do better." She punched him in the arm and he winced.

"The ladies sure loved it, though," she continued. "I've never seen so many women at a Blandon rally before."

"Tell me about it," I said, rolling my eyes.

We all laughed, except for Gloria, who was pulling my other arm out of my socket and glaring at Larry for holding her up.

When we made it to the car, Alex turned and hugged Larry again, then told her he'd call after the election and we could all get together for dinner. I hugged her too, even though we had just met.

"Nice to meet you, Larry," I said, before sliding into the car.

"Nice to see you again, Abbey," she corrected. And then, with another tip of her hat to Gloria, she was off.

On the ride home, I was curious. And maybe even a little jealous. Alex seemed to light up when he saw her, and they had such easy camaraderie. I asked him to "refresh my memory" of who she was and learned she was the daughter of a Jewish real estate tycoon from New Jersey and a beautiful Haitian artist who had come to Philadelphia in the late 1960s with no coat, forty-two dollars, and a scholarship to Bryn Mawr College. They lived on the Main Line in the 1980s while Larry's dad developed the Granite View Mall, and later half of Newtown Square. Larry and her twin older brothers were sent to Mercersburg Academy, the same rural Pennsylvania prep school as Alex, and they all shared a ride home to Philadelphia one spring break.

And though Alex was the boys' age and they played lacrosse together, it was Larry and Alex who became best friends. They bonded over their mutual love of early hip-hop, skiing, and social justice. They also both grew up with immense wealth and never had to be embarrassed by it with each other.

She and Alex lost touch during college, when she went off to Columbia and he stayed behind to go to his safety school, the University of Pennsylvania. ("Safe" for Alex, whose grandparents endowed the library.) But recently she had come back to Philadelphia, discovered Alex was running for Congress, and reconnected with him via e-mail. He hadn't had a chance to see her in person—until today.

"Larry helped get the press off our back when you were in the hospital," he explained.

"How nice of her," I said, remembering the e-mails I'd snuck a peek at. "It's always good to have someone on the inside, someone you can trust. Some reporters would do anything for a good exclusive. And don't even get me started about bloggers…"

"Larry's not like that," he said, cutting me off. "She's one of the good guys. She's always helping people." He sighed and looked out the window.

"Last time I checked, congressmen help people too."

"Yeah, but not like she did. Does."

"Well, let's not exaggerate reporting. I mean, it's one of the noblest of professions, but it's not the Peace Corps."

"It is when you do it from Afghanistan."

Before I could catch myself—"She was in Afghanistan?"

Alex coughed an annoyed laugh. "Uh, yeah? Remember she sent that woven blanket thing when Gloria was born."

"Oh, right."

"Abbey?"

"Yeah?" I braced myself for a question about why I was so forgetful. But, thankfully, he asked something easy.

"What's that smell?"

It was the diaper, deep inside my bag, swaddled in cashmere, where it had been cooking for hours in the afternoon sun.

"Must be Van," I lied, pushing my bag across the floor of the car to the other side. "I'll take him upstairs to change him really quick. You and Gloria can get started trick-or-treating."

But when we arrived back in front of the apartment, Alex didn't move.

"Aren't you coming?" I asked, standing on the curb but leaning into the backseat like a high-class hooker.

"Don't get mad, but I have to do some debate prep," said Alex. "Frank is insisting."

"But you promised. And Gloria has been so patient all afternoon. Can't you just come for half an hour?"

"Abbey, don't make me the bad guy. It's just trick-or-treating. It's not a big deal."

"Don't make me the bad guy"? Was that every husband in America's go-to rebuttal? I was so tired of that line I wanted to send out a press release: *Attention, men of the world: If you don't want to be made the bad guy, don't be one.*

I pulled Gloria out of the car and plopped her on the curb, unbuckled Sam, and slung him on my hip. "For the record, Halloween is the most important day of a five-year-old's life," I said. "It is a *really* big deal."

"Since when do you care so much about Halloween?" he said, tossing his head back in annoyance. Then he blew out a long sigh and looked up, sheepish. "I promise I'll make it up to them."

"When? After Tuesday?"

But he just powered up the window and sped off.

I watched in disbelief as the Suburban disappeared around the corner. But when I saw Gloria, her expression for once anxious and unsure, I tamped down my anger and dug deep. Setting Sam down on the sidewalk, I pulled my sad little rag dolls close.

"Guys," I said, squatting so I could look them in the eye. "Daddy had to go do some really important election stuff, so I'm going to take you trick-or-treating, okay?"

"But I want Daddy...," whimpered Gloria.

"I know, sweetie," I said. "And he's really sorry. But let's not let it ruin Halloween. Let's go get some *major* candy, okay?"

Gloria, never one to lose focus, agreed. "Candy!" she shrieked, and ran toward the revolving door.

But it turned out that trick-or-treating in the city wasn't as much fun as it sounded. Hitting all six apartments on the second floor, we came up with three fun-size candy bars, a dollar bill, and some cough drops. The next floor resulted in an apple, an ancient lollipop, and a confused elderly lady who kept asking if we were there to fix the faucets. The next two floors were equally disappointing. By the time we reached the fifth floor—where a young couple hosting a party offered the kids sushi and virgin pumpkin-tinis—I knew we'd had enough.

"C'mon, guys," I told them. "Let's get out of here."

We went back outside, flagged a cab, and headed to the one place I was sure would be having a *real* Halloween.

As the cab wound its way past the city limits into the suburbs, I began to feel nauseous, and not just from the winding roads. There were the familiar row homes along Radnor Avenue, the orange-and-black Flyers flags, the rusty deathtrap of a trampoline on Kenmore Street, and the giant blow-up ghost on the county commissioner's front lawn. I saw the playground where I used to take Sam, the house where our babysitter lived, and the ancient corner store where we went for hot dogs on rainy afternoons.

The sky was catching the last rays of fall sunshine, that magic hour on Halloween when children pulled their mothers away from hastily eaten dinners and dads from the six-o'clock news. When pillowcases were snatched from beds and Mom's makeup and hairspray were raided. When photos were snapped and the sun was just beginning to touch the trees. Go time.

Grange Hill was just the way I left it. My life might have turned upside down in some unexplainable and metaphysical way, but here life remained unchanged. Like the first page of a picture book you've read a thousand times.

I couldn't yet face my house, couldn't even look in its direction, so I asked the driver to stop a few streets away. We all piled out, and I punched in a huge tip, promising the driver another if he came back in an hour and a half. The kids were wide-eyed with astonishment at the gangs of costumed kids, the large green lawns, the swing sets, and the yard decorations, some clanging, some shrieking, and some blowing strange-smelling smoke. I was wide-eyed too, looking for neighbors, friends, or other inhabitants of my former life.

But of course it wasn't really "my former life." In this world, no one knew me and I had never even set foot in Grange Hill. The realization made me feel sad. Anonymous. Like a ghost.

En route to the suburbs, we had stopped at Walmart on City Line Avenue, eager to ditch Raggedy Ann and Andy for some real costumes. The inventory was slim, this being Halloween night, but we clawed through the white cardboard bins and messy racks until we found what we needed. We covered Gloria's face with white body paint, painted "bloody" drool on with lipstick, and replaced the itchy red yarn wig with a long silky black one. We even stuck candy corns on her bicuspids for fangs. The only cape we could find was adult-sized, so it dragged behind her like a coronation robe. She loved it.

There were only two costumes left in Sam's size: Iron Man and

Merida from Disney's *Brave*. Since he wouldn't let me pull either of them out of his tiny fists, we bought both. He wore them with pride, not realizing he looked more like a pint-sized cross-dresser than an action hero. I got in the spirit too, topping my smooth hair, gray suit, and high heels with a flaming red cape and plastic devil horns, transforming me from candidate's wife to hell's receptionist. We were a motley crew, but it didn't matter. In Grange Hill on Halloween, anything goes.

Fence by fence, walkway by walkway, and door by door, the kids filled their buckets. They ran along in gleeful abandon, their feet barely touching the ground. I walked a few steps behind them, reminding them to watch for cars and say thank you.

And the closer and closer we got to 1662 Sagamore Street the more anxious I became, as if I was about to come face-to-face with a long-lost lover. Finally we stood on my neighbor's wide wooden porch. My heart was beating so fast, I almost turned and fled.

But before I could, Mary Anne answered the door in an enormous fluffy pink robe and crazy hair. She was always one of my favorite people in the neighborhood, and my eyes lit up when I saw her face. As she bent down to say hello to the kids and drop candy into their buckets with one hand, I saw a pink newborn hidden in the folds of her robe.

"You had your baby!" I exclaimed. "And it's a girl!"

"Yes," she said proudly as a tiny hand escaped the robe. "Four days ago. Her name is Elizabeth."

"I just can't believe it. After three boys."

"Me neither," she said, laughing and shaking her head, then trying to inspect our backlit faces. "I'm sorry, have we met?"

"I...I used to live around here," I said, not thinking fast enough. "My daughter used to go to Grange Hill Elementary."

"Oh, what grade?"

"Kindergarten. Mr. Cleary." I was digging myself deeper, but it felt so natural to say those words.

"No, Mommy. My teacher is—" corrected Gloria, but I pulled her close and she quieted.

Mary Anne stared at my face, trying to place it, then shook her head with a laugh. "I'm so sleep deprived, I can't remember anything or anyone. I'm Mary Anne Evans. At least I think so."

"I remember those days. I'm Abbey." I stuck out my hand and then pulled it back, remembering her hands were full.

We both laughed, but then the baby started to fuss.

"Well, happy Halloween," she said, stepping back into the house.

"You too," I whispered back as I ushered the kids off her porch. I felt strangely guilty. My kind and sweet neighbor had had her baby, the little girl I knew she was dreaming of, and I wasn't there to bake her an oversalted casserole or take the boys off her hands for an hour.

We walked out to the sidewalk and turned right. To Sam and Gloria, it was just another house. To me, the only house. Ours. Jimmy's and mine.

Taking a deep breath, I forced myself to put one foot in front of the other.

It came to me in pieces, its walls and windows appearing in glimpses behind the branches of a large pine tree. Then it came fully into view, its silvery stone chimney and speckled gray roof gleaming in the light of a newly risen moon.

I stared, taking it in. The windows were streak-free, and the trim was green, not white. A flag hung jauntily from the porch and the front walk was smooth new concrete, not slate stone. In the yard, the hedges were bushier and less manicured, and the black oak, the one that threatened to take down our porch every time the wind blew, had been cut down, its pale stump the only reminder of its former glory. And there were no flying bats, no bales of hay, and no keg of pumpkin beer. Just one leering jack-o'-lantern, its grimacing face daring us to enter.

"Let's go," said Gloria when I hesitated. "What are you waiting for?"

We trailed up the walk, me moving slowly behind little kid feet and dragging polyester. We neared the porch, and I stopped to help Sam up the one big step, the same way I had done a thousand times before. I lifted up Gloria so she could reach the doorbell, but she just hung there, not knowing what to do. I put her down and pushed it myself. *Brrrrrnnng.*

"Oh, well. Looks like no one is home. Let's move on." I took Gloria's hand but she didn't budge.

"But they have a pumpkin. You said that means they are 'open for business.' " She turned back to the door.

I was about to grab her arm and yank her away when we heard footsteps. The door swung open and a man in a bright green shirt, plaid golf pants, and a bushy red beard appeared before us. I don't know who I expected to answer, but this was not him.

"Trick or treat!" sang the kids as he plopped a ring pop—one of the most coveted of all Halloween treats—into each of their monogrammed canvas bags. He gave me a smile and a hearty "Good evening!"

Even though I knew he was a stranger, and I knew he couldn't answer me, still, when I looked up at his friendly face, I wanted to ask him how he finally fixed the chimney, why he mowed over those last few daffodils, and whether his family buried their fish and turtles under the cherry tree too. I wanted to know how long he had lived here, whom he had bought the house from, and if he knew a man named Jimmy Lahey. But mostly I wanted this nice man to explain to me why it was he—not I—who graced this doorway, who lived and laughed and loved inside.

A group of teenagers came up behind us, forcing our little trio to the side. I managed one last look, then followed Gloria out and clicked the gate behind me, knowing that you had to lift the latch at just the right angle if you wanted it to stay closed.

The rest of the evening, I moved around the neighborhood in a daze, memories ambushing me from every direction. I remembered Gloria's first Halloween and Jimmy parading his tiny bumblebee around in a red wagon. Gloria when she was two, so proud of her sparkly shoes and princess dress that she slept in them for a week. The year Jimmy's brother Patrick and his girlfriend of the month stopped by, him too cool for a costume but her dressed in a tiny French maid's uniform. (The neighborhood dads lingered a little longer that year.)

And I remembered three years ago, before Sam, when I miscarried a ten-week-old baby the day before Halloween. Jimmy and I had gone through the motions of pumpkins, costumes, and candy for Gloria's sake, but we both felt numb and fragile, as if the light October wind might blow us away. The keg of beer was there on the porch as always, but neither of us could touch it. I was the one who took Gloria out in her little wagon that year, glad that the evening clouds hid my pale face and shiny eyes. It was times like these when Jimmy and I were glad of the noise and chaos of Grange Hill; this place could hide a river of tears, an ocean of sad good-byes.

Now, moving from street to street, a stranger to everyone I passed, I saw Grange Hill as if for the first time. It was not the sit-com version of suburbia, of prom date mix-ups and Little League pop flies and moms grousing at football-obsessed fathers. It was not the movie version either, a purgatory of missed opportunities, angsty teen poets, and middle-aged malaise. It wasn't even what my mom promised buyers in those ads of hers: *The perfect suburban oasis for young families—and retirees too!*

It was just rows of houses, filled with people and their things. A place where you could make the most of it, or the worst.

In Grange Hill, it was up to you.

CHAPTER TEN

In the bathroom mirror, I watched Alex pace back and forth behind me, his face grave and his lips moving. With his navy suit, stiff cuffs, and combed hair, and me in my white silk robe luminous under the rows of lights, we looked like a scene from an old movie—his Clark Gable to my Jean Harlow. I leaned in close and finished my mascara, then applied a light coat of Chanel lip gloss. After one last look, I got up from my tufted stool. I had to wait for him to pass before I slipped across into the long closet to get dressed.

He followed me inside, still muttering to himself.

"What's up?" I finally asked. "Do you want me to help you with some practice questions or something?"

"No, it's not that," he said, adjusting, then readjusting, his red tie.

"Are you sure?"

"It's not the debate," he said, cracking his knuckles. "It's my dad. He's back from Florida. Showed up at Bloemveld this morning. My mother didn't say anything, but I could hear him in the background."

"Oh."

"I just don't get it. He agreed—we agreed—he would stay away until this was over," he said. "I'm stressed enough as it is."

Having never met Collier, and not having any idea why his presence would be so agitating, I didn't know how to respond. But having a renegade parent myself, I certainly sympathized. I went to Alex, grabbed his hands, and peered at him until he looked me in the eye.

"It's going to be fine," I said, giving his hands a little squeeze. "I promise."

He took a deep breath and smiled, then gave me a quick kiss on the forehead. "Thanks, doll," he said. "You better get dressed. We have to leave in forty-five minutes."

"I can be ready in five," I said, hurrying back to my row of clothes.

"Yeah, right," he said, rolling his eyes. "When have you ever taken less than an hour?"

An hour to get dressed? I hadn't even taken that long on my wedding day.

But when I tried on outfit after outfit, they wouldn't cooperate. A wine-colored pencil skirt and matching blouse were uncomfortably snug. A second skirt, this one of thick gray wool, didn't zip up all the way. And even the stretchy cotton dress from Diane von Furstenberg, its interlocking-circles pattern poised to disguise a multitude of sins, wouldn't quite lay flat over my stomach.

Back in my underwear, I examined my reflection in the long mirror and realized that in just one week, I'd managed to add a few new curves—unwelcome ones—to this perfect, lithe frame. Nothing too obvious, but enough to make Abbey van Holt's body-hugging, natural-fiber clothes a bit tight. Making a mental note to forgo May's incredible Thai cooking and start drinking those weird green drinks I found in the fridge, I rustled around for a pair of Spanx.

I was pulling on some control-top tights, the best tummy-trimming tool I could find among the tiny bits of silk and lace Abbey van Holt called underwear, when Gloria burst in, dressed in a pink-and-black bike helmet, shiny zip-up biking shirt, and the tiniest black bike shorts I'd ever seen. I had to stop myself from laughing when I saw her serious expression.

"I'm going for a ride," she told me as she adjusted her helmet strap.

"Well, you're certainly dressed for it."

She frowned at me in annoyance, then stared wide-eyed in anticipation. I realized she expected me to retrieve her bike. From where, I had no idea.

"Can't Daddy get it for you?"

"He's on the phone."

"What about May?"

"She doesn't have the key. And besides, you said *you* are the only one allowed to go down there, remember?"

I nodded as if I did.

Finally dressed, and walking aimlessly around the basement parking garage having no idea if this was the "down there" Gloria was referring to, I searched for a bike rack. Finding none, I asked the attendant if he knew where we kept our little girl's bike. He just shrugged, his English not very good, but then pointed toward the slope that led to a lower floor.

I walked carefully down the curving concrete into the darkest bowels of the building. It was damp and cold and eerily quiet. I couldn't imagine why Abbey van Holt insisted she be the only one to come down. Weren't there people to do this for her?

Among the rows of luxury cars I found a black Porsche with an "AVH 1" license plate and figured I was on the right track. A few feet in front of it, I spied what at first looked like a chain-link fence but on closer inspection revealed a storage unit. Inside was the stuff of family life: a jogging stroller, luggage, a snowboard, booster seats, and to the side, a silver bicycle with a shiny bell and training wheels. Bingo.

A small key from my ring easily unlocked the padlock; the door swung open with a metallic creak. I stepped in and began to wrestle with Gloria's bike when something farther back caught my eye.

It was a tall cherry dresser, one my aunt had given me when I graduated from Villanova, the first piece of grown-up furniture I ever owned. I stared at it for a while and shivered in the cold. What other remnants of Abbey DiSiano had been banished to this dungeon?

Letting go of the bike, I stepped around some oversized Christmas wreaths to reach the dresser. I ran my hands over its soft, satiny wood and touched the little dent where I'd accidentally gouged it with some nail clippers. I opened the drawers, half expecting to find them filled with clothes from my Lahey life, where we still used the dresser in our bedroom, but found them empty, save a few faded receipts and a blue hair band. In the bottom drawer, though, tucked behind a crumpled plastic bag, was a half-empty pack of Marlboro Lights.

I had never really been a smoker. Never had a real habit. But post-college, in the late nineties, when smoking hadn't yet been banned in bars, Jules and I would sometimes buy a pack to split when we were out on the town. I opened the pack, and a whiff of tobacco took me back to those nights, the two of us sitting at the latest hipster bar we couldn't afford to be in, nursing our one sticky-sweet cosmopolitan for hours and thinking we were the height of urban sophistication.

As I went to put the cigarettes back in their hiding spot, I noticed that tucked under the plastic wrap was a book of matches marked "Sushi RX." I tried to picture Jules and myself at the place but couldn't. Then I realized that was because Sushi RX was new; it had opened just a few months ago. But if these cigarettes were recent, who had put them here?

I looked down to find a narrow path between the stacked boxes and followed it to the back of the unit. There, someone had arranged a box of old vinyl albums as a seat and a plastic tub as a kind of coffee table. On the floor was a Snapple bottle, half-filled with water and cigarette butts, and beside it was an empty bag of Herr's sour cream and onion potato chips—my favorite.

Apparently Abbey van Holt's favorite too.

The hair on the back of my neck stood up. It was spooky; I could almost sense her presence. It made me feel like I was trespassing. But when I sat down, the little nook was cozy and quiet, like the blanket forts I used to build as a child.

The lid of the plastic tub was askew, so I lifted it off. Inside was a mess of papers, photographs, and manila envelopes. A copy of a lease for a junior one-bedroom apartment, effective November 1998. Some old photos of Roberta and me at an amusement park in Ocean City. My college diploma. A letter of recommendation from Sharon and Barbara, the ladies who had owned Salmon & Sisley, the firm I worked at when I met Alex.

I was about to close the lid when my eyes landed on a newspaper article folded carefully and slipped inside a clear plastic protector. I took it out to find it was from an October 2003 *Philadelphia Business Journal*, its paper softened from age but its type still bright and clear, thanks to the well-sponsored weekly's thick white newsprint. On the front page, below the fold, was a headline: "Ones to Watch: DSX Agency Launches Strong with Six Clients."

I read a few paragraphs and then my eyes jumped to the accompanying photo. In it, Jules and I were standing in front the same office door I had visited earlier this week, except instead of one large pink X, there were two others letters before it: D and S. Jules wore an uncharacteristically conservative suit with her wild red curls, but she looked pretty. And happy. I looked happy too. And with good reason: According to this article, just a few weeks after hanging out our shingle, our little agency was killing it.

It was hard to believe that this article was all that was left of that partnership. And the friendship.

Judging from the softness of the paper, and the worn creases that indicated it had been unfolded and folded often, it seemed Abbey van Holt couldn't believe it either.

I realized then that was why she had insisted that she be the one to come down here. The little nook, and all that it held, certainly wasn't glamorous, but it was all hers. And it served a purpose.

Down here—many floors below her life as a society maven and political wife—she was free. No cameras; no catty friends; no in-laws. Unobserved, she could steal away to eat her favorite chips, smoke illicit cigarettes, and riffle through old photos and articles.

And just for a few moments, remember who she used to be.

Today's debate was being held in the auditorium of Walter Wilson Community College, a school about twelve blocks south of Rittenhouse Square. The row homes surrounding the city campus were small and covered in siding or faux stone, their bay windows decorated with plastic flowers and statues of the Virgin Mary. The businesses I saw looked small and family owned: plumbers, salons, and attorneys specializing in DUIs and divorces.

The community college, endowed by a wealthy Philadelphia widow and built just six months earlier, was a bright spot in the neighborhood. Its facade was a mix of glass and artfully slanted steel, circled by saplings tied down with yellow string. Though the houses around it seemed to sigh in jealousy, their roofs and balconies sloping sadly toward the street, the residents stood up straighter as they walked by. It was one reason why this debate was important; it was the first one ever held this far into southwest Philadelphia.

Local debates didn't generally have much impact on congressional elections, and yet according to Frank, if a candidate was asked to participate, he or she had better accept—or risk looking like he or she had something to hide. And the candidate had better take it seriously, because even though few voters watched, the press would cherry-pick the best and worst sound bites to play over and over again on the local news, if only for the next twenty-four hours.

As a public relations professional, I knew that ninety-nine percent of the questions would be routine. But those weren't the ones you prepared for. You prepared for that one percent. No wonder Alex, sitting onstage beside his opponent, looked a bit pale.

Amanda Bullock was in her early sixties, with silver bobbed hair and a sweet expression that belied her booming voice, deep intellect, and biting wit. Next to her, my husband looked more like a young legal clerk than a political rival. I knew Alex preferred to stand, and I wished the two candidates would face off at podiums instead of seated at a table draped in ugly maroon polyester. And worse, with the new building's thermostat set to a perfect sixty-eight degrees, Alex had no reason to take off his jacket and roll up his sleeves.

Soon the lights flicked on and off to quiet the audience. The news cameras lifted and turned toward the stage. The moderator, the lead anchor from our local PBS affiliate, welcomed everyone and, seconds later, lobbed her first question.

"Thanks, Trudy," said Alex with a smile. "And thank you, Judge Bullock, students, and everyone else for coming today and giving up your Saturday morning." He paused a beat, turned more serious, and continued: "I'm glad you asked that question, because jobs are the most important issue in this election..."

Watching Alex field questions with ease and confidence, I was glad it was him up there and not me. Even though I had spent countless hours helping clients learn to deftly deflect unwanted questions, politely say "no comment," and know when to go for the jugular, public speaking was not something I relished. I was a classic example of the shoemaker with the shoeless children: I could teach anyone how to ace an interview, but when the cameras turned on me, I either froze or, worse, acted manic, like an infomercial hostess on uppers.

For the better part of an hour, Alex and Amanda debated the finer points of the tax code, economic recovery, teen pregnancy, college scholarships, speed limits, prescription discounts, recycling…even the fiber content of school lunches. I sat beside Amanda's partner, Lori, who, like me, nodded and clapped at the appropriate times. The debate never got ugly, but a few times, I could tell Amanda was getting under Alex's skin, especially when she mentioned his family's money.

I wondered if Alex wished he had been the son of a teacher or a carpenter, or even an ex-con. Voters loved rags-to-riches stories; Jimmy and Miles always had. In fact, I was sure Miles had been at yesterday's rally for Senator Blandon, not Alex.

And what about Jimmy? Would he vote for Alex? He usually hated "trust-funders," nepotism, and anyone who tried to "game the system." He hated country clubs, made fun of his older brother John's BMW, and even refused to wear the Polo shirt I bought him the first Christmas we were together.

Not that my life with Jimmy had been one of constant deprivation. In fact, Lahey Landscape & Design proved to be profitable from the start. Nothing at all like what Alex had, but a steady monthly income that kept our little trio in turkey bacon, Netflix, and eco-friendly lightbulbs.

Jimmy might have been surprised by Lahey Landscape's success, but I wasn't. He was a born entrepreneur. He had the small business owner's instinct for thrift, but enough of a dreamer's bold thinking to take chances. Clients loved him, taking his design advice, giving referrals, and gladly parting with another two hundred dollars when a project went over budget. He was also a perfectionist, personally inspecting every lawn and requiring his employees to wash their shirts, and their trucks, every night.

His only flaw was organization. His office—first in our kitchen and later at the renovated barn that became his company's headquarters—was a mess. Stacks of invoices, mail, tax documents, and newspapers joined tools and product samples to create hills and valleys all over his desk. Shelves that started out holding neat rows of maintenance binders now stored a little bit of everything, including year-old magazines, half-drunk Snapple bottles, clumsily folded maps, and dusty snapshots of the kids. Jimmy's accountant said he was one of the most disorganized clients he'd worked with, even worse than the baker and his wife, with their shoeboxes full of sticky, flour-coated receipts.

I tried to help, but it only ended up in an argument. I sent Jules in, too, her tolerance for messes much higher than mine, but even she left perplexed and annoyed. Jimmy argued that he hated being indoors and that he didn't have the time for paperwork, but I think the real reason was his mother.

Originally, the plan had been for Jane to handle the books, but now that she was gone, Jimmy couldn't bear to deal with them. Every time he looked at a ledger book or mailed a set of invoices, he was reminded of her and how she hadn't lived to see him become a success.

And what a success he was becoming. Those first few years, it seemed he could do no wrong. The economy was good; home prices were rising; and business seemed to fall into Jimmy's lap. Most of it was suburban homes and estates, not the coveted corporate accounts every landscaper dreams of, but as word of mouth spread, he added bigger renovations and installations. And armed with a shiny new landscape design degree, he now had the knowledge to back up his creativity. His reputation, and confidence, grew.

In two years, Jimmy was able to pay off his start-up loan, and soon after, he had enough to rent the barn, purchase two new trucks, and hire four staff. He was so enamored of small business ownership, he even suggested I quit my job and work with him, or better yet, start my own public relations agency with Jules.

"You can have half the barn," he joked.

"Gee, thanks," I said. "I always wanted to work somewhere with a dirt floor."

He threw a sweaty towel at me and I ducked.

"You could call it the PR Farm," he replied. "Where ideas grow and grow."

"Don't quit your day job."

"Seriously, Ab," he said. "You guys could do it. Then you wouldn't have to commute; you'd have a more flexible schedule. And you could pick and choose the clients you want."

"I've definitely thought about it," I said. "But with the baby, and if we have another, I just don't know. Having clients is a twenty-four-hour thing."

"You think? I had a guy call me this morning at five because there were acorns in his birdbath." He dropped the teasing tone and touched my hand. "But in the long run, it's worth it. And if anyone can make it work, you can."

Starting my own business had always been intriguing to me, but now the pull wasn't quite as strong. It was just easier to let someone else find the clients, okay the plans, and tell me what to do and where to be. Maybe it was the sleep deprivation talking, but I heard myself tell Jimmy, "I think we've had enough big changes in our lives lately." Then I pretended to hear Gloria in her crib, scurrying off before I could see his disappointed look.

Jimmy never mentioned it again, and neither did I. Instead, we enjoyed taking Gloria to Disneyland, renovating the kitchen, and paying off Jimmy's school loans. That Christmas I gave Jimmy a new computer; he gave me a gold locket with a photo of Gloria inside.

While I pulled the dainty chain over my neck, he said, "I know it's not the thing you really wanted, that fancy army watch, but—"

"Army watch?"

"You know, army or armor or something like that?"

It took me a moment to figure out what he meant. "A tank watch? From Cartier?"

"Right," he said. "That's what I meant. I priced it, but I'm gonna need a couple years on that one. Actually, a couple decades."

"Deal," I said, and kissed him.

Little did we know, just a few months later, the economy would crater, dragging thousands of small businesses like Jimmy's down with it. By the following Christmas, the Laheys would barely be able to pay the mortgage, let alone save up for some fancy watch with a funny name.

The debate ended with a round of applause. Onstage, Alex shook hands with Amanda and I said good-bye to her partner, Lori, and then went in search of a bathroom. I queued up behind some college students and took out my phone, switched the volume back on, and checked my messages. I saw five missed calls: one from the apartment, two from May's cell phone, and two from an unknown number.

Oh shit.

Shaking, I hurriedly dialed the apartment number, but no one answered. When I tried May's number, the call went immediately to voice mail, as if the phone were uncharged. I called the unknown number and got a recorded greeting from the Children's Hospital of Pennsylvania.

Oh God, I thought, my chest constricting in panic. *Gloria. Bike. Something has happened to Gloria.*

I ran over to Alex and tugged at his sleeve. He was talking with a voter but stopped mid-sentence when he saw my ashen face.

I blurted out what I knew: missed calls, May, hospital.

He grabbed my hand and we started running.

Eight agonizing minutes later, Oscar screeched the SUV to a stop outside the entrance of CHOP and Alex and I leapt out, charged inside, and sprinted for the admissions desk—where a heavyset nurse moving in slow motion searched for any patients named "van Holt."

We stood frozen, our eyes locked on her face as she clicked and waited, clicked and waited. Finally, the computer blinked blue with a new screen, reflected in her glasses.

"Room 413."

She started to give us some instructions, but we didn't hear them, already racing toward the silver elevators, narrowly missing a bloody bike messenger. Alex kept pressing the up button over and over, but nothing happened.

"Stairs," he said, pointing. I followed.

He made it up the four floors in a few bounds, but I trailed behind in my heels. As he opened the door to the hall and looked down at me on the stairwell below, I waved him on while I took off my shoes. My mind repeated *please, please, please* over and over again as I made it to the top and started running down the fourth-floor hallway.

Inside Room 413, I saw Alex, Mirabelle, and a nurse surrounding the bed. I braced myself and pushed my way in. Looking incredibly tiny in the large hospital bed, with bright lights illuminating the sheets and metal rails, was my twenty-month-old son.

Not Gloria. Sam.

He was awake and alert, and he smiled weakly when he saw me approach. I rushed to him and grabbed his little hands, then stood back and examined him like a lioness with her cub, running my hands along his arms and legs and fingers and feet, checking closely, and even leaning down to put my nose and lips against his face. When I pulled back, I noticed he wore the same bemused expression as always; the only sign something was amiss was the IV taped to his pudgy arm. He was still wearing the undershirt I'd put him in this morning, its tiny blue planes patrolling the hills and valleys of his torso.

I caught my breath and looked up to find Gloria in her tiny jersey and bike shorts, standing beside my grim-faced mother-in-law.

"He had a reaction," said Mirabelle in a calm tone that belied her expression. "Went into shock, so May called 911. He's stable now."

"A reaction? To what?

"Peanuts. He must have gotten ahold of some candy." Then under her breath, she added, "Apparently, no one was watching."

"What?" I repeated, confused.

"The candy. From Halloween," Mirabelle repeated. "He found some and ate it. But luckily, just a tiny bite. Doctor said he is going to be fine."

A tiny bite of candy? This is a kid who took a softball to the face and kept on toddling. Who once ate an entire tub of cream cheese and asked for more.

Then it dawned on me. Peanuts. Reaction. Shock.

Sam, I mean Van, was allergic to nuts. Apparently, very much so.

I thought of last night's trick-or-treating and blanched. That candy could have killed him; *I* could have killed him. I grabbed the metal bed rails to steady myself. What else didn't I know? What other frailties had my children inherited from the van Holts?

Standing beside me, Alex put one hand on the bed and the other on my arm, calming me. I looked at him and we exchanged relieved and concerned glances. Alex then tickled Sam's feet, promising him new toys, some ice cream, a Mercedes.

"He turned red like a tomato," said Gloria, smiling with excitement. "I saw him. I told May."

"Good job, sweetie," I told her, struggling to find my voice again. "Thank you for watching out for your brother." Then, looking around, I asked, "Where is May, by the way?"

"I sent her home," said Mirabelle. "And told her we won't be needing her anymore."

"What?"

"She is obviously unfit to watch these children. Just think of what could have happened."

"She didn't do it on purpose," I said. "It was an accident. And he's going to be okay."

Mirabelle ignored me, turning to Alex: "It was a mistake to have someone who can barely read English watching my grandchildren. It's not safe."

"She can read it," I corrected. "Her English is excellent."

Mirabelle waved her hands dismissively, swatting away my comment as if it were an irritating fly.

"Alex?" I said, looking over to see if he was as stunned as I was. But he pretended not to hear, even though he was inches from me.

"Alex?" I repeated.

"What?"

"Your mother just fired May."

"Yes, I heard."

"The kids love her. She's a great nanny."

Alex ducked my questioning look and pretended to be interested in the IV bag, which was empty. "I'm going to find the doctor," he muttered, then walked out of the room.

I turned back to my mother-in-law. "I know this was really upsetting for us all and I am grateful you were home when we couldn't be reached. But I think you're overreacting. May is great with the kids. She loves them."

For a second, I thought Mirabelle was going to reach across the hospital bed and physically close my lips with her pointy, pale nails. But instead, her face turned placid, her voice as smooth as honey.

"They'll love the next one even more."

It was scary to be on the receiving end of such condescension. And if the subject had been anything other than my children, I would have backed down.

"Mirabelle, with all due respect—"

"Abbey, that's enough," a voice spoke sharply. It was Alex, standing in the doorway, jaw set in anger.

"But, Alex, I just don't think it's fair to blame May." Especially since I was the one who left the candy bag on the dining room table, easily reachable and irresistible to an insatiable toddler.

"I said, that's enough!" he barked, glaring at me.

I flushed bright red, embarrassed. Also shocked. It wasn't just that he took his mother's side, but that he yelled at me like I was a naughty child.

Just then the resident on call—a young brunette with the demeanor of an army sergeant—entered. She briskly assured us that Sam would be fine, told us they were releasing him, and was gone. Mirabelle leaned down and kissed Sam perfunctorily, then gathered her things. Alex walked her out. I turned my attention back to Sam, humming his favorite songs and kissing his head. He pulled at my earrings as I blinked back tears.

Motherhood could be frightening and exhausting and lonely, but at least the reward was always having the last word. Even as much as Jimmy was a modern dad—getting up for middle-of-the-night feedings, going to Fancy Nancy birthday parties, clipping diaper coupons—he deferred to me when it came to major decisions involving the kids: day care, doctor, bedtimes. But just now with Alex, I felt stripped of any power, as if my opinions on child rearing were sweet and well meaning, but negotiable. As if I had been demoted from mother-in-chief to a mere advisory role.

It made me feel helpless. And unimportant.

The van Holts had their own code, their own version of right and wrong, and, if you wanted to live in their world, you'd best learn it and live by it. There was no veering off the script, no questioning of their divine right. And no forgiveness for a wrong, however innocent the mistake.

Looking at Sam's sweet face, and knowing his easygoing disposition and the purity of his spirit, it sickened me.

We returned to an eerily quiet apartment and moved around as if afraid to disturb the silence. The only sounds were the occasional truck: one lurching down Walnut Street outside, and the large red one Sam pushed along the floor in the kitchen. Even Gloria seemed subdued, quietly playing hospital with her Barbies by hooking them up to IVs made from dental floss and Scotch tape.

After I had double bagged and discarded all the Halloween candy, including the tiny Snickers bar Sam had gnawed, its wrapper soft and still wet, I washed my hands vigorously as if to remove not just any nut residue but the memory of today. Of the terror of those twenty-five minutes from phone call to hospital room to all clear. When I was done, my skin raw and red, I turned and opened the fridge. I figured a quiet family dinner was just what the van Holts needed.

I pulled out eggs, pancake mix, milk, syrup, and bacon, and placed them on the counter. Tonight we would have "breakfast for dinner," my go-to meal when time was tight. I started to open boxes and slice packages, but standing between the stove and the sink— May's domain—I found myself frozen with guilt. Was she horribly upset? Would she ever see the kids again? If I could convince Alex to take her back, would she even come? I thought of her limitless patience with Gloria, the sweet way she sang to Sam, and how empty the kitchen seemed without her shuffling around in it.

I listened for Alex, and when I heard nothing, I slipped into the pantry.

Pulling up the recent calls on my phone, I found May's number and tapped. I didn't know exactly what I was going to say, but I knew that at the very least, she needed to know that Sam was okay.

When she didn't answer, I left a long, rambling message about how Sam was fine, how sorry I was about Mirabelle, and how much we would miss her. I had wanted to add that, in time, when everyone got over the heated emotions of today, we would hire her back, and if not, then she'd find another, better job. But I wasn't sure I could make either promise.

I had also wanted to assure her that she did nothing wrong and that it was me who had left out the candy. But standing in the van Holt pantry, the bottles of Perrier lined up perfectly and even the trash smelling faintly of lemon, something—instinct? fear?—told me not to admit that to anyone. A mother who so carelessly allows her deathly allergic toddler access to a huge bag of Halloween candy would raise red flags. Ones that might not ever be lowered. And I had made too many mistakes already.

So I ended the call feeling even shittier than before. With a sigh, I slipped out of the pantry and began cracking eggs into a bowl with one hand. I was just watching the last of the yolks join its brothers and sisters when Alex walked in wearing gray swim trunks and carrying a towel.

"What are you doing?" he asked, staring at me in disbelief. He was surprised not only to see my cooking but how effortlessly I was doing so.

"Making dinner. Well, actually it's breakfast. But it's all I could whip up on short notice." I offered him a slight smile as I took in his attire. "Why? What are *you* doing?"

"Going for a swim."

"Where?"

"Upstairs. Where do you think?"

Oh. I'd always wondered what that extra button in the elevator meant. I guess there was a pool—either heated or enclosed—on the roof. Maybe I could take Sam up there sometimes. He loved floating around in my arms in the water, feeling gloriously weightless.

"Right. Sorry." I began beating the eggs. "So, you don't want dinner?"

"Just save me a plate."

I sighed in annoyance but let him go without another word. But then I saw Sam crawling on the floor below me—rolling his truck and gurgling with glee—and I changed my mind. The kid had been through a lot; he deserved a family meal. I ran after Alex, catching him just before he slipped out.

"Alex, wait. Your son was in the hospital today. I think we should all eat together."

"What?"

"We haven't had a family dinner in…uh…a very long time. After today, I think a little normalcy is in order."

"I *normally* exercise every day. You're the one who's always saying she doesn't want a pudgy husband."

No one does, I thought, *but what difference does it make what my husband looks like if he's never around? Especially after a day like today?* I wanted to take his towel and wring his handsome neck, but instead, I gave him the "I'm not mad, just disappointed" look I had perfected after ten years with Jimmy.

It worked on Alex, too. He let go of the door handle and came back to the kitchen. But instead of picking up Sam or playing with Gloria, he slumped in a chair and took out his phone. Not quite what I had in mind, but at least he was here. Physically, anyway.

I placed strips of bacon in a hot pan, then yelled over to Gloria to come set the table. She didn't look up, so I walked around the kitchen island to the family room and stood over her. She pretended to be engrossed in her dolls.

"Gloria," I said. "I know you can hear me."

No response.

"Gloria. I need you to come set the table."

"I'm busy."

"I don't care if you are solving the world's energy crisis; I'm your mother and you will do what I tell you to." I took the Barbie from her, but she grabbed another. When I confiscated that one, too, and tried to tug her to her feet by one arm, she went limp. It was infuriating.

"You have two choices," I told her, overarticulating each word like a hostage negotiator. "Either you can set the table or go sit on the time-out stair."

Gloria wrinkled her brow and asked, "What stair?" In my anger, I had forgotten this place was all one level.

"I mean the time-out...*area*." I'd figure out where to put her later. Hopefully it wouldn't come to that.

But she didn't move, digging in her heels. I detailed her options again, then gave her five seconds to get moving. As I counted aloud, inside I secretly pleaded with her to move her tiny white ass. Nothing.

Eventually, she left me no choice.

In a stunning blur, moving the way only a furious mother can, I had shoved the Barbies, dental floss, and tape in a drawer, then lifted Gloria and carried her—kicking and screaming—into the hallway. I found a boring section of wall, plopped her down to face it, and told her she could sit there until she was ready to set the table.

She jumped up, so I grabbed her and set her back down. She jumped up again, so this time I pinned her to the floor like a wrestler, my arms around her waist and my knees grinding into the hardwood. As she kicked and clawed and fussed like a trapped raccoon, it took my best effort not to hurt her. Finally, she stopped flailing and thrust her hands into her lap. She looked at the wall defiantly and then gave it a delicious smile, as if it was the most interesting white paint she had ever seen.

What a little pisser.

I stood up and gathered myself, pulling down my apron and smoothing back my hair. Then I ran toward the smell of burning bacon.

Alex was waiting for me, pacing.

"I don't get it. You never made her do chores before."

"That's the problem."

"But why all of a sudden?" He wasn't wrong. It was unfair to introduce the concept of discipline at age five. But better late than never.

Gloria heard us and cried out, "Daddy! Daddy!" Alex looked at me in exasperation, starting to cave. "Abbey, please—"

"No, Alex. She has to listen. To respect me. Us."

"But it's been such a long day. She's tired. It's not fair—"

He started to walk toward her, to rescue her, so I grabbed his arm and pulled him back. He kept going, but I stiffened my legs as a counterweight until he slowed. I was prepared to subdue him too, if necessary.

"Abbey, what the hell?"

I lessened my grip and implored, "Alex. Don't."

He thought for a moment, considering, then told me, "Fine. Have it your way." Then he walked back to the kitchen and to his phone, sighing in disgust.

Good thing, too, because Gloria stuck to her post, and her faux satisfaction, like the most practiced member of the Royal Guard.

The rest of us ate dinner without speaking, and with me trying not to look at Gloria's empty place at the table. Sam seemed confused and, for the first time ever, ate just a few bites. The sound of forks and knives seemed overly loud, and the smell of the cheesy eggs and syrupy pancakes was nauseating. I tried to act like I was in total control of the situation, but inside I felt sick.

But if Gloria could hold out, so could I. All through dinner and Sam's bath time, I didn't give in, stepping around her like she was a box someone left in the hall. The thought of that slap at her school fueled my resolve, even as the first hour turned into the second. Funny, I'd always thought she got her stubborn streak from Jimmy, the man who refused to talk to a cousin who wronged him for *seven* years, but I guess she got at least part of it from me. Alex couldn't stand it; after gobbling down dinner, he left to go swimming after all.

Finally, it was Sam—or envy of Sam—who got through to Gloria in the end. When she saw me putting him to bed, reading a *Frozen* story and doing a perfect imitation of the little snowman, she couldn't take it anymore. She'd already missed a family dinner with both her parents and a super-bubbly bubble bath. But Olaf she couldn't ignore. I guess every criminal has a breaking point.

I was just lifting a droopy-eyed Sam into his crib when I saw her silhouette in the doorway.

"Mommy?"

"Yes, Gloria?"

"I'm ready to set the table now." *Hallelujah!* I scooped her up and carried her triumphantly to the kitchen, then helped her pick out knives and forks and spoons for tomorrow's breakfast. She quietly set four places, even folding the cream cloth napkins into triangles and remembering Sam's giraffe-handled silver spoon and fork.

I was giddy with relief. We took our time, chatting about the day, as we heated up and ate the leftover eggs, pancakes, and bacon, time no longer noticeable, or cruel, now that our stand-off was over. Then I took her and the *Frozen* book into my bed, just like I always did at home when she—or I—needed some extra attention.

She fell asleep almost immediately. I stared at her doll-like face for a few minutes, then carried her to her room, sliding her little body into the embroidered sheets.

Kissing her curls, I whispered, "I'm only tough on you because I love you so very, very much. And I know that you can handle it."

Later, after I had showered and there was still no sign of Alex, I tiptoed around in my bare feet looking for him. I was about to go up and find the mystery pool in the sky, when I noticed damp footprints on the hardwood. They led to Sam's room.

In the dim glow of the night-light, I could make out Alex's face, and glimpsed in his profile both the young man he had been and the old man he would become. When he moved to look at me, the images blended into the Alex of today.

I walked in and stood beside him. "She finally caved," I whispered. "She set the table. Even apologized for not listening."

He didn't respond, his eyes locked on the baby in the crib.

"Is everything okay?"

"Yeah." His voice was choppy and guttural, as if he was trying not to cry. *So he* does *have emotions.*

"Is it Van? Alex, he's fine," I assured him. "The hospital wouldn't have released him otherwise."

He nodded and swallowed but didn't move. Finally, he spoke. "It's not that."

"What?"

"I just want our kids to be happy."

"Oh, Alex. They are happy. Gloria's just stubborn. And have you met our son? He's literally the happiest kid on the planet." I grinned at him, but he ignored me, his eyes still fixed on Sam.

"For now, maybe."

I started to respond, but stopped. I let him continue.

"I just want them to be the people they really want to be."

"They will be. I'm sure of it." Though deep down, I wasn't.

"Remember all these plans we had? How we were going to be different than our parents? Look at us. I'm never around. You're never around…and somehow we seem to be doing all the things we said we weren't going to."

"Like what?"

He turned to me and rolled his eyes. "C'mon, Abbey." He gestured at our surroundings.

I lifted my hand off his shoulder and gazed around the room. I guess all of *this* wasn't in the plan. I guess we were supposed to be in New Orleans or in West Philly or Guatemala or somewhere. Building schools or putting bad guys away or just living a simpler kind of life. Looking good and doing well, but not this good, not this well. And perhaps not standing on the bow of this Titanic congressional campaign we had no idea how to slow down.

Even after just seven days in this world, I knew exactly what he meant. The fancy clothes. The fancier apartment. The spas, the lunches, the organic juice cleanses. The fund-raisers, the publicity, the political ascent. It was like a movie I'd seen again and again. So well plotted. So expected.

Alex took one last look at Sam and left the room.

That night, as we slipped into the crisp, cold sheets, we didn't touch or speak, the heavy silence broken only by the drapes moving slowly on their hidden track. They ground toward each other, stopping just before they crashed, leaving only darkness.

CHAPTER ELEVEN

On Sunday morning, the van Holts piled yet again into the Suburban. But this time, we weren't heading to a campaign event—we were going to church.

I was still worried about Sam, so I kept him near me and washed his hands every chance I could. Though I had to admit he seemed his regular perky self, gobbling down his usual trucker's breakfast of waffle, eggs, toast, avocado, and strawberries before chasing his screeching sister from room to room.

Also waking perky that morning was Alex. As soon as I heard him stir, he snuggled up to me and brushed his lips against my hair. He slid his arms around my stomach, which I instinctively sucked in before remembering I didn't have to. I knew what he wanted, even before I felt his hard-on straining against his thin pajamas. But I wasn't in the mood, so I ignored him and got up out of bed. He groaned in annoyance but was distracted by a ringing phone. Luckily, calls from Frank started early.

I thought we would be worshipping at one of the Waspy old churches near Rittenhouse Square, or perhaps the stately historic Saint Christopher's in Old City, but instead Oscar drove northwest, toward the art museum. We passed the wide ochre steps that Rocky made famous and wove our way up Kelly Drive along the Schuylkill River, past bikers, rowers, and dog walkers enjoying the quiet, misty morning.

We drove a few more miles, before Oscar slowed the car and cut a sharp right, up a hill lined with colonial-era row homes and wide-windowed corner stores struggling to stay upright on the steep slope. We were in the village of East Falls, a storied neighborhood where Grace Kelly had been born, though now out of fashion and mostly forgotten, housing only the most loyal "Fallsers." It was an old area, once the highest point overlooking the river, where early settlers traded with Native Americans. But in recent decades it had struggled as young families moved over the hill to Roxborough or farther down the river to hipper Manayunk.

But now, according to a recent *Philadelphia Magazine* article, things were changing. A group of young African American families had moved in and were attempting to invigorate the area. They established a neighborhood watch, began pumping money into the local elementary school, installed a tot-lot playground, and even launched the first annual East Falls Arts & Music Festival last June. Their hope was to turn East Falls back to what it had been centuries ago: a safe yet eclectic village for families looking to escape the harried pace and high prices of Center City.

At the top of the hill, Oscar pulled up in front of a previously abandoned Quaker meetinghouse that was now East Falls Baptist, the de facto hub of the community. Members of the congregation were lining up to enter the small red doors, and we joined them. Leaving the house this morning I felt a bit overdressed, but now I was glad I decided on the exquisite Jil Sander suit, its pale taupe wool as graceful as the whitewashed church I was entering. I fit in perfectly with the ladies in their long dresses and belted coats, some with matching wide-brimmed hats, and the men with their equally formal suits and polished shoes. It was a far cry from Annunciation Catholic Church in Grange Hill that the Laheys frequented (infrequently). There, the only parishioners who dressed up were the families with children to christen. Even the priest wore jeans under his vestments.

Inside, we squeezed into the narrow pews, me first, then the kids, with Alex taking a seat by the aisle. Though it was not every Sunday that a young white family joined the congregation, only a few people glanced over at us, most keeping their curiosity in check.

The pastor was about Alex's age, and just as handsome and well dressed, but instead of a full head of hair, he was bald, his smooth black skin gleaming in the light from the tall windows. He sat on the maroon-carpeted steps that led to the pulpit as the worshippers took their seats. Eventually he stood, clipped a small lavaliere microphone to his navy lapel, and welcomed everyone with a hearty "God is good!" The congregation immediately quieted and concentrated, except for Sam, who, within one minute, began to climb all over me, bored. I struggled to keep him quiet with some snacks from my bag, but he yelped and whined while Alex looked over, annoyed.

After some announcements, a trio of teenage musicians began to play a gold-and-black drum set, an electric guitar, and a shiny trumpet, and the choir began to sing. They were so loud, nothing short of a siren could be heard over them. Later, too, when the pastor began his sermon, his forceful tenor drowned out Sam's whimpers and Gloria's whispers, along with everything else.

The pastor was no older than forty, but his demeanor was one of experience and assurance. And though his tone was powerful, it was also melodic, casting a spell over the congregation. His effect was similar to the one Alex had over people, but with an added intensity, more urgency. I found it funny that when he came to the crescendo of his sermon, he also took off his suit coat and rolled up his sleeves.

When I read his name in the program—William Wallace—I

smiled to myself. William Wallace was the peasant turned knight who fought and died for Scottish freedom in the 1300s. Though to most, he was probably better known as the character portrayed by Mel Gibson in *Braveheart*. Jimmy's favorite movie.

He—and therefore I—had seen it at least twenty times. It also happened to be the catalyst for a huge fight we'd had last spring. It was the type of fight that comes around in marriages every few years; the one where you say too much, go too far.

I had just gotten home from a business trip: a two-night hand-holding junket to DC with Maxim Pest. Normally, I didn't travel with clients, but Max DiSabatino was being honored as Pest Professional of the Year, and I had to be there to help him with his speech, take photos, and coordinate media interviews. Charlotte had insisted on coming along as well, and she had nitpicked and second-guessed and talked over me the entire time. She had also stolen my female thunder with her tight skirts and glossy lips.

I stepped into the house after three twelve-hour days and a two-hour-delayed train ride and found the house in tragic disarray. Half-eaten dinners sat on the crumb-coated table; the kids' shoes and socks littered the floor; and the dog's food and water bowls were empty. I ran to the bathroom to pee and found no toilet paper, the laundry bin overloaded, and so much smeared aqua toothpaste in the sink it looked like a Smurf murder/suicide.

Jimmy was in the living room sprawled across the couch drinking a beer, watching *Braveheart* for the umpteenth time. Scottish lords fought valiantly for their birthrights and professed love in the face of gruesome torture, but here in our living room, the only movement was Jimmy's arm as he lifted and lowered his beer bottle.

"Hello," I said to him.

"Hey," he said, eyes glued to the television as he muttered the obligatory: "How was your trip?"

"Awesome," I said with a thick frosting of sarcasm, then turned on my heel, returned to the kitchen, and started shoving dirty dishes into the dishwasher.

Jimmy came in a few minutes later.

"What did I do this time?" he asked with a loud sigh.

"More like what you didn't do," I muttered under my breath.

"What?" he asked. "I'm sorry. I didn't quite hear that."

I stopped with a crusty plate in midair and turned to him. "Were you waiting for me to get home so I could clean all this up? Or did you not notice that it looks like a bomb went off in here?"

"Are you kidding me? What do you think I've been doing for three days while you were gone? Taking care of the kids, cooking, shuttling them around, cleaning up after them, and all that other shit. God forbid I sit down for a minute."

"But that's just the thing, Jimmy," I said, turning off the water. "I *never* sit down. Ever. When was the last time you saw me sitting around, drinking beer, watching a movie while the house looked like it was hit by a fucking tornado?"

"You can't have it both ways, Abbey," he said. "I can't work all day and all night too."

"Why not?" I replied. "I do."

And then, before I could catch the words, I added something I knew would wound—"Someone's got to."

All these months, I had never spoken of our financial situation, or how Jimmy's reduced client list was affecting our lifestyle. I tried to be positive, promising him it would turn around, that things would improve. I knew that for any small business owner, watching hard-won clients leave would be tough enough, but for Jimmy it was agony. I also knew that he was this close to losing his business entirely, and soon he would have to go back to working for someone else, maybe even take an office job.

I knew all this, understanding it was the sorest of sore subjects and thus should have been off-limits. But I was exhausted and angry, and at that moment I wanted to hit below the belt.

Like my ratty cashmere sweater, I was worn thin, and I couldn't keep on pretending. I had watched my once ambitious and positive husband become lost and unhappy, unable to accept the reality of the situation or do anything to stave off the pile of second notices that had grown even taller in my absence.

"Someone's got to?" He repeated my words back to me, but his were filled with pain, not just anger.

"Forget it," I said.

"Oh no, Abbey. You're so smart; you've got everything all figured out. Please, enlighten me. Please, Miss Perfect, tell me all the ways I'm failing you."

"I'm not perfect; I just try harder!" I screamed. "I try harder with work! I try harder with the house! I try harder with the kids! You phone it in half the time."

"Well, maybe you should try a little less," he said as he glared at me. "I didn't sign up for a lifetime of not measuring up. God, you can be such a … such a … *bitch*." That last word came a second later than the rest, as if he knew that he, too, was crossing a line.

I stood motionless, feeling the sting. Jimmy's voice softened, turned sullen and defensive. "And I don't phone it in," he said. "Everything I do, I do for you and the kids. Everything."

"Except earn a fucking paycheck."

He walked over to me, and for a second, I thought he was going to hit me. But instead, he took the dirty plate out of my hand and flung it against the wall, where it exploded, sending white shards and tomato sauce everywhere. Then he walked past me and out the back door, flinging the screen door open so hard it popped off one of its hinges.

"Great," I shouted after him. "Another thing for me to take care of!"

My ears were ringing and my heart pumping hard. But as I calmed down and my anger drained like the outgoing tide, what was left was despair.

I sat there for twenty minutes, until my tears were used up and my body was drained and limp. By then, my rage had turned to guilt and my guilt to hopelessness. I knew we had unleashed the resentment that had been gnawing inside both of us for months, maybe years.

Thinking about it now, my memories underscored by the sounds of the choir and a man of God preaching forgiveness, I wondered when it was in our marriage that Jimmy and I stopped working together and instead started working beside each other. When it was that we lost the push and pull and began to only push.

And when exactly our concern for each other had turned to contempt.

After the service at East Falls Baptist concluded, we stood in line with the other families to shake hands with Pastor Wallace and the church elders. As the line moved and we neared them, I saw Wallace eye Alex with interest.

"Brother van Holt," he called. "What brings you all the way to East Falls this morning? Don't they have God in Rittenhouse Square?"

"I thought I'd come out and see for myself why so many people like it out here," Alex said with a grin. "I hear they have some preacher who's really stirring things up. Got a real fire in his belly. In fact, maybe he should be the one running for Congress."

"Maybe so, maybe so," Wallace said slowly, thinking it over. He leaned closer to Alex and continued: "But I've got more than fire in my belly. I've got a hunger. So do a lot of folks out here. Hunger for something better. Hunger for what you got, Mr. van Holt."

"I know," said Alex. "And I think they'll get what they want. What you want." And then, almost in a whisper: "What we both want."

"I hope that's true," Wallace whispered back.

"I'm certainly trying my best."

"Well, then, God bless you," he said, a smile breaking across his face. "And God bless your lovely family. We hope to see you back sometime. Even after November fourth."

Wallace shook hands with Alex, smiled at the kids and me, then turned to the next group. I walked in silence, wondering what had just happened.

In the Suburban, I tried to put the pieces together when Alex called Frank with updates. It was something about a new tech company—named Ariel, like the Disney princess—moving their headquarters to Philadelphia. Wallace hoped the company would buy one of the old warehouses along the river, bringing hundreds of tech jobs to his community, not to mention new customers for the area's restaurants, shops, and apartment buildings.

The whole coded conversation with Wallace was political: Alex would sway Ariel to East Falls and Wallace would ensure his four thousand or so congregants made it to the polls. Seemed like perfectly normal political bargaining to me, but I also wondered if my husband would really have that kind of influence over a commercial business from another state. He wasn't even a congressman—yet.

When Alex dropped his phone and leaned back, I asked him about it. "Do you really think you can get Ariel to move here?"

"Maybe."

"You don't seem so sure."

"Well, it's not that. It's just that Jonathan Brindle might have something to say about the matter."

Mr. Brindle from the cocktail party? The one whose wife didn't know the Eagles? Why would they care? I stared at the river, so low and still from lack of rain, trying to understand.

Unless...They were the same Brindles as the Brindle Department Store on Market Street, the very same building where I worked when I was just out of college. Where I first met Alex. And the same building that had been slowly losing occupancy since their flagship tenant, Philadelphia First, moved to the Cira Centre in 2007. I knew that because I still sometimes had lunch with my old bosses, Sharon and Barbara, and they told me their building was like a ghost town.

Suddenly it dawned on me. "Do the Brindles want Ariel for their building?"

"Of course," he said. "Why else would he give me one hundred thousand dollars for my campaign?"

One hundred thousand dollars? That was a lot of money, even for the Brindles. Even for a godparent. The car quieted as it stopped at a traffic light, the only sound Sam chewing on his stuffed giraffe. Alex turned to me and spoke in a low voice: "Don't judge me, Abbey. I feel sick about it. But there is nothing I can do."

"Sure you can. You cannot give in to the Brindles. They'll find other tenants. Their building is in Center City. But East Falls really *needs* this."

Alex turned angry. "Why do you care all of a sudden? You certainly didn't feel bad about East Falls last week when you were in the Brindles' box at the symphony. Or when we borrowed their private plane to go to Vail."

I realized then that I, too, was culpable in this mess.

"Seriously, Abbey," said Alex, repentant. "You know I don't like this. I'd rather it go to East Falls too. But I never promised Wallace it was a done deal. I only said I'd *try*." He sighed and cocked his head, then added, "And you know what they say: 'Don't hate the playa...hate the game.'"

He seemed to expect me to laugh, but I just stared at him. Once again, he was joking his way out of an uncomfortable situation.

"It's Jay Z," he explained. Then he rapped the line again.

I continued to stare, cringing inside. He smiled and corrected himself: "Oh, that's right. It's Ice T. I always forget now that he's on *Law and Order*—"

"Whatever, Alex; that is not what's important. Quit trying to change the subject!"

I touched his arm, not willing to let the conversation end, but the car arrived at the apartment and Oscar ran around and opened my door, the kids' and my cue to get out. As I watched him drive away, I thought about what other false promises he might feel the need to make.

I walked the kids into the wide, elegant lobby of our building, past the uniformed doorman, smiling and courteous even on a Sunday, and I realized that for Alex, at least in part, this campaign *was* a game. For rich folks like him—and now me—things like economic development and tax hikes and gas prices were just talking points. Losing out on Ariel, and the jobs that could transform William Wallace's neighborhood for good, would have no effect whatsoever on our quality of life or that of our friends. It was just one of many spins in this colorful game of political Life.

And even though Alex professed he couldn't do anything about it, I couldn't help but think he could. The real truth? He just couldn't be bothered.

As for me, I couldn't get William Wallace out of my mind. I knew Alex thought it was only a sin of omission, but I could see it for what it really was—lying. He wasn't trying to get William Wallace what he wanted; he darn well knew which way the chips would fall. But I did believe him when he told me he felt bad about it, and that gave me some comfort.

Up in the apartment, I turned on lights and some music to try to make the monotone space more fun and, as a special treat, figured I'd order the kids some pizzas. I searched for take-out menus but, finding none, called down to the front desk for suggestions. They obliged, and after double-checking that the place would take credit cards, I ordered two larges: a meat-lovers supreme for Sam and a plain for Gloria and me.

I turned to tell her, then jumped, not knowing she was behind me. All day, she had clung to me like a little shadow.

"They are going to bring the pizza here?" she asked, confused.

"Yeah, that's how it works," I told her, surprised that the van Holts had never ordered pizza before.

"That's so cool! Is it coming now?"

"They have to make it first. But it should be here in thirty minutes or less. Or we get it free."

"How long has it been?"

"Thirty seconds. So twenty-nine minutes and thirty seconds to go. Twenty-nine. Twenty-eight..." Her eyes flew open in excitement; then she turned and ran into the family room to find the computer and its clock. She sat staring at it until finally, with just seconds to spare, the intercom system buzzed, letting us know someone was coming up. Gloria grabbed Sam and they ran out the apartment door toward the elevator.

When it opened, Gloria cheered. "You made it with one minute to spare!"

He laughed, handed us the pizzas, and, more graciously than he should have, accepted a tip of three dollars in change. (Tomorrow morning I would *have* to get this bank card situation sorted out.)

After a hearty lunch, and Sam in a sausage-induced snooze, I returned to put away the leftover pizza. I then sat down in front of the computer to check my e-mails. There were still none from Roberta, so I e-mailed her again.

Then I started to compose an e-mail to Jules. First, I tried inviting her to the animal rescue benefit next week. (Since it was "BYOP"—bring your own pet—there was a chance she would come.) But when I imagined her surrounded by society types and their little shih tzus, I reconsidered. I tried a peppy lunch invite but deleted it with a sigh. I composed a chatty e-mail about the kids, but that, too, seemed fake. Finally, I settled on just three words in the subject line: "I miss you." I hit "send" and watched it take off toward her in-box with a *whoosh* and a silent prayer.

I then checked the *Philadelphia Inquirer* for election news. There was none, but my eye did catch a Larry Liebman story on city worker pensions. I pictured her typing away or on the phone, the closest Philly would ever get to having its own Lois Lane.

Gloria walked in carrying a red T-shirt and black leggings, wanting to play "pizza deliverer." I laughed as I pulled off her church clothes and helped her slip on her "uniform." As I pulled up her pants, I noticed her underwear had little mermaids all over it. Little Ariels, to be exact.

Ariel. Larry. *Inquirer.*

An idea began to form.

I finished helping Gloria, even tying back her hair and drawing on a little mustache, and watched her run off to deliver the two empty pizza boxes around the apartment. Then I turned back to my computer, anxious to learn more about Ariel.com. Apparently, the company offered a traveling Wi-Fi device that worked all over the world and was one of last year's hottest American tech firms. It was named not for *The Little Mermaid* but for Ariel Morganstern, the company's founder, who just happened to be a University of Pennsylvania graduate, class of 1998. Same as Alex. So that's how he would use his influence. He and Ariel were friends. And the Brindles knew it.

I went back to the *Inquirer*'s home page and searched for Ariel .com, sure that some reporter would be tracking the developments. But strangely, there was nothing about Ariel or Morganstern. Not one mention.

It would seem that the deal would be negotiated over the phone, at private dinners, and behind closed doors. And the press wouldn't know about it until the deal was signed. Unless…

I opened up Gmail and set up the most anonymous e-mail account I could think of: "johnsmith65@gmail.com." Then, using the new address, I typed a message: "Did you know Ariel.com is looking to move their headquarters to Philly, specifically East Falls? Could mean great things for the community. Find William Wallace at the Baptist church for details." I signed it: "A concerned citizen."

I then addressed it to lliebman@philadelphiainquirer.com.

If Larry bit, and I was pretty sure she would, the headline alone could get everyone in this city thinking Ariel and East Falls. Then if the Brindles subsequently made their own play for the lease, they'd look unsporting, trying to woo away jobs from a black preacher trying to build a community. Rather than risk the bad press, or the fight, they would most likely back down and maybe not even bid at all. But more important, Alex could face the Brindles with a clear conscience, himself having no idea who'd tipped off the *Inquirer*. A win-win for all.

God, I loved it when public relations actually worked for the public. I hit "send."

Feeling a surge of energy, I turned my attention to the apartment. May had been gone only twenty-four hours but already the place was a mess. How had she ever cleaned this place *and* watched the kids *and* cooked those elaborate meals? I felt myself getting angry again, especially when I pictured Mirabelle's smug face, and began shoving dishes in the dishwasher in a fury. When I saw Gloria slink into the family room and click on the television, I barked at her.

"Not so fast, hot stuff."

"What, Mommy?"

"I need your help."

"But I *always* watch cartoons while Van's napping."

"I don't care. I need your help. We have work to do."

"What do you mean 'work'?"

"Chores."

Her eyes widened. "You mean together? You and me?"

"Yep. You and me."

She put down the remote and ran over, excited. I kneeled down and grabbed her hands.

"Hey, GloWorm," I said in my super-duper mommy voice. "Think you could drive a vacuum?"

Her eyes grew even wider and her mouth dropped, as if I had just offered her a ride on Space Mountain.

"Really?"

"Really," I said. "But first you'll have to show me where it is."

And so, the world's first millionaire mother-daughter cleaning service got to work, starting with the master suite in an effort to not wake the baby. I wiped counters, watered plants, folded towels, scrubbed the toilet, sprayed down the shower, and shoved dirty clothes and towels into tall hampers. Gloria followed behind me with the Dyson, and even though it was taller than she was, she didn't do a half-bad job.

I was gathering some of Alex's clothes in the bedroom closet when something that slipped out of a pair of dress pants caught my eye.

Scribbled on a crumpled cocktail napkin was the name "Jennifer." And a phone number. I stared at the white square, slowly beginning to comprehend. I then checked the rest of his clothes and the trash and came up with two more notes and three business cards, all from women. One even included a pink lipstick kiss. Really?

My confusion turned to fury. The thought of all these women propositioning Alex—even *thinking* he could be theirs—was maddening. I was tempted to call every number and announce that Alexander van Holt was a happily married man who adored his wife and two small children.

It was admittedly some small consolation that the cards and notes were left in pockets or in the trash, discarded or absentmindedly forgotten. But still it gave me pause: How long would he be able to resist these women? Especially if he won the election and spent long weeks in DC without me? And what about before…had he ever succumbed? Just *how* happily married was my husband?

These were questions any reasonably aware married woman could answer. But of course, most women had known their husbands for longer than seven days.

Gloria walked in and announced that her brother was up. Together, we went to retrieve him, enlisting his help for our next challenge, the living room. Sensing Gloria was losing interest, I tied Swiffers to her and Sam's feet with rubber bands and handed them each a feather duster. As they skated around the floors giggling, I tried to join in on the fun, but my mind kept rereading the tawdry notes.

I moved to the windows and looked down at the sidewalks below. As Alex traversed the city, jumping for event to event, did he pass any restaurants or bars or a park bench—our "special spots"—and think of me? When he saw young children, did he miss us and long to be home? Was he still "in love" with me?

And did he ever feel jealousy—like I was feeling now? It was a strange emotion, and one that left me scared and vulnerable. A feeling I'd *never* felt with Jimmy. Not once.

"Mama," said a tiny voice from below. It was Sam, already wanting a snack.

I walked to the kitchen pantry and scanned the shelves for something easy. I reached down for some crackers, and in a corner, I saw a Drexel University tote bag stuffed with books and clothes—May's. I carried it to the kitchen and plopped it down on the large island.

Inside was a blue sweatshirt, a pair of black plastic sunglasses, an umbrella, some diapers, a notebook, some highlighters, and a sippy cup. Also two textbooks, one on biology and one a review of American literature from 1920 to 1968. I stared at it and felt a rush of guilt. In getting Sam to the hospital, she must have left her things. And now was too scared or mad to retrieve them.

Gloria ran into the kitchen, demanding to know what was taking so long. I shoved the books back in the bag, and before she could say anything else, I grabbed her by the shoulders and spun her around toward the door.

"Get your shoes on," I told her. "We're going out."

It was the second time the taxicab passed the same antiques store. And the third time it passed the old man walking the beagle in an argyle sweater. And the umpteenth time we bounced along the uneven bricks along Jewelers Row.

"Are you sure it's this street?" I asked my daughter again. "Maybe it's one farther that way?"

I pointed south toward Washington Square, but she just shook her head and continued to scan the streetscape. I was beginning to think Gloria was just toying with me, and that despite her loud avowals otherwise, she had no idea where May lived.

"I know it has lots of shops," she said, her brow crinkling in concentration. "And signs like that one." She pointed to a pink neon scrawl: "We Buy Gold."

Shops and signs. Well, that narrowed it down to just about every city street on the East Coast.

We had spent the last thirty minutes driving around under Gloria's direction. The Russian taxi driver seemed confused but not especially irritated; I think he was enjoying the hunt as much as Gloria. Me, not so much. I was losing patience. And feeling carsick. I told the cabbie to pull over.

"Think, Gloria. What else is on the street? A restaurant? Or a park? It's very important. Only you can find her."

And we had to find her. So we could return her bag and textbooks. But mostly so I could apologize for her unfair and abrupt dismissal. Especially since I suspected she knew I was the one to blame for leaving the candy out.

Gloria tilted her head to one side. "What do I get if I tell you?"

"You get to continue living in our home rent-free," I told her. "How's that sound?"

Her eyes turned serious, not sure if I really meant it, but also not sure if it was a risk worth taking. She scrunched her brows, the same way I do when I'm really trying to remember, and finally blurted out one word: "Lambs!"

"Huh?"

"There are lambs there," she said, proudly.

"Like at Bloemveld?"

"No, dead ones."

Dead sheep? I struggled to translate the clue into something meaningful.

"And cheeses, Mommy. Big cheeses."

The cabbie turned around in his seat and said something in a thick accent.

"Excuse me?"

"The Italian Market," he said louder. "She means the Italian Market."

Gloria smiled, then high-fived the driver through the open Plexiglas divider. Then we all braced ourselves as he put the car in drive and screeched off toward South Philly.

Just one block south of the famous Ninth Street Italian Market, where they sold everything from vegetables to spices to sausages and—*yes!*—lambs, Gloria had found May's building. It was a turn-of-the-century leather goods factory converted into six floors of apartments, the authentic version of the factory turned lofts that attracted yuppies elsewhere in the city. It was quiet and dark save for a few signs of life: weekly grocery circulars, a padlocked bicycle, and a stack of delivery boxes from Amazon.com.

Once again, I had to rely on a five-year-old to direct us. But this time Gloria had no trouble, bounding up the five flights of stairs with confidence as I struggled to keep up with Sam in my arms. On the sixth floor, she stopped by a metal door with two pairs of shoes lined up outside, grinning and proud that she had finally solved the case. And obviously eager to see her beloved May. Her small fist turned pink as she knocked and knocked.

After reaching her and catching my breath, I pulled Gloria's hand down in time to hear May's voice call out a Thai greeting.

"May, it's Abbey," I said through the door. "Van Holt."

Silence. I tried again. "May?"

Finally: "What do you want?"

"I have your bag."

No response.

"You left it at our place. Your textbooks and clothes and stuff."

"Just leave it outside."

Sam and Gloria looked up at me with confused, puppy-dog eyes, not understanding why they could hear May but not see her. For their sake, I tried again.

"Look. May, I know you are upset with me. But could you just say hi to the kids? They miss you so much already."

The dead bolt clanked open and the door swung inward. May appeared in a close-fitting T-shirt, a long black cardigan, and army green cargo pants, with her hair long and loose. In these clothes, she looked so different, and I realized she was close to my age, maybe even younger. She knelt down and the kids ran into her arms, almost knocking her over. As she held them, laughing, the door swung shut, leaving me alone in the hall. I expected her to open it back up, but she didn't. Man, she was mad.

A few minutes later, she stepped out with Sam on her hip and Gloria's hand in hers. She didn't look at me, but I could tell she was near tears. As she hugged them good-bye one last time, trying to be cheerful, I almost couldn't watch.

May's hold over them was magical, almost primal. Just like a mother's. As I watched my children cling to her, a colorful jumble in the drab hallway, I thought I would feel jealous. But I didn't.

I realized then that I had been judging Abbey van Holt for having a nanny, for outsourcing the work of mothering, when what I should have been thinking was how lucky the children were to have someone else to love them. Especially someone like May, who had no preconceived ideas of what being a van Holt meant and just let them be kids.

And May's reward? Being fired for something she didn't do. I felt helpless. Worse—like the villain in a Dickens novel. The evil employer who brings ruin to a well-intentioned innocent. I had to do something.

"May, I realized that we never gave you any severance." I whipped out my checkbook, ready to write a check with a lot of zeros. But when I saw "Mr. and Mrs. Alexander van Holt" at the top of the check, I paused. When she deposited this, Alex would know. And he was quite clear on the subject of May. In his mind, her carelessness nearly killed his son.

I shoved the checkbook back in my purse. "Funny! I'm out of checks. I'll have to send you one later. Or I'll just bring you cash. Tomorrow. Actually, maybe not tomorrow. Later this week."

"I don't want your money," she said flatly.

"A recommendation, then? I am happy to write one—"

My words were cut off by the slam of her door, leaving me open-mouthed and stunned in the cold hallway.

As the dust swirled and then settled again, I realized what she wanted. The truth.

I grabbed each child by the hand, moved toward May's doorway, and started shouting through the heavy door. "May, listen to me. It wasn't your fault. It...it was mine. I should have been more careful. And I should have admitted it to Mirabelle. And fought for you."

I paused and leaned my head against the cold metal. "The truth is...I was scared."

There was no response, no sound. Even the children were still and quiet, staring at me. Their sea blue eyes were wide and anxious, as if to say *Please, Mommy. Please, make this right.*

I knew I had to. But as I turned to leave, guiding a shell-shocked Gloria and a bewildered Sam down the stairs, I realized I didn't have any idea how.

CHAPTER TWELVE

Meeting Collier van Holt, I didn't understand why everyone was so nervous about him. He seemed harmless and sweet and slightly confused, and I liked him immediately.

He was shorter and stouter than Alex, and his thinning hair was wispy and silver, combed gently over his smooth, tanned head. He wore a caramel-colored suit with a subtle navy pinstripe, a smooth light blue dress shirt, and polished brown shoes. He had an elegant but lost look about him, like a nobleman from another era flung into the modern world of skinny lattes and keyless entries.

He seemed especially awkward among his own family, almost shy, as if these people were strangers, not his flesh and blood. When his hands were not in his pockets or holding a glass, they shook.

"Abigail," he said warmly, as we entered the mahogany-paneled library, the same room where just one week ago I sat with Father Fergie before downing a few dog biscuits. "How are you, my dear? Mother tells me you had a little accident."

I gave him a hug and a peck on the cheek, and he seemed taken aback—but pleased. Gloria and Sam ran up and began circling and clawing, playing a game only the three of them knew. He feigned surprise as the kids found two peppermints hidden in his coat pocket.

"Careful, my little lobsters," he whispered to them as he helped unwrap the cellophane. "If Grandmère sees the candy, she'll be cross with me for spoiling your dinner."

At the mention of Mirabelle, Collier glanced toward the kitchen nervously, then headed toward the bar to fix himself a drink.

Mirabelle burst into the room in a cloud of creamy silk, gardenia perfume, and mock exasperation. Her spotless outfit was topped with an equally spotless black apron with the words "Kiss the Cook" embroidered across the front. *You're not fooling anyone, lady,* I thought. Behind that door were at least three hired helpers; the only thing Mirabelle would be cooking up tonight was opinions.

"Finally," she said as she saw us, throwing up her arms for emphasis, as if we were hours late, not fifteen minutes. She walked straight to Alex for an embrace, and then went through the motions of air-kissing me before dropping on one knee to greet Gloria and Sam.

"It's going to be a while. Your *father* wanted steak, so Cook had to go back out," she instructed Alex. She whispered the word "father" as if there was some question as to Alex's parentage, and she avoided looking in the old man's direction.

Next she was beside me, signaling she wished to speak privately. "So, my dear, how is our boy?"

"He's fine. Slept well, ate a good breakfast. Drank lots of milk per doctor's orders."

"No, I don't mean Van. Alex."

"Oh. He's fine. Why?"

"Well, I heard he skipped the Ed Rendell dinner last night."

"His son was in the hospital, Mirabelle. Of course he skipped it."

"But there's only two more days. Alex just doesn't seem himself… I can't tell if he's just exhausted or distracted. Something."

I had a feeling her "concern" was about me, not Alex or the campaign. This woman's instincts were too good. She knew something was off, but she couldn't figure it out. And it was killing her. I smiled inside, knowing little old Abbey Lahey knew something she didn't.

"Really? I hadn't noticed," I told her, watching her eager expression drop.

She pretended to hear a noise in the kitchen, and then turned on her heel, annoyed. I'm not sure if anyone else felt it, but the room seemed to sigh with relief, suddenly warmer, when she disappeared back through the swinging door.

Collier walked over to Alex and extended his hand as if greeting a business associate. "Son," he said. "I hear it's been a tough race but you're standing your ground. Within six points I hear."

"Six and a half," Alex corrected.

Unbelievably, this was all they said to each other. Each of them retreated to different sides of the room, Alex returning his attention to his phone, Collier to his single-malt scotch. I wiped the sticky drool off Sam's chin and walked back over to the older man.

"You're right," I said quietly. "Alex is making great headway. He could actually pull this off."

"I like your attitude." He smiled and nodded his head. "Positive thinking."

"It's more than positive thinking. You should see how people respond to him. They can't get enough."

"He always was such a charming boy. Smart too. Nothing like his old man."

"I'm not so sure about that," I said with a wink.

"Well, his mother is," he said, swirling the last of his drink and gulping it down. "And around here, that's all that matters." He paused, then added, "Surely you know that by now, Abigail."

I smiled at him, then looked down, unsure of what to say. It was apparent that for whatever reason, this man wasn't welcome in his own home, and I was taking a risk fraternizing with the enemy. I stepped away to pick up the kids' discarded boots and coats off the wool rug.

I pulled out some Matchbox cars from my boxy Prada purse and ushered Sam toward the hardwood. Gloria was banging out "Chopsticks" on the Steinway in the corner, her tentative, clanging tune adding to the uncomfortable vibe of the room.

And my sister-in-law Aubyn's arrival moments later didn't improve it. She came in dressed in a black velvet coat, riding pants, and boots, with her hair in a low ponytail. Her face was makeup-free and pale, her bright blue eyes the only pop of color. She ignored all the adults, scanning the room. Eventually her eyes fixed on Gloria, peeking out from the piano.

"*Tu veux voir les moutons?*" she asked her.

"*Oui!*" shouted Gloria, hopping up with a clang and running toward her aunt. Then, remembering, she turned back and asked, "Is it okay, Mommy?"

"*Oui,*" I said, though I had no idea what I was agreeing to.

Aubyn and Gloria left hand in hand. When their voices grew more distant and some faraway doors slammed, I realized they might be heading outside. I grabbed Gloria's forgotten jacket and headed after them. Though it had not begun to rain, the skies were ominous.

Glancing back to Sam before I left the room, I saw Collier awkwardly bouncing him on his knee while Alex watched from a corner. I guessed Collier would watch Sam; Alex would watch Collier.

When I reached the wide front hall, I didn't know which direction

Aubyn and Gloria had taken or which of the three doors they had exited through. Then I remembered the dark stairwell from my first night here, and headed toward it. I was right; when I opened the door, I heard the faint sounds of riding boots and little-girl chatter.

Descending the worn stairs carefully, I found myself in a dim corridor lit by bare bulbs, the air several degrees colder than the floor above. The walls were rough-hewn brick and the wood floorboards soft beneath my feet. Beside me on the wall was a modern gray fuse box hung next to a dusty wooden case of brass bells, like the kind I'd seen on *Masterpiece Theatre* to summon servants. Two of the bells were tilted, hanging askew in anticipation, whoever triggered them still waiting for that cup of tea, those shined shoes.

The rest of the hallway revealed more contrasts of old and new. One room held antique furniture, a locked case of long shotguns, old fishing equipment, and dented, dusty steamer trunks, as well as outdoor heating lamps, sports equipment, and gold-tone party chairs stacked to the ceiling. Another held bikes, skis, and sleds, all relics from Alex's childhood, plus an old Victrola, its lily-shaped amplifier tarnished and silent. The last room was the largest, and as I stepped inside, I noticed it still smelled faintly of soot and cooking grease. Shelves lined both walls, and on some stood crockery and jars, while others housed only empty hooks and cobwebs. Long, rough-hewn tables were pushed into a corner along with a giant barrel with "B.V." stenciled on its side. I stepped closer and saw a date etched into the worn wood—1883.

I tried to imagine this gloomy space bustling with servants filling soup tureens for a formal dinner or roasting turkeys for a fox-hunting party. I would have loved to see Bloemveld as it would have been a hundred years ago, with the people and animals and commotion that give a house like this purpose. I could not imagine growing up here—then or now.

At the end of the basement hallway was another flight of servants' stairs. As I climbed them and emerged outside, I saw Aubyn and Gloria slowly making their way up the hill in the distance. Two of Aubyn's three wolfhounds trotted ahead of them.

As I started after them, my heels sinking with each step, I watched my daughter and her aunt intently. With her niece, Aubyn seemed more relaxed, almost jovial. At one point, they both climbed and jumped over a low stone wall, Aubyn seeing Gloria over safely and then hopping over with a laugh. Then they both disappeared over the hill.

I picked up my pace, curious to see where they were headed and where this vast estate ended. After awkwardly managing the same low wall, I saw a gray stone barn, a stable, a fenced pasture, and several pebbled paths leading in different directions. And dotting the hillside were what they must have come for—sheep.

Gloria ran toward them with a little squeal of joy. I gasped as she threw her arms around the largest one, which stood motionless as she snuggled into its yellow-beige neck. Aubyn watched her and smiled, then began to feed a lamb something from her pocket. A Canadian goose took off from a shallow pond and the dogs ran after it. The scene was bucolic and beautiful, as if that hallway had transported us magically—like a Narnia wardrobe—from suburban Philadelphia to the English countryside.

"Gloria forgot her jacket," I called as I got within earshot. Aubyn looked up and eyed my clumsy, heel-sinking approach with cynical amusement. Finally reaching Gloria, I helped her put on her jacket.

Just then two chestnut mares emerged from a patch of trees and came trotting over. Gloria ran toward the smaller one and I limped after her, ready to throw myself between her and the beast if necessary.

"Careful, love bug," I told her, wary of the animals' long legs and heavy hooves.

But Gloria reached up and rubbed the horse's neck with ease. I relaxed.

"She's just waiting for Gloria, whenever you say the word," said Aubyn, wiping her hands on her khaki-colored riding pants and walking over.

"Waiting?"

"You told me you didn't want Gloria riding yet."

"Right. I guess you think she's ready?"

"She's *been* ready. Even though she's small, she can do it. Petal will know who's boss."

Wow, I thought. *Someone in the van Holt family who actually understands my daughter.* I was about to speak when Gloria interrupted.

"Mommy, please, please, please…" She hopped up and down. "I can do it. I know I can."

Both Aubyn and Gloria looked at me with matching blue eyes, wide with anticipation. How could I say no? But I also wasn't sure. Gloria might have inherited a love of equines from her aunt, but she was only five. And so small.

"Not just yet, GloWorm," I told her.

Gloria's smile faded and she ran off toward the dogs in a huff. Aubyn looked away, her face taut with anger.

"Of course," she said under her breath.

"Excuse me?"

She lifted her head. "Do you really think I'd let her do something dangerous? You're only saying 'no' because I bought her the horse."

I was so tired of these van Holts dictating what was best for my children. I stared at her and told her, "You're not her mother. I am."

"Yeah, you're mother of the year."

She said it under her breath, but I caught it. My heartbeat doubled up and my face burned.

"What did you say?" I hissed.

"Nothing."

"How dare you? You don't know anything about me."

"I know enough. You and your liquid lunches and your spending sprees and your constant complaining. My brother deserves better."

Her words hung in the air, then reached like little fog hands to choke me. I gasped for breath as the quiet evening turned into a hurricane in my head.

"You van Holts," I seethed. "You think you know everything, don't you?"

"All I know is that you were supposed to be different," she sneered. "But you're just like all the rest."

Then, again under her breath: "You're just like my mother."

The freight train in my head drowned out all sound. I stomped over to her, about to do I don't know what, when I slipped on the sloping wet grass, landing on my side with a painful thud, then rolling a few yards down the hill. I tried getting up, but the slick grass became slicker with each attempt and several sheep trotted over, their black faces and feet nudging me all over.

Aubyn walked over and tried to shoo the sheep away. As she got closer, I saw that she was smirking, biting her lip to keep from laughing. Her derision fueled my rage. All the stress and worry and angst of the past week—hell, the past decade—came together into a little ball of fury in my gut. I looked at her glossy hair and cold eyes and they reminded me of my old boss Charlotte. I did something I had wanted to do for a long time, to both of them.

She extended her hand to help me up, but I grabbed it and pulled her down hard. She landed beside me in the wet grass in surprise, a high-pitched yelp stark against the low grunts of the farm animals. I felt her hand hit my chest with a thump as she pushed me. I pushed her back, then pushed her facedown in the mud.

We tussled in the grass like little boys in the schoolyard, rolling even farther down the hill into a muddy puddle. The herd followed us and with their hooves and fur all around us, we had to separate from each other or be trampled. We then made comical attempts to stand, slipping and falling on the mud like sled dogs on ice.

By the time we were upright, dripping and disgusting, Gloria had run down between us, her hot pink jacket stark against the green grass and darkening sky.

Oblivious to what had just happened, or not caring, she asked again about the horse.

Neither Aubyn nor I spoke as we tried to sneak back into the house unnoticed. Our clothes and hair were peppered with mud and grass, our faces flushed with anger and exertion. We tiptoed across the black-and-white tile and almost made it to the stairs. But Gloria ran ahead of us into the library and announced, "Mommy and Auntie Aubyn had a fight!"

I guess she *had* seen it. I really was mother of the year.

One after the other, Alex, Mirabelle, a wobbly Sam, and a wobblier Collier came rushing into the hall.

"What happened?" asked Alex, confused.

"Girls, what took you so—" added Mirabelle, stopping mid-sentence when she saw us.

Only Collier seemed amused, asking, "Is that sheep shit I smell?"

Aubyn and I stood there like naughty schoolchildren, me in a disheveled dress and ruined heels in hand, my sister-in-law with springy, wild hair over dirty velvet. Sam toddled over, but I didn't dare pick him up.

"We slipped in the mud," I said.

"The grass was wet," added Aubyn.

Mirabelle cut her off before we could continue our truth stretching.

"Now what am I supposed to do?" she said, her eyes flashing with anger. "Dinner has already been plated."

"Give us five minutes to change," Aubyn said. "Abbey can borrow something of mine."

Aubyn took a step up the stairs but stopped when Mirabelle began again: "Honestly, Aubyn. You and your animals. I swear you do this on purpose."

"You think I fell on purpose? Thank you for your concern, Mother."

I felt relief, and both surprised and grateful that Mirabelle was focusing her ire on Aubyn, not me. Still, I barely breathed, hoping not to attract attention.

"What if Kipper were here?" continued Mirabelle. "What would he think?"

"I can assure you he wouldn't care," said Aubyn defiantly.

"You think he wants a wife who smells like a barnyard all the time?"

Maybe he does, I thought. From what I could see at the Ballantine Ball, Aubyn had her fiancé pretty well trained—a russet-haired spaniel nipping at his mistress's black patent heels.

"It's just so disappointing," continued Mirabelle, woundingly. "As usual."

My eyes flew wide with disbelief. The words weren't directed at me, but I felt the blow. I hoped Aubyn would throw a verbal counterpunch, as I certainly knew she was able, but her tone turned quiet, demure.

"I was just taking Gloria to see the sheep," she whispered. Her face was that of a little girl who had been scolded.

My anger turned to pity. I couldn't help but feel sorry for her. My mother and I had certainly had our disagreements, but I always knew that no matter what, she was proud of me. That she always considered me her greatest achievement, never a "disappointment."

Against my better judgment, I moved out of the shadow of the stairs and spoke up: "It was my fault. I was wearing these silly shoes and Aubyn was just trying to help me up. You know what a klutz I've been lately."

Mirabelle's withering gaze turned to me. But before she had a chance to speak, I blurted, "Don't hold dinner. We'll be back in five minutes," then pushed Aubyn the rest of the way up the stairs.

Out of the corner of my eye as we turned on the first landing, I saw Mirabelle sigh, throw up her hands, and then turn and march toward the smell of roasting meat.

Upstairs, in Aubyn's Wedgwood blue bedroom, I stood beside the tall, pineapple-topped four-poster bed as she disappeared into a closet. It was neat and tidy, but there were enough shoes, books, and power cords lying around to tell me she still lived here full-time. There were also enough red and blue ribbons and gleaming silver cups to indicate horseback riding wasn't Aubyn's hobby, but her vocation. I thought it odd that this dazzling array of silver plate was hidden in her room and not displayed downstairs alongside Alex's lacrosse trophies and law school diploma. Even the giant cup marked "USEF National Dressage Championships: First Place," so big Sam could have bathed in it, was on the floor, half-filled with leather gloves and headbands.

Aubyn returned from the closet and handed me a blouse and some black capris.

"You can change in there," she said, pointing to the bathroom. I took the clothes and walked past her.

"Wait a minute," she said with a gasp.

"What?"

"Don't move!" she said. "You have something in your hair. Some, uh, poop. From the sheep."

"Aaaaah!" I whined, flipping my hair back and forth as if a bee were attacking me.

"Stop! You'll get it everywhere." She pushed me toward the bathroom. "Just go in there and I'll help you."

At her mercy, I obeyed. She draped a towel around my shoulders and instructed me to lean over the wide oval sink. She then began to rinse the offending substance from my blonde strands with her bare hands.

A few minutes later, as if she had been working up the courage, she said, "Thank you."

"For what?"

"For stepping in down there."

"You're welcome."

"Honestly, I didn't know you had it in you."

"Neither did I." We both laughed.

"Reminded me of the time you told Mirabelle I was with you when really I was out with, well...you know."

No, I didn't. But I was certainly intrigued. Me covering for an illicit tryst of Aubyn's? Did we used to be closer? Seemed unlikely we were ever best friends, but perhaps there was a time when we weren't pushing each other down into the mud, either literally or figuratively.

"Aubyn?"

"Yes?"

"If you really think Gloria can handle that horse, I'm all right with her riding. As long as she wears a helmet. And you stay with her every second. And no hills. Or jumps."

"Really? Are you sure?"

In the mirror, I saw her smile. She looked so much like Alex.

"I promise I won't take my eyes off her. I would never let anything happen to that little girl."

"I know."

Now it was her turn for apologies. "I'm sorry about what I said earlier about Alex. It's just that..." Her voice trailed off.

"Just what?"

She hesitated, mistrust warring with something else—hope?—in her eyes. I leaned back down over the sink and told her, "Go on. I want to know. Please."

"It's just that, in the beginning, you were so different from the girls he used to bring home. You lived in the city and you had your own job, your own money. You saw Green Day at the Tower. And the first time you came to dinner here, you wore *jeans*."

I knew she meant it as a compliment, but I cringed inside. Mira-belle must have been aghast.

"Well, that proves it. I can't be *all* bad." I said it as a joke, though inside I was dead serious and hoping she'd keep talking. My neck hurt but I didn't dare move.

Her voice turned quiet, pensive. "Alex would have never taken that DA job if it weren't for you. And he never would have gone to New Orleans. It still cracks me up to think about the day you guys told Mother you were moving down there."

In the mirror, I saw her stand up straighter and imitate Mirabelle, complete with raised eyebrows and hand clutching heart: " '*My* son is going to live in the Lower Ninth Ward and work pro bono? I won't have it!' I swear, she almost spontaneously combusted."

She laughed, but then her tone turned more somber: "Seeing him get away from her, if only for a little while, made me feel like I could do it too. Maybe if Dad hadn't gotten worse…" She gave a sad shrug, suddenly looking older than her years.

Then, almost to herself, she added, "I have to give it to her, though. Now everything is back just the way she wants it."

In the mirror, our bodies were motionless for a moment, her words hitting home: for me, the realization that Mirabelle's pull was stronger than I thought, and for her, another reminder of how unhappy she was.

"We better get going," she said, remembering dinner.

"Are you sure you got it all? I can't be in the same room with your mother with you-know-what in my hair."

"You're fine, I swear," she said. "Besides, she can't smell anything over that horrible perfume she soaks herself in."

We looked at each other again and cracked up.

I changed into the borrowed clothes; then we marched downstairs, falling in line, one behind the other, like soldiers.

Back downstairs, the meal was under way, with Collier holding court at the head, in the middle of a rambling story. Aubyn and I took seats on either side of him, while Alex and Gloria flanked Mirabelle at the opposite end, and Sam split the difference between Alex and me. The table was so large I had to strain to reach my son, who was strapped into a carved wooden high chair with a wicker seat, a tiny white tablecloth over the tray. I pulled the contraption closer to me, scooped some bright green peas into his mouth, then tried to catch up to the conversation.

"I said to him," Collier boomed, "I want that filly for twenty grand, not a penny more! She had the most beautiful natural gait I have ever seen, but she'd also ruptured her left tendon at some point. And they knew it, and they knew I knew it." I noticed that Collier's tone and demeanor, fueled by alcohol, had coarsened.

He took another big sip of his drink and put it down with a thump. It hit harder than he expected, sloshing golden brown liquid onto the white tablecloth. He continued, eyes on Alex: "But I got her for twenty grand. Wrote the check and took her home. Your old man might not know much, but he knows horses!"

Alex was silent, his face downcast, so Aubyn responded. "Yes, Father. You know horses."

Collier rattled his now empty glass to get the attention of a passing server. The woman put down the soup tureen she was carrying and went to take the glass—but froze as Mirabelle shot her a warning look. Collier cleared his throat and rattled his ice again. The poor woman stood there, afraid to move, caught in the cross fire of the van Holts' opposing glares—Collier's sodden, Mirabelle's stern.

Alex finally spoke. "Don't you think you've had enough, Dad?"

"What?" Collier's head snapped around. "What did you say, boy?"

Alex waved the server away, then attempted to reason with his father: "It's just that you're monopolizing the conversation."

"Don't start with me," he slurred. "This is still *my* house. My great-grandfather built it, *goddammit.*"

"Calm down, Collier," Mirabelle interjected. "And watch your language." She nodded toward the kids.

Collier's watery gaze slid from Alex to his wife. His voice rose an octave as he addressed her with mock solicitousness: "I don't need to watch my language in my own home, *darling.*" After a brief pause to peer into his empty glass with longing, he continued, his tone antagonizing: "If my son has something to say, let him say it *to me.* You're always jumping in to fight his battles."

"Hush," she hissed. "I do no such thing."

"Ha! It's a wonder he ever learned to tie his own shoes."

I stopped chewing, not wanting to miss a word. This was getting good.

"Christ, I remember when he was eight and he begged and begged you to let him play Little League. But no, baseball wouldn't do. He had to do crew or lacrosse or some such bullshit."

"I *said* watch your language," shouted Mirabelle, her voice uncharacteristically loud and shrill.

Collier leaned back in his chair with a grin, enjoying watching his wife lose her cool.

"Shit, the only thing the boy has ever done without your approval is marry this one." He jerked his head in my direction.

"Dad!" shouted Alex. The old man jumped from the sound, and, in an instant, his expression changed from preening to remorseful. He looked at me. "Abbey, I'm sorry...," he whispered. "I didn't mean that."

Of course, I had already guessed I probably wasn't Mirabelle's first choice for Alex. She would have chosen someone born from a better bloodline, educated at boarding schools, clothed in one hundred percent cotton, and able to navigate awkward situations like these with ease. But even so, it stung.

Normally, I would make a joke or offer a snappy retort, but after a week with the van Holts, I knew what was expected. I acted like I didn't hear the remark and pretended to wipe invisible peas from Sam's mouth.

The old man started to stand up, but his chair wouldn't slide on the thick Oriental. It rocked backward, almost taking him with it, before he righted himself on the table with his swollen red hands. A knife and fork flew upward, sending meat juice across the table. He attempted to wipe it up, then gave up and let his napkin flutter to the floor.

He shuffled toward the sideboard, then stumbled into it, sending the ice bucket down with an incredibly loud crash and a scattering of ice. Unbelievably, everyone remained seated and continued eating, undeterred, though Gloria followed her grandfather with wide eyes.

"Luis!" Mirabelle called toward the kitchen door. "Luis!"

In walked a dark-eyed, honey-skinned man in sneakers, red track pants, and a black T-shirt, with headphones snaking around his neck. As he strolled slowly toward the old man, I saw a full sleeve of tattoos on one arm and a techy-looking wristwatch/thermometer on the other.

"Party's over, *papi*," he said gently. "Let's take a walk, you and me."

Collier looked up and shrugged off the younger man's arm. He clenched his glass with a death grip and put his hand on the crystal decanter, all the while cursing under his breath. But as the young man continued to speak, his words audible only to Collier, the old man's agitation subsided. He let Luis take the glass, and his expression turned from combative to remorseful.

"Luis, the ice...," he blubbered. "The ice is everywhere."

"It's okay, *papi*," soothed Luis. "But let's go, maybe take a rest."

And holding on to Collier's arm, he guided the family patriarch toward the large paneled doors that led to the foyer.

Before the two men disappeared entirely, Collier grabbed the doorjamb and turned back to us: "I'm sorry, Mother. So sorry," he said quietly to his wife.

Mirabelle pretended not to hear, just picked up her fork and resumed eating. The room fell silent, the only sounds those of her utensils as she dissected and downed her bloodred steak. After a few moments, she dabbed the corner of her mouth with a starched linen napkin and looked up at us all with a smile.

"Now!" she said brightly. "Who's ready for dessert?"

CHAPTER THIRTEEN

Once again, I found myself on the floor of the closet, but this time not in postcoital bliss. Once again, I was looking for that *goddamn* earring.

The night before, as she'd walked us out, Mirabelle asked me to return the diamond earrings that belonged to her mother. Turned out a cousin who was getting married the following month wanted to wear them. When I sent the children out to stay with her on Election Day, would I be so kind as to send them out as well? If that wasn't too much trouble?

It was as if that woman had a sixth sense for my screw-ups. Wearing the wrong shoes, feeding Sam the candy, and now losing half of a family heirloom that was probably worth more than the vehicle we were climbing into. I told her, "Of course," lying through my teeth in front of Alex, Gloria, and Sam.

But this morning, after combing the halls, the seats of the Suburban and every inch of the apartment on my hands and knees, I still couldn't find it. Father Fergie was wrong: Things don't always eventually "turn up"; some things are lost forever. Alex found me head down and ass up on the closet floor, giving it one last attempt, even though I knew it was fruitless.

"Hey, doll," he said, returning from his morning run. "What are you doing?"

"Looking for something," I told him, sitting up and separating the hanging clothes so I could see him.

"What?"

"A piece of jewelry."

"Not anything expensive, I hope?"

I paused, unsure. I could have told him the truth—even asked for his help—but I was scared to put any more stress on him. Tomorrow was Election Day.

"No, nothing important." I stood up and brushed the carpet fibers and stowaway sequins off my pajamas.

He leaned against the dressing room island and smiled a roguish grin. "Are you ready for this?" he asked, pulling me toward him and lifting me with ease. My heart began to beat faster as I felt his body against mine, still warm from his run. God he was sexy, even when sweaty.

"Now? Okay," I said. "We have to be quick, though. I've got to get Gloria to school." I slid my hands down into his silky workout shorts.

"Whoa," he said, laughing, then dropping me to the carpet. "Tempting, but that's not what I meant. I have news."

"Sorry. What?"

"CNN called. They want to do a story on me, on us, today. They'll be here in an hour. Something about 'the continuing van Holt political dynasty.' I guess somehow they think I'm a national story." He rolled his eyes.

"Oh my God!" I said, wide-eyed. "That's huge! And perfect timing. All those undecided voters. What do you need me to do?"

"For starters, you can get your hands out of my pants."

* * *

The cameras, cables, and lights, as well as a small army of producers and cameramen and assistants, crowded into our apartment, making the huge space seem small. Earlier, before any of the CNN crew had arrived, Frank and Calvin had rearranged the furniture and taken down some of the more expensive-looking art, attempting to tone down the opulence to something more ordinary. But there was no escaping it; the place looked like an interior designer's wet dream. Eventually, Frank agreed we would sit on one of the beige couches, but he made me replace the funky Jonathan Adler pillows with plain blue ones from the guest bed. He also replaced the stone-and-silver Buddha heads with potted plants and strategically scattered Sam's toys in the background.

The crew needed more time linking up with the satellite, so we took the kids to find refuge in our bathroom. Alex reviewed some notes while Gloria modeled the outfit she deemed perfect for her television debut: a hot pink sweater, hot pink leggings, and matching sparkly shoes. I had started to suggest a more subdued color palette but she shut me up with a sharp little-girl glance. Sam, however, looked appropriately adorable in his toddler jeans, red-and-blue sweater, and leather booties. Meanwhile, I stressed over my hair and makeup, wishing the Bacco Brothers had been available for an emergency styling. Eventually I settled on the "safest" outfit I could find: a pale pink tweed suit with a double strand of gray pearls.

"Now, remember," I told Alex as he paced behind me. "If they ask you something about military service, just be open and direct—not defensive. And if they want to know your position on fracking, don't take the bait, just speak to 'energy independence' in general."

"Thanks, doll, but I'm good. Frank's already been over this."

"Well, with all due respect, Frank was a newspaperman, not TV.

And besides, he's old school. It's different now. Any screw-up will be on YouTube in thirty seconds."

"Well, someone had their coffee this morning." Then he leaned over in my face, blocking my view: "Do I have any food in my teeth?"

"I'm serious, Alex. You have to be ready. CNN is national. And today is the day before the election."

"I know. I *am* taking it seriously. I just mean, well, you haven't worked in, like, ten years."

I put down my hairbrush and turned to him. "Well, funny you should mention that, because I've been thinking—"

"Uh-oh," he said, turning toward me with faux worry.

"I'm serious. Now that the campaign is almost over, maybe it's time for me to go back to work."

I couldn't quite believe I had just uttered those words...that I was actually considering stepping back into the hectic life of a working mother. But even after just a week, I missed having something of my own. Something that didn't involve my husband or children. I studied his face, anxious for his reaction.

He certainly seemed to be giving it serious consideration, his brow furrowed, deep in thought. Encouraged, I continued: "I was thinking I might get back into PR. Maybe reteam with Jules part-time or just do some consulting. Only with nonprofits or women's groups. Something that helps people, makes a difference."

He was silent a few more minutes and then looked at me.

"Why would you do that?" he asked. "You're my wife."

"What?"

"You're my wife," he repeated.

I waited for him to elaborate, but he turned his attention back to his teeth.

"Alex," I said, touching his arm to get his attention. "Wife is a title, not a job."

"It is when you're married to me," he said with a grin.

He laughed as if he were joking, reverting to his favorite method of avoiding tough topics. But this time, something told me this wasn't just avoidance; there was truth behind the words. Or if not his truth, then Mirabelle's. Her opinions seemed to permeate all the big moments in the van Holts' life like her overly sweet perfume. Me stuffing press kits and calling reporters and billing time by the hour while my husband toiled in service to his country? It. Just. Wasn't. Done.

He walked over to me and patted me on the butt before adding, "But don't get me wrong. You sure look cute talking PR."

I watched him check his large platinum Rolex, adjust his cuffs, then walk out of the bathroom, a tiny bit of swagger in his step.

Don't hate the playa... hate the game, I reminded myself.

"Mr. van Holt?" repeated Bailey Phillips, the pretty blond reporter sent by CNN. "Mr. van Holt? Do you understand the question?"

I couldn't believe it. My confident, charismatic, and cool-headed husband was freezing up on national television. When the lights had come on and the reporter first began the interview, Alex had seemed stiff, but I brushed this off to him just warming up. But now, four questions in, I realized something was wrong. He was responding with one- or two-word answers, and sweat had begun to bead on his temple. Behind the cameras, Frank and Calvin wore matching expressions of worry.

The stress of the campaign, the pressure to perform, the eighteen-hour days, not to mention last night's dinner, must have finally caught up to Alex. He was cracking. But why? He had done hundreds of television interviews by now. Perhaps it was because this was CNN and the piece would play nationally? Or maybe the kids and I were distracting? Or perhaps the reporter had thrown him for a loop: winking and laughing ahead of time, then hitting him with one tough question after another once the red camera light blinked on. For a second, I was secretly relieved to see he had a weakness, and that it wasn't me who was screwing up. But then I saw the look of a frightened child on his face, and I felt a sudden protective impulse to rescue him.

I had to do something. But what? This was live television. I put my hand on his, hoping to steady him. It was ice-cold.

The next question was about gun control, a subject Alex usually spoke on with eloquence and confidence. But he continued to blow it, badly. Bailey must have felt sorry for him, because next she lobbed a softball about the economy, but he started rambling incoherently about the price of milk. I looked to Frank and Calvin for guidance, but they both stood motionless with mouths agape.

It was up to me to save this sinking ship.

"I think what my husband is trying to say," I blurted, cutting in, "is that everyone deserves a chance to succeed and make a better life for their kids. And government has the responsibility to help working families when they need it."

I smiled widely, hoping it was enough. But I could feel Alex as still as a statue beside me. Bailey, who seemed relieved that at least someone was speaking, turned to me: "Mrs. van Holt, I understand you had a little accident earlier this week? Are you feeling better?"

"Yes, thank you. I'm fine. It was just a little fall. And my husband took great care of me."

"Quite the Prince Charming, isn't he?" She crossed her legs and turned to him with a look that was not hard to decipher. She was hot for him.

Um, hello? I'm the wife and I'm sitting right here. Beside his two little kids, thank you very much! The only benefit of Alex being so comatose was that he probably wasn't registering her long legs and bedroom eyes.

Thinking not only of this woman, but of all the women who thought it okay to hand my husband their phone numbers, I decided to mark my territory, once and for all. I responded with a gentle laugh and slid my arm around Alex. "Oh, he is. Such a wonderful husband and father. A wonderful man." I gazed over at him, lovestruck, then added, "I live quite the fairy tale." What she couldn't see was me digging my nails into his back, trying anything to get him to *wake the fuck up*.

It worked. As I turned back to Bailey with a painted-on smile, I heard Alex start talking. He was back.

And not just back—he was in the groove. He fielded Bailey's remaining questions with ease, even cutting her off at one point to finish his thought on Cuban American relations, and concluding with a moving anecdote about foster care. Later, Gloria provided the icing on the cake, informing the reporter that her daddy made "the best waffles ever." And even Sam played his part, sitting quietly on my lap and tooting only once, silently.

By the time the interview concluded, Frank was so giddy he hugged me.

"Thank you," he whispered in my ear. "I don't know what happened to Alex but you saved him."

"No problem. But I hope I didn't sound like too much of a jerk. All that 'fairy tale' stuff."

"No, no. It was great. Nice to see a woman standing by her man." He meant it as a compliment but I cringed. I was officially a Stepford wife.

And yet, as I watched the crew and the camera equipment trundle out of the apartment, keeping a sharp eye on Bailey as she attempted—*but failed!*—to corner Alex, I was pleased that I'd said what I'd said and saved the interview. For the first time in this world, I felt like a part of it, not just an accessory. I picked Sam up and tickled his belly, whispering to him that his daddy had a real shot at becoming a congressman and that we all might live part-time in Georgetown, visit the Air and Space Museum, ride bikes along the Potomac, and have lunch together on Capitol Hill.

When Alex mouthed "thank you" at me from across the room, I felt another strong emotion—happiness. I was settling into life here, and it wasn't altogether bad. I had my children, everything money could buy, a distracted yet doting husband, and I was *this close* to becoming the wife of a congressman. Abbey Lahey and her out-of-work husband, stacks of bills, and bulging muffin top were becoming more distant, further away.

For the first time in a week, I allowed myself to feel excited about the future, even if it wasn't really mine.

That last time I remembered feeling this happy—truly happy—was five months ago when Gloria, Sam, and I took Jimmy skating for his thirty-seventh birthday. He loved to skate, but lately, with business pressures overwhelming him, he didn't have much free time and was rarely in the mood. I browbeat him into going, hoping it would give him a respite from worry, if only for a few hours.

It was June and already excruciatingly hot in Grange Hill. The Skatium parking lot was so full we had had to park at the church across the street and run across Darby Road. It was just enough exercise to develop a sheen of sweat that turned cold on our faces when we stepped inside the rink.

Jimmy slipped into his fifteen-year-old skates and immediately hit the ice while the rest of us lined up at the sagging, blade-battered counter for rentals. Gloria bemoaned that her skates were brown, not white, though Sam seemed happy with his beat-to-hell double-bladed baby skates. I squished six feet into unforgiving brown leather, tightened twelve long red laces, and adjusted Sam's helmet before leading my wobbly brood across the worn, wet carpet to the rink.

On the ice, the Laheys became different people. Behind his big plastic skate helper, Sam glided weightlessly while Gloria raced and roughhoused with her dad like an NHL pro. Even I relaxed, my perpetually tense shoulders falling and my head bobbing to the music. I enjoyed the cool air, the sound of my kids' laughter, and watching our teenage babysitter try to impress the rink guard with a half loop. And, as always, I loved to watch Jimmy skate; it reminded me of when we were young and falling in love.

We stayed on the ice for about an hour before heading to the snack bar for a break. I had texted some of Jimmy's buddies and they had stopped by as well, those who didn't skate keeping the bartender busy pouring drafts and analyzing point spreads. As the kids found friends to chase, Jimmy and I talked and joked with his high school buddies. I could see my husband turn back to the more relaxed, easygoing Jimmy from years ago, feigning protest at the birthday fuss but secretly loving the camaraderie and free beer. I was glad he was happy, especially since the next morning would mean negative balance sheets and begging for business.

When the hockey leagues came in at seven thirty, we said our good-byes and made our way back to the car. I drove home and Jimmy turned around to regale Gloria with tales of skating on real ponds, not rinks, while Sam snored in his car seat. Back at the house, Jimmy carried Sam up to his crib while I directed Gloria to the bathroom and then to her room for pajamas, reminding her it was a school night. She protested and I raised my voice, but when she tried to belabor bedtime with just one more birthday kiss for Daddy, I said it was okay.

Once they were finally asleep, Jimmy and I snuggled in the hammock on the front porch, watching the sun set beyond the oak trees across the street. A lone butterfly, out late and hurrying home, flittered over us.

"I can't believe how well the kids did today," I said, thinking about Gloria and Sam in their skates.

"They get it from their old man," joked Jimmy. "Definitely not from you."

"I'm not that bad. But yes, they get it from you. And yes, you are an 'old man.'"

"How many old men can still do this?" he asked, setting the hammock rocking as he humped my leg.

"Sexy," I said, rolling my eyes.

He laughed and stopped moving, his face golden in the setting sun. He took my hand, raised it to his mouth, and kissed it. *Now, that is sexy,* I thought. We swung for a few more minutes, silent and content, watching the evening turn darker.

We began to kiss, slowly at first and then more urgently. He moved his hand down the front of my shirt, over my stomach and to my hips. I rolled closer, giving him better access to my body. His hands found my jeans and unsnapped them, and he slid his hand inside as he whispered in my ear. I let myself enjoy the pleasure that was building, and the naughtiness of being outdoors.

Turned on, and forgetting the motion-sensor light by the door, I rolled on top of him—then froze as the spotlight came on, illuminating us in eight hundred watts. We remained motionless for fifteen seconds, our hearts beating loudly as we waited like scared teenagers for the light to switch off.

When it did, I reached down and, very slowly, stroked him over his jeans. When he was hard, I carefully unbuckled his belt and loosened the zipper, reaching inside. We both started to breathe deeply, both wanting release, but knowing any quick move might set off the light again. It was delicious agony, the threat of exposure restricting our movements to sexy centimeters.

After a few more minutes, Jimmy couldn't take it anymore.

"Oh God," he moaned, then stood up and twisted around.

As he stood up, his pants dropped to his ankles and the spotlight snapped back on, illuminating his lower half for all the neighbors to see. I had a view of the back side; any passersby were getting the X-rated version.

Beyond caring, he lifted me from the hammock and carried me into the house like a new bride—which wasn't easy given that his pants were tangled around his ankles. I was laughing so hard my shoulders shook.

But Jimmy wasn't laughing; his expression was all business.

Once inside, he kicked shut the door, laid me on the floor, and finished the job.

The CNN crew was long gone, Alex was off shaking hands at a diner, Oscar had run Gloria back to school, and an exhausted Sam was crashed out in his crib. The van Holt apartment was quiet again. It was also unusually dark, even at midday, as gray clouds blew in and settled over Rittenhouse Square, creating a warm, cozy feeling inside the softly lit apartment.

I did something I hadn't done in almost ten years—took a nap. Stretching out on the wide couch in the family room, I covered myself with a cashmere throw and fell asleep, dreaming of my childhood, of days spent at our neighborhood pool under Roberta's sort-of-watchful gaze.

"Stay where I can see you," she yelled between puffs of a menthol cigarette. She rarely got in the water, preferring to bake in the sun for hours with the other ladies banished to the "single mom" area.

To trick her, I would dive low and swim to the deep end, emerging far away from where she was watching.

"Here I am," I'd call to her, relishing her look of panic before she spotted me at the far end.

I was still floating in that pool, enjoying my weightless body and the sounds of children splashing, when a lifeguard signaled the start of Adult Swim. His whistle blended into a ring and I woke up. It was my iPhone. I answered, still groggy.

"Turn on CNN," barked Alex. "Now!"

"Okay, okay," I said, fumbling for the remote.

I clicked on the TV, already set to the right channel. But instead of Anderson Cooper, it was my face filling the screen. I saw myself sitting beside Alex in the living room, smiling like a constipated 1950s housewife while the words "Like a fairy tale" appeared underneath us.

"Oh my God," I whispered as I listened to my voice coming through the TV. "I'm so sorry, I was just trying to—"

"Are you kidding? Frank is over the moon," he said, cutting me off. "He says voters love happy couples. Thinks it will really help." Then dolefully, he added, "It looks more and more like this thing has a chance of breaking our way."

"Doesn't sound like you are too happy about that."

"I am. I guess it's just dawning on me. I could end up being a congressman."

"Yeah, you could," I said sarcastically.

"Well, there's still another day to get through," he said. "Which reminds me, I need some shirts for tomorrow. I'm out."

"Okay. What do you need?"

"I like those ones you got before. The blue ones."

"Sure," I repeated. "I'll pick some up this afternoon." I made a mental note to check the tags on the dirty shirts in his hamper.

"Thanks, doll."

"No problem."

"And, Abbey," he said, his voice sobering. "Thanks again for saving my ass today. I love you."

I started to say "I love you" back, almost as a reflex, but the words caught in my throat.

Did I love him? I certainly liked him. A lot. And he seemed to genuinely care about the kids and me. But despite living with him, campaigning with him, surviving our child's near-fatal health crisis, and twice having "marital relations," I still felt I barely knew him; I didn't really know what made him tick.

I guess the bigger question was, "*Could* I love him?" Because if that was a possibility, even just an early inkling, then I could say the words back now—like practicing for a future feeling—and they wouldn't be a lie. Or quite as big a betrayal.

For now, I decided on a more diplomatic response: "Me too."

"You sure?" he said, confused by the long wait time, but laughing. I laughed too.

I also sensed that now, with him in a good mood and my stock high, was a good time to unburden myself of my secret.

"Alex, I have to tell you something," I said. "Something you need to know."

"What did you do?" he teased. "Buy another bag?"

"No, nothing like that," I warbled, my throat constricting. It was time to fess up.

"What then?"

"I lost one of your mother's diamond earrings. The ones that were made special for your grandmother. It was the night of the Ballantine Ball and I've looked everywhere and, well, it's gone. And I feel sick about it."

"I know," he said nonchalantly. "I have it."

"What?"

"It's in my shaving kit in the bathroom," he said. "I was trying to teach you a lesson. So you'd learn to take care of nice things."

"What?" I said again.

"Gotta run, doll," he said. And then the line went dead.

CHAPTER FOURTEEN

I didn't know what was wrong with me. I should have been relieved. The earring wasn't lost after all. Now I could send it out to Mirabelle and forget it. Instead, I kept replaying his words—*I was trying to teach you a lesson ... so you'd learn to take care of nice things*—over and over in my mind. How dare he?

I was desperate to get out of the apartment and clear my head, to find a quiet place where I could think. But I was due to attend an important "afternoon tea" at an auction house and couldn't back out now. Frank was counting on me to work the influential, all-female crowd and hopefully turn the fifty or so Friends of Lafayette into friends of Alex van Holt.

After leaving her ample instructions and practically frisking her for nuts, I left Sunita—our college campaigner turned temporary babysitter—in charge of Sam and Gloria. She seemed capable enough and Sam was already in love with her long black hair and high-pitched giggle. I knew Gloria would be equally excited for a new babysitter whom she could con into treats, unlimited Nickelodeon, and lip gloss.

Downstairs, Oscar was waiting with the door open, so I crossed the windy sidewalk quickly and slid inside, my pink bouclé suit bright against the black leather of the backseat. As we pulled out into the midday traffic, I wondered how long this afternoon tea would last. I also wondered if they would have any real food. I had been too distracted by the interview, then too upset over my phone call with Alex, to eat anything. I was starving.

At the end of our block, Oscar turned right, immediately took the next right, then stopped. I leaned forward and looked to the sidewalk in disbelief. I could have walked faster.

"Thanks for nothing," I told Oscar as he opened the door.

"Sorry?"

"Just a joke," I said. "Obviously not a good one. But seriously, I won't need a ride back. I can just walk."

"Are you sure?" he said.

"I can walk two blocks," I told him. "I have run a marathon, after all." I wasn't sure if that was true, but Oscar didn't blink.

"Okay," he said. "But call me if you need me."

"Just get Gloria from school and bring her up to Sunita."

"And Mr. van Holt?"

"What about him?"

"Will Mr. van Holt be needing me?"

"I have no idea," I said. *And I don't really care,* I thought.

A city bus honked, sending Oscar jogging back around to the driver's side. He pulled away, leaving me in front of a windowless concrete building, its fortress-like appearance made even more menacing by two large bronze sconces flanking a deep-set wooden door. A tiny brass sign announced the "T. Th. Davis Auction House" in a small, ornate font, warning any passersby against casual inquiries. Whatever treasures were inside, they would be bought and sold by a few Philadelphia families, priceless objects moving from one mansion to the next with a casual flick of a paper paddle.

Inside the cool, dark foyer, a willowy blonde in black glasses stepped out of the most recent J.Crew catalogue to greet me.

"Mrs. van Holt! So good to see you again. Mr. Davis was sorry to miss you, but he and Mrs. Davis are in Vienna looking at silver. But he hopes he might arrange for a private showing of our new Alice Neel next month."

"That would be lovely," I told her, though the thought of next month hung heavy in my mind.

"May I take your jacket?"

"No, thank you, it's pretty chilly in here."

"I know. We keep it cold because of the art. That's why I *only* wear cashmere." *Of course you do,* I thought. *God forbid any man-made fabric touch that perfect skin.* I forced a smile, though, as if we were members of the same obnoxious club.

She motioned for me to follow her down a long hallway, and we walked briskly, passing a medley of animal paintings (horses, sheep, and owls), bucolic landscapes, framed coins, threadbare tapestries, and a faded American flag with the stars embroidered in a circle, not rows. Finally, Miss J.Crew paused in front of two oak doors and swung one open.

"Here they are," she sang, then turned on her low heel and disappeared.

The main gallery space was dotted with round tables set with delicate white china and bowls of purple irises. A large antique mirror reflected light from six low-hanging brass chandeliers. Farther away was a raised dais with a wooden podium, a few chairs, and a "Friends of Lafayette" banner.

Wealthy women of all ages stood in pairs or trios, their bright dresses and shoes reminding me of a fruit basket spilled on its side. Only two women were sitting, a silver-haired matron in a stiff gray suit and her caregiver, a young black woman in large silver hoops and a purple velour sweat suit. Under the table the caregiver held the older woman's frail hand, a silent act of kindness drowned out by idle chatter and tinkling glasses.

I lingered near the entrance, in no mood to be sociable, and hoping to remain inconspicuous. But apparently this was impossible for Abbey van Holt, and within fifteen seconds of my arrival I was spotted. "Abbey!" a voice called, and next thing I knew, I was surrounded.

Luckily, their questions—"How are you?" "Is the beach house finished?" "Are you just exhausted?" "How's Alex holding up?"— were pretty easy to answer, and if they weren't, I ignored them and turned the tables with my own questions: "How's the family?" "Where'd you get that sweater?" "Do you know anywhere I can get a good facial?"

I was pretending to be aghast at one woman's description of a recent hotel stay—*Just imagine, no room service!*—when I felt a tap on my shoulder. I turned around to find Alex's high school friend Larry, standing with an older woman whose ebony skin contrasted with the tropical-colored fabric twisted around her head and body, the Haitian version of a power suit.

"Hi, Abbey," she said. "I thought that was you."

"Yep. It's me," I said. "Having some tea with the ladies."

"You mean you don't do this every afternoon?"

"Actually I don't really like tea. I only drink it at night. When I'm trying not to eat Oreos." I tried to sound down-to-earth. For some reason, I wanted her to like me.

She laughed but then stopped when her mother cut her off.

"Lawrencia," said the older lady, the Caribbean lilt in her voice so bewitching. *"S'il vous plaît nous présenter."*

"Sorry, Mother," she said, sheepish. "This is Abbey van Holt. Alex's wife."

I shook her hand while she looked me up and down, taking me in like an artist examining a potential model. She must not have liked what she saw, because as I attempted to ask her if she still painted, she excused herself and floated off toward a group of ladies nearer her age. Larry and I stood awkwardly at first, but then we started in on some small talk, which, thanks to her, turned into the most interesting small talk I'd ever heard.

Larry had not only been a war correspondent; she was a painter in her own right, an avid triathlete and was investigating a story about a city employee who bankrolled his beach house, and the hookers who visited him there, with HUD money. She also loved to cook, was a Big Sister to a nine-year-old West Kensington piano prodigy, and was happily single again after her latest relationship ended over conflict of interest (she didn't have any). She was also clearly exasperated by her artist turned socialite mother, who insisted she attend events like this one, even when the *Inquirer*'s daily deadlines loomed.

When she mentioned her five-o'clock deadline, I couldn't help but wonder about the e-mail I had sent and whether she was already investigating the East Falls Ariel story.

"Working on anything for today?" I asked nonchalantly.

"A few things."

"Anything interesting?"

"Yes."

"In town?"

"Maybe." She furrowed her brow, cocked her head, and leaned closer. "Why?"

We both looked at each other, suspicious. But I didn't dare expose myself as "a concerned citizen." I looked away dispassionately. "No reason."

She touched my arm and leaned in close. "If you want to know if I'm doing anything on Alex, I told you before, I'm on the city desk, not politics," she whispered. "And I can't tell you what other reporters are doing. I just can't."

"Oh no! That's not what I meant," I replied, aghast. "I would never put you in that position." I hoped she believed me. I didn't want her to think I was the kind of person who would use friendship for inside information.

Luckily, she smiled and told me, "It's okay. I understand it's hard not to ask. Now, let's go get some crumpets or cucumber sandwiches of whatever other poor excuses for food they have at these things."

I followed her toward the buffet, and between bites of dainty sandwiches, we continued to talk easily, like old friends.

For an heiress, Larry was delightfully down-to-earth and funny and had an endearing way of talking with her hands, her thin arms jerking up and down, over and around. At one point, she got so excited she smacked a passing woman in the face. She apologized profusely, and after the woman moved on, annoyed, she gave me a bug-eyed look and we both struggled to stifle our laughter.

She was also beautiful despite her "Plain Jane" outfit. I wondered why Alex had never made the moves on her. Before I could stop myself, as we made our way across the room, now filled almost to capacity, I found myself bringing him up.

"You've known Alex a long time. I bet you have some good stories."

"Maybe a few. Though mostly stupid high school stuff. Nothing too shocking."

"Knowing Alex, I believe it. He seems...I mean, he's a pretty straight arrow."

"Even though he longs to be crooked. Dangerous." She laughed like it was a joke, but her words hit home. Perhaps Alex did long to be more like her...out in the world, investigating wrongs, working in foreign countries, and living life to the fullest?

I probed even more. "You guys understand each other so well. Hard to believe there never was anything between you two."

Her cheeks flushed and she looked down with embarrassment. Shoot. If not torpedoed already, my plan to become her new best friend was ruined. No one wanted to be buddies with the jealous wife.

"Oh God, no," she said. "I could never be with someone so into his looks. Always working out all the time and having to have just the right suits and shirts. He's such a girl."

I laughed and she relaxed, but I wasn't so convinced of her rebuttal. Perhaps, deep down, she harbored a crush. Or used to long ago.

The ringing sound of a fork tapping a glass signaled it was time to take our seats. I found my place at a table in the front as Larry escorted her mother to one farther back. I poured myself some tea, then settled in for what I figured would be a long, boring program. I even kicked off my shoes under the table and stretched my tender toes.

A lady in a checkered suit and glasses attached by a thick gold chain walked to the podium and began to speak. I sat up straighter in an effort to hear her better, but I still didn't understand, her words nonsensical. Then I realized it wasn't gibberish but French, spoken at a rapid pace and with a flawless accent. I looked around to see the crowd's reaction, but there was none. They were all listening intently and nodding along. Apparently the "Friends of Lafayette" took their friendship literally.

I took a sip of tea and pretended to follow along, though I couldn't understand a word.

Except my name. I looked up and saw the woman at the podium watching me expectantly. As was every other woman in the room.

And then it dawned on me. They were waiting for me to get up. I wasn't being mentioned; I was being introduced.

My mind raced, unable to focus on anything but the thunderous sound of clapping as I forced myself up and toward the podium. My heart was beating so hard I was sure people could see it thumping under my thick wool jacket, and the cool room suddenly felt tropical. I reached the stage and turned to the crowd, feeling sweat form between my breasts and shoulder blades. To make matters worse, it was only then that I realized I was barefoot.

The woman turned and welcomed me—"*Bienvenue*, Madame van Holt"—and left me onstage. Alone. With all eyes on me. And time passing one horrible second after another.

Of all my phobias, public speaking wasn't one of them, but still, it wasn't my favorite way to spend an afternoon. Because I often had to give presentations at work, I had forced myself to become somewhat competent through training and practice. I'd even managed to get a few laughs at last year's PRSA Pepperpot Awards, thanks to a few hundred bathroom mirror rehearsals and a few sips of Jules's gin and tonic.

But this was something else entirely. This was an anxiety nightmare come to life. Try as I might, I could not remember one word of high school French. I then tried to speak English, racking my brain for what to say, but even that language eluded me. The room grew quiet, the only sounds a few cups hitting their saucers. A heel scratched the floor. Someone coughed.

I took in the sea of faces, their two-hundred-dollar haircuts and their silk blouses with tiny box pleats. I knew I looked just like them in my beautiful suit. But I was nothing like them. I was a fraud.

I was supposed to charm them, flatter them, and give them a multitude of reasons to vote for my wonderfully kind, smart, and noble husband. I attempted to speak but only got as far as "I . . . I . . ."

The whole room leaned in, unsure how to react. Expressions turned from confused to concerned.

"I…I…" Again, repeating one syllable was all I could manage.

The room became even quieter. No one moved, or seemed to breathe.

It was so hot. My face burned and I was sweating. Before I melted, or burst out in tears, I had to get out of there. I turned to the woman who introduced me and mouthed a feeble "Sorry"; then I dashed down the steps of the podium, the microphone announcing my exit with a terrific screech.

I was halfway out of the room when I remembered my shoes, so I spun back around and snatched them from under my seat. Everyone watched, bewildered, as I hopped awkwardly on one foot and then the next, mashing my feet into my pointy-toed heels.

As I fled, face burning, the scandalized crowd whispering, I noticed a familiar face. Mirabelle was sitting at a table in the back; she must have slipped in late. Her face was immobile, but her eyes were glittering with rage.

Finally a word of French entered my head: *Merde.*

Back on Chestnut Street, the November air cooled my burning cheeks. I walked as fast as my heels would permit, desperate to put some distance between myself and the scene of my humiliation. I didn't know where I was going, but I didn't care. I just wanted to get away. To lose myself in the city.

Of course Abigail van Holt spoke French. Of course she frequented auction houses, where everyone fawned and fussed over her as if she was the First Lady. And of course she addressed large groups flawlessly and without hesitation, her perfect hair and perfect clothes inspiring in her audience a mixture of admiration and envy. At this moment, I kind of hated her.

Soon I passed a station wagon filled with car seats and wished I was sitting in my old Subaru with the kids strapped safely in the backseat. I walked by a teenager tugging a golden retriever and wanted desperately to hear the jingle of my own dog's collar as I opened the back door of my house in Grange Hill. I was so homesick.

I turned left, fighting tears, and headed toward the convention center complex on Market Street, eager to disappear into the crowds of tourists and conventioneers. But among them I only stood out even more, my pink suit and blond hair bright against their faded jeans and sweatshirts. I stepped inside the building, weaved around commuters heading to the center's underground subway station, and slipped out the other set of doors into a narrower street. Into another world.

Above me stood a massive red wooden arch with ornately carved dragons, red and green symbols, and gilded lettering: the gateway to Philadelphia's small Chinatown. Crowding the sidewalks were vendors and their rickety tables of sunglasses and paper fans, men smoking in groups or hiding behind outstretched newspapers, and children darting from one stoop to the other while the rich smells from restaurants, noodle bars, and flower stands filled the air. Horns honked, music spilled from open doorways, and mothers called to children from second-story windows. I felt miles away from the van Holts, safely anonymous at last.

I slowed my pace and caught my breath. I stopped in front of a dark sliver of a bar with a neon Tsingtao sign in the window. The lure of alcohol beckoned. I slipped inside.

Once my eyes adjusted to the dim lighting, I took the first seat at a honey-colored bar, placed my purse on the ground, and looked around. In front of me, shelves held a United Nations of liquor bottles, jarred olives and cherries, and printed pint glasses. On one wall, posters of pretty Chinese models suggested travel destinations and cigarette brands, while a large aquarium separated the small bar area from the even smaller "dining" area in back. I looked around it to see tables full of neighborhood businessmen drinking out of small ceramic cups and laughing loudly at one another's jokes.

It felt too early for happy hour, but the flat-screen television behind the bar announced that it was just a few minutes until five o'clock. Close enough.

A slim young man with spiky hair and a silky button-down, who looked more like a DJ than a bartender, offered me a menu. I pointed to the men in the back and told him, "I'll have what they're having."

He looked at me quizzically, shook his head, and handed me a menu filled with photos of pink and blue drinks, each topped with cherries or a parasol.

"Really, I want the same as them," I insisted.

When he didn't move, I assumed he didn't speak English. Again, I pointed to the little blue and white ceramic cups on the nearest table. I had no idea what was in them, but whatever it was, it was working. The men in the back seemed to be feeling no pain.

The bartender finally spoke, his voice accented only by the lazy inflection of a teenager. "Lady, you're not gonna like it. It's old school. Stupid strong."

"Perfect," I said, ignoring him. "Set me up."

Sighing, he moved to a small fridge and pulled out a thick brown bottle with a cork stopper. He poured a small bit into a cup and placed it in front of me. He waited, hands crossed in front, while I took a sip. The men from down the bar watched as well, their conversations stopping.

I brought the cup to my lips and gulped it back. It tasted like hot, spicy licorice mixed with pine needles and it burned so badly it almost triggered my gag reflex. I put the cup back down, my eyes watering.

The bartender gave me a "told ya so" look and handed me a napkin. I looked up at him sheepishly and whispered, "Beer, please."

He returned with a frosty Yuengling lager and told me it was on the house. I drank a third of it fast, the cool malty liquid quenching the fire on my tongue. When I stopped for air, I set the pint back down on the bar and exhaled loudly.

"Been that kind of day, huh?" said a voice beside me.

I was about to respond blandly and pull my purse over to make room for the newcomer when the voice registered somewhere deep in my body, like a punch to the gut.

Jimmy.

My head snapped up. My heart stopped.

He stood just inches from me, one tanned arm leaning on the bar, the other slipping a phone in his pocket. I almost said his name aloud but caught the word before it escaped. Instead, I stared wide-eyed, not even blinking.

He tilted his head, puzzled. "Do I know you?"

Such a natural thing to say, such simple words, but they stung almost as badly as the shot I'd just downed.

"Sorry, no," I told him. "You just reminded me of someone I used to know."

"Good guy, I hope," he said with a grin.

"The best," I whispered back.

I motioned for him to sit and he squeezed onto the tiny stool beside me, the tips of his work boots banging the flimsy underside of the bar. He took off his jacket and waved to the bartender, giving me time to glance at him from the corner of my eye. My heart beat fast at the nearness of him.

"Lager, please," Jimmy instructed the bartender. "And a menu."

The young man stepped away, leaving Jimmy looking around and drumming his fingers on the bar, me silently exploding.

"What brings you in here?" I asked, cringing inside at the cheesy line.

"The noodles. Best in town."

"Oh, I meant into the city."

"What makes you think I don't live around here?"

"Do you?" In this world, he just might.

"No. You're right. I live out in Delaware County. Just in town for a trade show."

"What kind?"

"The boring kind," he replied. "Seriously, it's for construction. To be more specific—paving."

"Paving? Like, roads?"

"No. Like pavers, concrete, bricks," he explained. "I work for a construction firm. I handle the outdoor stuff. Hardscaping, landscaping, patios, that kind of thing."

"I like patios," was my genius reply.

"Yeah?" He laughed. "A lot of people do. Or at least they used to."

"Used to?"

"The recession hit the business pretty hard. We're still reeling from it."

"I've heard."

"You have?"

"Yeah, someone I know is...was...is a landscaper. Ran his own business."

"Good for him," he said, sipping his beer. "Hope he is...was...is doing okay." We both laughed. I caught my breath.

Jimmy leaned back on his chair and squinted at the small whiteboard advertising today's specials, allowing me a better look. He was wearing a white button-down shirt tucked neatly into khakis, and his face was clean shaven. But he also wore his same beloved and battered Phillies hat I used to OxiClean once a week. When he saw me looking at it, he took it off, smoothed his hair and popped it back on, a nervous habit I'd seen him do a million times. Same old Jimmy. My Jimmy.

He leaned a tad closer and studied my face. "Are you sure I don't know you? I swear you seem familiar," he said.

Yes! I wanted to tell him. *Yes, yes, yes! We know every inch of each other; we can finish each other's sentences; we've spent every day and night together for the past nine years; we have two beautiful children.*

But I just stared into his golden brown eyes and said the only thing I could: "No. I don't think so."

We continued talking, sipping our beers. He told me he loved what he did but wanted to focus more on landscaping, on environmentally friendly installations, maybe run his own business someday. He said he liked his current boss but that the paperwork and politics of a big company were tough. He explained what I already knew—he had three brothers, was born and raised in Upper Darby, played ice hockey since he was three, and had a dog named Walnut (Wally, for short). But I also learned new things. That he loved Chinese noodle bars, for one, and was really into mountain biking. Also, that he had plans to go on an eco-tour of Iceland over the Thanksgiving break.

Who knew my husband had interests outside of me and the kids? Shocking.

A server brought Jimmy his food order, giving me time to look for a wedding ring. He wasn't wearing one. That didn't tell me much; few landscapers wore them since they spent so much time using fertilizer and chemicals. But then again, it seemed unlikely that a man who was married with kids would be hanging out at a bar at dinnertime.

When he wasn't looking, I slipped my heavy diamond wedding rings to my right hand. I didn't want anything to scare him away.

"So you know all about me," he said. "Why are you here? Somehow, I wouldn't peg you as the dive-bar-in-the-afternoon type." Was he flirting with me? It was too cute.

"What type do you think I am, then?" I said, tilting my head coyly, giving it right back to him.

He looked me up and down, taking in my pink suit, high heels, and sleek hairstyle. "Hmm...I'd say you are a lawyer. Or one of those mergers-and-acquisitions finance types."

"Not even close."

"Something more creative? Like advertising or something?"

"Bingo. I was in public relations."

"Was?"

"Yeah. Not anymore."

"So what do you do now?"

"Funny. I'm having a hard time figuring that out."

"Aren't we all." He lifted his glass and we toasted, our beers making more of a clunk than a clink.

"You're right, though," I explained. "I'm not usually the drink-in-the-afternoon type. I just needed a break."

"From?"

"My life."

"Husband? Kids?"

"Public embarrassment. I just royally screwed up a speech."

"Like bored everyone to death?"

"Like freaked out and bolted."

"Wow. I'm sure it wasn't as bad as you think."

"It was worse." I grimaced and hung my head.

A second or two passed, as if he was contemplating what to say next. Then he leaned toward me and attempted to peek around the sheet of my hair that separated us. When I looked up, and my hair fell away, we were inches from each other.

"I can't imagine you screwing up anything," he said quietly. "I can't imagine you being anything less than"—he paused as he struggled to find the word he was searching for—"remarkable."

The word hung in the air, silencing us both. I knew he wasn't giving me a line; his tone was earnest and honest. Besides, Jimmy didn't blow smoke. And he always did think better of me than I thought of myself. When he looked away, shyly, I leaned toward him and breathed him in, so later I could remember everything about this moment.

Jimmy waved to the bartender, who had been ignoring us in favor of his iPhone. The young man trotted over and asked, "Another round?" We said "yes" in unison.

Outside, the light faded and the streets grew quiet, but we didn't move from our stools, so deep in conversation. Tucked inside the small bar so far from our respective homes, it felt as if the world outside that flimsy red door didn't exist. Even the other patrons seemed to fade into the background, their exotic, unknowable conversations softening to a hum. I finally understood what Buddhists meant by being in the moment; I was so alive I thought I might vibrate off my stool.

But it was my phone that started vibrating, bringing me back to reality with an incoming text: Sunita couldn't find Sam's giraffe and could they order pizza? I read the text as Jimmy glanced up at the television above our heads.

"Excuse me, I have to go to the ladies' room," I said as I stood, slipping off my stool and taking an ever-so-slight stumble as the blood returned to my legs.

"Careful," he said, his tanned hand catching me by the elbow. Our eyes locked and I fought a powerful urge to kiss him.

In the bathroom, I texted answers to Sunita, then peed out two and a half beers and washed my hands. Looking at myself in the mirror, I started to fix my makeup and limp hair, then stopped, remembering that Jimmy preferred the natural look. Maybe it was the alcohol talking, but I decided then and there that if he asked for my number, I would give it to him. There was no reason we couldn't be friends, right? I unbuttoned one button of my prim blouse and hurried out, anxious to be beside him again.

But when I got back to the seat, he was gone.

I scanned the bar and the tables in the back. I even ran back and pushed open the door to the men's room, but it was dark and empty. I then ran toward the door and flung it open, searching up and down the sidewalk, but found only a few street vendors packing up their wares. I sighed and walked back to where we had been sitting. There were the two half-drunk beers plus two twenty-dollar bills.

And then, very quietly, I heard my own voice, and it wasn't inside my head.

On the television above where we had been sitting, I caught the tail end of a repeat of today's CNN interview: me sitting between Alex and Gloria while Sam played on my lap.

Jimmy must have seen it. And the plain white font identifying me as "Mrs. Abigail van Holt." Very much a wife and mother. Not to mention, Philadelphia's "political royalty."

I had lost him again.

CHAPTER FIFTEEN

After relieving Sunita and putting two chocolate-milk- and cartoon-drunk children to bed, I slipped into my own sheets, even though it was only half past eight. Alex had texted he would be home late, but just to be sure, I turned off all the lights in the bedroom. If he did come home soon, I wanted to pretend to be asleep.

I settled in and pulled the covers up to my neck, anxious to get to my thoughts. Of Jimmy.

I replayed the scene at Wok Ling's over and over. I thought of his words, his smile, his smell. I wondered if he liked me, if he thought I was pretty, and if he felt the connection too.

I also thought how funny it was that despite my new marriage, new clothes, and awesome new body, underneath it all I was the same person I was a week ago. He was the one who was different. He had a different job, lived somewhere I'd never seen, and had interests, tastes, and hobbies I didn't know about. I couldn't picture his hefty frame on a mountain bike or him the lone blue-collar guy on a hipster tour of Iceland. But apparently he enjoyed these things. I wondered if all the responsibilities of our life in Grange Hill—or even me—had stifled this adventurous streak.

But then again, without me, Jimmy wasn't a small business owner. He worked for someone else and probably hated it.

I'd always assumed Jimmy had done those things—started his own company, gone to night school to get his degree—on his own initiative. But now, seeing him working for someone else, I thought that perhaps I had something to do with it. Maybe I helped bring out his ambitious side? Or perhaps, as a couple, we were able to tackle challenges that alone seemed insurmountable. I'd always assumed that people were just who they were, but I was beginning to think that we influence those around us even more than we could ever really know.

Thinking that made me feel good and a touch wistful. Sighing, I stretched my knees down from their fetal position and fell asleep.

Rain.

It fell in torrents, pounding the windows and drowning out the sounds of the city below.

I got out of bed, padded across the carpet, and yanked open the heavy drapes. The trees in the square below were barely visible and the lights from cars blurred together in pretty pink and yellow streaks. And the sky—usually bright blue, even at seven thirty in the morning—was an angry slate gray.

Election Day was off to a bleak start.

Alex had slipped in late last night but was gone again when I woke up. Wherever he was in the city, I imagined him pacing back and forth and cursing the weather, his hands in his thick dark hair. For days now, Frank, Calvin, and he had obsessed over the forecast, and I knew barring a hurricane or a tornado, this downpour was the worst-case scenario.

I knew that in addition to a strong showing from middle-aged men, Alex needed at least forty percent of the female vote. Normally, this would not be something we were too worried about—we all knew the ladies loved Alex—but rain would keep women, especially older ones, home. Despite their different ethnic and socioeconomic backgrounds, there was one thing South Philly, West Philly, and Main Line ladies could agree on: no matter how cute their future congressman might be, he wasn't worth wasting a good blowout.

As badly as I wanted to crawl back in bed, I knew I had to get moving. An insanely long day waited. On today's schedule were visits to a library, senior center, high school for the deaf, and two churches, one of which was our polling place and where we would cast our own votes. Along with the campaign staff and our favorite volunteers, we would smile and shake hands and squeeze the last bit of energy out of the overworked, overtired campaign machine.

And then tonight, win or lose, we would party. The big ballroom at the Ritz had been reserved, and at this moment, hotel staffers were probably blowing up hundreds of red, white, and blue balloons, while inside the kitchen others pulled the shells off an equal amount of shrimp, cut cheese and bread into tiny triangles, and iced down cases of champagne. Across the city and deep into the Main Line, our friends and family went about their day, some waiting more anxiously than others for tonight, when they would don their suits and cocktail dresses, then jump into taxis and town cars on their way to congratulate, or sympathize with, Alex. As for me, I knew that it didn't matter if Alex won or lost, how tired I was, or how heavy was my heart. I would remain by my husband's elbow, clad in satin-backed wool and the softest silk, playing the part I now knew how to play. Kissing everyone hello. Smiling and nodding. Making small talk. Doing what I had learned so well to do—pretend.

In the hall, on my way to rousing the kids, I heard a noise, like water running down a drain, coming from the kitchen.

"Alex?"

No response. I pulled my robe tighter and followed the sound, only to find my mother-in-law at the sink pouring a bottle of Macallan 25 down the drain. She was still wearing her khaki trench coat, the sleeves dotted with rain.

I knew the kids were heading to Bloemveld for the day, but I had thought I was supposed to send the children out with Oscar. I had already gathered their necessities—plus the diamond earrings, which I had retrieved and reunited last night—and the kids' bags, as well as the velvet box, waited in the hall.

I cleared my throat, still froggy from the morning, and asked, "Mirabelle! What are you doing here?"

She set the empty bottle on the marble countertop and looked up at me. "I think you know."

But I didn't. And that worried me.

I noticed that my purse was open, as if she had just searched through it. Then I saw that in addition to the bottle in her hand, she had emptied *all* of our liquor bottles and thrown them into a recycling bin at her feet.

"I'm afraid I don't."

"Don't think for a minute I'm not on to you."

On to me? For what? She couldn't possibly suspect the real truth. "What are you talking about?" I asked blithely.

"You're an alcoholic."

I stared at her, flummoxed. But also relieved. Alcoholism was something I could refute. Masquerading as a woman whose life I had suddenly jumped into? A little harder to explain.

"An alcoholic? That's ridiculous."

She continued: "Then you're *on* something. Pills."

I couldn't help but laugh, but then I saw she was serious. I straightened up. "Mirabelle, believe me, I'm not an alcoholic. Or on drugs of any kind."

She picked up the last full bottle—an aqua blue bottle of gin—and upended it over the sink. The pine smell filled the room as it hit the stainless steel.

"If it's about what happened yesterday at the tea, no one is more embarrassed than me. I just wasn't feeling well and I needed to get out of there fast. My head was hurting again."

As I waited to hear if she bought the lie, I walked around to the coffeemaker, placed a cup under it, and began pressing buttons. Hopefully, this was the end of this ludicrous discussion.

"This isn't just about yesterday," she continued. "You've been acting strangely for some time." She set down the now empty bottle and pointed her bony finger at me. "You are on something. I know it." Then, her eyes widened as if the thought had just come to her. "Or it's something worse."

"Worse?"

"The bizarre fall off the escalator. That mess with Aubyn. And you asked Dr. Cohen all sorts of weird questions about 'alternate universes.' And then this embarrassment yesterday. If you're not on something, you are *mentally unfit*."

I had to hand it to the old broad—she was right. I *was* unfit to be a van Holt. I was Abbey Lahey, suburban sweatpant mom, bug publicist, and walking klutz. Funny that of all people she was the one who was suspicious. Women's intuition, I guess.

I picked up my coffee cup and took a sip, buying time. Then I took a deep breath and used the same tone that Jimmy used when talking to an irate customer, the same tone I'd heard *her* use many times: "Mirabelle. I can assure you I am *not* abusing drugs. Or alcohol. And I am one hundred percent sane." I put down my cup and walked back to the other side of the island, looking her in the eye. "And besides, if I was a drunk or a pill popper, don't you think Alex would know? Ask him. He'll tell—"

"Leave Alex out of this," she interrupted. "I don't want him side-tracked. Not today."

"Leave him out of this? He's my husband."

She blanched, then regained herself. "Alex has a blind spot when it comes to you. But I *know* something is wrong. Very wrong. And I'm not going to allow it to ruin this family. Or his future."

Her voice had that same patrician lilt she always used, but her meaning was as clear as a prison yard threat. I didn't like being bullied in my own home. I matched her lethal charm with some of my own.

"Mirabelle. *Mother.* Thank you *so* much for stopping by." I pulled my phone out of my purse and pretended to read e-mails, making her wait, a tactic I'd learned from Charlotte. Eventually, I looked up. "If you'll excuse me, I have a busy day ahead. Alex is waiting for me. He *needs* me."

I'd never seen her so mad. Or speechless. We glared at each other across the island like two lions seconds from ripping each other apart.

But then Gloria came stumbling in, yawning and rubbing her eyes. When she saw her grandmother, she ran over and threw herself into the stiff khaki fabric of her old-fashioned trench.

Mirabelle smoothed Gloria's hair and turned the little face up to hers. "Good morning, my dove. Are you all ready? While Mommy and Daddy finish campaigning, you and Van are coming to stay with me."

Gloria smiled, anticipating time with Aubyn, the sheep, and, above all, her horse. "For how long?" she asked.

"All day." Then, Mirabelle looked over at me with a wide smile and triumphant eyes. "And if I have my way, maybe even longer. Maybe a good, long time."

Take my kids away? She couldn't do that, could she?

Every time I tried to think clearly, to figure out if that was in any way legally possible, my mind became jumbled by fear. This was my worst nightmare coming to life, and it gave me chills, even while I stood under a steady rain of hot water in the van Holts' giant marble shower.

So I fell down an escalator. So I asked strange questions. So I botched a speech. That doesn't mean I'm an addict. Or insane. And this isn't the 1800s; no one can lock someone up in an institution without just cause.

Still, I was worried. If you added them up, I had had more than just a few screw-ups this week. And who knew what ones were still to come. I slid to the floor of the shower and curled my knees up under me. I felt so alone. Scared. And with that horrible feeling of not knowing what's to come.

Suddenly, I heard men's shoes cross the bathroom floor, then the pop of the glass door as it opened. It was Alex, and he looked like he was in a rush.

"Where are my—" He scowled as he looked down at me on the floor. "What are you doing on the floor?"

"Uh, meditating."

"Seriously?" He watched, annoyed, as I stood up and tried to shut off the water but couldn't remember how the fancy control panel worked. He reached in and waved his hand underneath it. The water stopped, then gurgled down the drain.

"Where are my shirts? Did you get my shirts?" he asked as I stepped out.

I winced. "Oops." I reached for a towel and pressed it to my face.

"You're kidding, right? Abbey, it's Election Day! And I have nothing to wear. I wore this one yesterday and now there are coffee stains all over it. Frank's waiting downstairs."

"Sorry. With the interview and the speech and everything, I just forgot."

He followed me into the closet and tore off the stained shirt angrily. I grabbed a robe and tied back my wet hair, then began to flick through his hanging clothes, hoping there was a clean button-down hiding among all the navy blue blazers.

"Where were you yesterday afternoon anyway?" he asked. I froze but managed to come up with an excuse. "I had that tea at the auction house, and then I stopped to get something to eat."

He bought it, or didn't care, because he kept on.

"And you couldn't stop by Brooks Brothers? I've had to wear the same shirt for two days because someone hasn't been keeping up."

I turned to him incredulously. "It was *your* mother who fired May, not me, remember?"

He was about to say something back but stopped himself, realizing I was right. It felt good to respond with confidence instead of confusion. After ten days in this marriage, our fights were a little fairer.

Still, given the day, I offered an olive branch. "I can run out and get you some," I said cheerily. "Just let me get dressed."

"But we're supposed to be in Springfield in twenty minutes," he said. "Then that deaf school and the church. And we have to cast our ballots at noon."

"Just go on ahead in that shirt and I'll meet you wherever you are," I said. "Alex, trust me. No one ever lost an election because of a coffee stain."

"Can't Sunita go? I want you with me."

I started to say okay, but he cut me off. "Actually, never mind. I don't want her driving my car." He reached in his pocket, tossed me some keys, and told me, "Get me three. And remember, white or blue. No pink."

I scrambled through my drawers and found a sweatshirt, sweatpants, and some well-worn lime green running shoes. I jogged into the kitchen, filled a travel coffee mug, and rushed to the elevator. But then I remembered the rain and turned around.

I rustled through the hall closet for an umbrella or a jacket but found only wool coats, a full-length fur, and ski pants. I tramped back to my closet, set my coffee mug down, and scanned the shelves and hangers, then rifled through some drawers. There was no umbrella, no raincoat, not even a baseball cap.

How can a woman with twelve pairs of J Brand jeans, six Hermès scarves, and a rainbow of Nordstrom pashmina not own a raincoat? Then it dawned on me. Nordstrom, raincoat. Hadn't I seen a raincoat in the bag when that nice man—Bingley Cowan-Smith or something—returned my things?

I crawled around under the hanging clothes and found the large silver bag on its side behind some boots, exactly where I'd shoved it a week before. Inside was a navy Tory Burch raincoat lined with coral and white geometric silk and a matching umbrella. I grabbed them both and slipped on the coat. I started to push the bag back where I'd found it, when something caught my eye. I flung off the remaining silver tissue paper—and gasped.

There was the red leather Marc Jacobs bag. The same one Abbey Lahey had bought on the sly for $598. The one that caused the fight. The one that was on its way back to the store just eleven days ago. I stared at it in disbelief, lifting it out and setting it on the marble top of the dressing table. I examined it as if it was a wild animal, about to bite or run away.

My thoughts ran to the last days I had used it…Gloria in her laundry basket…Sam toddling up the walk toward Miles…the lunch with Jules…even the fight with Jimmy. I picked up the bag and held it to my chest, the thick, shiny leather cool in my warm hands.

Emotion built and then crashed over me, like an ocean wave that looks small from far away but clobbers you anyway. I began to cry, quietly at first and then harder, my shoulders shaking and my hands and lips trembling. Tears dripped down my face and onto the purse, then rolled off and disappeared into the cream-colored carpet.

With every cell of my body, I wished I was holding that bag in my own room, in my own house, with my own husband seething downstairs. Actually, no. I wished I was home *without* that bag. Wished to God I'd never bought it, had never even laid eyes on it. In fact, I'd never want another fancy purse again. If I could just get home, I swore to God I'd carry my keys and wallet in a brown paper bag for the rest of my life.

Quick as lightning, my sadness turned to rage. I threw the purse down and kicked it. Then I turned and began to tear down hanging clothes in a fury. I pulled sweaters off their perch and pulled out the trays from the island, dumping T-shirts, lingerie, even jewelry on the ground. One twinkling diamond stud pinged across the marble-topped island and stopped just before it slipped to the other side. Another lost earring, I thought, then ran around to fetch it.

Picking it up, my anger found its focus. I knew why Alex's words about the lost earring haunted me so badly. It wasn't just what he'd said—*To teach you a lesson...so you'd learn to take care of nice things*—so much as the casually cruel manner in which he said it. It was that he'd been waiting to say it—planning to say it—for all those days. Perhaps he even enjoyed watching me crawl around on my hands and knees, amused by all my angst and stalling and lying. Who the hell does that to someone—let alone his spouse?

Hitting below the belt in the heat of an argument is an unpleasant but normal part of marriage. Everyone has a temper. I had said plenty of things to Jimmy I immediately regretted. But I had never tried to "teach him a lesson"—or even considered it. Because that was something you did to a child. And he was my partner. My husband. My *equal*.

Across the island, I caught a glimpse of myself in the opposite mirror. The lipstick-red bag looked shockingly bright next to my gray sweatshirt, black sweatpants, and makeup-free face. The now messy closet looked like my old closet in Grange Hill. My feet were cushioned in workout socks and sneakers. The smell of coffee scented the air.

It all felt so familiar, startlingly so.

I glanced at my watch. Nine forty-five. What time did Nordstrom on City Line Avenue open?

It was amazing how many women were waiting outside of Nordstrom on a Tuesday morning, even in the pouring rain. They seemed anxious to get in, checking their watches and peering into the glass, like nineteenth-century factory workers eager to get to their looms before the first bell.

At two minutes until ten o'clock, a woman with a crisp silver bob, square red glasses, and a black pantsuit opened the department store doors with a clunk and a clack. The other shoppers and I lined up to go inside, and together we streamed into the brightly lit building. They dispersed to the shoe department, children's wear, and contemporary fashions, leaving me shuffling toward the escalators, my eyes fixed. Today the siren song of fur, silk, and cashmere would lure many a woman to financial ruin, but not me. I wasn't here to shop.

The escalators looked taller and steeper than I remembered, crisscrossing back and forth up a three-story atrium. My resolve weakened and I stood motionless as I gazed up at them, examining the Plexiglas dividers, the speed of the stairs, their looming height.

I closed my eyes and tried to remember the sound of Jimmy's voice, the smile in his eyes. I took a deep breath, held the bag in my right hand, just like I had done before, and stepped onto the moving metal.

Halfway up, directly over the piano, I leaned over the railing and willed myself to flip over the rubbery handrail. But I couldn't do it.

It felt so unnatural that my body physically resisted...the mind's instinct for survival trumping a heart's ache. Next thing I knew, I was at the top.

I circled around through the store, went back down, and tried again, this time with a little jump when I reached the midpoint. But once again, I couldn't do it. From that height, the piano looked really hard, almost menacing. Down again. A few salesladies eyed me, suspicious of the wild-eyed woman in sweatpants who neared the escalator, then veered away, then approached it again.

Sweating now, I forced myself back up. But this time, I stepped off, walked to the women's contemporary section, and plotted. Perhaps I should take a running leap? Bribe someone to push me? Close my eyes and step off?

Another shopper came by, clutching her Louis Vuitton satchel and staring at me as I mumbled to myself. I moved myself farther back into the fall collections, losing myself in the forest of merino wool and triple-knit cashmere. Before I knew what I was doing, I fingered a Céline jacket. I checked the price of a black Jason Wu sweater. I paused in front of a row of slinky Alexander McQueen dresses. Wasn't that the designer Kate Middleton wore on her wedding day?

"May I help you?" said a voice. "Can I get you a size?"

I turned to see a handsome woman with the hopeful look of someone who works on commission. I stared at her, saying nothing, even though a part of me wanted to say, "Yes, size six, please."

The saleslady looked confused: "Do you want to see something else? We have some gorgeous suits that just came in. They would look lovely on you."

"No, thank you. I'm just browsing."

"Are you sure? We just got the new Zac Posen line. Some really nice things."

Nice things. So you'll learn to take care of nice things.

I shook my head and stepped back from the saleslady, determined now to do what I'd come to do.

I marched back to the escalator and rode it down. I waited for the other shoppers to clear off, then went up again, this time determined.

But once again—*Goddammit, Abbey!*—I froze. This time because of a glance at the children's section. What if this really *was* my life and Grange Hill was the dream? And what if I ended up seriously injuring myself, leaving Gloria and Sam with a paraplegic mother, or worse—motherless? I couldn't bear the thought of them being raised by Mirabelle and a rotating array of nannies.

I dropped my arms and head in defeat.

My bag slid off my shoulder, its gold chain falling down and catching between two of the grooved silver steps. I pulled it back but it didn't budge. I pulled harder, my arms taut, trying to use my body weight to yank it upward.

When I reached the top of the escalator, the stairs just beginning to flatten into one another, the plated gold chain creaked with the strain. Then I heard a snap.

Untethered, I flew backward. Clothes and lights and shoppers and metal and my own shoes rotated before my eyes like images from a viewfinder.

"What happened?"

"Is she okay?"

"Don't move her."

When the world stopped spinning, I tried to get up. But then I felt a sharp pain in my hip and hands gently holding me down.

"Don't try to get up, dear."

My eyes followed the voice and focused on an older saleslady spackled with makeup. Her kind concern was echoed in the faces of her coworkers, all leaning over me as I lay on the floor at the foot of the escalator.

It took me a moment to gather my wits and remember what had happened. When I did, my heart soared.

I'd done it! It may not have earned points for grace, but I'd succeeded in re-creating my tumble down Nordstrom's escalator. I thanked God for my inherent clumsiness, which had triumphed—*finally!*—over fear.

Too excited to just lie there, I forced myself to sit up, waving off protests from the salesladies and a barrel-chested security guard. There seemed to be a lot of concern about whether I'd sustained any broken bones. And whispers about lawsuits. But I was too full of endorphins to care.

The light seemed different: everything a little brighter, more vivid. It took me a moment to realize why. The front doors at the far end of the store. When I'd entered Nordstrom it had been overcast, rainy. Now the sun was shining.

I was back!

I wanted to sprint for the doors and back to my real life, but the Nordstrom employees surrounded me, insisting I wait for the paramedics. Then with hands on my elbows, they escorted me to the employee lounge and plopped me down on a metal chair. Someone brought me water. I gulped it down. The most delicious water I'd ever tasted.

The ladies continued to fuss. Their expressions were a mix of anguish and pleasure, upset that someone got hurt, but also happy to have an excuse to leave their posts.

"I promise you I am fine," I told them. "I'm just more embarrassed than anything." I smiled for emphasis, though my shoulder throbbed and my right knee felt like it had been Tonya Harding–ed.

Before they could respond, a British accent addressed them. "Thank you, ladies. I can take it from here."

As the women dispersed, disappointed, I looked up and saw Mr. Cowan-Smith, the regional vice president, the same man who had hand delivered Abbey van Holt's gown and personal effects a week before. This time he wasn't smiling and effusive, but stoic with concern.

His light blue eyes flicked down at my sneakers and then up to my flushed forehead. I stared, looking for any sign of recognition, but his face was expressionless. Did he know me as Mrs. van Holt—or as one of the nameless, faceless mothers who perused the sale racks every day, staring longingly but never buying more than a MAC lipstick?

"I don't know what happened," I said. "Must have been my shoes, wet from the rain."

"Well, perhaps next time, you should use the elevators. Or take the stairs."

"I know what you're thinking," I said as I stood up and pulled my purse over my arm. "That I'm going to sue Nordstrom or something. I can assure you that is not the case. I'm not some crazy lady; I'm just an average mom from Grange Hill…"

I let my words trail off and studied his face, waiting for a reaction. But he said nothing, just offered a crooked arm for me to hold on to.

"The mall paramedic is on his way," he urged. "Please."

"I'm fine. Really." I gave him a little shuffle ball change to prove it.

"If you insist on leaving, I certainly cannot stop you," he said with a sigh.

Taking my arm, he guided me around the escalator, the piano, and the shoe department toward the store entrance. "Before you go, let me please reiterate that Nordstrom values your business and is happy to offer any assistance you might need in future shopping endeavors. But, Mrs. van Holt, I think from now on, it's best if you shop online."

We looked at each other as the words sank in.

I couldn't believe it. It hadn't worked. I was still Mrs. Alexander van Holt.

Only now I was Mrs. van Holt with a tender forehead, an aching knee, and a full day of election events to fake my way through. Then a lifetime of three-hour lunches, overcrowded fund-raisers, ten-mile jogs, and marathon shopping sprees.

Except, of course, at Nordstrom.

Driving back to the city in Alex's sleek cockroach of a car, some hastily purchased shirts boxed and ready in the backseat, I felt so helpless. And hopeless.

I merged onto I-76 eastbound in a daze. I drove slowly, well below the speed limit, while trucks honked and whizzed by me in irritation. After a teenager in a gold-trimmed Honda Civic flipped me off, I pulled over at an exit, moved to the shoulder, and turned off the engine. I opened the door and leaned out, feeling nauseous.

The last time I had felt this way was eight months ago, when Jimmy's best account, an office park with a monthly retainer large enough to cover half our mortgage, canceled its weekly service. Turned out the office park had been sold and the new owner, an absentee landlord from New York, was "making some changes." Jimmy still had other clients, but this was a major blow, not only financially, but to Jimmy's ego. The new owners didn't care that the grass was now naturally weed-free or that the new pear trees shaded the parking lot in summer. They didn't care about my husband either. When they called to tell him they were canceling the account, they called him Johnnie the whole time.

Soon after that, Jimmy began to let his employees go, until finally, it was just him and one part-timer. The company of five, sometimes nine in summer, was now down to one and a half. And the one person was killing himself to get more work, calling in favors and asking for leads from everyone he knew, but unable to land any new accounts.

One evening, about two weeks earlier, when I was boiling the kids' toothbrushes and sippy cup lids in a saucepan, Jimmy sat down on a stool at the end of the kitchen counter. I knew the look; he wanted to talk.

"Ab?"

"What's up?"

"The business isn't doing so good."

I pretended to be engrossed in my witches' brew of plastic, giving him breathing room to speak his mind, but inside I was listening intently. It was unusual for Jimmy to bring up the state of his business unprompted. I may have complained about my job and my boss every chance I got, but Jimmy always left business behind when he stepped inside our kitchen door.

"And I don't really know how to fix it," he continued. "I've bid on every job around, but the competition is tough. Every firm out there is looking for work too, and they're offering cheaper rates."

"Maybe you could cut yours."

He sighed heavily. "I wish I could. But I have a wife and family to support. And a school loan and this fucking house—"

He stopped himself and looked away. I was surprised, this being the first time ever that Jimmy had indicated he was anything but ecstatic to be married, with two kids and a fixer-upper. But the shock quickly gave way to more practical concerns. "I could ask my boss for leads. Or Max at Maxim Pest. He works with a lot of—"

He cut me off. "No, babe. Please don't *do* anything." I smarted but kept quiet.

"I have to make a decision soon. Keep going and hope it turns around or go back to working for someone else. I don't know what to do."

Our eyes met and he added, "Ab, I'm scared."

Then he put his head in his hands.

Looking back, I know now what I should have done. I should have taken him in my arms and reassured him that everything would work out fine. I should have told him I was proud of him no matter what. I should have promised we'd do whatever it took to keep the business open…that we'd sell the fridge, the car—hell, even my sad, middle-aged body—if it meant keeping his dream alive.

But I didn't. I just stood there, too focused on my own worries to offer any solace. Too busy formulating a plan to find him a new job with a regular salary. And figuring how much we could get for the mowers and the snowplows on Craigslist.

Now, sitting on the side of the road, the new-car smell mixing with exhaust, I felt lower than low. Ashamed. I would have given anything to go back in time and tell him what I should have that night: *I know it's hard. I know you're scared. But no matter what, we'll get through this. Together. Because I love you and that's what love means.*

The sun moved in and out from the clouds, casting shadows around my feet. I watched them come and go, still too numb to move.

Finally, I rubbed my face, took a deep breath, and folded my limbs back into the low bucket seat. I turned the key and steered the car back toward the city.

There was nowhere else to go.

CHAPTER SIXTEEN

He had been here, maybe even today. He had brushed aside the leaves and cleared away debris. He had wiped the stone free of the last of the late summer pollen. And alongside the purple chrysanthemums he had planted in front of her gravestone, he had added a small Phillies flag.

Miles always knew what would make Jane smile.

I read the epitaph again and sighed. "Jane Louise Lahey 1953–2008. Beloved wife, mother, friend."

Silently, I added one more: beloved mother-in law.

When Oscar had turned the Suburban onto this street and pulled up in front of the Church of the Holy Redeemer, at first it looked like just another improvised Delaware County polling station. It took a few minutes for me to realize why the church looked familiar. After all, it had been five years since Jane's funeral. But looking closer, I remembered, and remarked how nothing had changed: a restaurant-style sign advertising Mass times like today's specials; thin metal handrails trailing up wide concrete steps; and silvery gray stone covering just the facade, with weather-worn brick everywhere else. As if God couldn't see that they had used cheaper materials on the sides and back.

My memories colored the church much darker, more somber, than it really was. The sign out front might have offered eternal life, but to me it offered only an ending. Jane was the only person whom I truly loved who had died. Hers was the only funeral service I had ever attended.

And now I stood looking at her grave, while Alex shook hands with voters. I had told him I had to call to check on the children, and I did, but then stole away to the adjacent graveyard, ducking under tree limbs and walking worn pathways until I found Jane's grave. And now my hand touched the same dirt that Miles had touched, maybe just days ago.

Miles and Jane had weathered so much...put four boys through Catholic school and two through college...survived car wrecks and chicken pox and layoffs...managed to put a little aside for themselves...and finally reached retirement together like two marathoners crossing a finish line holding hands...only for Jane's cancer to come back and rob them of what should have been their victory lap. Jane held the ultimate marital upper hand. *You're mad because I didn't take out the trash? Well, how about I get cancer and die a slow and painful death in front of you and your children? How about that?*

But to them, it wasn't about comeuppance, wasn't even about which one of them got sick. They were so intrinsically bound by four decades together, it was as if they had both been sick, with Miles feeling every pain, losing just as much hair, and matching her pound for pound, both of them growing gaunt.

I'd never even seen them make jokes at the other's expense or snipe at each other under their breath. They were devoted to each other their entire lives, and, according to Jimmy, they had been since the day they met on the corner of Forty-Sixth and Market in 1964—when they were turned away from the last *American Bandstand* taping in Philadelphia. Though they didn't make it on the air with Dick Clark, or get to do the South Street Shuffle they had each been practicing all week, they would end up falling in love. A pretty awesome consolation prize, plus a great story to one day tell their grandchildren.

I was sure they fought—Jimmy said they had some real screaming matches, both with fiery tempers—but by the time I met them, their relationship was one of bemused adoration and steadfast loyalty. And even now, separated by death, the devotion remained. Miles tended this grave carefully, creating an arrangement that looked just like the window boxes she had fussed over for forty years, as if telling her, *Despite the separation, you still matter to me. You're still my number one person.*

I thought of the countless times I had silently cursed Jimmy because he wasn't someone like Alex. And how I might now curse Alex because he wasn't Jimmy. But how did each man really feel about me? If I died, would either of them visit my grave, covering it with wildflowers and fashion magazines and Krispy Kreme doughnuts? Was I capable of earning this type of devotion? Was I capable of giving it?

I reached out and touched the wet headstone. "Good-bye," I whispered to her. "Rest in peace. You deserve it."

As I walked back to the group, I noticed they were no longer standing near the church door greeting voters but huddled beside the black Suburban in the parking lot. As I got closer, I saw their eyes were glued to Calvin's iPad. Good news, I hoped.

"What's up?" One by one they raised their faces to me with

bewildered expressions, though no one said anything. Alex started to but then stopped himself. Instead, he opened the Suburban's back door and barked, "Get in."

Oh shit. I ducked into the truck and scrambled into the backseat. Alex folded his long limbs and scrunched in beside me, Frank and Calvin hit the middle row, and Sunita sat up front. Oscar slipped into the driver's seat and started the engine.

Beside me, Alex's face was grave. He wouldn't look at me, even when I touched his arm.

My heart began to beat faster. What had I done now? I reviewed the past few days. Had Alex heard about the Friends of Lafayette debacle? No, I couldn't imagine him really caring about that. Had he found out I'd gone to see May? If that was the case, I had an excuse ready—we were just there to return the lost bag. Then I remembered. The e-mail to Larry. Somehow he had found out about me leaking the Ariel story. Oh no. That would be much harder to explain…

"Alex, please don't be mad," I said, even though I could tell he already was. "I wanted to help you. I hated seeing you so conflicted."

He looked at me with disbelief.

"And no one knows it was me. I swear." I held my hands out in emphasis.

"Really?" He grabbed the iPad from Frank and shoved it under my nose. "Not you? This I have to hear."

I forced myself to look at the screen, expecting a front-page Philly .com story linking Alex to Ariel to Father Wallace to the Brindles to God knows who else. But instead I saw a grainy YouTube video. I pressed play.

The scene looked familiar. But it took me a moment to figure out why. And when I did, I felt my stomach turn over.

It was cell phone video of me sitting at a bar in Chinatown, laughing, drinking, and awkwardly flirting with the man beside me at five o'clock on a Monday. It was shot from an angle, and from behind the bar, but even in the dim light my pink suit, gray pearls, and blond hair were unmistakable. Beside me, his face half-hidden by his cap, was Jimmy.

To my horror, the video had a title: "Candidate's Wife Caught Canoodling."

But the words didn't make sense. It was all so strange. "What is this?" I whispered, still struggling to understand.

Frank asked, "Did you go to a bar yesterday? Some place called Wok Ling's?"

"No! I mean yes, I mean—" I was still too shocked to make much sense. "I went there. For a drink. But it was just a drink. I swear."

I looked down at the iPad again, and reasonable thought began to percolate. I guess Jimmy hadn't been the only one to recognize me from CNN. So had that young bartender. The whole time I thought he was texting or playing games on his phone, he was filming us. He must have posted it online—Instagram, perhaps—and from there it went viral. Already this YouTube video had more than seven hundred views.

Frank was frantic with disbelief. "How could you not notice someone filming you?"

"I saw a guy with a phone, but I thought he was just texting or something," I replied, anguished. "He was just a teenager. I can't believe he knew who I was. And even so, I was just stopping in for a beer and a bite."

"Well, the problem is it doesn't look like that," Frank continued. "It looks like you and this guy are—" He stopped himself to look back at Alex for permission to keep speaking, knowing he was treading on something that was personal, not just political. But Alex nodded, as if everyone in the car had a right to hear, and Frank repeated his thought: "It looks like you and this man are...

well...*together*." The word hung in the air like a sickening smell. Like something lurid and altogether nasty.

I couldn't tell Frank what I really wanted to: *That's because we are together. He's my husband!*

But, of course, that was the problem. When you looked at the two people in the video, they looked to be more than friends, more than just two strangers sharing space at a bar. The shy smiles, the laughter, how we leaned into each other, the moment I closed my eyes and breathed him in.

The video was burning up the Internet, implying I was cheating on Alex, because there *was* something to it: Only a woman in love looked at a man that way.

Still, I also knew I hadn't done anything wrong. Jimmy and I had barely even touched. And besides, I wasn't the one running for office. My husband was. "Why does it matter? Who cares what it looks like?" I asked defiantly.

"Who cares?" said Frank. "The whole goddamn Internet; that's who." He lifted up his phone and started reading from a Twitter feed:

" 'The van Holts join long list of political hypocrites...' "

" 'I thought they were so in love...' "

" 'If she doesn't want him, I'll take him...' "

" 'Not quite the fairy tale after all...' "

He started on the next one—" 'What a...' "—but Alex cut him off. "Frank!" he shouted. "We get the picture."

"Sorry. But we don't have time to candy coat this," Frank explained. "And that's not all. There's even a meme. Someone cut together her 'fairy tale' comments from the CNN interview with clips of her at the bar. It's all over the place."

He pulled the iPad out of my hand and started to cue it up. I put my hands to my face in embarrassment, then started to cry. Alex asked the others: "Can you give us a minute?"

Frank, Calvin, Sunita, and Oscar clicked their belts and somberly exited the car, leaving Alex and me alone.

I quieted myself and waited for him to speak. When he didn't, I began to plead with him.

"Alex, I only stopped in that place for a beer. I wasn't even gone an hour. Please don't tell me you think I'm having an affair."

He frowned in annoyance, then raised his hand to cut me off. "Calm down. I know you're not having an affair." Thank God whatever problems the van Holts had in their marriage, suspicion of infidelity wasn't one of them.

But he was still furious. "What those Internet trolls say doesn't concern me," he said. "I just don't understand how you could be so stupid. You of all people should know better."

I hung my head as he continued, his fury giving way to exasperation. "I don't get it. For the past six months, you're the one who has been telling me to watch every move. That I can never be too careful. That everything I do sends a message. And now, one week before the election, you turn into a PR disaster. First, you fall down an escalator. You write Fergie that check. And now *this*." He looked at the iPad in disgust, then looked back up at me. "If I didn't know any better, I'd say you were trying to sabotage this campaign."

"Oh, Alex, no. I swear I'm not. I just made some mistakes."

"Mistakes? Abbey, please. It's more than mistakes. This week you've been acting so...*strange*."

So he had noticed. And honestly, I couldn't blame him. Viewed individually, every misstep had a reasonable explanation. But collectively, they added up to some seriously schizoid behavior. I realized I owed him a real answer, and one that was more convincing than "I'm just tired."

I looked down at the carpet, avoiding his eyes. "The truth is, Alex, I am completely overwhelmed," I told him. "I thought having all this help and money and the best of everything would make things easy, but they don't. I guess I'm just feeling the pressure." To say the least.

"Pressure?" He leaned toward me like he couldn't believe what he'd heard. "You think *you're* under a lot of pressure? What about me? You think I don't want to call a time-out sometimes? Get lost in some dive? That sounds pretty fucking nice to me right now."

I looked down, face burning with shame. He was right. I hadn't thought of what he was dealing with: months of campaigning, a child in the hospital, a rogue father, and—let's face it—a disaster of a wife who had now turned into his number one political liability. He continued: "But no. Not me. I'm out here killing myself every second."

"I know you are," I said, my voice wretched with regret. "And I'm sorry. I just messed up. I wasn't thinking."

"Well, I hope it was worth it. You may have just cost us the election."

Then he rapped on the window, signaling to Frank and the team he was ready to go. Signaling to me that the conversation was over.

The fully loaded Suburban swung back and forth around double-parked cars and slower traffic as Oscar tried to get us to Center City quickly. I was being taken back to the apartment, where the plan was to keep me under house arrest for the remainder of the day. My ears blazed in humiliation as I sat listening to the "grown-ups" decide how to fix the damage of my childish disobedience.

"There's no time stamp on the video, just the date it was uploaded," pointed out Calvin. "Maybe we can spin it that this video is old… from a few years ago."

"No, it's pretty obvious that it was taken yesterday," said Frank. "She's wearing the same outfit she wore on CNN."

From the front seat, Oscar began to speak, and because it was out of character for him to chime in, his deep voice startled us. We listened intently. "Maybe you say family is off-limits. Like Obama did when Sarah Palin's daughter got pregnant."

"I hear you, Oscar, but it wasn't Alex's kid in the video," Frank replied. "It was his wife." The way he said "wife" made me feel invisible, as if the person he was referring to wasn't sitting two feet away from him.

"The Bullock camp must be thrilled," he added. "God—what a gift for them. On Election Day, no less."

"Maybe we use that against them," argued Calvin. "Talk about how Amanda's spreading the video. Slinging mud."

"No," interjected Alex. "Leave her out of it. We can't prove she had anything to do with this going viral. Besides, it's our mess, not hers." Alex was taking the high road and it made me feel sick inside. Once again, he was showing why he would make a great congressman. And now, thanks to me, he might never get the chance.

Everyone was quiet, thinking. Then Sunita asked, "Should we just deny it was Abbey? Say the video was faked? Photoshopped or something?"

I rolled my eyes at this one but remained silent.

"No," said Frank, sighing. Then he looked out the window and down at his watch. "But it's noon already. Polls close in nine hours. Maybe we do *nothing*. Just let the clock run out and hope for the best."

That was it. I couldn't hold my tongue any longer.

"You can't," I muttered, shaking my head.

Frank heard and swung around. "What was that?"

His tone was patronizing and sarcastic, but I continued. "I said, you can't 'do nothing.' Not with something like this."

"Abbey, with all due respect, let us handle this."

"I'm just saying that if you ignore this, it will only escalate," I argued. "I mean, that's why they're called 'viral videos.' Unchecked, they spread and spread, taking on a life of their own. And then what was gossip starts looking like the truth. And if the mainstream press then picks up on it..."

Frank's cheeks turned the color of red wine and his eyes bulged. He looked like he was about to explode. And he did, letting loose a full campaign's worth of disdain for Abigail van Holt: "I don't tell you what color to paint your nails or where to eat lunch, so I would appreciate it if you wouldn't try to tell me how to do my job. Especially after all the trouble you caused."

I couldn't believe he was speaking to me like this in front of my husband, or that Alex was letting him. But Alex seemed not to hear, lost in thought.

"Alex," said Frank, trying to get his attention. "Alex!"

"Yes?"

"Let's cancel the photo op of you guys voting. It's our only option. We'll avoid the press at all costs and pretend this never happened."

The car pulled up outside the apartment. Frank hopped out and held the door, signaling me to leave. I scrambled out of the car and onto the sidewalk.

But just before the car door closed completely, Alex pushed it back open. "Abbey, wait."

"Yes?"

"If we can't ignore it, what should we do?"

I stood up straight and looked him in the eye.

"Face it," I said. "Head-on."

After much debate, we decided the best place to confront the issue of the video was at the Holy Trinity Church voting station, where Alex and I were scheduled to cast our votes—and where we knew there'd be at least some media in attendance for the obligatory "candidate smiles, waves, and votes for himself" photo op. Normally, these standard photo ops were done first thing in the morning, but the morning's rain had washed out Kelly Drive and backed up the Schuylkill Expressway so badly, the press had asked us and the other candidates to postpone until noon. Frank had agreed, but only with the promise of definite air time. In just this one instance, this morning's rainstorm had worked in our favor.

So it was just Alex and me who crossed Rittenhouse Square and trotted up the wide steps of the church, me struggling to keep up with his long-legged stride. He hadn't looked at me since our conversation in the Suburban, and he gripped my hand a little too tight. But—ever the gentleman—he held the heavy wooden front door for me, as well as the metal door that would lead us to the basement polling station. I figured he was either saving his full ire for later— or pushing it down deep in his gut, where it could fester for days. Maybe months.

We walked down a red-carpeted hallway with gray stone walls and the occasional purple banner, so regal compared with Father Fergie's scuffed linoleum and painted cinder blocks. We were greeted by volunteers, excited to meet the candidate himself, and then led into the fellowship hall that housed the voting booths. As we walked in, we forced wide smiles, as if we were the two happiest people on the planet.

Inside the voting room we were met by a phalanx of reporters, and if there had been any question about whether the press had seen the YouTube video, this dispelled it. Usually this sort of staged photo op would warrant only a camera or two, and even then, the local affiliates' B teams. But today, I saw many of the city's most recognizable faces, including reporters from all four news stations, both the *Inquirer* and the *Daily News,* and our local news radio station. There were also some faces I didn't know—bloggers, most likely.

It didn't feel good to be proven right. I made a mental note to never read another gossip magazine again.

Still, I was glad I had coached Alex to fight this. Not just to defend my honor, but to stop this sordid snowball before it gathered even more speed. If Frank had gotten his way, and we had ignored it, who knew what kind of rumors would be circulating now? Next thing I knew, they'd be saying I was leaving Alex for Jimmy. And pregnant with his baby.

And whatever happened, at least this way we wouldn't go down without a fight.

When it was our turn to vote, Alex let me go first. I wanted to stay behind that flimsy blue curtain forever, but I pushed the button for an all-party ticket, hit the "Cast Your Ballot" button, and exited the booth. A moment later, when Alex emerged, he grabbed my hand and pulled me toward the waiting crowd. The reporters stepped closer as well, hoisting television cameras, opening notebooks, and thrusting microphones under our chins.

I could feel my neck getting blotchy with nerves. Sitting on your own couch in your own apartment talking to an on-the-make CNN reporter was one thing. But confronting a wall of Philadelphia media as they jostled one another for space, their expressions aggressive and accusatory, was terrifying. Luckily, Alex took charge.

"Wow. All of you came just to watch Abbey and me push a button? We're honored, really."

A few polite chuckles. He was following the script exactly as I'd coached: *Open with a joke. Use my first name. Don't mention the video directly, but also make light of it, as if it is so ridiculous, it's not worth anyone's time. In short, defuse it before anyone even gets the chance to lob a question.*

Alex continued: "It's been a long journey to get to today. Lots of ups and downs. But nothing, and I mean nothing, will stop me—stop us—from what we set out to do. And that's get to Washington to fight for Philadelphia families."

The strategy worked. The *Daily News* asked Alex what he thought his chances were. WPVI-TV's newest cub reporter pitched him a softball about the economy. And a graying old veteran from the *Inquirer*, who had been reporting for the paper long before "viral videos" became news—long before the Internet, even—asked about an upcoming tax reform proposal in the House. Alex fielded these easily and then started to make motions toward the exit. My hopes soared, and I was beginning to think we might escape without any direct questions, when someone yelled, "Just one more!" from the back.

The group stepped to either side, exposing the culprit. It was Jeremiah Lehane, a gossip blogger whose ThePhilth.com site was our local version of TMZ.

He smiled creepily from beneath his dirty black baseball cap and looked squarely at me: "Been to any good bars lately, Mrs. van Holt?"

I felt the color drain from my face and my throat go dry. Also, Alex's hand tightened on my own. Though whether in anger or solidarity I couldn't tell.

"I know what you're referring to, and it's ridiculous," interjected Alex, trying to remain calm. "You are trying to make something out of nothing."

Jeremiah smirked. "Nothing? Yesterday morning, you and your wife were on CNN pretending to have the perfect marriage. And then a few hours later she was cuddled up to some other guy at a dive bar in Chinatown. You gotta admit that if anything, it doesn't paint the best picture. Ain't like any 'fairy tale' I've ever read!"

He was throwing my own words back at me. What an asshole.

"I don't care what it looks like to anyone. My wife is not running for office—I am. And my wife can eat and drink anywhere, and sit down next to anyone, she wants. The real story here, and what most Philadelphians care about, is helping their families to..."

He was blocking and bridging to another topic. Great.

But Jeremiah had opened the door, signaling to the others that the elephant in the room could now be acknowledged. The cub TV reporter interrupted him with a blunt "So you two aren't getting divorced?"

Alex stiffened for a second, then gathered himself. "Of course not," he said. "Our marriage is fine." He put an arm around my waist and pulled me close. "Better than ever. Isn't that right, doll?"

He looked over at me, his eyes a tad wider than normal. As if he wasn't quite sure he could trust me to say the right thing. But I did.

"Absolutely," I said, looking past the cameras into the crowd. "It's perfect." I forced my most brilliant smile.

While I stood, flashes popping off, I noticed a woman in a bright yellow raincoat scribbling furiously in a little notebook. Her pencil tip snapped off and she scrambled in a big black purse for another, frantic. Beneath her parka she wore a half-buttoned maroon cardigan sweater and a rumpled skirt over rubber boots. Her hair was still damp from the morning's rain, or perhaps from sweat, and it clung to her bare face in little strings.

I stared at her, realizing that even though I didn't know her name or what paper she represented, I recognized her immediately. I knew all about her. She was a tired, overworked, underpaid, frazzled working mother trying desperately to get the story, get back to the office, finish it, file it, then pick up the kids by five and get dinner on the table by six.

She was the woman I used to be. And to look at her made me feel like such a phony. Like such a liar.

In those few seconds, I decided enough was enough. I had to set the record straight. And unlike the disastrous speech at the Friends of Lafayette tea, this time, words wouldn't fail me. This time, I would say what I wanted to say.

I shimmied out from under Alex's arm and stepped closer to the bouquet of microphones. "Actually, I'm not sure 'perfect' is the right way to describe our marriage. I'm really not sure *how* to describe it. But I can tell you, perfect isn't it."

The room went silent; I could hear my own breathing. My hands trembled but I kept talking, partly to the woman in the yellow slicker and partly to myself. "*I'm* not perfect either. In fact, more often than not, I'm a mess. My kid is so spoiled she slapped me. My mother-in-law thinks I'm certifiable. And my husband, God bless him, doesn't know *what* to think of me. Sometimes I don't think he even knows who I am."

I looked over at Alex. His smile was fixed but his eyes were worried about where I was going with this. Mine probably were too, since even I didn't know. Only, I knew I had to keep going, or forever hold my peace.

"So let me tell you exactly who I am. I am just the same as any of you. Trying to raise my kids right. Trying to be a good wife…daughter… mother. Trying to keep all the plates in the air, day in and day out, only instead of PTA meetings and job interviews, I'm juggling campaign events and fund-raisers and interviews. With all the city watching.

"But sometimes I get tired. Sometimes I say and do the wrong thing. Sometimes I feel sorry for myself, even though I know I shouldn't. Sometimes I want to give up and throw in the towel. Or have a good, long cry."

I took a deep breath. "And sometimes, like all of you, I just need a break. Need to get away from everything, sneak off, and steal a few minutes to myself. To sit on a barstool, have some friendly conversation, and down a nice, cold beer."

No one spoke. Or moved. It was if they didn't know what to do. Neither did I. All I knew was that I had lifted the veil on Abigail van Holt and shown the world the real woman underneath, and it felt good. Especially when I saw that the woman in the yellow raincoat was smiling at me. I smiled back. My only regret? That Jules wouldn't see this. But then again, the cameras had been rolling the whole time. Maybe she would.

Only, Jeremiah was not so easily thwarted. "But, Mrs. van Holt, what about the guy in the bar? Who was he?"

The question sent me reeling. For the past two hours, I'd been so fixated on crisis control and fixing my screw-up, I'd forgotten there was another person involved—Jimmy. What if he had seen it? What if it was causing problems in his life too? What if he felt used, like a pawn in a political game? And worse—what would he think about what I was about to say?

The guy. The guy. Who was the guy? It should have been simple. But for me, the question was so complex.

"The guy" was a guy who would be mortified to be caught in a video "canoodling" with a married woman, who would probably never live this down to his family and friends. He was a guy who always offered a kind word, some commiseration, maybe even a joke or two, whatever the situation called for, even when he was dead tired, and even when he might have wanted a moment alone. He was a guy who made people feel special—or, always made *me* feel special—and never asked for anything in return.

That was the guy. My guy.

As I stood there in Holy Trinity, I silently begged the man I had promised to have and to hold, for better or worse, until death do us part, to forgive me for what I was about to say. It didn't matter if it was meant in part to protect him from the jackals; I still felt more unfaithful at this moment than I had when I first slept with Alex days ago.

I leaned into the microphones and lied: "He was no one."

CHAPTER SEVENTEEN

What the hell happened?" gasped Bobby Bacco as he gazed from the door of the bathroom into my closet. He and his brother, Francis, had been doing my hair and makeup for tonight's post-election party but had yet to see the rock star–style trashing I had given the closet earlier.

"Jesus," added Francis. "It looks like you got robbed. Or a tornado came through."

I stood behind them in a towel and strained to find an excuse. But after the long day, my mind was blank.

Luckily, both men just sighed and waded in. I had completely forgotten about what I had done, but looking around now, I was as shocked as they were. The room was like a designer debris field, fabric strewn and twisted, shoes upended and scattered from their partners, a lone G-string caught on the chandelier. Except for Alex's side. His beautifully tailored suits and polished shoes were still lined up perfectly.

"I...I had a little trouble figuring out what to wear this morning," I said finally.

"A little trouble?" asked Bobby, looking back at me. "This is more like a...a...couture crime scene."

He leaned down to poke a wrinkled Armani jacket for signs of life.

"Why didn't you Skype us?" cried Francis. "There was no need to do this to these...these innocents." He scooped up a beaded Reem Acra sweater, held it close, then shushed it like a baby.

By now I knew that the Baccos' overdramatic shtick was part of the service they provided, but tonight I was not in the mood. I was exhausted from the emotional roller coaster of the day, and I really just wanted to be alone. Trying to hurry them along, I plucked a simple black ponte knit dress off the floor and asked, "So, how about this?"

"Another night, maybe," said Bobby, back to the business at hand. "But even if Alex loses, you're not going to a funeral. Something more fun."

I pulled out a short, sparkly number with fringe, a sarcastic smile on my face.

"Definitely not," replied Bobby, not realizing I was joking. "Not after today, missy." He scanned the dresses and pulled out a slate blue A-line Victoria Beckham dress. It was so prim and ladylike, I knew right then that they had both seen the video. I nodded my head in approval and understanding. From now on, there was only one "look" we'd be shooting for: demure.

I dropped my towel and the two men helped me into some lingerie and a slip, and as I felt their cold hands on my arms and legs, I realized that it had become perfectly natural for me to be naked in front of them. To them, I wasn't flesh and blood, but a window that needed dressing. But then I remembered the extra pounds I'd put on recently and sucked in my stomach.

They pretended not to notice, their indifference to weight fluctuations an important part of the stylists' code, but I saw them exchanging a glance. Luckily, the dress zipped up easily. They snapped on a Tiffany T bracelet and some chunky platinum earrings, rolled a lint brush over my torso, and placed a pair of black patent Christian

Louboutin heels in front of me. I stepped into them dutifully and turned to face the brothers.

Suddenly, Francis let out a little gasp. "What about a bag?"

"I don't care," I said. "Anything is fine."

He looked aghast. "Oh no, no, no. This is a big night. You need something really special."

He perused my shelf of bags, a finger to his lips, rejecting a woven Bottega Veneta, a boxy black Balmain, and a petite cream Chanel, until he arrived at the orange-and-brown box at the end of the shelf. His expression turned reverent.

He lifted it down and set it gently on the marble-topped dressing table. He took off the lid, brushed aside the tissue paper, and using just his fingertips—like an archbishop lifting a jewel-encrusted crown from its pedestal—brought out the red Hermès Kelly bag.

"Hello, gorgeous," he said, addressing the bag in a hushed tone.

"Don't you think that's a little much?" I asked. "I want voters to like me."

"Who gives a shit about voters now?" said Bobby. "Polls are closed."

"No, she's right," said Francis. "What about four years from now? If we're going to get to the White House, she's got to be careful."

White House? I wasn't sure I was hearing correctly.

"Look at all those photos of Hillary Clinton. Do you think she would have worn those awful padded headbands if she'd known she'd have to see them again and again for the next thirty years? You have got to start thinking about your look now."

I continued to stare, gob smacked.

"Don't look at *me* like that," said Francis, offended. "*You're* the one who always talks about it. You and Mirabelle."

As I continued to process, Bobby jumped in. "Ha! I never thought I'd ever hear those words—'you and Mirabelle'—together. God, how you used to hate her."

332 • Leigh Himes

"She still does," added Francis. "She just doesn't want to piss off the golden goose!"

"What?" I asked, interrupting.

"Well, sure, darling. If Mirabelle quits funding you guys, you're going to have to get out there and beg," he said, swatting my behind. "Even more reason to look amazing."

Mirabelle "funded" us? My face reddened under its NARS blush. The room suddenly felt smaller. And warmer. I pulled at the neck of my dress, but Francis slapped my hand down with a scowl. He slipped an iPad mini out of his jacket pocket and held it up to take a photo.

Bobby joined his brother behind the iPad and the two men chirped in unison, "Smile like you mean it!"

As I forced a smile and waited for the digital click, I flashed back to the last time I'd heard this catchphrase from the Baccos: a little over a week earlier, when they had styled me for the Ballantine Ball. At the time I'd assumed they were photographing the moment because it was such a special occasion. But now it occurred to me that this might be something they did whenever they styled Abbey van Holt.

I was suddenly curious about what else Francis's iPad held.

"May I?" I asked him, nodding to the device.

"Sure," he said, then hesitated, cautioning, "but it's too late to change your mind about the outfit."

"I won't. Promise."

He handed me the iPad and then turned to assist his brother in straightening the closet, hanging clothes back up and reuniting shoes with their mates.

I retreated to a corner of the closet with the iPad. On its home screen was a pink folder icon labeled with my name. I tapped it and a window opened with the picture Francis had just taken. I swiped it away to find a photo of the night of the Ballantine Ball—me wearing navy satin and diamonds, as well as the shell-shocked look of a woman who had just woken up in a stranger's life.

Finding the word "All," I clicked to bring up the entire contents of the folder and watched as the screen filled with dozens and dozens of tiny photos, each labeled with a date going back nearly a decade.

I was holding a "look book" of Abbey van Holt's life, a high-fashion catalogue of couture dresses, exquisite shoes, elaborate updos. And yet it wasn't the clothes I was interested in.

With a shaking finger, I scrolled through the thumbnails until I found the earliest photo in the file—more than ten years ago—and tapped it open.

The thumbnail bloomed open into a photo of a decade-younger me, ears still double pierced, hair long and loose, eyebrows untidy. She had the dazed look of someone in a mug shot, like a debutante being booked on a DUI.

The clothes and hair were different in the next photo, but the expression remained the same: a little startled, as if I'd just been ambushed by paparazzi.

I began swiping faster and faster and found images of me wearing a flowered sundress; a serious-looking suit; jeans and braids (some sort of charity hoedown?); an embroidered cerise sheath; a green suede pencil skirt, crisp white blouse, and tall brown boots; and a lovely gray chiffon gown, its beaded bodice reflecting light in white pinwheels.

Viewed in quick succession, like a child's flip-book, the photos showed my transformation from the newlywed Abbey into the thinner, sleeker, more polished version—one with the poise of a moneyed heiress, the confidence of a future congressman's wife. It was impressive to behold, even a little awe-inspiring. But it was also unsettling, as if with the transformation came a curse: the woman in the photos slowly morphing into something inanimate, like a marble statue.

I lingered on the photo dated "October 18th," taken just days before I tumbled down Nordstrom's escalator and fell headlong into Abbey van Holt's life. In the photo, she was elegant as always, in a Valentino red silk cocktail dress and black satin pumps. But the uncertain look of her earlier days was gone, replaced by a weary resignation.

And something else.

I enlarged the photo to its maximum amplification so I could peer closely at Abbey van Holt's gray-blue eyes—the only parts of her that hadn't been touched or tweezed or tweaked by the Baccos, and Botox, and self-tanner, and personal trainers. The only parts of her that remained unchanged.

I knew those eyes. They were mine. *Ours.* Knew the look in them too, though it took me a few moments to find the word to describe it.

Loneliness.

"Finished with that?"

It was Francis—suddenly appearing beside me—making me jump. I must have looked ashen, because his eyes widened with concern.

"What's wrong?" he asked. "I told you; we're not changing the dress. It photographs great."

"No. Yes. I mean—the dress is fine. I'm fine. Can I just have another minute?"

His lips formed a disapproving pout. "Just one—you're late as it is."

He grabbed the iPad, then left to join his brother cleaning up in the bathroom.

I looked around the now-tidy closet, clothes and shoes returned to their proper places, order restored. I ran my fingers along the row of clothes on padded hangers, setting the satin and silk sleeves rippling like a wave.

I shut my eyes and leaned my forehead against the dressing mirror's cool glass, steeling myself for the night ahead. And suddenly knew, with the spooky intuition of a twin, that Abbey van Holt had done the same—on more than one occasion. I understood then, at some primal level, that she and I were the same.

This time it didn't take as long to find the word for what I was feeling toward her: sympathy.

I opened my eyes. Saw her looking back at me from inside the mirror. For a few heartbeats, neither of us moved. Then I silently swore to her—to both of us—that things were going to change.

"All done!" the Baccos shouted from the bathroom. I followed them out to the living room, the suitcase wheels rumbling on the hardwood, and walked them to the door.

"Good luck!" said Francis, giving me an air-kiss.

"See you Friday!" added Bobby with a wink.

"Actually, boys, before you go—I want to tell you something."

Their heads cocked in unison.

"Thank you for everything. I really appreciate your hard work—"

"Don't mention it," said Bobby. "Our pleasure."

"You *are* our favorite client," added Francis.

"Was. I *was* your favorite client," I said. This got their attention. I took a breath and broke the news: "With the election over, I won't be needing you guys anymore."

Their mouths dropped in shock.

It was a small step, but for the first time in forever, I knew it was in the right direction.

CHAPTER EIGHTEEN

The polls had only just closed and it was anyone's game. Only the first few districts had reported, and those along with the mail-in ballots put Alex and Amanda in a statistical dead heat, though technically Alex trailed by half a point. Even though this was still within the margin of error, and even though we were waiting it out in the calm luxury of the Ritz-Carlton penthouse suite, tensions were understandably high. No one laughed or made jokes; no one ate or drank. Everyone just stared at computers, phones, and the television, waiting for news.

At least the weather was finally cooperating. The rain had stopped and voters who had stayed away all day now stood under tranquil skies to cast their ballots. Our volunteers at all the major polling places had reported long lines, some even extending down sidewalks and around buildings. And according to minute-by-minute updates from Alex's overeager groupie, Gerald, the longest line was in East Falls, where William Wallace had made good on his promise. In a video texted to Alex's phone, we watched as voters stood patiently in a quarter-mile trail running from the tiny post office polling station down to the churning, rain-sodden river.

I thought of my e-mail to Larry. Would anything come of it? Had she even gotten it? So far, no story had run. So far, only Wallace was keeping up his side of the bargain. But given the day's events, maybe it was for the best.

As the clock slowly wound down on the election, and the air got even thicker with worry and dread, I mostly hid out in the suite's tiny kitchen or in the bedroom. I was trying to stay out of the way, trying not to cause any more trouble. But mostly I was trying to avoid the television, where the local news programs had been rerunning clips of my Holy Trinity speech all afternoon. I was terrified to be in the same room as Mirabelle when she watched the same sound bite—"down a nice, cold beer"—being played over and over again.

But every few minutes, I had to step into the main room to check on the kids, and when I did, I could see my van Holt world as it had become. And all the players in it.

There was Frank, on his phone and computing poll numbers on the back of a room service menu; Calvin toggling between his iPad, BlackBerry, and laptop for updates, and Sunita flipping between local affiliates on the TV. In a corner, Aubyn babysat her father, plying him with diet Sprite and gin rummy. The only person who was relaxed was Collier's nurse, Luis, who tuned everything out with his iPod. He knew, as did everyone else, that he wouldn't be needed until, well, he was needed.

The only character in this cast who was missing was May. I knew that if she had still been working for us, she would have been mouthing a silent Thai prayer for Alex's sake, picking up dishes and newspapers, and following the kids around with a washcloth. It was hard to believe I was the only person, besides Sam, who felt her absence. When he asked for his beloved "May May" for the fortieth time today, all I could do was hug him close and whisper, "Sorry, Mr. Magoo. You're stuck with me from now on."

Mirabelle flitted around at a faster pace than normal, fussing over the food and barking at the Ritz staff while eavesdropping on everyone's conversations, anxious for any news in our favor. She also toyed with me, making comments like "such an unusual day" and referring to me as "Alex's outspoken wife" when I came up in conversation. I could tell she was only biding her time for when she would try to convince Alex of her troubling theories. I felt like I was trapped in a cage with a viper, waiting for the day that she would strike.

And of course, there was Alex, perched on the edge of a sofa beside Frank, staring blankly at some notes, the television, or his phone. He seemed subdued, as if saving his strength for what was to come later tonight.

Despite the close quarters, everyone except the children ignored me, speaking to me only when they needed to, or to ask me for more shrimp/napkins/tonic. Because of the trouble I had caused, I was no longer to be trusted and therefore barely worthy of acknowledgment. I felt the same way I had felt in high school and, lately, at my PR job: invisible.

Now I understood why Abbey van Holt had changed so much over the past ten years. She must have learned, through her own missteps, that being yourself, making your own decisions, and occasionally going rogue carried a price tag. It meant being questioned, watched, worried over, and, eventually, excluded. A person made to disappear in plain sight.

Just like Collier, I was living in a world where I was tolerated but not really wanted. And funny, he was the only one who seemed to be able to see me. When I passed by him, he took my arm and whispered, "Don't look so glum, Abigail. Sometimes being the black sheep has its advantages!" I smiled and sat down beside him, watching his hands shake as he placed one card after another on the deck.

My eyes found Alex again, and I studied his face. He was the only one in this group whose opinion mattered to me, the only person whose forgiveness it would be impossible to live without. And though he had been polite to me these past few hours—he was *always* polite—I knew he was still trying to process the day's events. As well as the current state of our marriage.

But, honestly, so was I. Was he still angry with me? When would we move on? Would I even know? And where would we go from here? With Jimmy, I always knew where I stood. With Alex, it was infinitely more confusing. I sighed and continued to move around the party like a ghost.

Never in my life had I felt more alone.

"Precinct six is in," announced Frank. "Bullock took it." There was a collective groan, but this was no surprise, precinct six—the opponent's own neighborhood—never really being in play for us.

When Gloria walked by, I attempted to pull her into a hug, but she wriggled out of my grasp, too busy exploring the suite. Faithful Sam took her place, toddling up with a smile when I beckoned to him. We played horsey and tickle spider, and for a short time, I forgot the election. But then suddenly Frank, leaning over Calvin's laptop and squinting, barked out more updates: "Precincts two and ten are all in. Eleven too. This is it, folks."

A hush fell. Even Sam went silent. Beneath his glasses, Frank's eyes moved left and right as he read the screen. Finally, he dropped his head and closed his eyes. Exhaled loudly. Then spun around to look at Alex.

And grinned. "Congratulations, Congressman."

The room exploded in cheers. Then hugs, laughter, sighs all around. Aubyn offered a rare smile, Mirabelle threw up her hands to the heavens, and Collier beamed. Calvin, usually so reserved, stood up on a sofa and fist pumped while he shouted, "Fuck, yes!"

before remembering the children. I stood awkwardly, clapping, then knelt down to check Sam's diaper for the thousandth time that evening.

When I stood again, Alex was there, pulling me into a stiff hug and giving me a perfunctory kiss, then whispering a quiet "It's over." It was the first contact I'd had with him since we left Holy Trinity, and to have him acknowledge me physically, even if it was just for show, made me want to cry with relief. Then he was on the phone, fielding a string of congratulatory calls—from the party leaders, the mayor, the governor—as well as a concession call from Amanda Bullock.

Someone popped champagne and Frank walked over to me with a glass.

"A peace offering?" He looked at me with a hangdog expression, his eyes peeking out above his glasses.

"Sure." I took a small sip, then put the glass down, aware of Mirabelle watching from the corner of my eye.

"I'm not afraid to admit when I'm wrong," he continued. "It *was* better to face the issue. And as it turns out, your little speech at Holy Trinity gave us the bump we needed. Delaware County came in strong. Record numbers."

"Really?"

"Really." I couldn't believe it. Finally, I had done something right. And it just may have given Alex the edge over Amanda.

Frank lifted his glass in a toast, took a sip, then cocked his head to one side. "But from now on, can you please be a little more careful?"

"Sure." I gave him a genuine smile. He smiled too, then returned to Alex. I knew he didn't really care for me, but at least now we weren't at each other's throats.

Behind me, I heard another champagne cork pop. Then another. The party had officially begun. And one by one, people started talking to me again, greeting me as if I had just arrived. With Alex's win—and, more important, his show of affection—I was visible again. Even Mirabelle managed to acknowledge me, offering a stiff "Excuse me, Abigail," as she passed to pick up a plate.

I shuddered to think what would have happened if he had lost.

Feeling as if I had just been let out of purgatory, I relented on my "no jumping on the furniture" policy and let the kids bounce away. As I watched them chase each other through the apartment-sized suite, I was glad to see they were oblivious to what the night meant. There would be time later to discuss the changes coming; tonight was supposed to be about celebrating. I forced a smile on my face and began to circulate through the room, thanking supporters.

The suite became cluttered with crumpled napkins, water bottles, half-smoked cigars, and discarded newspapers. Every few minutes, Ritz employees swept through to clear glasses and plates and check with me to make sure everything was "satisfactory." "Fine," I told them the seven times they asked. I guess these were the types of stimulating questions I'd have to answer in my new role as congressional wife.

It was getting late, and I was worried the kids might melt down, but Frank assured me we would leave for the victory party very soon. I told the kids they could each get a cookie from the dessert buffet, hoping some sugar might pep them up for the home stretch. Gloria picked a sugar cookie, but Sam went right for the chocolate éclairs. He grabbed two, grinning at his good fortune, then escaped under the table before I could check the chocolate topping for nuts.

Mirabelle ran up and dropped to her knees on the other side, trying to reason with him. But the more she begged, the harder he gripped his éclairs, the cream and chocolate running down his arms and dangerously close to his navy-and-white sailor suit. She stood and flashed me a look of disgust. "I don't know why you let him have things like that. Now what are we to do?"

I ignored her and rushed around to the other side of the table to cut Sam off, only to see him slip out under a chair and take off toward the bedroom. He ducked past Calvin and Sunita—busy flirting over beers—then breezed by Aubyn and Collier, still hard at their card game.

"Run, Van, run!" cheered Frank from across the room.

"Look at the little stallion go!" slurred Collier. Aubyn looked up from her cards and tried not to laugh.

I followed Mirabelle, surprisingly nimble in her kitten heels, as she cornered Sam in the bedroom. "My tweat!" he shrieked in outrage. "My tweat!"

"Give them to Grandmère," she said menacingly. He shook his head and retreated farther into his corner, clutching his gooey prizes but, luckily, not yet putting them to his lips.

Finally, Mirabelle, who was closer, grabbed him hard by the shoulder. But he wrestled free and escaped. As he made a break for the door, I crouched to catch him. But at 122 pounds and in four-inch heels, I didn't stand a chance. He barreled into me, knocking me backward off my feet and onto the carpet.

Mirabelle, ever the lady, offered her hand. I pulled down the hem of my dress and pushed the hair out of my face, hot with embarrassment. Around me, a few onlookers, curious to see who would win the battle of the éclairs, stood motionless and stared. I noticed they weren't looking at my face, but farther down. My eyes followed theirs.

Across the front of my beautiful blue dress were two perfect little ganache handprints.

As I stood in my bra and underwear in the bathroom, Mirabelle and a woman from the Ritz housekeeping staff tried their best to clean the dress with club soda. They dabbed and rinsed and dabbed and rinsed, but the stains only got bigger and darker, happy to make their home in the finely napped wool.

"I should have known something like this would happen," said Mirabelle.

I knew what she was thinking—that I was drunk again—but I said nothing in rebuttal. By now, I knew she was going to believe what she wanted to believe.

Still scrubbing, she continued her tirade: "The Baccos told me about earlier. Your little moments 'alone.' The closet all torn apart."

Though I had just fired Bobby and Francis and would probably never see them again, her words stung. I was in fact *not* their favorite client... Mirabelle was. I shivered in my slip, then wrapped my arms around my waist.

"So I have a messy closet and sometimes I need a few moments alone. That doesn't mean I'm a drunk."

Ignoring me, she threw the stained dress onto the ground in disgust. "This is ruined."

"I'll just run back to the apartment. Or send Sunita."

"There's no time," she said. "Frank says they need you downstairs now."

"Well, I guess this will have to do, then," I said, irritated. I picked the dress up from the floor.

"No," said Mirabelle, snatching it back from me. "It won't do. I've worked too hard—" She caught herself. "You represent our family. I won't have us be laughed at anymore today."

Her face was white with anger.

"It's not a big deal," I assured her. "Alex won. There's no more—"

"Quiet," she said. "Let me think."

She sighed and took off her jacket—a beautifully tailored peacock-colored wool—and handed it to me. "Here. Take this."

She slipped off her white silk blouse and the matching blue-green skirt and handed those to me as well. Against her knee-length beige slip, her body was pale, the flesh clinging on tiny bones, as if she was about to be mummified.

"Put them on," she hissed. "For heaven's sake, just put them on."

I slid on the blouse and skirt, then the jacket. The skirt was shorter on me and the blouse strained over my breasts, but they would do.

"Thank you."

She waved away my words imperiously as she pulled on a robe from the back of the door. "And whatever you do, don't throw those into the wash. *Dry. Clean. Only.*" As if I was an idiot.

I sighed and rolled my eyes, then noticed that her hands were clenched in tight balls. She was so tense, and shaking, she could barely tie the robe.

"Can I help you?" I asked as she struggled with the fuzzy fabric. She might have hated me, wanted me locked up, but looking at her—so flustered and overwrought—I couldn't help but feel for her.

Why couldn't she just enjoy what was happening? Her son had done it. He had won.

"Don't touch me," she barked, jumping back as I reached out to her. "You...you...almost ruined it all."

"But I didn't," I told her. "Alex is a congressman. Aren't you happy?"

She looked up at me, and for just an instant, and for the first time, I saw confusion in her eyes. Vulnerability, even. I saw the young woman she used to be, one full of soft white hopes and red-hot exuberance. The person who existed before all her dreams—and her honest affections—hardened into glass.

I realized the answer to my own question. She wasn't happy. She could never be happy. She was holding on to this family so tightly, she was past emotion. And after today, and all the added stress I had caused, she was this close to shattering.

I wanted to take her in my arms and hold her like a small child. Tell her there was still a chance for her, if she would just take her hands off the wheel. If she would just let herself, and the people around her, coast for a little while. But before I could, she was gone.

"Do you need anything else, miss?" I had forgotten the maid was still in the bathroom. I looked up and told her, "No, thank you," then turned toward the mirror. The woman slipped out quietly, leaving me alone. I washed my hands and patted them on the thick white hand towel. I looked at my engagement ring, one that might have even been Mirabelle's, and felt its heaviness more than ever.

Mirabelle had planned for this moment her entire life. But what she didn't know, what she probably wouldn't realize until later, was that Alex's win—the thing she so desperately wanted, the thing she thought would tie him to her and her money forever—might also be his escape. Our escape. Living in Washington, DC, would put 150 miles between us and Bloemveld. Between us and her toxic, smothering kind of love.

But then I looked up to check myself one final time and shuddered. In the mirror, I realized Mirabelle might always be close, closer than I would have liked.

In her suit, and with my razor-sharp bob and heavy jewelry, I looked just like her.

A plainclothes security guard escorted us down a dark hallway, through a service area, and into a blanket-lined freight elevator that would take us—Alex holding Gloria, me holding Sam—to the celebration below. The guard listened to chatter on his earpiece and the kids giggled with excitement while Alex and I rode in silence, still overwhelmed by what had just happened. My husband had become the next congressman representing the second district of Philadelphia, a post that could be traced all the way back to 1791.

"Wow," said Alex, breaking the silence. "We did it."

"Congratulations," I told him. "I'm so proud of you."

"Thanks."

We were speaking again. Perhaps now was the time to clear the air. I decided to go first.

"Alex. I'm sorry again about yesterday. I promised Frank from now on I'd be careful. Check with you guys whenever I do anything that might be taken the wrong way."

I waited for him to tell me he was still mad, I was officially forgiven, or somewhere in between—*anything*—but instead he waved his hand in the air and said, "Forget it."

That was all I would get. It wasn't like I expected a big proclamation, but this wasn't a small thing; I'd nearly ruined the campaign. I wished he could give me more, and if not in words, then in actions: a real kiss or a real hug. I swore then and there I would never take those three little words—"I forgive you"—for granted again. I would offer them whenever I got the chance.

The elevator stopped on a mid-level floor to reveal an older couple holding hands and about to step on. The security guard demanded they wait for the next car and the doors slid shut on their confused faces. I changed the subject. "Maybe this weekend, we can all get away for a few days, just the four of us," I suggested. "Before things get crazy again."

He lifted his brows and tilted his head as if considering it, but didn't respond. He turned his attention to Gloria, tickling her until she squealed. Once she quieted, he turned back to me. "Abbey…"

"Yes?"

"I've been thinking that maybe it would be good for you to go back to work. Not full-time, but..."

"You sure?"

"I am. For starters, I know a freshmen congressman who could really use some help. With appointments and events, that kind of thing."

It wasn't really what I had in mind—I was a publicist, not an administrative assistant—but it was a start. "Will you put in a good word for me, then?"

"My highest recommendation." He winked at me and I understood that he had put today's events behind him and was ready to move on. We both exhaled heavily.

The *baloop* of his phone indicated a new text. He looked down and his brow furrowed. "That's weird."

"What?"

"Ariel Morganstern texted me. Says the *Inquirer* just posted a story linking him to East Falls. For the new headquarters."

My face turned hot and the elevator walls seemed to close in, but I forced myself to sound nonchalant. "Really?"

"This isn't good. Brindle is going to be pissed."

"Well, it's not your fault."

"But *someone* tipped off the press. Who?"

"People talk. Things get out. That's just the way it is." I barely breathed, waiting for his response. But he said nothing, thinking, the static from the security guard's earpiece and Sam's strenuous thumb sucking the only sounds.

Alex looked over at me, at first suspicious but then somewhat bemused. "Is it?"

Watching his expression, I knew I could have confessed. But I was tired of explaining myself to this man. I returned his gaze with a blank stare and then asked, "What?" as if I had no idea what he was alluding to. As if inside I wasn't doing a little happy dance, knowing I'd done something good for East Falls.

Alex opened his mouth to speak again but stopped himself. He was tired too. He shrugged, then pressed off his phone and slipped it into his jacket pocket. Whatever else was on that phone—whatever other fallout he would have to deal with—could wait until tomorrow.

The elevator doors opened and the roar that erupted from the supporters lining the hallway drowned out any further conversation. We began to walk, and soon the article on East Falls was forgotten in the *beat-beat-beat* of the professional sound system and the cheers and clapping of a party in full swing.

As we followed a few steps behind two rent-a-cops on the red-and-gold-carpeted hallway, people turned one by one to see us and then began to cheer, clap, and chant our name. The guards tried to maintain control, but soon we were engulfed by ecstatic supporters and well-wishers. Alex shook hands, waved, and gave a few hugs. A teenage boy threw confetti; a middle-aged lady in a "Van Holt for Congress" T-shirt started to cry; and two inebriated college girls giggled and hugged each other in excitement as Alex passed by. Flashes from iPhones blinked all around us. Sam tucked his head into my neck.

When we entered the ballroom, filled to capacity with people, tables, balloons, and servers, cheers rippled through the room. There must have been a thousand people there, all taking selfies, enjoying the free liquor and soft pretzels, and dancing to a five-piece band butchering a Van Morrison song. Disco lights swirled, and the entire room seemed to pulse to the music. It felt like a frat party, except for all the sports coats and stiletto heels. Everyone here was a supporter of the campaign, and from the looks of it, most supported with their checkbooks, not canvassing door to door.

We shook hands on the way to the stage and braced ourselves as animated faces came in close for hugs and kisses. I recognized some people from the week's events, and some from that first Bloemveld cocktail party. Even Betsy and Ellen were there, both having seemingly forgotten the incident at lunch. Alex was only two minutes into being a congressman and already I was feeling the power.

Beside the stage, while Alex conferred one last time with Frank, Mindy rushed up to me, panting with excitement. She enveloped me in a hug, then planted a bloodred stain on Sam's blond wisps.

"*Loved* your speech today," she told me. "I'm happy to know I'm not the only hot mess in town." She gave a loud laugh/snort, then put her hands to her face as if to say, *See what I mean?*

"You're not a mess," I told her. "You're great."

"Thanks. But you wouldn't have said that if you saw me earlier. The boys were out of control today. I almost didn't think I'd make it tonight. I still haven't solved my nanny problem."

"Your nanny problem?"

"Mine moved back to Sweden, remember?"

"That's right!" I said, more excitedly than the situation called for. She looked at me funny, so I quickly explained: Alex and I had recently let May go. It was time to try life without a full-time nanny for a while. Any chance that *she* might be interested in hiring her?

She looked at me wide-eyed and excited. "Yes! I would love that!"

I explained the one caveat: May was much in demand, with several women already fighting over her...If Mindy wanted her, she would have to make a really nice offer. Maybe even throw in a shorter workweek, say, only thirty hours, and never on nights or weekends, just to edge out the competition.

My friend's face turned grave with understanding—and determination. She thanked me profusely and then ran off, pushing her way through the crowd. I knew she was looking for her husband, eager to tell him the good news: They had a lead on a new nanny. And not just any nanny—*the van Holts' former nanny.*

I did it to help May, but also us. I knew that since Mindy's children went to the same school as Gloria, my kids could at least see their beloved May from time to time. And the van Holts would never have to know. I smiled at my own cunning, then moved quickly to stand beside Alex, who was waiting for his big moment.

Onstage, Alex gave the cheesy campaign-speak a rest, instead giving a funny, self-deprecating speech made twice as long by bouts of laughing and clapping from the crowd. When it was over, he grabbed my hand and lifted our arms together over our heads, and I heard the crowd cheer harder than ever. And when he leaned over and kissed me, they went crazy. The noise and flashes and exuberance were amazing.

And yet, despite the win, despite the adulation, despite how gorgeous Alex looked with his loosened tie, weary eyes, and five-o'clock shadow, I felt detached from the scene, as if I was watching us all from afar, looking down at myself from the giant crystal chandelier. Alex leaned over and whispered that he loved me, his voice warm and sincere. It was the forgiveness I wanted, but, strangely, I struggled to feel relief. I struggled to feel anything.

Alex put his arm around me and I looked up and imitated his wide smile. Even though we had won and I had ended up being a small contributor to our success; even though May would have a better job than the one she had with me; and even though I was no longer afraid of Mirabelle or any of her threats; I smiled back with my lips and cheeks and eyes, but not my heart.

Deep down, my heart was somewhere else.

CHAPTER NINETEEN

Alone at last.

Oscar had taken the kids and Aubyn back to our apartment immediately after the speech; a triumphant Mirabelle, a stumbling Collier, and the noiseless Luis were in a cab back to Bloemveld; Calvin, Sunita, and the rest of the twentysomethings were making the rounds of after-parties; and Alex and a gleeful Frank were fielding television interviews in a lobby corner. I found myself in the silent suite, with only a few lost coats and *Action News at Eleven* to keep me company.

I kicked off my shoes, opened a Heineken, and commandeered a platter of leftover desserts. I deserved a treat. I had worked hard for this win too.

Sam was right, I thought as I bit into a gooey éclair. *These* are *worth fighting for.* I was about to devour a second when a knock at the door froze me mid-bite. I kept quiet, hoping whomever it was would go away, so I could resume drowning my sorrows in pastry cream. But whomever it was knocked again: *rat-a-tat-tat-tat.* I sighed and got up to answer the door, my stockinged feet slick on the thick carpet.

"Yes?" I called, putting my eye to the peephole and finding four inches of cleavage, distorted to Dolly Parton–like proportions in the curve of the fish-eye lens.

Roberta. In the van Holt world.

I swung open the door, dropping my beer in surprise. I saw her smile at me, then look down and frown at the puddle fizzing at our feet.

"Shit!" she said as she looked around for a napkin, before pulling out a *People* magazine from her bag and blotting the carpet with it. As she patted, then gave up with a short sigh, I drank her in.

She looked the same as always: overly tan, overly blond, and in clothes that even Barbie might reconsider: a purple faux-Juicy sweatshirt unzipped to reveal a low-cut silver studded tank top, stretchy white jeans, and fuzzy black boots. Her nails were long and bloodred, her lips pursed and glossy.

Normally, she reminded me of a past-her-prime ski bunny or an airport cocktail waitress. But tonight she looked like an angel.

I reached over and touched her face, just to make sure she was real.

It was her "tiger spirit" that told her to come.

As luck would have it, Roberta had caught yesterday's CNN interview via the shipboard satellite TV and immediately sensing something was "off" about me, she got herself helicoptered to the closest Greek island (Mykonos), where she was able to book a puddle jumper to Rome and then a red-eye flight home to Philly.

"I just can't believe it's you," I told her once the initial shock had worn off. "I've missed you."

"Wow, now I *know* something is wrong," she deadpanned.

"What? I'm fine."

She gave me the same look she always gave me when she knew I was lying. I turned back toward the couch and my éclairs, and she followed.

"Abigail, tell me what's going on. I didn't fly seven thousand miles for you to act like everything is okay."

I stared at her for a second, honestly not knowing where to begin. I bought some time by opening another beer and taking a sip.

"I swear, Mom. Nothing's wrong."

"I haven't seen you drink a beer in ten years. Out with it."

I considered telling her the truth. The whole truth. This was not my life. This was just an elaborate joke or delusion or an incredibly lifelike dream. And part of me felt that if anyone could believe in alternate realities, it was Roberta. But I also worried she would do what any other good mother would do: listen attentively and nod, and then, when I wasn't looking, call 911 and have me hauled off to a psych ward.

"Let's just say I'm confused," I told her.

"Confused about what? Prince Valiant won. I thought you'd be ecstatic."

"I know. I should be. It's…complicated."

She started to respond but stopped. Instead, she reached over and put her hand on my shoulder.

"I don't care about complications," she said. "I care about you. Are you okay?"

"Yes. No. I don't know," I stammered. "I'm just confused. And tired. So tired."

"Well, you don't have to do anything this minute," she said. "The election's over. You can take a few hours off from being Mrs. Alexander van Holt. For the next little while, why don't you just be my daughter?"

"Gladly," I said. And for the first time in a very long time, I curled up under her arm and put my head on her shoulder.

And I cried.

* * *

Roberta held me in her arms, rocking me and shushing me like I was a heartsick teen. She smelled of coconut lotion and hairspray with just a hint of something medicinal. The skin of her neck felt soft and loose, the only part of her like a traditional grandmother, though she would have been horrified if she knew I thought that.

When my sobbing had quieted, she looked straight ahead, lost in thought, and began to speak:

"When your father and I got married, I thought I had it all—a nice husband with a good job, a cute little house, and a beautiful baby girl," she said. "I baked tuna casseroles and sewed curtains and washed and dried and ironed. Trying to be the perfect wife, the perfect mother, the perfect neighbor. I even went to church on Sunday!"

She sighed to herself and continued. "I did everything I was supposed to do…and still my husband left me."

I sat up in surprise. "Dad left *you*?"

"I know I've always made it sound like I was the one who did the leaving. That I happily left the rat bastard behind. But it's not true." She took a breath, and I could see the effort it took for her to admit the truth. "Your father left me a note written on the back of an unpaid oil bill. He said he had fallen in love with a woman named April Dawn and he was moving to Florida with her. Can you imagine? He left me for a woman named after dish soap."

I couldn't believe what I was hearing. I had a million and one questions but kept quiet, letting her finish.

"For weeks, I refused to believe it," she continued. "Big-time denial. When I finally realized he wasn't coming back, I was devastated. And then really depressed. I couldn't get out of bed. Couldn't take care of you. My mother had to come up from Virginia and live with us."

Roberta depressed? I couldn't imagine it. She was always so capable, so positive. I'd never even seen her cry.

"Life went on—as it does—but I was holding on by a thread. Then, a few months later, you started to talk. And talk and talk and talk. And scream and laugh and run around the house bellowing like you owned the place. I swear, you were the loudest kid ever. And the funny thing is, you didn't care a hoot about casseroles or clean sheets or any of that shit. All you wanted to do was wear tutus and sing songs and eat as many marshmallows as humanly possible.

"One day I woke up from a nap to hear you playing outside with the hose. You thought it was funny to spray Grandmom Gloria and she was getting really pissed off. Every time she went to grab it from you, you would dash out of reach and then hit her again. Finally she caught you and was about to spank you, when you let out the loudest, most primal scream I've ever heard. It's a wonder no one called the cops. I got up out of bed and went to the window, and I'll never forget what I saw." She closed her eyes, as if the scene was replaying in her head. "You were standing in the sunlight in your underwear. Water dripping off your golden curls. And you had your arms out like this"—she demonstrated—"and this look of sheer defiance on your face. I couldn't take my eyes off you. At two years old, you looked so powerful. So incredibly fearless. Scared the shit out of Grandmom."

She laughed at the memory.

"And that was the moment I decided to get out of bed. I went outside, picked you up, and told your grandmother we wouldn't need her anymore. It was as if everything suddenly became clear to me. I was done being perfect. From then on, I was going to be just like that little girl with the hose. I was going to do what I wanted and the world would have to deal with it."

She sighed, and after a moment said quietly, "I know people make fun of the way I dress and the younger men and the sports car and the bikinis. But I don't care. I really don't. The way I figure it, I earned it."

She let the words linger for a moment before shifting toward me. Her hands moved up and grasped my tear-stained face, turning it toward her so she could hold my eyes with hers.

"I know you say you're confused. That everything is complicated. Maybe you even feel as hopeless as I did when your dad left," she said, her voice soft, almost a whisper. "But, my darling, maybe your rock bottom isn't made of rock. Maybe it's soft. Hell, maybe it's made of marshmallows. Why don't you push your way through and see what's on the other side?"

After my mother left to go sleep off the jet lag, I went outside onto the suite's wide balcony and admired the view of city hall, its round clock face glowing yellow beneath a navy sky. After the stuffy suite and crowded ballroom, it felt good to breathe in the cool night air.

I thought about what Roberta had told me. All these years, I had never known she suffered so much after my father left. She always made her divorce seem so unimportant, a minor plot point in the glamorous and exciting movie that was her life. It made me feel embarrassed, and selfish.

I put my hand on the thick concrete parapet and looked down at Chestnut Street. From where I stood, fourteen floors up, the streets below looked peaceful and dreamlike. Occasionally, a few cars moved past or a young reveler pierced the hum with a shout. But mostly, the city was beautiful and silent and anonymous.

Behind me, the slam of a door made me jump. It was Alex returning. I stepped inside the suite and slid the balcony door shut.

"How did the interviews go?"

"Fine," he said, as he filled half a glass with gin and dropped in an ice cube. I realized then, watching him take a sip and grimace, I'd never seen him drink alcohol before.

"Just fine?" I asked.

He nodded, took another sip, then looked past me toward the balcony. "Is it raining again?"

"No, it's just cold."

He dropped his iPhone on the table and stripped off his tie, slipped off his jacket.

"Guess the morning rain didn't keep voters away after all," I continued. "Frank said it was a record turnout."

"Looks like it," he said. "They came out. In droves. And now I'm their man."

"You don't sound all that excited."

"It's just a lot to take in, a lot of changes coming for us."

"But just think of all the good you can do—"

He cut me off quickly: "I know, I know. It's a great achievement. A tremendous responsibility. An honor for the van Holts...blah, blah, blah."

I smarted at his tone. And stared at him. It was not the face of someone who had just won an election. I walked over and sat beside him, picking up his free hand.

"Alex?" I asked, my eyes looking into his. "Do you even *want* to be a congressman?"

He looked surprised and—for a fleeting moment—something else: afraid. As if I had uncovered something he was trying very hard to keep buried. Suddenly, so much of the past week made sense. The passive-aggressive arguments, the freezing up on national television, even the strange obsessive-compulsive behavior about clean shirts. He was running for Congress because he *had* to, not because he wanted to. Deep down, there was nothing he wanted less. And his unhappiness, and suppressed defiance, bubbled up at the most inopportune of times.

Still, he kept to the script. "Of course I do," he said testily—and unconvincingly. "What did you think...I was just in it for the free stationery?" He gave a halfhearted laugh.

It wasn't the first time I had seen him charm his way out of an uncomfortable emotion. And though I had known him only a week, I suspected it was a lifelong instinct for avoiding painful truths. I felt a pang of sympathy for him. Alexander van Holt. Newly elected congressman from the second district of Pennsylvania. Trapped in a life—and a family—he couldn't escape.

An imposter, just like me.

"Well, it is really nice stationery," I said, taking his lead. "I hear it's embossed." I pretended to swoon.

He laughed, grabbed my hand, and kissed it. We were partners in this charade.

"We'd better get home," I said. "It's late." I walked over to get my purse.

"Not so fast," he said, not letting my hand go. "I was thinking we could stay here tonight. Seems a shame to let this big suite go to waste."

"But what about the kids?"

"They're at home with Aubyn. She can handle them until morning."

"Oh, Alex. I don't know..."

"I do," he said, turning my face to his and kissing me.

I tried to respond, but my lips barely moved.

"What's wrong?" he asked.

"Nothing. Sorry."

He kissed me again. He tasted of gin, and his stubble was rough against my lips and throat. I closed my eyes and tried to give myself over to him, waiting for my burners to ignite. But nothing. I kissed him harder, hoping to kick-start the flame.

"Room service," called a voice from outside.

"I almost forgot!" exclaimed Alex, with a boyish grin. There was the old Alex, the one I'd met by the elevator all those years ago.

He jogged to the door, letting in a white-coated waiter pushing a cart topped with a champagne bucket and crystal flutes. Alex tipped him a twenty and pushed the cart in a little farther.

"How about a little champagne, Mrs. van Holt?" He looked proud of his romantic surprise, as men always are. He popped the cork and filled two flutes, the bubbles reaching the top but not flowing over. He handed me one as he raised his in a toast.

"To the future," he said, clinking his glass with mine.

"The future," I repeated. I took a small sip, then noticed a silver dome on the cart. I looked up at him, confused. He grinned again—a little boy with a secret—and said, "For you."

I put my hand on the cold silver handle and lifted the dome, expecting fresh strawberries or caviar or, God willing, another plate of éclairs, but instead saw a red leather box sitting in the middle of the tray.

"What's this?"

His grin gave way to sincerity. "I know it's been a tough road, so I just wanted to say thank you. And I love you." If he was conflicted about being a congressman, he certainly wasn't conflicted about me. Even after what I put him through today.

When I hesitated, he picked up the box and put it in my hands. Inside, cradled in satin, was an antique platinum-and-diamond Cartier tank watch—the one I had bid on at the Ballantine Ball auction but lost.

"Aubyn told me you were bidding on it, so I found the couple and made them an offer they couldn't refuse," he said with a wink.

"You did?"

"Well, Calvin did. Here, let me help you."

He slipped it out of the case and onto my wrist. Then he looked up at my face, anxious for a response.

I should have said thank you, but I couldn't. To Alex, this watch was just another expensive bauble for his wife. There was emotion behind it, and some gratitude, but no sacrifice, no real significance. Coming from Jimmy, it would have meant so much more: a shared journey, obstacles overcome, and a love that flickered but never blew out.

I looked down at the watch's pale face and slim black hands and noticed it was one minute to midnight.

It was time for Cinderella to leave the ball.

I closed the top of the watch box and took a deep breath to steel myself.

"What's wrong?" he said, "Don't you like it?"

"It's beautiful," I said quietly. "But…I can't accept it."

I took it off and pressed it into his hands. He cocked his head, still smiling, as if I were playing a game.

"Alex, you are a good man. A good father," I said. "And whether you want to or not, you're going to make a wonderful congressman."

He stared at me, his smile fading.

"I want to thank you from the bottom of my heart. You've helped me more than you could ever realize. But…"

"Abbey, what's this about? Are you drunk? My mom says she's worried you are drinking too much."

"No. I am perfectly sober, I promise."

"Well, what, then? Is this about someone else? Is it that guy in the bar?"

"No. There's no one else. You know that." It was the truth. This wasn't about Jimmy. This was about me. And the kids. I took a deep breath and continued: "The truth is…I'm leaving you."

For a moment he didn't speak, as if he couldn't process what I was saying. Then he took my hands. "I know things haven't been great between us. But now that the campaign is over, they'll get better. I promise."

I looked over at his questioning expression, the hurt in his eyes, and felt sick. But I forced myself to continue.

"They won't. They'll only get worse," I said. "Be honest, Alex. You can't pretend things have turned out the way you wanted. Deep down, part of you is relieved."

"Relieved?" His voice choked with emotion. "Jesus Christ, how can you say that? We're great together. Look what we just accomplished."

"No. We're not great together. Maybe we were once, but not anymore. Now we bring out the worst in each other."

"No, we don't!"

"It's true! I've known all along you didn't want to be in politics. But instead of putting on the brakes, I let it go on, even though you were miserable. And you've known all along I really never wanted to leave my job and have full-time nannies and work on charity events for dogs. We should have stood up for what each other wanted. But we stopped fighting. Settled. Just gave in and gave up."

"But I love you. You know I do."

"I know," I said. "A part of me loves you too."

"A part? Just a part? What part?"

"Not the part that matters."

"Stop speaking in code," he said, suddenly angry. "What is it you're saying? You want a divorce?"

I nodded.

"Why?"

I looked at his face and saw anguish and despair. I chewed my lip to stop from crying, but I couldn't. Tears slipped out. But I had to go on; I had to finish before I lost my nerve.

"Because this life isn't mine. And it never will be."

CHAPTER TWENTY

I had arrived at the Ritz-Carlton as Mrs. Abigail van Holt. Now, a few minutes past midnight, in the dark, earliest hour of a new day, I was leaving as Abbey Lahey. No, that wasn't right; I wasn't married to Jimmy either. I was Abbey DiSiano, someone I hadn't been for nearly a decade.

I wondered if I could remember what it was like to be her. But instead of feeling worried and sad and plotting my next steps, I felt calm. Even-keeled.

I exited the elevators into the Ritz's lobby, its marble floors amplifying my footsteps in the soaring rotunda. The place was empty except for a bored bellhop checking his phone and a few late-night partiers. *Good-bye, Ritz-Carlton,* I thought, *good-bye Ritz life.*

I walked to the reception desk and was greeted by a briskly efficient night clerk.

"How can I help you?" she asked.

"Can you do something for me?"

"Of course, Mrs. van Holt."

I took my wallet, keys, and iPhone from the red Hermès bag, dropped them in my pocket, and asked to borrow a piece of paper and pen. I scribbled a note, dropped it inside the bag, and buckled it up. I then scribbled an address on another note and slid it over to her.

"I need this delivered as soon as possible to this address," I told her.

"FedEx?" she asked.

"Courier, please."

"Yes, ma'am." She glanced at the address and then, more covetously, at the handbag.

"Nice, huh?" I said.

"Very."

"Trust me. It's not worth it."

I turned and strode away. It made me smile to imagine Father Fergie's confusion later that morning when he received a package containing a woman's purse. I hoped when he read the note inside it, he would be pleased and that he'd forgive me for the canceled check. I hoped, too, to confirm his first instinct about me: that I wasn't a spoiled princess who broke "cocktail party promises." That when I told him I wasn't quite what I seemed, I meant it.

But mostly I hoped that he—or someone at the Holy Rosary Settlement House—knew how to use eBay. In my note, I told him not to accept a penny less than thirty-two thousand dollars.

As I walked down Walnut Street I savored the night air, the rare quiet of the city streets, and the exhilarating lightness I felt.

Looking at my reflection in the shop windows I passed, I marveled at myself. I had done something extraordinary tonight: I had turned down Alex van Holt for the *second* time in my life. Only this time I hadn't done it for the sake of some college boyfriend but for myself.

My heels clicked loudly on the sidewalk, brisk and purposeful, the sound of a woman striding with confidence into a new life. A woman knowing that whatever the future held, it would been seen clearly, and without hesitation. And hopefully, it might even be something like my past.

Funny how different your life can look after ten days in someone else's. It wasn't long ago I'd sat in that bagel shop with Jules, looking at a photo of Alex in *Town & Country* and fantasizing about how much better my life would have been if I'd only gone out with him. Now I knew better.

Alex wasn't the one that got away—I was.

My life with Jimmy might have been messy, but it was *mine*. I'd chosen it and it wasn't a mistake. If anything, my mistake had been allowing the messiness to become an excuse. For not standing up to my bitch of a boss. For claiming to be "too busy" to start a firm with Jules. For not supporting Jimmy in his darkest hour.

For all the moments, big and little, when I played it safe. When what I should have been was bold.

As I neared the center of Rittenhouse Square, I slowed, feeling a sudden urge to see Jules. Or at least hear her voice. Leaning against my favorite statue, a bronze lion subduing a serpent with gleaming teeth and heavy paws, I dialed her number.

"Hello?"

"Jules?"

Silence. Then, "Hello, Abbey."

"Hi. How's it going?"

"Uh, it's going fine." Then, "Why are you calling me so late?"

"I'm sorry, I forgot what time it is. Did I wake you up?"

"No, I'm up. In fact, I'm still out."

"You are? Me too. Where?"

"The Rittenhouse Hotel. Lucas has a gig so I'm just hanging out waiting for him to finish up."

"That's funny, because I'm standing in the square right now. Mind if I join you?"

There was a brief pause, but then she answered. "I don't know... he's only got one more set—"

"I'll be right there."

I hung up before she could say anything else, then ran full throttle across the damp grass toward the glass-fronted hotel.

The Rittenhouse Hotel's Oak Bar was a cozy little space that few Philadelphians knew about—a secret watering hole closely held by the hotel for its cosseted guests and permanent residents. I found it at the top of a wide staircase, on the second floor, just before the hallway got smaller, leading to conference rooms, ballrooms, a gym, and a spa.

On the other side of the heavy oak-and-glass door, I found Jules. She was sitting in the corner by the fireplace sipping white wine with her eyes glued to the black-haired, black-clad bass player. He fronted a trio comprised of a another man tapping on a snare drum and a woman playing a keyboard, all swaying slightly, eyes closed, and seemingly unaware of anyone else in the room.

But maybe that was a good thing, because besides Jules, a bored bartender, and a handful of barflies, the place was empty. The bluesy tune added to its speakeasy-like intimacy.

As I approached Jules's table, she looked up and smiled shyly, pulling her sweater around herself as if she was suddenly cold.

"This is a surprise," she said. "I thought you'd be out celebrating the big win."

"There was a party," I said. "But I needed a break."

"Yeah, I hear you need one from time to time." She smiled cautiously, hoping I could take her joke.

I put my hands to my face in mock embarrassment. "I guess you saw that?"

"Yeah. I did. Pretty hard to miss."

We both laughed and I took that as permission to sit down. I settled into my chair and looked over at the musicians in the corner. The man with the guitar was performing an impressive solo. "Your boyfriend is really good."

"Thanks. But he's not my boyfriend. He's my fiancé."

I glanced at her left hand and saw a cool sapphire-and-diamond engagement ring. Engaged!

I opened my mouth and my eyes went wide in a silent scream of joy. She tried not to laugh, but her green eyes sparkled.

I could tell she was trying to keep her emotional distance and stay mad at me, but as she got talking—telling me about the engagement (this past Saturday night, on the roof of their apartment in Old City), their plans (a spring wedding), and the flowered dog collars she was planning for her terrier "bridesmaids" (hot pink, of course)—I could see her resistance weakening. I loved hearing her talk, the rise and fall of her voice as rhythmic as her fiancé's music.

Eventually, she came up for air—and laughed.

"Guess you can tell I'm kind of excited."

"You should be. Marriage, the right marriage, can be amazing."

"I would guess so. How does it feel to be a congressman's wife?"

"Uh, fine."

"Just fine? Aren't you guys thrilled? Where *is* he, by the way?"

"I don't know." I took a breath, bracing to say the words aloud for the first time. "Actually, I left him."

"What?" Now it was her turn with wide eyes and an open mouth. "Oh God, Abbey. When?"

"About fifteen minutes ago."

"You left him?" she repeated, disbelieving.

"Yep, I did. But it was a long time coming. And it's for the best. For both of us."

"But I thought you guys were happy."

"Sure looked that way, didn't it?" I said with a sad smile. "But we weren't. At least not the way you are supposed to be. Not the way I would want for you. Or for Gloria. Or for me, frankly."

A silence fell. She pushed her glass over to me. I took a sip before continuing. "The thing is . . . it's hard to settle for anything less than perfect when you've had the kind of love that really fits, even though it's messy and ridiculous and complicated. The kind worth fighting for, the kind that makes you feel truly alive."

Like in Braveheart, I thought. I smiled to myself, realizing I'd never really gotten that movie until just now.

Jules looked at me with a mix of dismay and concern. She put her hand on mine. It was warm. I looked down at it and then back up at her sympathetic, worried face and realized that I wasn't alone anymore. My best friend was back.

"What are you going to do?" she whispered.

"I don't know," I admitted. "I haven't thought that far ahead. But the kids and I will figure it out. We'll probably have to stay with my mom for a while until we get sorted out. *That* should be interesting."

She couldn't help but smile at the mention of Roberta.

"How is the old broad? Still breaking hearts and busting balls up and down the Main Line?" she asked. "Seriously, though, let me know if I can help. I can't imagine divorcing Alex van Holt is going to be easy."

She was right. The thought of divorce, and the heartbreaking work of disentangling two lives, brought me down to earth from the high I had been on since walking out of the Ritz.

Jules noticed my face. She gazed around the almost-empty bar and suddenly stood up.

"C'mon!" she said. "This place is fucking depressing. Let's go somewhere more fun."

"But what about your fiancé?"

She wrinkled her nose. "He knows I can't stand jazz."

I laughed as I let her pull me to my feet.

"Where are we going?"

"Dancing."

"I'm not exactly dressed for dancing," I told her. "And where in the world can you go dancing at one in the morning on a Tuesday—I mean Wednesday?"

"Are you kidding? Jesus, you *have* led a sheltered life," she said. "I can see I've got a lot to show you."

"Here. Finish this." She pushed her white wine over to me and I gulped what remained, then told me: "Let me just say good-bye to Lucas and I'll meet you outside."

I gave her fiancé a shy wave, then headed out to the hall. I pulled out my iPhone, checked for any messages, then pulled up a mirror app. I checked my makeup and ran my fingers through my hair.

I heard shoes on the stairs behind me and moved aside to let a hotel guest pass. But instead he stopped and spoke.

"Nice suit," he said.

"Thanks." I looked down at the peacock-colored fabric as if for the first time. "But it's not mine. I just borrowed it."

"It's Dior, right?" he said. "Nineteen sixty-eight? Seventy? And in such great shape."

I looked up into a handsome bearded face. He was wearing a dark T-shirt and silky gray gym shorts with funky silver sneakers. Not tall, and slight, but so taut and tan it was as if he alternated days at the gym and the pool. But what set him apart was his eyes: warm and moss colored, but with a mischievous golden gleam.

It was a face I'd seen many times in my fashion magazines. Marc Jacobs.

"You're...you're...Marc Jacobs," I said, my voice constricted by surprise. Then louder: "I mean, are you Marc Jacobs?"

"I am," he said with a nod.

"Wha...What are you doing here?" I stammered.

"Just squeezing in a workout." He hooked his thumb in the direction of the hotel's gym and explained, "Still on Tokyo time."

"No, I mean, what are you doing *in Philadelphia*?"

"We're opening a new store on Walnut Street."

All of a sudden I remembered: the construction worker who had ogled my chest, the white mannequins, the long silver shelves.

"The old Ochs store!" I said. "I saw the construction last week."

"Yeah, just under the wire as usual." He smiled and extended his hand. "You are?"

"Abbey van Holt; uh, Abbey Lahey; I mean Abbey DiSiano."

"Are you sure?" he said with a laugh. I laughed too.

"Nice to meet you," I said, gathering myself. "I'm a big fan."

"Appreciate it." He then turned and moved down the hall.

He was almost to the gym door when I found myself, or maybe the wine, continuing to speak: "Actually," I yelled after him. "I *used* to be a big fan. Not anymore."

"Oh, really? Why not?" he said, pausing and looking back.

"Well, I bought something of yours, a bag, and, this sounds weird, but it cost me something. It cost me something very dear."

"Sorry for that," he said as he moved slowly back to me. "But how do you know that you lost it? Are you sure it's not still out there? Maybe it's closer than you think."

I froze and stared at him, wondering if we were talking about the same thing. He stepped very close to me, his lips near my ear.

I smelled a hint of expensive shampoo and felt his beard tickle my cheek. I heard his breathing, and my own.

"I've built an empire giving people what they *think* they want, what they *think* they need," he whispered. "But it's all just an illusion. A beautiful illusion. Isn't it?"

I felt a chill crackle through me like lightning. I stepped back from him, startled. But not realizing the stairs were right behind me, I lost my balance, the heel of my shoe hooked around the wide top step like a claw.

As I tipped backward, my hands pawed the air for help, then grasped the front of his T-shirt. His diminutive frame was too light, though, and instead of acting as a counterbalance, he fell toward me. We tumbled down the pinky-brown steps in a flurry of black, silver, and peacock green.

At the bottom, my head struck the floor and rolled to the side. I saw little yellow lights detach themselves from the flowers in the flocked wallpaper. They floated over to me and surrounded my head, like Gloria had blown them over from a dandelion.

I studied them and felt their warmth. Then everything went dark.

A long and lonely piece of dust, or maybe a long-abandoned spider's silk, drooped from the corner of a perforated ceiling panel. Beside it, on the muted wall-mounted television, a late-night talk show host told jokes that no one could hear. Near it, some Mylar balloons stirred in the current from a heating duct while a vase of carnations drooped, their graying stems aching for water.

I raised my head off the pillow.

There, dozing in a beige vinyl chair beside the hospital bed, his legs stretched out before him, arms crossed and hat covering his eyes, was my husband. He was breathing quietly, his chest rising and falling, while one arm extended toward me, his palm and work-calloused fingers ready to be grasped.

I watched him until the image blurred with tears. When I found I could speak, I whispered his name—"*Jimmy*"—first softly and then louder.

His eyes fluttered open and he looked at me, then leapt to his feet.

"Oh my God!" A smile broke over his tired, unshaven face. "You're awake."

Then he pulled me up gently into his arms, folding me into him.

"You're awake," he repeated. "You're awake."

I began to sob with the pounding, overwhelming joy of coming home.

"I got you, honey, I got you," he said, mistaking my cries for pain. "You're going to be okay."

I pulled back and looked at his face. "I'll never leave you again," I told him.

He smelled of sleep, stale coffee, and unconditional love.

EPILOGUE

Any questions?"

I looked for any raised hands in the large conference room of the law firm of Smith, Weldon, Adams & Tuvonec, which everyone around town called SWAT to their faces and SWeAT behind their backs, on the twentieth floor of a colossal glass skyscraper in downtown Philadelphia. The room belonged to a prestigious Center City law firm, but today it was being loaned to an association of nonprofit agencies, some of which were the firm's pro bono clients.

Jules and I had been asked to speak on the topic of "Small Budget, Big Impact" communications, even though our two-person PR firm was less than a year old. Recently, we had helped raise substantial amounts of money for a community health clinic and landed one of their docters a spot on *The Daily Show*, so we had become rock stars among the nonprofit set.

It was a crowd of about seventy-five people, some sitting at the U-shaped tables directly in front of me and some in rows of folding chairs in the back, some even standing behind them. It was much more than we expected, and the butterflies danced in my stomach.

But so far, I was doing great—speaking confidently and with passion for my subject—and when I did stumble, Jules was there to cover.

At the end of my presentation, several hands shot up.

"How long does it take to get a PR program going?" asked a young woman from a homeless shelter.

"I know people hate to hear this, but you have to be patient," I said. "Take the time to plan your attack and know your message. Remember, stories live forever online, and every person—more important, every potential donor—is going to find that story. So it had better be a good one."

Someone standing in the back near the windows cut me off.

"But reporters write stories every day where people aren't prepared. Isn't that the whole point? Get press whenever and wherever you can?" The voice came from a man in the back, but I couldn't make out his face in the darkened room.

"There is that old saying, no PR is bad PR…," I said, slightly annoyed. "But I think you should aim higher than that, don't you?"

I shifted from foot to foot—I really had to pee—but continued. "A lot of firms will come in and promise you ink on day one, but anything you get that easy is kind of like that second bottle of wine. It seems like a good idea at the time, but the next morning maybe not so much. And believe me, I should know." I pointed to my rounded, protruding belly and the crowd cracked up.

We took a few more questions; then Jules walked over to switch the lights back on. I started to search for my heckler but got caught up in a conversation with a museum president. When I finally could break away, I moved around the long table and peered down the hallway, but whoever he was had slipped out.

When the crowd was mostly gone, I motioned to Jules that I would see her tomorrow, then waddled to the bathroom. I made good time in the long hall in my old scuffed flats, the only shoes that my seven-months-pregnant feet could fit in.

When I came back, the crowd had dispersed and I stood alone in the hallway. I pressed the elevator button and waited, my body relaxing now that the presentation was over. I heard footsteps move down the hall, turn toward me, and stop. I looked up and took in the thick, dark hair, lean physique, crisp shirt, and genuine smile of someone very familiar.

It was Alex.

"Great presentation," he said casually. "Nice to see someone with an eye on nonprofits. They really need the help."

I stood there silently exploding, memories moving through my mind like a grainy filmstrip.

"Believe me, I know," he continued. "All my clients are nonprofits...much to my partners' dismay."

As he punched the elevator button again, I managed to eke out a quiet "Thank you."

He extended his hand. "I'm Alex van Holt."

Then he cocked his head to one side and peered at me with a half smile: "You look familiar. Have we met before?"

We had sex against a mirror in a walk-in closet, I thought, blushing. "No. I don't think so. But I think I saw you in *Town & Country* once."

Now it was his turn to blush. "God. That. Me and a bunch of polo players."

The elevator door opened. He held it for me, then followed me in, lugging a worn leather satchel bulging with papers. He looked as handsome as I remembered, only dressed in jeans, a basic blue blazer, and sneakers. He smelled of soap, not cologne.

"I thought your ideas were really creative," he said. "My family's foundation could use someone like you. Any chance we can lure you away?"

"I'm flattered. But I'm happy with my little firm. We're doing pretty well. And it's hard to beat working with your best friend."

"Bring her too!"

I laughed, then shook my head. "Tempting, but I've got enough changes coming in my life." I patted my tummy.

"When are you due?"

"April."

"Your first?"

"Third."

"I have three too," he said proudly. "All girls."

"Really?"

"We love it. My wife only had brothers, so she's in heaven." He whipped out an iPhone and showed a photo of himself with three adorable curly-haired little girls. Beside him, smiling widely, stood Larry Liebman.

"Larry!" I said, before I could catch myself.

"Do you know her?"

"Uh, I know of her. She's a reporter at the *Inquirer*, right? She's great. And she's perfect for you."

"Thanks," he said with the same funny/sweet look that always made me smile. "I certainly think so."

We fell silent as the elevator clinked to a stop on the ground floor. He put his hand over the door for me as I exited, and we walked into the lobby.

"Well, it was nice to meet you, Abbey," he said. "Even if you are turning me down. *Again.*"

He winked at me, acknowledging our encounter by the elevator and the awkward phone call all those years before. He *did* remember.

I looked up at him, tears starting to well, not with sadness but with a knowing certainty that all was as it should be. We shook hands, each taking a long last look before he turned and walked away. I watched him cross the marble floor and disappear, the city sidewalk swallowing him up like a ghost.

The baby kicked inside, and I remembered I had a train to catch. I turned and joined the rest of the commuters rolling on the escalator down to Suburban Station. If I hurried, I might make it home before five, maybe even before Jimmy and the kids. I would wait for them in the kitchen, bracing myself for the clamor of footsteps, the collision of voices, the cold hands and flushed, pink cheeks.

I held tight to the railing.

ACKNOWLEDGMENTS

Thank you to Theresa Park for her belief in this book, and for pushing me to dig deep.

Thank you to Stacy Creamer, for her thoughtfulness and enthusiasm, and for helping me to find my way when the path went dark.

Much appreciation to the early readers who advised me on everything from Congressional elections to Thai endearments to Louboutins: Tobey Pearl, Heather Jacobs, Amy Fonville, Jody Weber, Emily Morrison, Laura Getty, Nimpa Bosch, Gretchen Regan, Sandra McClintic, Sopee Conard, Olivia Rabe, Carol Gangemi, Sara Himes, Rebecca Timme, Katharine Bolt, and Natalie Blanning Weber.

Thank you to Abigail Koons, Emily Sweet, and everyone at TPL, and to Howie Sanders for his passion.

Thank you to my mother for showing me that anything is possible and for always being there, to my father for his joie de vivre and steadfast support, to my brother for his humor, and to my sister, who knows everything and loves me anyway.

All my gratitude to Lulu and Will for their patience—and for being such good sleepers.

But mostly thank you to Joseph Gangemi. You make me want to live this life forever.

DISCUSSION GUIDE

1. Leigh Himes's novel poses a question: are you happy where you are, or are you still thinking about the one, or the turn in life's path, that "got away"? Why does this person or moment stick with you?

2. Abbey's *Sliding Doors* moment happens in a split second during a boring errand. Have you experienced a moment like that, in which an everyday task becomes life-changing?

3. There are many forces working against Abbey in both her lives. But what do you think is her real problem? And what does she have to learn?

4. When Abbey wakes up in her new life, she has to set aside her former marriage vows and take on a new loyalty to Alex in order to keep up an appearance of normalcy. Do you think this was hard for Abbey at first, or was it easy for her to "start" a new life? How does this change over time?

5. Why do you think the author allowed Abbey's children to remain very much the same in both worlds? How do their very different lifestyles change the children and Abbey's relationship to them?

6. Abbey experiences life as both a working mom and a stay-at-home mom. Moms, if you could switch your own situations (working in the home or out of the home) for a day, what would you do first? What do you think you would miss the most?

7. Striking to many early readers is the remarkable change in Abbey's friendship with Jules. Women's friendships are powerful: what would happen if you found out that your best friend, or closest confidante, was suddenly out of your life?

8. In early chapters, Abbey is trying to "fake it" at the party and with her family. Have you ever found yourself in a situation where you have to fake understanding what's going on? Were you successful? Did you learn something surprising about yourself, your closest friends and family, or someone else?

9. Alex and Jimmy are good men, and they care for Abbey, each in their own ways. But one brings out her best qualities, while the other only amplifies her worst. Who in your life challenges you to be a better version of yourself?

10. Have fun with this one: If *The One That Got Away* became a film, who would you cast to play the primary roles?